central square

central square

A NOVEL BY

George Packer

Graywolf Press
Saint Paul, Minnesota

Publication of this volume is made possible in part by a grant provided by the Minnesota State Arts Board through an appropriation by the Minnesota State Legislature, and by a grant from the National Endowment for the Arts. Significant support has also been provided by Dayton's, Mervyn's, and Target stores through the Dayton Hudson Foundation, the Bush Foundation, the Andrew W. Mellon Foundation, the McKnight Foundation, the General Mills Foundation, the St. Paul Companies, and other generous contributions from foundations, corporations, and individuals. To these organizations and individuals we offer our heartfelt thanks.

Published by Graywolf Press
2402 University Avenue, Suite 203
Saint Paul, Minnesota 55114

www.graywolfpress.org

Published in the United States of America
Printed in Canada

ISBN 1-55597-277-2

2 4 6 8 9 7 5 3 1
First Graywolf Printing, 1998

Library of Congress Catalog Card Number: 98-84450

Cover photograph: Paul Clancy

Cover design: Julie Metz

For Gordon Harvey

money

one

November breaks up a Northern city into its separate lives. No one lingers on granite planters, strangers stop making conversation, pigeons go unfed. Murk settles over the river and dusk comes midmorning. Buildings lose their heads, faces grow indistinct. In the evening, trains and buses fill up with individuals, and the bodies layered in bulky clothing shrink from the coming winter and one another. The yellow glow in windows lights them safely home. This is the new center of life: The household becomes the temple, the family the god. Even those who have no home disappear, crowding the shelters. Every November, when the sky turns leaden and the clocks have been set back, the larger body dies and the idea of the city becomes a memory, an accident of warm weather. More than the fall of leaves and the flight of geese, this memory explains November's sadness in a Northern city.

That November in Cambridge, across the river from Boston, people started noticing signs. Teal-colored flyers, recognizable from a distance on lampposts, in the windows of Laundromats and discount clothiers and walk-in clinics, or around the new construction site. Cryptic phrases in small black type.

> No One Is Excused.
> Do You Know Where You Live?
> Who Is Your Neighbor?
> You Could Be Anyone.

No one claimed responsibility, and the signs became a conversation piece and source of speculation—a terrorist cell with a sense of humor, an ad campaign for a blockbuster movie, a millenarian lunatic.

Their appearance, just at the moment when cold weather and early darkness arrived to close up windows and doors, worked strangely on people's nerves. The signs irritated and disturbed some; in others they woke nameless longings. The feelings were rawest where the signs were thickest, in the heart of the city—the several dingy blocks of Massachusetts Avenue, its main artery, growing dingier toward the river—known as Central Square. By late November, these nerves and signs were all that remained of the idea of the city.

In her blind basement office in Central Square, Paula Voorhees sat listening to Gladys Dill.

"Uh-uh, not intimidated. Maybe scared sometimes. Like last night when he comes home all depressed from being dissed at the garage and I don't know how to make him feel good. And he starts screaming at me and Michael and that's when the feeling is like, I must be crazy to be here even though I love James, like I'm enabling him by being passive and all. I don't know."

Paula's eyes shifted from Gladys to the wall clock behind her. "It sounds like you feel both responsible and helpless." She watched the last minute tick down. "No wonder you think you're going crazy."

"I don't know. OK, I know, time's up."

The chairs were arranged in the room—windowless, a midsized closet—so that only Paula could see the clock. Between her and Gladys there was a low table with a box of Kleenex on it. Today no tears had accompanied the catalog of James trouble and money trouble and childhood trouble. Gladys had come in with one lens missing from her plastic-frame glasses. It made her look crazy. The naked eye was a little unnerving—half of Gladys's face seemed to be analyzing *her*. But Paula was an expert listener even when she wasn't listening.

She sat forward. Gladys Dill slumped, unbudging. Paula imagined hauling her large body out of the room, heaving it out of the basement, into . . . life. Her stuckness was maddening.

"I don't think I can keep coming."

Familiar stuff; and the hour was up. "Why not?"

"Michael's asthma medicine. They're fixing to shut the gas off."

"Next time let's talk about adjusting your fee again."

"I'm just trying to figure out what we accomplished today."

Paula's mouth went dry. "You made a connection between James's troubles at the garage and your stepfather's anger. Don't you think that's something to pursue next week?"

Now the lensless eye reddened, and the other disappeared behind fog. "But what did that accomplish?"

Paula edged out of the chair. Her own vocabulary was boomeranging. We need more black therapists, she thought, this one really ought to be seeing a black woman. "If you can feel these things in here," she said, passing the Kleenex box, "you'll have a safe place to work on them. That will make it easier to get what you want out there."

Paula had resorted to talking shit.

Suddenly Gladys gave back the Kleenex box, gathered herself, and stood up. "OK. See you next week."

Gladys Dill was nearly six feet tall, thick-bodied and short-haired. In her beret and long winter coat she looked like a different woman, maybe the one Paula never saw, the one who was raising a child and had trained as a nurse's aide before cocaine messed up her plans. The transformation came as a rebuke.

After showing her out, Paula sat and stared at the Cape Cod beach that Fran, her office-mate, had hung over the desk. She felt like tearing it down—its beige and blue calm enraged her. Her progress file lay open on the desk. Gladys Dill was her last of the day.

At the very least she could have said, "You're mad at me." And then Gladys would have denied it, and the notion of being mad would have hovered over her thoughts for a week, and by next week they might have finally reached Square B. But it wasn't nice to have people mad at you. It was nicer when they teared up and you passed the Kleenex. So instead Gladys had left the way she always left, depressed.

And what good *have* you done her?

Once, she got the gas turned back on in Gladys's apartment in the Columbia Street projects. A call to Com Gas, her professional voice informing some clerk that Ms. Dill suffered a disability, and it was done. A seductive revelation—more power than she knew she had. But it was just crisis management, not the real work, which was supposed to take place in Gladys's mind, a slippery, perilous place that couldn't be fixed with a phone call. This real work never seemed to get done because there was always an eviction crisis or a violence crisis or a drug-relapse crisis, the crisis that had sent Gladys via the hospital to the Problem Place and Paula's office.

She would be taking this one home. It was working on her nervous system like a third cup of coffee.

"Staff meeting, sweetheart."

Fran stood in the door. Her peasant skirt and bonnet of frizzy gray hair suggested an embittered hippie turned Puritan.

Paula said, "All we ever do around here is talk."

"Who did you just have?"

"The asthmatic's mother."

"She sounds very damaged."

Every one of Fran's clients turned out to be an abuse case. For all Paula knew it was true, but her own overripe sense of ambiguity compelled her to explore other regions for the sources of human misery. Irritated and chairbound, unable to make Fran go away, Paula rashly decided to unburden herself.

"She wanted to know what good it does her to talk to me."

"Hey, great! You can really work with that."

"It's a good question, isn't it? Talk doesn't pay for Michael's asthma medicine. It doesn't stop James from scaring the hell out of her. It's a fucking good question."

Fran frowned. Profanity was the language of the clients, displaying lack of impulse control. "But you can help her see how the victimization works."

"Com Gas is going to cut her a break for self-awareness? At the very least that woman needs a shrink whose skin is thicker and darker than mine."

"This is very negative talk I'm hearing," Fran said. "Bring it to the meeting. We've all been there, sweetheart."

"You go ahead. I need to catch up on my notes."

Alone, Paula went back over the day. In the morning there had been Nick, her wordless mailman, whose wife had given him the get-help-or-I'm-leaving ultimatum. After that came Raul, her sweet closet transvestite who, she felt pretty sure, was developing a crush on his therapist. She had hope for Raul. He was able to love and one day he might be capable of loving himself. She felt not nearly so sanguine about Earl, overweight and unemployed, a victim of corporate downsizing on Route 128. Middle management had held Earl's being together. Now, having lost status, function, and wife, he'd turned to eating undistributed Halloween candy in front of late-night TV and shouting obscenities at the screen. Earl's life was a nonstop parade of comedowns and insults. The delicate move was getting past the paranoia without making him out to be a total failure. Today, through his Xanax fog, he let Paula know that she inspired homicidal feelings. This was progress, but it felt like training a drugged bear to perform tricks designed to put her life at risk. The one place in Earl she could reach was a spot of fear, for he was not so paranoid that he didn't grasp what was happening to him. But sometimes she flashed on his body crushing hers, pumping hard. In the tiny office their sessions were tense, and small-boned Paula had trouble drawing breath.

Then Gladys Dill, with her question.

Paula sat with her pen poised. She had been a good listener all her life, having been born, she was told, without making a sound. Sometimes she thought of herself as the priest she stopped seeing around her first period, his side of the confessional silent except for nasal breathing. Other times she felt like a hooker hired by the hour to coax vices, hand out Kleenex, make the client feel that she cared for no one else in the world. In return they told her about cruel fathers, indifferent mothers, devouring lovers, maddening children, humiliating bosses. Some were tormented by the lottery, some considered getting out of bed a victory. Many of them told her it helped them to talk to her—that they had no one else in the world to talk to.

Today this thought saddened her beyond words.

Entering the conference room, she was surprised by the color of twilight through the casement window at sidewalk level.

"We can't start without Paula." Peter Fine watched as she squeezed behind the chairs. "Paula is indispensable."

The executive director of the Problem Place sat gnome-like in his armchair at the head of the table, trim-bearded, plump in his sweater vest, his stocking feet pulled up on the cushion and cozily crossed at the ankles. Around the table sat his harem of dependent, resentful MSWs and PsyDs. Except for Philip, who was gay, Fine was the only man in the room.

"I have important news so I'll get straight to the point," Fine said—but first there was praise for his staff's dedication; a plug for a paper he was writing with Suzanne Martin, his associate director, on post-traumatic stress in children of divorced parents; a reference to the couples' treatment he was doing with a manic-depressive woman and her affectless husband (today both cried). Suzanne looked on smilingly; glancing at Paula, she rolled her eyes as if they were secret confidantes. According to Fran, Suzanne was the mother who refused to see that her children were being incested.

Paula looked around the table. Her colleagues were listening with attitudes of numb rage. She thought: What am I doing here? There were a hundred other things she could do. Like work at a big hospital where you didn't have to hear your boss go on about "therapeutic courage." Or just get out of the field. She could do that. She sometimes thought that her real talent, the one going to waste, was as a private investigator. She loved detail and had an infallible nose for guilt. She wasn't the type of therapist who was too weird for any other kind of work.

"OK," Fine at last getting to the point. "Unfortunately, today's topic is money." The harem stirred nervously. "Wouldn't it be great if we could do our work as healers without thinking about money? We know that's not the real world. The Department of Mental Health has decided not to renew our allowance."

With a mental clunk, Paula returned to the table. From Fran and Philip's corner came audible groans. Suzanne, who'd obviously heard the news and whose job was secure, dished around looks of pained sympathy.

"I don't have to tell you contributions are down—empathy fatigue, structural recession, I'm not interested in labels. Now the Commonwealth in its wisdom decides sports arenas are more important than the psychic wholeness of the underprivileged. No one here wants to get into short-term therapy and meds—"

"What's the bad news, Peter?" asked Sara Simon, Paula's one friend here.

Fine took a breath. "As of January first, all staff clinicians will move to a fee-for-service basis as independent contractors."

Around the table there was stunned silence.

"That means the Problem Place will no longer cover health benefits. You'll be doing a lot more paperwork. If a client doesn't show, you'll have to reimburse their part of the fee." Fine was nodding with the gravity of a clergyman comforting his flock in the face of collective tragedy. "I know this is upsetting. *I'm* upset—I'm *very* upset. There are going to be painful decisions about who can continue here. But some of you could turn this into a positive and pick up more client hours."

Paula's throat was burning—nausea coming on. There were no jobs, everyone knew that. Therapists were moving to other states. Social workers with union cards were living off unemployment or going into day care. It was cold and gloomy out there and once you were thrown outside you never got back in, unless you were willing to commute an hour to work with violent teenagers in Lawrence. But she didn't even have a car. She had no connections, hadn't even bothered schmoozing when she met the director of a psych ward at a party last week.

"Don't you sometimes think," Fine asked, "there's a plague on men and women today? And the symptom is a fearful and rageful hardening of the heart? And we in this room know the cure but no one listens? I think there is a plague and it's called All Against All, and it's killing us. America should be quarantined. This basement may be our last sanctuary."

Fine openly desired the status of therapeutic rock star. He wanted to counsel in stadiums or on public television, and he sometimes spoke as if the clients interfered with his work. He believed that shrinks suffered from lack of vision. Thousands of them toiling away separately in fifty-minute hours—if they looked up long enough to realize their collective strength, they could treat the nation's damaged psyche. His ambition mirrored Paula's restlessness, grossly magnified and distorted.

She had started out a favorite. With Fine there was never a clear line between supervision and foreplay, but his come-ons were always psychological. He stayed technically faithful to the childless wife no one ever saw—and Paula once told Sara Simon that it would be better for everyone if Fine just bedded one of the harem so he could abstain from mind-fucking everyone else. Still, she had refused even sublimated concubinage, and it was partly her fault that he decided she was an enemy. She lacked the therapist's gift for euphemism, not because she was confident but because she was shy. She hadn't been political. She should have been volunteering to do research papers with him, instead of walking into staff meetings late. Now she'd be the first one Fine cut. It was stupid and reckless to be superior to all the crap you had to do to survive.

Paula's stomach was turning over. How would she tell them? Gladys Dill would die without her. Earl would end up in Walpole Prison.

"We've been addicted to government," Fine was saying. "Now we're clean and free to create something totally new. And you know what? It's going on right now in this very city. This very room."

"Peter, there's private grant money out there." Paula was speaking rapidly and her voice sounded unnatural. "I could do some research on it."

In silence, a dozen therapists processed this event. Fran's stare accused Paula of betrayal. Fine's lips opened a pink hole in his beard.

"Beautiful, Paula."

She crossed her legs under the table. She felt dirty. No one got off free with Fine. But she could tell that he was relieved to have her on his side—she frightened him. At their core these megalomaniacs were little boys trying to please Mama.

Fine talked on, and the staff sank into depression. Outside it was night; trouser legs, coat hems, winter shoes walked past the casement window, people going home at the end of their workday. In the cramped conference room they were all sucking the available air into their self-monitoring, overheated brains. Paula felt a headache coming on. When the meeting broke up she made for the door, but Fine intercepted her.

"Stay late tonight." His voice was intimate. "Something's happened to my Wednesday evening group. This guy from out of town, a kind of organizer, he contacted me. He wanted me to open it up to new people. A new group every week."

"What about your old people?"

Fine smiled enigmatically and shook his head. He was standing so close that she could see the shaved bristles above his sculpted beard. "The whole focus is changing. It's outward-oriented, community-oriented. This is what we've needed." He extended a finger to within three inches of her sweater above the breast. "What *you've* needed, Paula. Other people. Isn't it?"

Her face grew hot; she knew she was coloring. She had no idea what he meant but felt utterly transparent. "I have something tonight. Next week?"

"OK." Fine released her with a wink. "I always knew you'd come back to me, Paula."

Fleeing up the exit stairs, she was pursued by Sara Simon.

"Dum-da-dum-dum," Sara said.

"The beginning of the end."

"For me. He'll keep you because you're prettier."

Paula was about to say that with Fine being pretty had its disadvantages. But she realized it wouldn't console Sara. "None of us will go. We'll have a revolution and throw him out."

"And tear him to pieces like the women in that Greek play. It really sucks—he and Suzanne stay on salary, of course. Want to have dinner at the new Mexican place?"

"I'm—going to the movies."

"Sounds like fun." Sara brushed a ringlet of hair from her face. "Do I know the guy?"

"It's not a guy," Paula lied again.

In the bad light of the stairway Sara looked pale and puffy. She was five years deeper into her thirties than Paula, and "Do I know the guy?" was both confession and rebuke. Sara was irremediably single. She had a body firmed up at the YMCA down the street, and a dry wit that appealed to Paula in an otherwise irony-free workplace. Yet her singleness had become a condition—suppressed panic with a whiff of cat hair. But Sara would never go to fat and enlist in the sisterhood with Fran. The tragedy was that she couldn't imagine happiness without a man. She never addressed the subject directly, but it never failed to come up, like someone dying of cancer, deep in denial, yet forever complaining about mysterious stomachaches. Paula sometimes caught in Sara's eyes the devouring look of the doomed: You too some day, you too.

"How about tomorrow?" Paula said.

"I have therapy." In spite of the lies, Sara wasn't letting her off easy. "Well, it's home to Lucy and Spike, the little ingrates. Have a good time, Paula. See you tomorrow at the shop of horrors."

Sara disappeared into the subway. Paula began walking down Mass. Avenue. The sidewalk was slick with rain, and a frozen mist descended on her hair. She'd forgotten her umbrella again. The traffic slid thickly by and at the corner the Number 1 bus wheezed to a stop, splashing the people waiting to board. Paula turned and saw a big man in a shapeless suit coming at her. For a heart-stopping second she thought it was Earl, smiling, approaching to kill with bare hands. The man mimicked her startle, throwing his shoulders back in stylized surprise. When she tried to pass, he stepped in her path. She went the other way and he moved to block her, his pasty face hugely amused.

"Fuck off," she said with false bravado.

"Only if you help."

She managed to get around him, head down, pushing on past the discount children's clothing store, where a secret pedophile was peering in the window. In the light of the bank machine a hooded teenager stared Paula down; she imagined a gun in his backpack.

It was the witching hour, when the whole world went mad. Out of the clinic into rush-hour Central Square, Paula encountered a city full of lunatics. They came out of the cold fog faster than she could keep track. This elegant woman waving for a cab to take her home to her husband's emotional blackmail. These little wailing children dragged along by their mother who was straining against the urge to infanticide. The men whose minds lurched from rape to rape, the women who tore out clumps of their own hair. The respectable alcoholics and the surprise addicts, the liars, self-deceivers, self-haters, the ones who didn't know about themselves half the things Paula knew from a glance at their public faces. The fog was electric with every kind of disturbance.

As she walked, the charge crackled inside her. In the clinic, talk grounded it and the basement's thick stone walls retained it. Here on the street it ran out of control, right through her. A few minutes ago the thought of not being allowed to spend her days bathed in the psychic ills of poor people had made her sick to her stomach.

Recently, Paula had begun to suspect that she lacked the talent of living—of simply entering the mindless stream of life. And that her job was the main expression of this lack, as well as its cause. Anyone who needed a job that badly deserved to be let go. Gladys Dill had handed her an opportunity and she had blown it.

As if the others could do any better. Fran would be so earnest that Gladys would have to kill herself. And Fine! Fine wouldn't last a minute with Earl, he'd say things like "community-oriented" and Earl would have to kill him.

Down the avenue, past the new building going up on what had been for years an empty lot. One day a crater appeared, and now two stories of skeletal steel gleamed in the streetlamps and head-lights. Chain link protected the site but hadn't kept a brigade of rats from escaping when a sewer was rerouted for the foundation. Paula read the latest blue signs on the fence. "Who owns the building?" "What is the building for?" Some paranoid grad-school dropout, hunched over his computer at 3 A.M. Soon she would read about the blue-flyer bombings.

She stopped by The King and I for the order Steve would have phoned ahead. His loft was next door above a photocopy store. He was a forty-year-old city planner, and there wasn't much else she knew about Steve Lorenz. When she rang she was instantly buzzed in. Being buzzed in without a question was part of the secret excite-ment of Wednesday night.

"You again," he said at the front door. She had forgotten the ponytail and earring, because she disapproved—wanted to tell him, "Don't do that, you don't need to." The strong stubbled jawline and sly gray eyes she remembered. In jeans and a bulky maroon sweater he cut a lean figure of advancing hipness.

"Yep, me. Quick, warm up my hands." She held them out and Steve gave a vigorous chafing. He pulled her toward him and then there was the unbelievable softness of human lips. So much of the time everyone had to keep their hands to themselves, brain-stuffed and sense-starved. Tonight, after her brush with a cold, jobless, clientless world, she felt more grateful than usual to be here, to be kissed.

Steve ran his hand through the back of her wavy black hair. Though he cultivated detachment, she knew it was the same for him—the surprise, the pleasure.

"It's wet out there," Steve said.

"Wet and wild."

"Central Square? Come on."

"It's all invisible."

"This city," he said, "is more repressed than Orem, Utah. First

Puritans, then Catholics, then liberals, then yuppies. Herbal or Earl Grey?"

He could be a bore on the subject of Old Cambridge before gentrification—apparently the Ford-Carter era had been a period of continuous debauch—but she didn't mind, because Steve wasn't her boyfriend. He was Wednesday night, the way a therapist only existed on the day of your session. There was an archaic word that she liked: *tryst*. Her pattern was either infatuation with men dimly aware of her existence or else apologetic and repelled flight from the heartbroken. But she and Steve had slept together immediately, without fear or regret. Having no future made them calm and generous. Why they had no future she didn't know.

"It isn't fair," she said as they sat on the wood floor to eat from his junk-shop coffee table.

"Of course it isn't. What?"

"Biology. Demographics. I have a friend who's thirty-six and—"

"Nope, too old. That's when they start to get scary."

His irony irritated her, too safe and smug. "That's what I mean. The other day I heard a man tell another guy, quote, 'I need to meet a woman who's ready for my intensity.' This guy had gray hair. He was at least fifty. Who the hell does he think he is, talking like that?"

"He's Educated American Male. He's pushing the evolutionary envelope."

"He ought to be helping his wife through menopause. It's obscene."

"While your friend's eggs go to waste. It isn't fair."

In Steve's good looks there was a sort of decayed youthfulness. All these years on the scene of his higher education, haunting the same bookstores, watching his favorite bars turn into boutiques, had arrested his growth. In ten years Steve would be telling someone about his intensity.

He was reporting on his current peeve: the half-finished construction site up the street.

"What's that building for anyway?"

"I just told you, Paula, nobody has a clue, that's the problem."

She had been thinking about Fine—Fine wanted the building for the Problem Place. Big ideas while they went down the tube. What the hell did he mean, "You've needed this"? What did she need?

"The owner was building office space," Steve said. "He had his problems with the IRS and lost it. The city took over and now no one can make a decision and the work's still going on. I'm surprised you don't know any of this."

"I should be more political."

"Now everyone's getting in on the act. An AIDS clinic, says the gay community. A youth center, says the—the African American community. Oh no, say the homeless advocates, a wet shelter. We'll buy it, says big bad MIT. Twenty developers want to bid for retail plus luxury housing. There's even a rumor a Florida gaming enterprise is interested. A casino in Central Square! And the city council is shitting its pants, like 'Building? What building?'"

Paula nodded, locked her eyes on Steve's, and timed her "Mm-hmms" as if, like a first-time client, he might clam up any second.

"Anyway, it's not important."

"I'm sorry, I was listening."

"Never mind. Let's hear about your day with the emotionally challenged."

Pouting made Steve's fork clumsy with the yellow-curry beef, and it blew away her fantasy of an insouciant at ease in a world that bewildered and threatened her. What, she wondered, was his fantasy of her? Dark pretty little sister of charity with a fun side. Tending to the poor and then to him. She told Steve about Fine and the cutbacks but left out the moment of her undoing with Gladys Dill.

"It scares me to need this job that much. I literally can't imagine how I'd live without it."

His eyes were unfocusing. She wondered if marriage was like this.

They watched a video. Nestled against his chest, she drifted in and out of sleep, feeling a vague urgency to keep him talking, and the characters in the movie too, afraid the tape would stop if she faded out, wanting to apologize to them all every time she woke up. Finally she gave in to the downward pull.

Paula jerked awake as Steve was rewinding. "Great movie."

"Do you always twitch in your sleep so much?"

"I don't know, I'm always asleep." She didn't like being seen unconscious, nerves discharging the day's electricity after the current is switched off.

"They say you have to trust someone to sleep in their presence."

"I think I'm just really tired." Not that I don't trust you, she thought. What could the word mean for them? He mimed a hurt face as he cleared the plates, mocking himself, and it was enough to make her like him again. When Steve came back from the kitchen she reached for his hand, pulling herself up into a kiss. She enjoyed her ability to please him; the sex itself she liked better than cooking, less than conversation. Before Steve there had been almost a year without—the period when the talent of living had begun to elude her. She knew that men liked the way she looked and the things she did, but a strange detachment from her own body had set in, as if it were made of foam rubber wired to her nervous system. Once sex had been an effortless pleasure, she'd jumped into bed with men she didn't care to remember now. She longed for this one to take her out of her head.

The ritual of undressing, condom-fumbling. His style of narcissism was to let her come first, but tonight, with Gladys and everything else, she knew it was hopeless and coaxed him along. "What about you?" "No, never mind, you." In the middle of his climax, the buttocks-tensing earnestness of it all struck her as extremely funny. She tried to stifle a giggle and dissolved in helpless laughter. She apologized, and for a moment it was touch-and-go whether he would take offense; then they were laughing together.

Shortly, under his warm weight, she was asleep again.

"Why don't you stay the night?"

Paula came to groggy and grumpy. Inside her he felt like an uninvited finger.

"Mm . . . that's tempting. Jesus, what time is it?"

The blue digits of his clock radio read 11:08. She thought of checking her office voice mail. Any disasters out there?

"I should probably get home."

"Bagels on the house," he said, "then you can walk to work. It's wet and wild out there."

And it was warm in here. And in the morning she would put on yesterday's underwear, and brush her teeth with his toothbrush, and he would still be there.

"Then a rain check? I don't have my makeup or toothbrush."

"I have a spare. I admit I'm out of lipstick."

"It's a nice offer."

"So accept it."

She eased him out and off her and sat up.

"Too spontaneous?" he asked. "Need time to analyze it?"

"No." As she covered herself with the wool blanket, irritation prickled her skin. She saw clearly the awkwardness of cream cheese, the false kiss at the door, the stale disorderly day. "I have nothing against spontaneity. I just have a thing about going home at night."

"Maybe I shouldn't have offered."

"No, it's sweet of you."

Dressing, she felt his resentful gaze in the darkness.

"I want to see if you turn into a pumpkin at midnight."

"Unfortunately, I never stop being me."

"'All you want is my body!'" Steve imitated female hysteria and pretended to find the reversal amusing. "'You never respected me!'"

Paula was hurrying with her snaps and buttons. There were a hundred things she didn't want to know about him, and now that the stuffing was pouring out she was furious. "You could just call me a little tramp."

"I like little tramps."

"That must be your problem."

"What's your problem, Paula? Because you clearly have one."

Paula stopped zipping up her skirt. She imagined the sneer on his handsome, preserved face. The hurt pride of demographically spoiled Educated American Male.

"You don't know me," she told him.

Steve fell silent.

In his bathrobe he showed her to the door. At the touch of the brass knob, Paula suddenly felt dizzy. Vertigo dimmed her vision, and then came the nauseous burning in her throat that she had felt in the conference room when her job had trembled and cracked. She paused in confusion and closed her eyes.

"I hope your building gets worked out," she told him.

"Thanks. I hope you don't get downsized."

If they'd only said this before then things would have gone as always, he wouldn't have asked her to stay, and they could now say good night without wondering if there would be another Wednesday.

To get home she had to take two buses and it was on the second, composing herself against the window and watching the rotten triple-deckers of Prospect Street tilt crazily against the night sky, that Paula understood what had gone wrong. Steve had asked for more than fifty minutes. She knew by heart the reasons why you respected the limit: You got more done in the available time, you both knew what to expect, the encounter remained under control. Pushed, she was ready to bring her authority to bear.

Paula lived near Union Square, in an old brick building whose long hallways and broad staircase suggested a boarding house from the Sacco and Vanzetti era. It even had a name, the Narconia, which was never satisfactorily explained to Paula but seemed apt. The Narconia housed a strange collection of tenants: Irish widows, immigrant families from Egypt and Haiti, single mothers on subsidy, pale quiet people working in marginal jobs as paralegals or teaching assistants. The damp smell of the hallway runner, the gloom of the varnish, the tinny slamming of mailboxes—all of it said that no one in the Narconia was getting anywhere.

Paula had moved into this building when she came up from New York, during the late-eighties boom. The Narconia was a temporary solution to the shortage of affordable apartments—a room and a half with a fine view of the Dumpster, a neighborhood of funeral homes and bathtub madonnas behind rosebushes in the tidy front yards of aluminum-siding houses. Her apartment never fully shed its odor of fried potatoes and lemon-scented air freshener. But Paula painted the woodwork white and replaced the yellowing curtains with bamboo blinds. Six years later it was still home.

Her key was hardly in the lock when the next door flew open. Mary's face, sagging from the dozen children who never visited, peered out. Scandal was magnified in her eyes by plastic glasses that reminded Paula of Gladys Dill's missing lens.

"Paula dear, thank God you come home. The super and his wife been fighting all evening with all sorts of language. Now Linda's catching her death outside in nothing but her nightie and Bud's been smashing the kitchenware and watching violence on TV."

Paula sighed. "What am I supposed to do about it?"

This checked Mary's titillated panic. "I just thought since you come home, and you work with them crazies and all—I'd go out myself only I ain't dressed and she don't like me anyway because I'm friends with Colleen in Number 17."

Paula withdrew her key. It was probably her own fault that people assumed she was willing to solve every problem, but at the moment it made her want to smash some kitchenware herself. Passing the super's apartment, she smelled beer and dead ash from under the door. The TV was on—a woman was screaming.

Around the side of the building the super's wife, barefoot on an upturned cinder block, was leaning over the Dumpster and rummaging furiously. Bags were torn, bottles smashed. Linda's nightgown, which Bud might have bought her during a tender mood, barely covered the tops of her thighs. As she disappeared over the side, a red bottom came into view. Paula recoiled.

"Who the fuck is no use around here, you useless fuck?" The voice was headless, as if the Dumpster itself were drunk and rebellious.

"Linda?"

"What!"

"Are you looking for something?"

"He threw my fucking prescription away!"

"What prescription?"

CENTRAL SQUARE | 21

"*Mine.*"

Levering herself up on her belly, the super's wife confronted her questioner. In their only previous conversation they had discussed a washing machine that was prone to overflowing; Linda had seemed simple and sweet.

"Can't your doctor write another?"

"He says he won't!"

Linda began to weep. Her face twisted with shameless, childlike sobs.

"It's cold, and it's starting to rain again."

"But I need it!" Linda looked at the Dumpster. "He'll steal it, the dirty bastard!"

She began lowering her body down inside.

"Linda, I'm afraid you'll fall in."

"Good, they can haul me away."

"Can you tell me what the prescription was for?"

"None of your fucking business!"

"Fine." Tired and cold, Paula had had enough. It might be tragic, but it was also a pain. With a strange feeling of satisfaction she went back inside. That was how it was done: The super's wife had told her to fuck off, and she had told the super's wife to fuck off. They had both connected with their feelings and gotten admirably to the point, using a minimum of jargon. It felt like her first real human contact of the day.

Mary was by her door, wringing the knot of her bathrobe. "What are you going to do?"

"If Linda wants to freeze in a Dumpster that's her business."

Paula's answering machine carried a message from her mother — a long account of an argument with her West Fourth Street neighbor who had complained that she was playing an Edith Piaf CD too loud. In the oldest corner of her being, Paula felt a flutter of panic. Too late to call. She told herself that her mother would survive until morning.

Mercifully, nothing on her voice mail at the Problem Place.

She sat on the edge of the tub while hot water steamed around her naked body. Half-dozing, she entertained the notion that the super's wife had shown her the same truth she had just learned with Steve. That she really *didn't* care. About anyone.

But it was supposed to be her business to care. For fifty minutes and a modest fee, within the rules. She was a fraud.

Paula imagined a man standing beside her in the bathroom, stroking her shoulder, telling her to stop being so hard on herself.

In the bath she scrubbed with her coarse sponge and the water darkened. She rid herself of the day's involvements so that she might sleep straight through the night without troubling dreams and wake up clean and shiny to go back into the fray. Because it was her contribution. She was good at it, they told her so, the ones who knew. In a murmur that she once used as a girl for prayer, Paula vowed to make Gladys Dill better, stronger, happier.

She walked in her kimono through her room and a half, absently tidying up. At the sight of the clutter on her table, sadness came over her. She took a muscle relaxant and turned on the radio. A novelist was being interviewed. She switched to music, then turned it off. The radiator was clanking to life. As she lay on the covers, Steve's doorknob flashed through her mind and she became dizzy again.

She had tricked herself. What she had felt at his door wasn't relief at all.

Fine said she needed something—he had a way of drilling into her brain. Weekly meetings with strangers? What she needed didn't come in groups. But she wouldn't go back to Steve's again, for her own good. Because a lover wasn't a client. Lovers loved. The thought of not going back frightened her, but she would do this; it would be decisive, like leaving Linda outside.

Paula switched off the light and lifted the blinds. Down the alley the Dumpster huddled in a dark mass, but the super's wife was nowhere to be seen.

two

In the heart of the crowd Joe tried to look like everyone else, but a man and woman had already spotted him. Beyond the glass booths their faces dissolved in his hunger and fatigue, but he saw the blue and white uniforms and felt their eyes tracking him in the crush toward Immigration. Among dull overcoats his shiny suit of African wax glared red and yellow and green. The windbreaker he had bought at Heathrow for the cold spread the British flag across his back like a target.

He thought speaking to the Dutchman might take their attention off him.

"Do you think it will be snowing?"

"Oh no, too early. Raining. It rains always in Boston."

The Dutchman said everything as if it was grim and funny and he had no doubt. Joe was the one who sounded like a foreigner. The Dutchman went back to his children's passports. On the flight from London he and Joe had talked about Africa, where the Dutchman had business in oil. They shared bribery stories and illness stories, and although the Dutchman's Africa sounded silly and unreal, Joe was grateful to have a seatmate who knew a little. Halfway across the Atlantic, in the hush of the cabin, he had closed his eyes and pretended the plane was taking him back there. But it was his first time, none of it had happened, everything still lay ahead of him.

They weren't seatmates here in the airport. Africa was just a place for the Dutchman, and now Boston was another—everyone tense, focused on the glass booths, thin clean-smelling air, the man and woman in uniform. But they had disappeared.

"My friend, it's the wrong line for you," the Dutchman said. "You see? Non-nationals."

Joe looked up into the blur of lighted signs and felt a hand on his shoulder.

"Would you step over here, sir?" Raccoon eyes staring under a black eyebrow grown together across the bridge of nose.

The man in uniform led Joe out of the line and over to a window. The wing of the plane was visible beneath a low charcoal sky. The woman was waiting, blond, square-faced.

"Sir, this is Miss Fargen. I'm Mr. DeSouza. U.S. Customs Service. We're going to ask you a few questions."

Mr. DeSouza spoke very carefully. Joe tried to smile and a Halloween mask stretched across the bones of his face.

"What was your port of embarkation, sir?"

"London Heathrow."

"And before that?"

"Lagos, Nigeria."

The Customs officers exchanged a glance. "Passport," Miss Fargen said.

It was in his backpack. He struggled out of the shoulder straps. "Did you check any luggage?" Mr. DeSouza asked. Joe shook his head. "How much currency are you carrying?"

He had to convert three different exchanges. Halfway through he lost track and started over. It came to slightly under a hundred dollars. Joe couldn't believe it was so little.

Miss Fargen said, "What's your motive for coming to the United States?"

Joe started to answer and nothing came. He couldn't think of his motive.

"Student?" Her eyes didn't believe it.

"I need a motive?"

Her mouth flickered, a laugh about to explode off her lips. "Passport." Joe had forgotten.

When he brought it out of the zippered pouch, Mr. DeSouza's jaw flexed. He grabbed the little booklet, a silver eagle fading on its cover, and fumbled through the pages. He moistened his finger on his tongue, touched a page, scratched at it with his thumbnail. Then he looked up at Joe in a new way, narrow-eyed.

Joe understood now and his heart began to beat fast. He heard himself say in a deep African voice, with a little African laugh: *No problem. You are doing your job. Oh that uniform suits a girl like you.* He would wipe that look she'd given him off her face.

What's your motive, fool? Who the hell are you, flying in here without a motive. They picked you out like a bad joke.

The Customs officers had moved a short distance away.

"Nigerian passport scam," Joe heard Mr. DeSouza mutter.

"Dressed like this?"

"They're good at accents."

"Roland, don't personalize."

"*And* they use Americans."

Miss Fargen turned away and approached Joe. He had become a nuisance to her. "Would you open your bag?"

If he really was an African, if this was an airport in Africa, it would happen like this: He would say that he was a busy man with things to do. They would frown and say it was going to take a long time. He would walk away for a few minutes, and then he would come back with a bill tucked in his passport like a bookmark. He would say he hoped there was some way for the process to be expedited. The passport would be taken away to be stamped and then returned without its bookmark. There would be a brief search that was really no search. Handshakes, laughs, good-byes. No one would ever mention the money, but it would make him the important man he had said he was.

The Dutchman and his family were gone. The sky was darkening over the jet's wing. By the window, Mr. DeSouza patted Joe down. Miss Fargen in her blue skirt knelt over his backpack like a doctor examining a corpse. Everything he owned was scattered around the shiny floor: a knot of clothing he hadn't had time to wash, insect repellent, foot powder, iodine tablets, a paperback book an Englishman had given him.

He felt that she was inspecting *him*, mouth, balls, asshole; turning him inside out, and the contact of heated air and artificial light and woman's hands was killing his Africa spirit, leaving meat and bones, a fool without a motive. The cut on his arm throbbed.

"Don't touch that," Joe said.

Miss Fargen had pulled out a block of dark wood hacked into the figure of a human being, with a cork stopper in its hollow skull. "What is it?"

"I said don't touch it. That's personal property."

"Let me see." Mr. DeSouza took it from Miss Fargen, turned it around, shook it, opened the head, sniffed unpleasantly. Then he put the statue in his shirt pocket, skull and stopper peeking out, as if he owned it.

"You're invited to continue this conversation in my office. I want you to think about your situation while you put those things away."

Packing, Joe thought about his situation and decided it could go one of two ways. He could snatch the statue, coldcock the raccoon face, elbow Miss Fargen through the glass, sprint to the gate where they had the next plane to Africa, and slip into his seat as the engines were starting up. Like in the movies.

Or he could just go with it. Because Africa was already a dream.

An abalone diver in San Francisco once told him about something called "neutral buoyancy." When you inflated your vest and cleared your ears, water and air pressure outside and inside you was equalized. You didn't float up or sink down against your will but moved with total freedom, gravity and all forces that act on a body canceled. So if it felt like you had to hit someone, or cry, you could pinch your nose, breathe out, and be free again. Neutral buoyancy was important for survival but very difficult. Joe could never sustain the state for long.

He finished packing and stood up. The terminal air was peppery in his nostrils.

"No problem. You are doing your job."

Another plane load was filling the room. In the passageway out of Immigration, a flag was suspended across the wall. Above it a sign said: "Boston Logan International Airport. Welcome To The United States Of America."

They walked for what felt like miles, through one terminal and then another, under lights and past mirrored walls that fractured him into hundreds of Joes, all of them startled and exhausted. People stared openly. He glided alongside Mr. DeSouza down a corridor, through a blank door, into a bright cramped office with a metal desk and two plastic chairs. Miss Fargen had disappeared.

"Where did you get that?"

Joe was taking off the British Airways windbreaker. A cloth scrap that had once been a piece of his underwear was glued to his left forearm by the dried blood of a short, deep, transverse wound.

"In Africa."

"What happened?"

"I cut myself."

"You cut yourself. Who are the Dodgers?"

"What?"

"Where do the Dodgers play?"

"L.A."

"Who plays here?"

"Red Sox."

Mr. DeSouza stared at Joe. He closed his eyes briefly and sighed. In the fluorescent light his face was a shade of gray.

"Look, I need your help. OK?"

"OK."

The Customs officer sat forward, gray face sagging. He waited.

"What do you want?" Joe said.

"Dammit, you knew at Immigration. What did you think we stopped you for?"

"Because—" Joe hesitated. "The stealing."

Mr. DeSouza was becoming extremely irritated. "What stealing?"

"Before I went to Africa."

"What did you steal?"

"Five hundred and seventeen dollars."

"For Christ's sake." Mr. DeSouza slapped his bony thigh and looked around for help. "You come off that plane like Joe Illegal African, scared to death. OK, maybe not, but you've *been* in Africa. Plus you haven't got enough luggage and cash for a day trip to Providence. Then this artifact in my pocket sets you off with Evie— you were ready to jump her, right? Now you show me this ugliness on your arm that looks like someone tried to make a pretty strong statement." He was watching Joe from under the eyebrow. "My opinion—you're the type of amateur that saw an easy way to cover airfare home."

It broke over Joe like a hot dirty rain.

"I'm carrying drugs?"

"Yes you are. Someone over there spotted you for a yo-yo, asked you to do a favor and you thought, hey, this once—"

"You don't know what you're talking about, mister." His tongue tasted sour. He got out of the chair. He had a picture of himself riding up and down on a string tied to Mr. DeSouza's finger.

"Take it easy."

"I don't have to sit for this. Give me my thing back."

"Sit down, please."

"You think you know all about me."

"I don't think anything. You could be anyone. You could be famous."

All of a sudden the anger drained away, leaving him weak on his feet, helplessly weak like in a dream. Mr. DeSouza waved him down, and Joe sat.

"Talk to me about your trip."

"What about it?"

Mr. DeSouza opened the passport to a visa page. "What were you doing in this country for a year?"

"Planting trees."

"Most people have something they need to be doing back home. What about your family?"

They're waiting for me, he almost said. It's been years and they're in that crowd outside Customs and they're starting to worry, because they have a big party waiting. But it still wouldn't be true.

"They died."

Mr. DeSouza moved his head to an angle. "All of them?"

"My foster parents. An auto accident."

"What about your real parents?"

Joe set his teeth and didn't answer. Mr. DeSouza was watching him sideways.

"No job?"

"I lost it."

"What kind?"

"A stupid job. Photocopying."

"How'd you lose it?"

Joe looked away. On the wall three posters were thumbtacked: a cigarette with a red slash through it, a height-weight chart, and a picture of the major food groups.

"You don't want to tell me about it?"

"I got caught stealing."

"Why'd you steal from your stupid job?"

Joe wanted to rest his head against his knees. Telling the truth was exhausting, facts were facts, dumb and leaden, always the same.

Mr. DeSouza edged his chair forward. "Joe, when someone falls under my purview I feel responsible for them. Evie—Miss Fargen—says I personalize. Guilty. I don't know you. But did those bastards in Lagos tell you what happens if one of the condoms opens before the mule passes it? When heroin enters your bloodstream from your stomach, it's like you've died and gone to heaven. Incredible feeling. Only problem is, you really are on your way to heaven. And the thing is, you *know* this, but you can't really *believe* it because you feel so damn great. Until the convulsions and the foaming start. If you're lucky you have a heart attack first. I bet those bastards didn't tell you that."

Half-listening, Joe had gone under water, gliding in the blue depth, turning somersaults. He knew what he was going to do. The strongest pressure in the room wasn't gravity or anger or the facts, but Mr. DeSouza's wish for him to be a mule with a nest of heroin-filled condoms in his stomach. He could go that way, if that was what they wanted. A lot simpler really.

He still mourned the African traveler at Immigration.

"If I'm doing this, what's the penalty?"

For the first time Mr. DeSouza smiled, showing gray gums. "We'll work something out. First offense, never charged on the stealing? You got in trouble over there and just did what you had to do to survive, like anyone, right?"

He patted Joe's knee, then he reached around and opened the desk drawer and withdrew a small flat box.

"What this is, Joe, is fast-acting Ex-Lax. You take one of these and in no time it passes out."

The rectangle wrapped in foil was chocolate, but as Joe swallowed it brought a taste of metal to his tongue, the trick in the disguise.

Half an hour later he was escorted down the hall by a policeman and a young orderly in a medical smock. The policeman stopped at the door to the men's room.

"I'm not going in with him."

"He could destroy the evidence," the orderly said.

"Jesus Christ."

Joe sat in a stall with his embroidered pants down around his espadrilles and the door wide open. The cop's back was turned. Iron-haired and furious, he was squinting into the mirror above the sinks.

Joe's chemically loosened bowels voided into the silver bag that the orderly had given him. And in the shock of release, he suddenly understood his motive. It was to sit on a cold toilet seat under the eyes of a policeman and feel these things.

The orderly would stare through the microscope and say, "Come here, look at this. The yo-yo was mad and sad and no one knew."

"Don't flush!" the policeman barked. He came over to inspect. The water in the bowl was clear. He set the sole of his polished black shoe against the handle and shoved violently. Joe held out the bag. "Give it to the orderly," the cop told him, turning away. "I got nothing to do with that."

"I'm frankly a little perplexed, Joe." Mr. DeSouza couldn't conceal his disappointment. "If you ever want to talk, anything you want me to know, here's my card." He raised his hands. "It certainly was not racial. Honest mistake, right? What are you planning for yourself?"

"I'm going to look for a job."

"Do you know someone? I mean, why Boston?"

At Heathrow, Joe had overheard two Americans talking about a huge digging project that was going on under Boston. They were building tunnels and roads right below the city. Joe had liked the thought of working underground. It had seemed like a way to start over.

Mr. DeSouza shook his head. "The Big Dig has been full for years. You don't know the situation here, there's competition for toilet-cleaner. No one's going to just pick you out of the crowd. I mean, the clothes, this thing on your arm. You need a strategy. Everyone has to be their own P.R. guy. Where are you staying?"

"If there's an inexpensive hotel . . ."

"You can't afford a hotel. Wait, I'm going to make a few calls."

The names of the places Mr. DeSouza called were Lifeline, St. Mary's, and Another Chance. None had a vacancy. "They fill up when the weather turns cold," he told Joe. "Let me try Rainbow House in Central Square."

"Is it like a flophouse? Where bums sleep?"

"This one's clean, it's safe."

Rainbow House had a bed.

Joe put on his windbreaker and swung the backpack over his shoulders. In the doorway he stopped and turned.

"I need my thing back."

Mr. DeSouza hurriedly gave him the statue, and Joe put it in his windbreaker pocket. Still he didn't leave.

"You thought I was African."

Gray gums flashed. "Hey, I apologize."

"But why did you think I was?"

"It must have been the clothes. Miss Fargen made the exact same mistake. Maybe you picked up an accent."

"It wasn't—my face?"

"Oh no, not at all. Nothing like that. Look, here's a subway token. You need warmer shoes. Watch yourself, Joe, it can get crazy out there."

Central Square ran with cars and lights and cold rain, and the rain raked down Joe's face and soaked through the windbreaker into his skin. The ink on Mr. DeSouza's little map was smearing. All around, people hurried along the sidewalk with their heads down. Joe was beginning to feel like a foreigner again when he looked up and saw the street sign halfway down the deserted block: a rainbow. It looked like a child's finger painting, ragged bands of color curving over a steel door.

The man who answered his knock wore a baseball cap and an army jacket and had a bandage on his face. When he saw Joe, he did a double take.

"Not a chance, brother, you way too late. Lottery's already started." He flashed his watch, which said 7:25.

"I'm here for a bed."

"Think I'm talking about Mass Millions?"

The man with the bandage glanced over his shoulder, and then he let Joe into an unheated and windowless entryway. By a lightbulb over the stairwell, Joe made out shapes wedged together, slouching, squatting. No one spoke. There was a trapped stench of dirty feet. He wondered what kind of people stayed here. He eased out of his pack and backed against a wall, shivering, the wound on his arm starting to hurt again. He waited for someone to come out of the gloom with fists flying.

"Can we please do one more count, people?" A high nervous voice from the stairs. "How many of you are presigned?"

Near Joe a stocky white man in a blue knit cap raised his hand. Other hands went up.

"You presigned?" asked the man with the bandage, who had let Joe in.

Joe started to nod, then shook his head.

"Me neither." The man was staring at him, unsmiling but not unfriendly. "Where the hell you in from?"

Joe said, "Africa."

"Holy shit! Lay it right there, brother." He seized Joe's hand in both of his. "Welcome to America, the real Third World. My advice is you should've stayed home, where you and me both belong." He lowered his voice. "They don't need to know you was late."

Joe opened his mouth to correct him, then shut it. Let the man think so if he wanted to. Funny thing, though, for it to happen twice.

The entryway was emptying. The people who had raised their hands shuffled toward the stairs and climbed. A dozen others were left behind. A broad-backed woman with frizzy blond hair sat on a duffel bag, scowling. A man on metal crutches leaned against the wall and whispered to himself. An old white woman with two shopping bags lowered herself onto the bottom step, looked up, and saw Joe. "My Gawd, he's beautiful!"

A young man in a crewneck sweater was counting the leftovers.

"Does everyone understand the rules? If you're not presigned and you were here by seven you go into the lottery. Tonight we have five beds left. So some of you won't be our guests tonight. I wish that wasn't the case." The high nervous voice cracked. "I wish we didn't have to turn anyone away. I wish we didn't *need* a shelter, because housing is a right and you all—"

"Start the fucking lottery," said the woman on the duffel bag.

"I'm just a volunteer here."

The volunteer walked around with a shoe box, from which everyone drew a balled-up scrap of paper. The woman on the duffel bag read hers and faked a machine-gun assault. A black kid in a hooded jacket waved his ticket and looked for someone to high-five, but the others were too preoccupied to notice.

When the volunteer reached Joe, a rashed face in a furry parka hood cried, "He was late, he don't get to play."

"Aw, give the brother a break, Bugs Bunny," said the man who had let Joe in. "He's from Africa, that's why he was late."

"I don't care if he's from the moon, he ain't taking my bed."

"You ain't got a bed, how's he going to take it?"

The volunteer stood before Joe, a smile pasted on his face. "I'm sorry, we have to stick to the rules." He hurried off with the shoe box.

"Tough luck, brother." The man with the bandage showed Joe his own scrap: 5. "I'm in," he said tonelessly. "Back in Africa bet you didn't think it was going to be like this. Let me tell you something, brother, this is *exactly* what it's like."

Joe sank against the wall, and the tile made him shiver violently. It was still raining outside. He would have to sleep under a tree. You could do it in Africa if you watched out for red ants, but here—cops, killers, cold, rain. Maybe Mr. DeSouza was laughing about it right now with Miss Fargen. "That yo-yo we thought was an African mule? I sent him to Rainbow House." "That's a good one!"

Joe said, "At the airport they told me there was a bed here."

"You got a referral?" The man stroked the bandage on his cheek and his eyes wandered off. He murmured, "This your lucky night."

Joe's name was written on the volunteer's clipboard. He was in—Number 5 was out. The man took it with a shrug.

"This ain't no problem for me," he interrupted Joe's thanks. "Lots of places I can stay. Just remember one of your American brothers helped you out. I know some of you come over here and avoid us. Don't you do like that, 'cause we the same. Remember."

He went out into the rain. Joe lifted his pack and started for the stairs. The man with metal crutches was sitting on the bottom step, eyes fixed on the floor, forehead scrunched up as if he was thinking of a way to make the lottery come out different. Joe was afraid he would look up and their eyes would meet—*give me your bed, buddy. Someone did it for you. Pass it on to a crip.* But the man didn't look up; he was trying to figure it out on his own. Joe stepped around the crutches and climbed the stairs.

"This is fucked-up," the parka hood said.

"It absolutely isn't fair." The volunteer was groping in his pocket.

"I didn't say that, did I? I said it's fucked-up. The system's rigged."

"Here's a token. They let you sleep at the international terminal out at Logan."

"I don't want your token. I want justice."

Below him Joe heard the high nervous voice trying to explain the rules. A familiar smell was warming his ascent. It was the most wonderful smell in the world. By the top step he had identified it as spaghetti sauce.

"Welcome to the house of the dead." Joe had set his paper plate next to a man with a bloodshot face and a thick sweep of graying hair combed over his jacket collar. His voice, a mix of slur and growl, sounded British, or some version of Bostonian, which was like no American accent Joe had ever heard. "Very much a Dostoyevskian experience, you'll find."

"Don't pay him no mind," an obese woman at their table told Joe. "He thinks he's superior but he's just crazy."

"Madam, my sanity may be in question but my superiority is not. You are devouring that pasta with extraordinary speed, young sir, next to a sometime faculty member of a well-known institution down the street, as well as one of the country's leading neoformalist poets."

"So what are you doing in here?" It was the stocky man in the blue knit cap, a sneer twisting up his doughy face. The poet twirled drenched noodles around his fork. "I said, what the fuck you doing in here?"

"Passing a bit of time between projects. I'm off to France next week to meet with colleagues about a film script that may be of great mutual benefit."

"You're off to shit. Looks like you been hitting the water pretty good."

"Respect the man's privacy," said the other person at their table, a black man with a tired face and two front teeth missing. He had nodded when Joe sat down. "And ain't nobody in here any different than anybody else, Mr. Poet, that's *obvious*. Take care of that," he told Joe, pointing at his arm. "They got a medical van coming tomorrow. I hope it wasn't one of our young bucks did that to you."

"I ain't ashamed to say why I'm here," the man in the knit cap said, "because it wasn't my fault. I was in Walpole six months for ripping off a faggot social club where this liar says he teaches. My apartment in Dorchester that my fucking cousin was supposed to be looking after was burglarized. Didn't leave me a fucking thing."

"What one might call poetic justice," the poet muttered over his Kool-Aid to Joe.

"Watch your language." The obese woman smiled sweetly at Joe. "Don't you listen to Kevin, dear. We're not all ignorant here."

"Ignorant's what I was before the joint," Kevin said. "But I figured things out inside. Number 1, the biggest problem with this country is mongrelism. What's a mutt good for?" No one looked at him. "Making more mutts, mental retards. Walpole's full of mongrels. I ain't prejudiced, this is scientific. Take him."

Kevin indicated Joe with a plastic fork.

"Like you're African, right? You're lucky, you come from a pure genetic stock."

Joe glanced at the faces. No one was giving him a look. They believed it. How did that happen?

"Blacks in this country don't have your advantages because of all that Mandingo shit. See, I ain't prejudiced," Kevin told the room. "These are facts."

"The fact," the black man said, patting his gap-toothed mouth with a paper napkin, "is you ain't the first I seen come out of there more messed up than you went in."

The poet mimed applause. Kevin pushed his chair out and stared him back into his spaghetti.

Talk died. Someone slept with his head on the table. A black girl wearing thick glasses smiled to herself as she buttered her bread. A woman with a ponytail and milky skin stared at the Kool-Aid pitcher.

The poet turned to Joe. "Am I given to understand you're from Africa?"

It had to be more than what he'd said downstairs, more than his clothes, his build, the tone of his skin. There had to be a look in his eyes. It was his face and the way he carried himself. They wanted his opinion, his approval, like someone important. But as soon as he opened his mouth, he would give himself away.

"I used to know Soyinka," the poet said before Joe could answer. "Wonderful chap, witty, serious, *engagé*—God, what a voice. Irresponsible teacher but they forgave him, with a voice like that."

"I'm out of here tomorrow," Kevin announced. "I got business. This place is more fucked-up than the joint."

Dinner was over.

Rainbow House had a basement full of used clothes and guests were allowed to browse under the exposed pipes. When someone found a fit, everyone got more tense, like a treasure hunt. Two men came close to blows over a down jacket with a broken zipper.

Joe lucked into a pair of jeans. The back pocket was white with the ghost of a wallet, a pen line ran across the left front. The Africans called the Goodwill "dead white man's clothes" and believed that traces of the former owner's power and wealth crossed the ocean inside. The former owner of these jeans must have had money in his pocket, a job that used his brain, enough comfort to get rid of a good pair of pants. A loving wife, maybe a child, maybe more than one. Joe felt his luck changing already.

Behind a coat rack he peeled off his damp clothes. A denim shirt missing two buttons, a navy pea coat with a ripped lining, and cracked workboots completed the transformation. He went back upstairs with his wax suit in a roll under his arm. No one seemed to notice—even in his strange clothes they took him for an African. He would keep the suit in case he needed it.

Rainbow House was a converted dance studio. In a large room that smelled of disinfectant and dirty clothes, cots were spread across the floor. On the cot next to Joe's the poet sat fully dressed, shuffling through a briefcase full of papers. The overhead lights flashed.

"All right, listen up." The director stood in the door, hairy forearms folded across his chest. "Who needs an early wake-up?" The man missing two teeth and a few others raised their hands for the five o'clock day-labor pickup. "From 9 to 11 tomorrow morning a free medical van will be parked outside. If you do not know about the Problem Place, it is a walk-in counseling center right around the corner with skilled mental health professionals."

Names, laughter, angry denials echoed across the dance floor.

"Cool it! It's not a stigma. Avail yourselves. Tomorrow's *Globe* job listings will be posted at breakfast. Everyone must be out of the shelter by 8. OK, good night everybody."

The lights went out. Joe began to undress when someone sat down on his cot.

"Would you care for some rather ill-used indigenous companionship tomorrow?" A hand fumbled onto his shoulder, a little scurrying creature. "I'm a bit worried, I haven't quite got the hang of this yet. My dear wife expelled me just last week for—" The poet broke into a laugh. "Intemperance, she said. I can't quite conceive how to occupy myself. And our friend from Walpole Prison has just promised to, as he expressed it, put a little fear in my life."

"You were going to France."

"Ah—until then. I'll introduce you to the Cambridge glitterati. I know everyone. They'll adore you. Africa is very big."

The creature on Joe's shoulder had died there. Darkness clarified the sound of the poet's voice: desperation. Joe was feeling desperate, too. The African Joe had disappeared in the darkness, leaving his own voice to betray him. He twisted and flung the hand off his shoulder.

Silence. The cot became lighter, the poet got to his feet. Joe started to speak, expecting his voice to break and leak out. But he sounded calm—it was Amouzou's night voice, when the kerosene lamps were lit and the bush just outside the hut.

"I have business."

"Apologies. One's alone out here anyway, on the heath." The poet moved away. "Fatuous scribblers. They have no fucking idea."

The big room was underheated and Joe huddled in his blanket with the pea coat drawn over him. He was too exhausted to sleep.

The town in Africa lay spread across a hillside, and when he arrived he was accepted there like an act of God, as if a place had always been waiting for him. The place was a whitewashed cement house on the lower edge of town. He filled it with furniture made from forest hardwood by Amouzou, a man whose shop was next door. Amouzou had learned an old-fashioned English from the BBC: "hale and hardy," "starvation cheap." He was round-faced and barrel-chested, and at the cinema house or in the Syrian hardware store Joe heard people call him "Monkey-Head." But the mockery stopped at sunset, because behind the shopyard littered with reddish wood shavings there was a room where Amouzou or Monkey-Head kept his cowrie shells, his horsehair flyswats, his hand mirrors, his Gordon's gin, and the wooden figure with the hollow skull. By day he made chairs, an unimportant man; by night he commanded the unseen forces of the dark, changing his shape and the shapes of others, the sick who came to him for help.

After three months, Joe finally was admitted into this room and the world of powders and incantations.

In the afternoons it rained. The red clay foamed and ran downhill. Afterward, the heat broken, the town smelled fresh, and Joe walked down the main road greeting women with babies lashed to their backs, farmers straggling home from the fields, and the bread lady with a grapefruit-sized goiter. Her hand-painted sign said "Modern Bakery," and the picture of a woman in a giant Afro and brilliant cloth turned her into a big-city businesswoman. Alongside her bakery stood a ditch where schoolchildren dropped their khaki shorts or hiked up their Goodwill dresses. The stench of the ditch mingled with the aroma of warm bread all the way down the road.

Joe supervised the planting of 500 trees. He formed a livestock cooperative among schoolboy dropouts who had become petty criminals. Townspeople made it known that their daughters were available. You must stay here, they told him, marry, have children, and when you grow old and die we will build a tomb for you in the forest where the chiefs are buried. No one asked what he had run away from, what he had to go back to. He lived at his surface, like a sketch of himself. Nothing was expected; and yet he was special, loved.

One morning—it was the day before yesterday—none of Joe's boys came to the hog pen. He decided he had forgotten a national holiday, so he locked up and headed home. On the way he passed no one in the road, no one, until he saw the bread lady's little boy standing naked in front of the Modern Bakery, crying his eyes out. Joe approached but the boy fled inside, and it was when Joe started after him that he saw the bread lady lying in the ditch. One arm was gone, and something terrible had happened to her goiter.

Joe found her son trying to hide in the mud-brick oven. He gathered the boy up and ran home.

On the road he saw the woman who sold batteries in the market and always scolded him for not marrying her oldest daughter. The woman was weaving as if she were drunk, trailing a zigzag of blood in the dirt. She was bleeding from the back of her head. When he called her name she looked in his direction without appearing to see him. He passed other people and everyone was in a daze. The sunlight looked all wrong.

In his house, Joe found someone crouched inside the shower stall. It was Monkey-Head, clutching the wooden figure between his knees. In a lifeless voice, Amouzou said that a man's death the night before had been blamed on his magic. Now everyone in that man's tribe was killing everyone in Amouzou's. The same thing was happening to his tribe in other towns across the region; the man's death was the excuse. For days everyone had been waiting for it to start here—and Joe had heard nothing, known nothing. Now it had started. Amouzou sat rigid and refused to leave the shower stall.

Joe left the bread lady's son with Amouzou and went back into town—went back, he realized later, to come across something that would undo Amouzou's story. He ran into one of his boys, a tall pimply youth who seemed to have just woken up. Joe described what he'd heard from Amouzou. The boy asked where Monkey-Head was hiding and Joe told him, then went to look for his other boys. What he found was a pile of corpses under the church wall. He started running down the hill, but even before he saw the crowd gathered outside his house he knew what he had done.

His boys looked at him without seeing. When he grabbed one by the shoulder, he was shown a machete. No one else threatened him, no one paid him any attention, what was happening was no business of his. He begged his friends not to go inside, but their faces had turned into carved masks.

After they left, he couldn't bring himself to look in the shower stall. He hunted single-mindedly for a very few things: his money, his passport, his open-return ticket. On his way out he noticed the bread lady's little boy standing in the shower stall, naked, mute, staring. Joe went in to get him. Amouzou's body was crumpled over the drain, his legs folded back under him. There was blood everywhere, yet Joe expected the magician to move any moment and get up, and he sensed that the little boy was waiting for the same thing. Where had Amouzou gone? Where was his voice? This wasn't the magician anymore; it was just flesh, heavy, inert. It would lie here for days, watched over by the little boy, as flies and dogs came to feed.

It was hard dragging Amouzou out of the house—a dead body weighed so much more than a live one. The little boy tried to help, but he wasn't any use and ended up just tagging along, his thumb in his mouth, as Joe hauled the body by a wrist into the part of the forest where the town kept its cemetery. Among high trees, over concrete tombs, stood the rigid painted statues of chiefs. Nothing stirred. Sunlight burned through the leaves. Sweating heavily, Joe pushed the lid off a tomb. It made a dry, grating sound. Under the chiefs' eyes he scooped out the bones; they crumbled in his hands like old paper. He scattered the chips and dust in undergrowth. Amouzou's body was too long and Joe had to prop up his butchered knees to make him fit.

When he began to replace the lid, the little boy, who hadn't made a sound, started crying. Joe turned to hush him and noticed something clutched in the crook of his arm: the wooden figure with the hollow skull. He held out his hand, and the boy gave it.

Joe tucked the figure carefully under Amouzou's folded arms. And then, looking around as if one of the statues might move and try to stop him, he took it back. When he was a long way off, he thought, the wooden figure might help. He already felt a terrible empty ache—not just for Amouzou, his teacher and friend, but for Africa and who he had been here.

Having nothing else to leave behind as a remembrance, Joe pulled out of his wallet a duplicate of the passport snapshot taken long ago in San Francisco and laid it on Amouzou's chest. As he shoved the lid back over the tomb, he kept his eyes on the magician's fallen face and avoided the old familiar one that was about to be his own again.

Then, feeling that he had done what he could for Monkey-Head, Joe went back to his house, washed off the blood, put the wooden figure in his backpack, took the little boy by the hand, and fled.

They traveled on foot to the next town, where they boarded an overloaded bush taxi. Every town had a roadblock, and at every roadblock the local men looked drunker and angrier and made more passengers get off. But Joe and the little boy were always let through. At the frontier, his passport and seventy-five dollars got them past the exit officials and dozens of people begging, weeping, or standing silent on the wrong side of the bridge over the border river. But at the other end of the bridge, the officials of the next country gave him trouble. The money they wanted to let the boy in was far more than what Joe had. He bargained, he pleaded—no one ever refused to come down. But the men were frightened by what was happening on the other side of the river. "You, America, OK," one of them said. "This little one go carry deat'."

Joe finally had to go back and leave the bread lady's son with a woman in a head scarf who was happy to add another child to her three for thirty-five dollars. He walked across the iron bridge over brown water. When his passport was stamped and the barrier lifted, a great clamor went up on the other side of the river. People were shouting and waving identity cards and money. In the front of the crowd, the little boy was clutching the skirts and looking up at the face of his new mother. Joe felt his own hands tugging the material.

He waited in a dusty bus stop for a truck that would take him to a city where there was an airport. While he waited he asked to borrow a groundskeeper's machete. The old man was no more astonished than Joe himself when he drew the blade across his own left forearm. He had an idea of atoning to Amouzou, but mostly he hoped the pain would make his ache go away. Instead, the sight of blood welling along the blade brought him to himself. And since that person wasn't an African after all, there was nothing to do but leave.

Around the floor guests snored, farted, murmured to one another or themselves. On the next cot the poet was moaning in his sleep. Joe sought the memory of his childhood bed, the smell of fresh sheets, the safe feel of pajamas with feet, the crack of light in the doorway, his foster mother coming in. She was still alive; he was nine years old. It was his first night in the house. The bed was strange, the corduroy bedspread. He looked up into the strange woman's face. She said, "Good night, sweet boy." And his own face opened with a smile and the strange woman smiled back, and he knew that as long as he was "sweet boy" this mother would let him stay.

Tears started in Joe's eyes. Softly he practiced the new voice. "They tried to kill me," he whispered, the cadences rich and liquid. "Po-li-ti-cal a-sy-lum." It was so easy. One of the secret powers had outlived Amouzou and come all the way here in the wooden figure and now it was inside Joe. A few hours ago this city had been the dead end of everything—but it turned out to be a city where anything was possible. Tomorrow he would go out and find a new life as Joe Amouzou. He was a survivor.

three

At 4:30 Eric Barnes turned off his computer, sat back in his chair, and stared at the blank screen. Outside his barred window, in the sky above the triple-decker that faced his building across a parking lot, early winter light was failing. Four-thirty and almost night: the hour of fatigue. And yet he was conscious of quitting too soon. His bones ached unwholesomely with things undone. Each day grew shorter, and each day he stopped work earlier. Going by the light, he might have managed an illusion of steady labor. But he was the kind of man to go by the clock.

"Getting late too early," he said aloud.

A few weeks ago the clocks were set back to standard time. The shorter days made him feel as if time was running out with the close of the year. He had spent the last hours this afternoon listening for the rats and waiting for dusk to come and declare the day lost.

He switched on the clock radio in the corner of his desk. "We're talking about marriage."

He turned up the volume.

"Kitty Di Angelo has published a book called *Hold On, You Can Have Everything!* The book says that marriages can be saved if husbands learn to share—not just help—*share* with the housework and child care." The host was shading from promotional brio to sarcasm. "That's what the book says."

"And what's in it for you men? Better sex, a happier marriage— real marriage, a partnership." Kitty Di Angelo sounded New York, middle-aged, soothing and prosperous. Eric imagined her photo on the back of *Hold On, You Can Have Everything!*: blown hair, pearl earrings, face-lift, excess smile.

Talk radio was all the illicit pleasure he allowed himself working at home. At the end of the day, he filled his study with the world's rage and hysteria for a few minutes while obscure anxieties and satisfactions spun in his head. Jane would be home in an hour; before then he would switch to the news on public radio.

"Car phone on the Expressway, you're on the talk station."

"Hello? Kitty, my husband and I split the chores even-Steven."

"Congratulations, darling. You have a real marriage."

Eric bent down and tapped on the wall just above the baseboard. No answer. He tapped again, and there was a sudden frenzy of claws on wood. The little rat was scratching at an implacable two-by-four. The noise continued for ten seconds, and then just as abruptly stopped. Eric felt that to tap one more time would be harassment. Anyway, the rat in there was still alive.

For months—something to do with a foundation dug near Central Square, or the river's closeness—rats had been commuting across the ceiling just over Eric's head: not mousey scampering but the heavy gallop of fattened city rats. He hated their hairy flanks and mocking arrogance and also felt, in a way he didn't understand and couldn't tell Jane, that these creatures spent so much time with him while he sat at his computer that they must somehow know him, that their presence a few feet above his scalp had taken on the quality of a relationship.

The one in his wall was smaller than the others, perhaps not fully grown, and that was its downfall. Yesterday, on its way to the kitchen, while trying to leap across the abyss where the study ceiling joined a wall, it had slipped and fallen in. For hours, limbs spread against the wallboard (Eric imagined) to brace itself, the little rat had slid inexorably down to the floor.

"We have a four-year-old and a two-year-old," the woman on the car phone was saying, "and we both work and we've worked it out so one of us is always home with the kids, except for child care ten hours a week. I'm on my way there right now—it's a dollar a minute if you're late and the traffic is unbelievable. But I think I'll make it," she laughed nervously.

"Perfect," Kitty Di Angelo told her. "You're doing exactly what the book says."

"I mean, we take it one day at a time."

"Let me ask you a candid question," the host's sonorous voice said. "How often do you have sex?"

"Ah-hah," Eric laughed.

"What's that?" the caller giggled forlornly. "We're too exhausted. We never see each other, and when we do we just talk about money."

"But you're sharing," Kitty insisted. "Cut corners."

"You didn't hear her," Eric snapped. He got angrier at the radio than at anyone he knew in flesh and blood. The caller's harried soul, linked to his by cell phone and airwave, had won his goodwill.

"We have our budget down to a science," she said.

"When was the last time you really enjoyed each other's company?" Kitty asked.

While the caller tried to remember, Eric got up, went to the closet, found his hammer and a flashlight, and carried them back to his desk. Picking a spot on the wall three feet above the place where the rat was trapped, he raised his hammer and delivered a sharp blow to the wallboard. A clean hole opened. There was a frozen moment and then wild scratching, unmuffled and so loud it gave Eric a vivid picture of the frantic little pointed face. He brought himself eye level with the hole and aimed his flashlight's beam downward. He couldn't see anything.

He went into the kitchen and cut a lump of butter. Then he poured out a spoonful of the rat poison he kept under the sink—it looked like health food. Kneading like a baker, he formed a soft round butterball with a lethal core.

"You need another vacation, darling," Kitty Di Angelo was saying in his study. "Just the two of you."

Eric approached the wall with his poisoned butter. The hole wasn't a problem, they were going to tear out the wall anyway when they started renovating. His study was destined to be the baby's room. He'd had iron bars bolted over the window for the same reason: A neighbor was burglarized and Jane said shouldn't they do something about the baby room? It was already the baby room. There was no space anywhere else in the house. Now Jane was after him about the rats—she'd heard stories of babies being chewed to death.

Sometimes the thump of rodents in the ceiling sounded like the heartbeat Eric had heard during an ultrasound.

"Somewhere warm and romantic," Kitty said. "Bring a favorite book. Spoil yourself. Sex twice a day."

"How the hell is she going to pay for it?" Eric demanded. He was standing by the wall like an assassin braced for his moment.

"The thing is," the caller said, meekly apologetic, "I don't think we can afford to right now."

"Darling," Kitty said, "you can't afford not to."

"I'm sorry, buddy," Eric said. Foolish tears welled in his eyes. "It's better this way." He fed the butterball into the hole and heard it drop with a soft squish. There was no reaction inside, but the starved creature would smell this gift from dark heaven and fall gratefully upon it. The little rat was going to die happy.

Then he realized it wasn't true: The poison worked by dehydration, the death would be agonizing. He was stricken with remorse.

This was what happened when you worked all day by yourself. He turned off the radio with a buttery finger and told himself that killing rats was one of the many duties of a father-to-be. Now at least he could get his work done.

In the kitchen, Eric did the dishes listening to the news on NPR. A murder in Boston, a massacre in Africa. News brought him to consciousness every morning: Communism ended, governments fell, countries ceased to exist, epidemics swept the cities while he lay crusty in the gray light and waited for Jane to roll over. All day long the half-heard reports ghosted him as if they were his dreams. This morning it had been the massacre; but the Africa that played along the borders of thought as he washed the dishes wasn't the bloody madness the reporter was describing. It was a place of sunlit greenery and vast open space, a long drive on a red clay road by a river whose wide bends were like the Charles.

By the time he finished, the sky between the window shade's slats looked like the bottom of the sea. He took a shower and came out feeling anxious. The house had been empty and silent too long. He wanted Jane to come home, wanted to walk the footpath by the river with her hand in his and he would tell her about his day and she would listen and know what to say.

Eric was correcting student papers at the kitchen table when he heard her come in. He was prepared for her tired, preoccupied face, yet there had never been a day in their years together when the sound of her keys didn't cause something inside him to fall back into place.

"Are you still working?" she asked, taking off her coat. There it was, the basketball under her dress. He couldn't get used to it.

"And did the dishes."

She kissed him on the head. "Good househusband." He saw with relief that she looked flushed and fond.

"That's me."

Jane went through the mail on the counter.

"Let's go for a walk." Eric stood. "I've been cooped up all day."

She exaggerated a look of disbelief. "Eric, it's late November."

"It's not that cold yet. Come on, before winter hits and then the kid comes. Last chance for eighteen years."

"Anyway, we've got Jerry and Rachel's tonight."

"Oh." Eric had thought they had the evening to themselves. He resented the instrusion. Jane flipped through a children's clothing catalog. Now he felt foolish for having stood up. "Well, let's not talk about babies the whole night."

"But they're so interesting. What else is there to talk about?"

"In the old days, people spawned and moved upstream, talking of other things."

"OK, you and Jerry and what's-his-name can solve the big picture. Talk talk talk, injustice, outrage, and not a thing ever comes of it. So since it's all just talk, why not talk about babies?"

"Who's what's-his-name?" Eric asked.

"That multimedia writer guy who came to the Whitset for a grant." Jane worked on the staff of a nonprofit foundation whose investment portfolio seemed to generate ever larger returns with each year of the endless recession. In October, the Whitset had enjoyed a windfall on the stock market and was looking for ways to rid itself of some before the end of the tax year. Eric wondered why he and Jane couldn't help. "Rachel told him we only fund social services, but he wangled an intro to Jerry and Jerry gave him an out-of-pocket grant. Paul Duffy."

He had met Duffy a few times at parties and readings. He remembered a crimson face and a confidence he'd found unwarranted. "I hate multimedia writer guys."

Jane was examining an envelope, frowning below her brown silver-threaded bangs. "How'd it go today?"

"Wrote two and a half sentences."

He ran his finger along the table's edge and waited. Look up. As soon as she looked at him everything would be fine. She was reading a solicitation from a nonprofit in New York. In a moment it would go into the trash, but for now it consumed her total attention.

When she finally looked up, her face had become chiseled, a ridge of muscle stood out in her cheek. He knew that muscle intimately.

She said, "We need to make some decisions."

Pregnancy had changed Jane in ways Eric had never anticipated. The maternity dress made her both older and younger, harder and softer. Her face was now dominated by the straight bangs and always looked either girlish or strict. Her levelheadedness, which he relied on, had become impatient, and her tenderness, which he loved, had become infantile. She focused relentlessly on the future, or else monitored the thrum of her blood and every tremor in her womb.

He said, "That's true."

His tone of insufficient worry drew a look. "Eric, we can't have saws and hammers going after I deliver."

"We'll start after Christmas, one way or the other."

Jane folded her arms. "What if you're not finished with the book? It sounds like you've slowed down."

"I'll wear earplugs and a dust mask."

"What about renting cheap office space?"

Even in his best years she earned more money. The imbalance was a delicate subject and generally off-limits, but it put a stress on his work getting done.

He willed an inner adjustment and became practical. "Four hundred a month minimum? It defeats the purpose."

"Oh, I paid AmEx. How much is in the account?"

"It might bounce. We're unfit to be parents. They have state agencies for people like us."

Her eyes suddenly looked tired. "Why doesn't that goddamn college give you an office?"

"Because I'm part-time labor and they're embarrassed about it, so they have to make things as unpleasant as possible. Besides, someone needs to keep an eye on the crew. They're all crooks."

Jane threw the letter away. "Can you finish in time?"

Recently Eric had become aware that, under pressure, he had a habit of looking away from the person's eyes, toward the ground. It bothered him, but he couldn't stop himself.

"I think so. But I won't see the rest of the advance for at least three months."

"Can't your agent get Ann to give you part of it now?"

"Jane, I don't want Ann to disengage completely. I doubt she even knows I missed the deadline."

"You've written three books for those jerks. Why are you afraid they're about to pull the plug?"

"Because they are. They have their hand on the plug all the time. They pull the plug at the first smell of rot."

In the middle of the kitchen floor, by tactical experience and common enemies, they had negotiated their way into a hug made slightly awkward by the swell of her stomach.

Jane sniffed his chest. "I don't smell rot."

"Fish-odor syndrome. Genetic defect."

"Is this what you're wearing tonight?"

"This" was a flannel shirt and old khakis, his uniform of prairie stubbornness. "You betcha. Jane—"

She raised her brows in a sort of skeptical amusement, as if he was going to say something eccentric and probably irritating for which she would nonetheless love him. The expression was so much hers that it recalled the exact texture of the delight he took in their life together, the reason he couldn't imagine sharing his with anyone else. And it stopped him from saying what he was about to say, which was either (he didn't know yet) "Should I change the shirt?" or "Something's gone wrong with my work."

"I'll finish the book," he said instead, "and we'll get our dough and live happily, happily, happily."

Jane kissed his neck. "No kidding, Eric. Between now and March, no major expenses except baby stuff and construction work."

He put his palms against the balloon of her belly and felt its tautness. "Little materialist."

"I killed a rat today," Eric said in the parking lot.

"Jesus, Eric. You and the rats."

"It was a mercy killing, poor guy. Anyway, I have to spend all day with them. You don't know what it's like."

"We need new garbage lids, they keep getting stolen."

Unraked leaves and twigs lay in soggy mats. Fall had already come and gone. The air smelled of the end of the day, car exhaust and gathering chill.

"It won't keep the rats out if the neighbors don't put their bags in barrels," he said. "'No one is uninvolved'—isn't that what the signs say?"

"'No one is *excused*,'" she corrected him. "'*Nothing* is uninvolved.' Meaning, it all fits together. There's a plan."

Eric picked up wet wrappers from their corner of the lot. Another gem of graffiti art had appeared on the end wall: "Brown Bomber Sucking Crew." In short order there would be replies, invitations. He would paint over them and the game would start again.

For a decade they had lived between Central Square and the river, in Cambridgeport. In those years they had seen the area evolve from peeling paint and windowless churches to a real-estate hothouse of renovated brick townhouses. Spandex joggers and power walkers passed silent old men on park benches. From the porches or upstairs windows of their triple-deckers, the longtime residents—Irish, black—watched gentrification advance. They were old and tired, and the childless invaders had money and energy to spare.

But the cycles of decay that used to take centuries among the Romans and Mayans had speeded up. When recession made their apartment affordable, he and Jane became owners and put roots into Cambridgeport's marshy landfill just as it was starting to sink again. Spray-painted glyphs appeared on their wall in lurid black and red, and there were other omens of decline: drunken street-fights at 2 A.M., rum bottles in the rhododendron, hooded teenagers leaning in the windows of idling cars, "For Sale" signs that never came down, and the endless battle against stray trash. Then Jane conceived; and for practical purposes they were stuck.

Not long ago, the blue flyers started appearing like harbingers of a mysterious new wave of invaders. "It takes a trust fund to raise a child," Eric would say, and Jane would answer, "Do you know what your husband does all day?" Tonight, as they drove along half-lit streets, past the triple-deckers and Victorians closed up for the long freeze, a drizzle starting to fall, dim shapes moving beyond the streaked windshield, he found himself looking for the signs. A decade here and it was still true—he didn't know who his neighbors were. He was at a loss to understand the pang of desire he was feeling. It felt like the loneliness of things unsaid.

They had a video to return, and the way to the Silvers' took them through the heart of Central Square. In spite of the cold and drizzle, it was alive with human activity. Two girls in shearling coats strolled out against the light, and one threw her head back and laughed when Eric braked and honked. In front of Purity Supreme, a knot of people huddled under the bus shelter. Farther along, down a side street, they were lining up for Rainbow House to open. Eric and Jane used to talk of volunteering there, if only on Thanksgiving, but it never happened. She was distracted by pregnancy, he by work, always telling himself that once his career was more secure he would get involved in the city. A guilty silence filled the car.

"Do you still want to live around here?" Jane asked.

Eric turned from the windshield. "Do you?"

She was gazing at the bright utopian mural of the public library. "Sometimes I wonder."

He decided that he wanted to stay.

At the front door, Jerry Silver greeted them both with hugs. He was a patents lawyer and yet deeply sentimental in a way, Eric thought, made possible by money. Eric made an awkward adjustment from an intended handshake and poked his friend's sweatered paunch.

"Jane: pregnancy is doing wonderful things for you. Eric: you don't look so hot. You can't infect us, we've been passing a bug around for three weeks. Plus, I think I've got carpal tunnel from holding Zach. We're a wreck here. Just wait till yours comes."

Jerry looked in the pink of health. Above his heavy black beard the color in his boyish cheeks was rich. He shambled into the living room like a bear retreating to his cave. Hibernation was in full display: Jerry's extra poundage, the dried spittle on his sweater, the plastic trucks and stuffed animals scattered around the floor, the slightly sour smell of nuclear family and long enclosure. The Silvers, once the most elegant of entertainers, had utterly submitted to the degeneration of style and dignity brought on by childbirth.

Zachary had descended on their late thirties like a new religion that initially cut them off from the world, as if eighteen months of home worship were demanded of converts. Now that Eric and Jane were about to enter the faith, Jerry and Rachel had taken an intense proprietary interest in them. The Silvers belonged to a different social category, attended the symphony and hosted fund-raisers for local candidates (until Zach). The women worked together at the Whitset Foundation, but the Silvers' cultivation of Eric and Jane was based on Jerry's misconception that a writer was automatically a person worth knowing.

"Zach honey! Come say hello to Uncle Eric and Aunt Jane."

"No!"

Silver shrugged in helpless affection. "His favorite new word."

Zachary had slightly crossed eyes and angelic blond curls that lurked recessively in his dark-haired parents' genes. At the moment, a little green worm of snot was inching in and out of his nostril as he stood transfixed before the living-room sofa, where Paul Duffy was making a marble disappear and reappear in his hand. Duffy's golden-haired date seemed just as charmed by the trick.

Duffy glanced up from his performance, hair cropped short, an ornamental lick tailing down his neck. Like one dog taking another's measure, Eric sensed that reserves of power were hidden in the compact body and deceiver's handwork, that they were being treated to just a tiny portion of Duffy's inventive energy.

"Eric, Jane—Paul and Heather." Jerry watched the two writers with the eagerness of a salon host.

Duffy put down the marble, rose, and shook Eric's hand warmly. "I'm a fan. *Soldier's Dilemma* convinced me I wasn't a novelist."

Startled, Eric muttered, "Thanks. Or sorry about that."

"It wasn't even envy. I just thought, he can have it, I'm not cut out for that quiet devotion to craft."

"Too quiet."

"No, I admired the integrity—no cheap effects. For a writer like you, that's its own reward. OK, maybe a *little* jealous. But I know myself, I need a bigger splash. Then your third one came out and it should have done so much better, it was like the first two never existed, and I thought, Yep, he's a camel and I'm a dog, gotta feed me twice a day."

"The deserts are full of corpses with humps."

Duffy laughed in delight. The overture had thrown Eric completely off balance, made him feel both puffed-up and on edge, seen through. Duffy was one of those people who already knew everything about you.

Rachel Silver came in from the kitchen. She looked rheumy-eyed and maternally stocky, with a 3 A.M. pallor and a grim lower jaw. It was clear that the sharing wasn't even-Steven here. "Zachary, be careful of the tabletop," she said before greeting her guests.

The grown-ups discussed toilet training while Zach smeared goat cheese on the leather ottoman. It took four tries for Rachel to coax her son upstairs to bed. When she came back down she activated the baby monitor on the coffee table, so that even as he slept Zachary's little whimpers provided material for the adult portion of the evening.

"Jerry's hopeless," she said. "If it were up to him, Zach would be awake till midnight."

"He's given my life so much meaning," Jerry said. "I know that sounds corny—I guess I've gotten corny."

Rachel looked at her husband. "Eric doesn't know yet. But he will."

"I'm beginning to figure it out."

Jane said, "Eric's going to be a great father."

"My partners say I've lost my killer instinct," Jerry said.

"Don't take the beast out of the man." Duffy's smile suggested a mischievous secret. "We're hunters from way back—women can never get that."

"Why can't you have both?" Jane was challenging his smile with her own.

Heather returned from some luxurious reverie. "Yeah, why can't you have both?" She was a head taller than Duffy and a decade younger, and she spoke and tossed her hair with a dream-bound vagueness, as if she floated in honey.

"The eternal conflict," Duffy said happily.

Eric watched as Heather squeezed Duffy's thigh. Duffy stroked her hair, which looked as expensive as cashmere. In the Silvers' living room, amid Zach's toys and the wrecked Wheat Thins, with the baby monitor gently hiccuping, this level of stimulation was almost intolerable. Lust and envy were firing up their cold engines. He and Jane had gone seven weeks now—eight—not a hint of sex in sight in this desert. The baby becomes the object of female libido, and as for the male . . . but Jerry didn't seem to mind.

Jane was looking at him for an opinion.

"Camels are vegetarians."

Dinner was already lukewarm, delivered from The King and I by a man in his fifties who also delivered the Silvers' *Times* every morning—he had been laid off after twenty-three years at GE. Silver, whom strangers trusted and who was astonished by the details of their lives, sadly reported this as he spread cartons across the table. And so as they doled out Thai food the men turned inevitably to politics, the economy, the awfulness of contemporary America. And nothing ever came of it, Eric remembered, annoyed, unable to resist.

Jane and Rachel were discussing ultrasounds. Heather drifted smilingly between the sexes.

"What are you working on, Eric?" Duffy suddenly asked.

Eric was on guard. "Oh, a sort of historical thing."

"About."

"Elizabethan London. Knife fights between playwrights in pubs, backstage double-crosses, comic seductions. Shakespeare makes a cameo appearance as a money-grubbing philanderer."

He was being glib, but as he described to Duffy the book that had consumed the past two years, he began to recall his excitement at the rich velvety textures of Renaissance fabric, the smell of fish and disease in alleys behind the Globe, the vivid and blessedly amoral world of the senses into which he plunged day after day. And something of this excitement got into his account, so that he was like a man describing a woman he loved as if she had not already left him—not just to protect himself, but in the hope that the force of this momentary remembering might be enough to bring her back. Once or twice he looked to see if Jane was listening, if she was pleased, if she heard a false note, if she knew that back in his study there was no smell of fish or disease, that Shakespeare was only the strange silent egghead of the woodcut.

But Jane was deep in talk with Rachel.

For half a minute Duffy had been extracting a shred of basil from between two molars.

"Is the novel still viable?" he asked when it was worked free. "Hasn't technology made it obsolete?"

"Christ, I hope not." Quit posturing, Eric wanted to say with the hardheaded scorn of men in his Iowa hometown.

"Writers are part of society too. Same economic forces."

"The novel as smokestack industry?"

Duffy snapped his fingers. "Exactly. No one uses coal, right? You start seeing wage cuts, job loss. Finally you go on strike and get killed."

"I think there's still a few coal-burning readers left." Eric felt Jane's hand on his. Maybe she had been listening. She gave a cautionary squeeze and then stroked his hand the way you calm an agitated horse. The gesture irritated him. "But if I have to be retrained, like the delivery guy, I'll apply for Charles River groundskeeper. Some human being has to mow the banks, plant annuals, keep an eye on the mergansers."

Duffy smiled, amused, tolerant. "Seriously, don't you have to be realistic about the market and Zeitgeist?"

"I am serious," Eric said. "This would be my perfect job."

"There's enough market and Zeitgeist where I work," Silver said.

Duffy turned on him. "Why do we have to be the purists, Jerry? Anyone who says they want to spend their life writing for *Wholewheat Quarterly* is a liar. Fifty thousand poets and who reads the stuff? Downsize them! I used to take months to sweat out a story, and then *shushhh*, into the void. So I got into video. The market decides what's worth keeping."

Stoked by argument, Duffy's scalp had burst into flame, his green eyes glowed with the internal heat. Eric knew that this exercise, akin to the thrill of the hunt, required a competitor. It wasn't personal. The second worst mistake would be anger, the worst seriousness.

"So you're with Kitty, Paul?" he said.

"Who's Kitty?" Jane said.

"Kitty says you can have dollars, sex, *and* critical appreciation because the market's always right." Eric felt another pulse from his wife's hand.

"Tell him," Duffy said to Jane.

"What do you want me to tell him?" she asked ironically. For an instant they seemed to be flirting.

"No one's bigger than the market."

"Eric knows that. You don't think quiet devotion to craft can succeed? What matters is if you believe in yourself."

Duffy laughed. "Now that is a bedtime story."

Eric wanted to say something witty and devastating to put an end to this man, but his next words would carry the deadly note of sincerity. The other thing would be to take Duffy's hair by its silly little tail and give a hard pull. What a shiver of satisfaction to see the head snap back! And he actually felt his hand leave Jane's soft imprisoning grip and begin a journey out into open air.

He diverted it midflight and found an alternate destination in the baby monitor lying on the coffee table. He brought the apparatus with its glowing red light to his lips.

"Zach? Zach, do you copy? Eric Barnes here. Uncle Paul is moving toward your location with Kitty Di Angelo's *Hold On, You Can Have Everything!* Pretend you're asleep. Do you copy, Zach?"

Jane's laugh was subdued, but Eric picked up the undercurrent of pleasure. He set the monitor down and returned his hand to hers.

"All this is reminding me of Eamon Connelly." Silver was toying gloomily with a stuffed panda. "Did you hear, Eric?"

"I heard Margot kicked him out."

Silver identified Connelly to the others—an eccentric acquaintance from an aging hipsters' bar called the Harp & Plume.

"Margot's had enough of his drinking," Rachel said.

"I think she finally figured out the majority of his projects were in his head." Silver looked at Eric. "Anyway, I saw Eamon in Central the other day."

"What were you doing in Central?" Rachel asked.

"He started talking about a movie he's going to produce in

France. And he smelled so bad I had to back off. It turns out he's staying at Rainbow House."

Eric was stunned. "Eamon's homeless?"

"Except for the smell he seemed just like himself. I gave him twenty bucks to help him get back on his feet. He pocketed it with some line from Shakespeare."

Eric murmured, "I ought to do something for him."

"I'm glad for Margot," Rachel said. "She put up with him too long."

Eric folded his hands together against his lips. He was remembering Eamon Connelly in waistcoat and cravat at the Harp & Plume, a picture of late-Victorian dandyism, waving a pint of Guinness and declaiming against the corruption of the poetry establishment. A whole life built on sand. Then he saw himself through the barred window of his own study, caught in electric light, bent over the computer, fingers paralyzed on the keys. He should have worked another hour tonight.

"Eamon won't get back on his feet, Jerry," he said. "He's not at Rainbow House because of money. It's where he thinks he belongs. Guys like Eamon end up dying in rented rooms."

"The world is what it is," Duffy said.

Jane turned on him. "It's a personal tragedy, not an excuse for selfishness."

The little set-to with Duffy had been pointless. And Eric felt it was somehow his own fault that a shadow of unpleasantness had fallen over the living room.

"Are you two still looking for a contractor?" Rachel coming to the rescue of her own party.

Eric roused himself from Eamon Connelly. "Do you know one?"

"One of Jerry's hunter-gatherer partners is redoing his house in Lincoln. A really creative contractor."

"He sounds expensive."

"Drive a hard bargain," Rachel said, "they need the work. You've got till when, Jane, March?"

"End of February."

Heather came to life. "It is *so* thrilling. Have you picked a name?"

"We have some ideas. We don't want to know the gender. The ultrasound didn't show it."

To Eric the ultrasound had looked like a flickering image from a cave painting—more amphibian than human. The recognition that this dim half-formed creature was his had filled him with confusion and awe.

"We're calling him Ashley if it's a boy," he said. "If a girl, Ainsley."

Jane cut him a baffled, angry look.

"Those are wonderful names," Heather said. She was sitting cross-legged on the rug at Duffy's feet, and she floated a hand upward for his. "I think women today can invent our lives any way we want. We can be hunters and nurturers." Duffy left her hand grasping air.

"To Ashley, or Ainsley," Jane said, raising her soda water toward her husband with light sarcasm.

"To Lincoln." Rachel smiled at the confusion. "Massachusetts."

Jane was the first to get it. "You're leaving."

"*Moving.* We're not even changing area codes."

"I was thinking you might."

"This house is just way too small. And your neighbors had that break-in. Jerry knows this is no kind of neighborhood to raise a child."

"I'll miss you guys," Silver said. "And Central Square, and the Harp."

"You haven't been to the Harp in years," Rachel told him.

"Well, I'll miss having it there."

"It will still *be* there."

Silver capitulated. "There's a lot Zach and I could do with a real yard."

Zachary chose this moment to finish off the evening by squawking through the monitor.

On the way out, Eric noticed awkward smiles. He was having trouble reading the mood. Had he quarreled unforgivably with

Duffy? Made a fool of himself? No, it was something else. The secret was out—the Silvers weren't their equals. What kind of friendship was possible when one couple could up and move to Lincoln whenever they wanted?

"The burbs, Eric," Silver murmured at the door. "Is that me?"

"You might like it there."

"That's what I mean. Let me know if you detect any signs of quiet desperation."

"You don't have to leave the city for that."

"Rachel's going to be proselytizing you guys."

"Well, Lincoln's out of our reach."

Heather and Duffy walked outside ahead of them. On the sidewalk, Duffy turned. In his full-length belted woolen overcoat, with his short forelocks, he looked vaguely Napoleonic.

"Eric, my friend George Feloni's an editor at *Edge*. I know they're looking for new voices. Use my name with him."

Later, Eric would appreciate the complex cunning of this move. Duffy was treating him to a put-down in full view of his wife, getting in the last thrust, displaying his own generosity, and impressing young Heather with his literary connections in time to warm her up for tonight's bang. And when Jane answered, "Oh, I don't think Eric's interested in writing for *Edge*," Duffy only smiled and shrugged, as if to say, "Then go on writing for *Wholewheat Quarterly*. It's not my problem."

"Good-bye to all that," Eric said when they were in the car. It was very cold inside, with a dank smell of standing water where rain had leaked through the hatch and collected in the spare tire well.

"I guess so."

"They'll fall off the map out there. White flight proceeds."

Jane shivered. "Makes me feel lonely. The tide's going out and we're stranded. It's like a jungle sometimes. . . ."

". . . it makes me wonder how I keep from going under," Eric finished the old rap they used to sing together. He thought of heading over to Memorial Drive and following the course along the river that they hadn't walked earlier. He wanted to prolong this moment together, between the party with its odd pressures and what awaited him at home. But he found himself following the usual route. Yellow fog hung under the streetlights as they drove.

"Zach needs to be knocked around a little," he said.

"Child abuser."

"The kid is going to be a terror. Lincoln must be crawling with those monsters."

"It'll be different with us. For one thing, it'll be fifty-fifty."

Stuck between his desire to avoid an argument on which she had the moral high ground as well as the hormonal passion, and his sense that genetically speaking it just wasn't in the cards, he didn't answer.

Jane said, "What was that about Ashley and Ainsley?"

A warning bell went off in his head. At the time he'd been perversely picking a fight; now he had no desire for one.

"Heather really liked those names."

"Proving you're not Jerry?"

Eric kept his eyes on the road. "Just a little put out by what's-his-name."

"You should have brushed him off."

"You seemed to find him attractive," he said recklessly, ashamed, wanting her to deny it.

"That slimy operator? What's with you?"

"But it's true, I only have myself to blame."

"Blame for what?" Jane was staring at him. "Paul Duffy is bad for you, Eric."

"I'd like to hold up my end. If I wrote for *Edge* we wouldn't have to worry so much about money."

"That's not who I'm married to."

"Then what should I do?"

"Finish your book, Eric. That's your end."

She said this as if it was the simplest thing in the world. Her calm voice made him desperate to believe her. He reached from the gear shift for his wife's hand and warmed her cold skin.

Eric stayed up in his study after Jane went to bed. It was past midnight and the heat was off. In the kitchen the rats were astir, but below his hammer hole there was no sound. He sat down with a complete sentence in mind, an unexpected gift that had come to him out of the peace with Jane. He typed it and waited for others to follow. On the street a horn sounded, trash was blowing through the dark parking lot. The image of Eamon Connelly came before him— pontificating, smelling bad. It happened so fast to some people. The world is what it is. He thought over all that Duffy had said, struggling to reject it. He had always worked in his own grain and let the rest take care of itself.

He shook out the thought and suddenly in his mind's eye there appeared green hills in sunlight, a clay road winding along a river. He saw himself walking down it. The river had stopped being the Charles; now it smelled like the lake where every summer as boys he and his friends hunted the reedy shallows for frogs and salamanders.

He returned to the computer and searched for another sentence. He started one blind and misspelled simple words. It was like typing with frozen fingers. But he would have sat for hours if Jane hadn't come in to tell him he was coughing and should come to bed.

When he was lying alongside her she murmured, "Hold me." Gratefully, he wrapped his arms around her from behind, cupping her in the old way. But she said, "They're a little sore" and moved his hands from her breasts down to the swollen center of her being.

four

"I've met this guy."

Sara Simon gazed at Paula over the rim of her margarita glass. Coyness unexpectedly rendered her irises a dazzling yellow-green, like tropical fish when the sun comes out.

"You have?" Apparently the idea was for Paula to pry the information loose piece by piece. "Does he have a name?"

"Lewis." Sara added, "He's Jewish. Lew the Jew."

"Congratulations."

"Exactly. I am to be congratulated." Sara raised her salted glass. "I met Lewis amid the gothic horror of a successful singles function. Don't laugh, Paula, it could happen to you someday and it's better than the bar scene."

"I'm not laughing."

"Fortified by spiked punch, our heroine forced herself to talk to five different guys. God helps those. Lewis didn't make much impression at first, but our heroine evidently did. Then I decided he was kind of cute. He's in computers and awkward, but very sweet."

Paula congratulated her again and busied herself with fragments of enchilada. Sara's gloomy self-appraisals had undergone, through the alchemy of whatever had come over her (it didn't seem like love), a transmutation into pushiness, which made it hard to feel undiluted pleasure. Tonight was Wednesday, and Paula had stopped her trysts. She had called Steve Lorenz to say she couldn't come back. He had accepted with grim curtness, and afterward she had felt every bit as lonely as anticipated.

"To be honest, there *are* things that concern me," Sara went on in answer to an unasked question. "He's humor impaired. He isn't at all psychologically minded. On the plus side, he likes cats, he's very good when I'm moody, and best of all—he wants kids."

"You've already established that?"

"It was like the third question. There's no time to waste, Paula. If he doesn't propose by mid-January," Sara said, "you're going to see one very depressed L.I.C.S.W."

The light in her eyes wasn't the helpless sparkle of joy but the gleam of calculation. It would never work. At some point Lewis would realize that the whole relationship was being programmed on the intricate little chip inside Sara's brain. But then Paula considered Lewis—his fumbling eagerness, hopelessly overmatched in interpersonal skills—and she realized that Sara's scheme might bear fruit.

"Sounds like you're in love."

"As a matter of fact, no," Sara said defiantly, as if she'd been waiting for the chance. "I am very fond of Lewis, but I have no illusions about him. I do not think about him all the time, I do not whisper his name as I lie in bed. Don't look that way, Paula. Get real. Marriage has nothing to do with infatuation."

"Or love?"

"I don't even know what it means anymore. I'd be panicking if I *was* in love, that's when it doesn't work out. You see these single women in their forties, buying salad for one at Bread & Circus. They should have cut their losses and compromised. In a few years you won't be such a romantic, Paula."

"I hate that word."

"What, you're holding out for perfection?"

"I'm not holding out for anything. I'm not planning on a loveless marriage either."

"You say that now. But why not be practical? Marriage is a numbers game. It's like real estate. You figure out your price range, the neighborhood, then settle on the closest thing available and move fast. Instead, girls grow up with this idea of true love and this other idea of independence, and we either end up hating men like Fran or else wake up at forty wondering what happened. You think I'm cold and heartless. But I'm the real feminist."

Paula was finding that she preferred Sara wry, envious, and depressed. "Does Lewis feel the same way?"

"I think Lewis actually is in love with me."

"Wouldn't he be hurt to know how you feel?"

"He doesn't need to know everything."

"You sound defensive."

Interpretation as attack, a cheap therapeutic trick—they all knew how to do it, and it worked every time.

Sara said, "Why does it bother you that I'm finally going to get what I want?"

"If this *is* what you want."

"It is."

Why not be happy for her? Paula lacked the talent of sisterly solidarity. Her friendships with women tripped on small personal failings magnified by her own relentless self-criticism. Men were easier to be with, easier to like—less spiky and defended.

"I wonder if we promise our clients more than we can deliver," she said, moving to common ground without really changing the subject.

"What do you mean?"

"Self-awareness equals change equals fulfillment."

"I don't promise my clients that." Sara was still arguing.

"You know. What Fine says about liberating the self from its shackles of repetition, et cetera. Maybe we should aim for less. Like that joke about the guy who has a compulsion to pee on fire hydrants, and so he goes into therapy and five years later a friend asks how he's doing and he says, 'Great. Therapy's cured me,' and the friend says, 'Great, so you don't pee on fire hydrants anymore?' and he says, 'Oh, I still pee on them, but now I don't mind.'"

Sara didn't laugh. She was staring into the well of her margarita glass, her face restored to its characteristic mood. Paula suddenly realized that Sara didn't believe a word she'd been saying.

"I don't know," Sara finally said. "One way or the other I doubt I'll be in the psyche business much longer."

"Why?"

"If things work out with Lewis, I'll quit and take a full-time job getting preggers. If they don't, I'm at the top of Fine's death list anyway."

"So am I."

"Paula, you'll do what you have to to stay and I don't mean that in a negative way. You always land on your feet." Sara looked up from her glass. Paula tensed for hostility, but Sara was pleading for something. "Not everyone can be as independent as you."

"Am *I*?"

"I always think of you as someone who knows how to take care of herself. I've always admired you for that. I'm so tired of the stationary bike, Paula. I'm like a galley slave at the Y. I'm tired of trying to keep five pounds off my legs. I want to give in."

Outside the restaurant Paula embraced her, kissed her cheek, wished her the best. Sara looked utterly grateful. Why was that so difficult? On the bus home Paula admitted to herself that she'd felt a little jealous—left behind to stew in her mother and her clients and her longings. Independent? It amazed her how wrong everyone was about everyone.

The Narconia was gripped with white-knuckled cold; the hallway smelled of frozen metal mailboxes and the damp of the carpet runner. The water pipe feeding the building's radiators had burst in the morning, but Linda and Bud had been too drunk to notify the plumber until late afternoon. The problem was solved, but it would take a building as old as theirs all night to warm up, like the ancient homeless man Paula heard about who was admitted to the hospital at 89 degrees and spent three days in intensive care under layers of space blankets.

Wrapped in her comforter and cradling a mug of tea, her frosty breath mingling with the steam, she called her mother—the phone's only preprogrammed number other than her office voice mail.

"I'll be down on the 22nd, Mama."

"Ai, that's late. Are you staying at least until New Year's?"

"I have to work the Monday after Christmas."

Her mother inflicted a brief silence. In the background Puccini was playing very loud. "Maybe you want to stay in Boston this year."

After thirty-one years it was a tedious humiliation to feel the familiar feelings gather as automatically as dog's drool. Paula identified them in real time like an emergency-room nurse: We have abdominal anxiety, we have guilt in the respiratory system, we are beginning to have signs of cerebral resentment. The organism is normal.

"No, I want to be with you. But I have to work, too."

"This is what I cannot stand about America, the total hatred of life. People in this country are machines for work."

Her mother was off on an old diatribe that signaled to Paula an abuse of Chianti. Not many things in her mother's life had worked out. Her career as a cabaret singer, for which she had come to New York thirty-five years ago, didn't work out. Her three marriages didn't work out—one husband died and two, including Paula's father, a Dutch painter named Voorhees, left her. Paula watched as America became the repository of all her mother's grievances. The one thing she had succeeded at was the thing she gave herself least credit for: motherhood.

"I don't blame you if you don't want to spend Christmas with a mother who was too young to raise you properly after your father betrayed me." The bottle on the kitchen table would be stoppered by a wad of paper towel. "But we also had a little joy and light and music in our house. I don't blame."

"Enough." Paula felt tiny and childlike, crouching in a corner, barely breathing. "I'll come down on the 20th."

In a minute her mother was talking about Christmas food in a voice full of joy and light and music.

"Do you have a boyfriend, *carina*?"

"Lots. I don't have time for them all."

"What about the anthropologist, that is a very good profession."

"That was years ago. I don't want to discuss this."

"The only men you see are *pazzi*."

"I like them better crazy. Let's drop it."

"Men need you to talk nice, not just to be so smart, American women are too smart."

"Mama, I want you to stop drinking wine after dinner."

"One glass—a small pleasure. . . ."

"When you talk this way I can tell. If you're concerned about me, lay off the red wine."

"What did I say so terrible?"

After hanging up, huddled in her comforter and chafing her icy toes, Paula brooded. She had been too pliable—or too harsh—the bottle of wine was unplugged again, her mother sliding into a black mood. She reached for the phone; before she could punch the programmed button she made herself hang up.

Who was she to help other people get free of their compulsions? When would she? Peter Fine liked to talk about the toxic people in our lives who poison us. He said we have to get rid of them as ruthlessly as taking antibiotics for an infection or cleaning up an industrial waste site. Tolerating the toxins was unfair to the healthy person, the healthy community. And if the toxin was your mother? Fine would say: Especially.

Paula had become a social worker because, growing up in New York, where misery was a given, she never developed the willful blindness or thick skin to accept it as such. She hated having options, however modest, when so many others had none; she hated the injustice of it, not as an idea but as a human fact in the face of an old man who politely asked for her doggy bag one night on upper Broadway. She had no politics to explain the poverty that put him there and no solution for it, but it upset her in the most elemental way. She felt no responsibility greater than to the face in front of her. For most of her life it had been her mother's.

Today was one of Paula's better days.

She had been brave enough to say to Gladys Dill, "I haven't helped you much, have I?"

Gladys said, "I don't see things getting no better."

"It must be pretty infuriating, coming every week."

"Hm."

"Finding a baby-sitter so you can come see me for an hour."

"Sometime I don't think you know."

"Know what?"

"What it's like. I don't think you know."

"I probably don't. Try telling me."

Gladys—a new lens in her old glasses—eyed Paula as if to figure out whether it was worth the effort.

"I could tell you but it wouldn't make no difference, you'd still go back to your house on Beacon Hill or whatever."

"That's right."

"You get home and what? Wait for some man to come over in a necktie and go out to a restaurant?"

"Italian."

"And he pays. Lot of money."

"Expensive meal."

"And you tell him about me. Stupid coke-sniffing black woman care of D.S.S. Stupid woman doesn't have enough sense to get rid of her man. Sit there drinking wine and telling him about me. And he says, 'How do you stand it?'"

And the valve began to open and let out some of the infected blood of her rage.

When Gladys stood up to leave she said, "That's funny, I feel better."

That was how it was done. After all, people changed. Life changed.

five

Eric worked his fingers into Jane's swollen skin, massaging one arm, the other, then the legs from feet to midthigh. Her circulation had been clogging up again. Head propped on a pillow at the end of the futon, she watched behind the rise and fall of her belly. Her lids were heavy and her lips pursed in a dreamy smile, and once or twice she ran her hand through his hair. It was like a pantomime of sex. A sitcom was on TV, and a week-old stack of papers lay unmarked on the coffee table.

"What are you thinking about?"

"Me?"

"You with the fingers."

"I was thinking about Oaxaca."

It wasn't true. Oaxaca was what he'd been thinking about before he started thinking about what had happened earlier in the evening. He had spent the day slowly destroying yesterday's work and had then gone out, intending to clear his head with a walk along the river. Instead, he wandered off the street into a bookstore vaguely hoping for some new idea. He ended up by the remainder table and was turning the prematurely brittle pages of unwanted books when he noticed a woman staring at him.

This happened so seldom that at first it didn't register. Before he could look away, enough eye contact had been made for her face to brighten. She was young, extremely pale, with a boyish haircut and a gash of brown lipstick. Pretending to examine a biography of E.M. Forster, Eric saw her move around to his side of the table.

When he looked again, her head was almost directly under his; her upward smile struck him as coy and provocative.

"Have you read this poet?"

She flashed the book cover at him: a name he didn't know, a painting of a violently fractured woman's face. He shook his head. "Good?"

Her laugh mingled contempt and sly promise, as if to say, "You don't know what good is." The odor of female shampoo had penetrated his airspace. Stunned, he reached for the book and opened to its contents. A grad student, he was thinking, the sweatjacket and leotard top. Sort of underfed, with big nocturnal eyes. Still.

"Here, read this, this one." Eagerly turning the pages for him she grazed his hand. The recommended poem was called "Deathday Girl" and Eric searched its ragged stanzas for verbs. *seeping weeping black blood/twice as absorbent as the other brand.* His wedding ring gleamed into view, and desire was yanked like a dog that forgot the leash. Nevertheless he thought: If she suggests coffee . . . technically within the rules? They'd discuss this morbid poet of hers, who apparently tried to self-induce toxic shock on her twenty-fifth birthday. But what if he did? Highly suspect, unless it *was* just coffee, but what if it wasn't, which of course it was?

The questions startled and overwhelmed him.

"Very nice." He returned the book and met her lemur eyes. Their vulnerability made him flash on cinder-block bookshelves, a disorderly bed, frantic lovemaking. His heart pumped with the consciousness of possibility. Deathday girl was offering herself.

He was preparing a sentence that began "Would you" and whose ending he didn't know, being a decade out of practice, when she said:

"This poem saved my life."

Sensing that she meant it literally, Eric became cautious. "I'm glad it did."

She closed her eyes. When she opened them they were drowning, or screaming.

"Do you know what it's like to be totally dark and open a book and feel a light shine?"

He understood.

"I haven't had that experience." She was insane. In Cambridge, only insane women came on to men. They were being observed from the mythology section by a man in an Indiana Jones hat. When Eric made a move toward the cash register she seized his arm.

"Are you really alive? Please! Listen to me. It's very important."

"I'm sorry, I have to go." The socially embarrassed solid citizen now, he gently withdrew his arm and made his way toward the exit. The cashier whispered, "Sorry, she's very troubled."

"My fault."

He walked home with his ears burning, wondering what had gotten into him, knowing exactly what had. On the way he spun out variations for Jane's amusement, but none worked because the meaning—what made it bizarre and funny—did not have to do with the girl but with him. He had moved from fantasy to plan and was unprecedentedly on the verge of words, which can be deeds. The will was about to get involved. These distinctions meant a lot. Jane had once set them down in great detail and Eric basically accepted her analysis. Morally he had already done it: gone to bed with Cassandra.

Foolish man. But the lemur eyes haunted him, the feel of her hand was imprinted on his forearm. "Are you really alive?"

So tonight he had something to conceal, and concealment made him guilty and restless.

Jane lifted her knee so that he could massage the calf. "What about Oaxaca?"

He scurried back to his Oaxaca thoughts. "Do you remember that traditional dance, when we sat in the blazing sun for five hours because it was too crowded to leave?"

"I remember I had my arms inside my shirt and you were covered in newspaper."

"That time we hitched to Guatemala and sat in the bus with the goats on the way back."

"It was a terrible ride."

"We had fun."

"I remember being sweaty and the goats smelled."

A slight change in the angle of Jane's knee told Eric that the subject irritated her.

"Every morning," he went on, "we woke up to the parrot and had our cafe con leche. You'd go off to your institute and I'd sit at my rickety little table. I can feel the tile under my feet. Some days I wrote ten pages." His posture had begun to seem servile. "Remember when we made love on Monte Alban, behind Tomb 103? And ten seconds later that guy with the burro showed up?"

Eric heard her exhale nasally: a warning. "Yeah, that was Mexico."

"That's what I'm saying."

It was one of those conversations that had them getting angrier the more they pretended to agree.

"Eric." Without looking up from her leg he knew the lineaments of disapproval across her face. "We were thirty. It won't be that way again. Can you live without it?"

"You mean, forever? No more good times?"

"I'm not saying that." Under his fingers her calf muscle felt rigid. "We had our year in Oaxaca. For me once was enough. I'll be thirty-eight when the baby comes. And frankly what worries me is you don't seem to understand what it's going to mean."

"Oh, I do. I totally accept Rachel's version. We'll move to Lincoln and have everything except sex."

Jane withdrew her leg and sat up. Now they were sitting side by side, but since looking would be a kind of concession they both addressed the TV.

Jane said, "What are you angry about?"

"I'm not angry. I'm having problems getting my work done."

"And why do I get the feeling you're blaming the baby and me? Oaxaca—"

"I didn't say that. There are lots of reasons, none of which seem to interest you."

"You assume that. But you don't tell me, so how can I know?"

"By asking."

"All right, I'm asking."

"You can't ask that way." The TV was too loud. His head felt feverish and cramped. He hated to fight, it always left him empty. "I'm about to lose my study, we need cash, God knows what this renovation will cost. And I can't talk to you without upsetting you."

"You can say whatever you want."

"You ask what I'm thinking, then it's unacceptable."

"I don't have to like the answer."

"At least you ought to listen."

This was their way now: he looking more and more to her, she thickening her rind to save the juice for the baby.

"I've been listening. You wish you were writing your first book in Oaxaca with the parrot again."

"That's not listening."

"You wish I wasn't pregnant."

The unanswerable truth.

"It's different for men," he started to say, but Jane had sunk into the couch. He turned around to explain how it was different for men. "Oh God, what's wrong?"

She was biting her lip. A tear fell from the tip of her nose onto her lap. When Jane wept she wept silently, against her will. His anger melted away and he leaned back and took her in his arms. She began to sob.

"I feel so alone." Jane's voice was muffled in his sleeve.

"I'm sorry, I'm sorry. Sweetheart. I'm right here with you."

She gave in to the pressure of tears and he stroked her hair and was happy.

"It's your child too, doesn't that matter?"

"Of course it matters," he murmured, and suddenly the congestion of trouble in his chest rose to his throat. "I don't know what I'll be able to offer."

"Love. You can offer love."

"Jane, you don't know what it's like. I can't write, I've lost my confidence. Every day I sit there fighting and nothing happens, this numbness comes over me."

She pulled away. There was terror in her eyes. "You'll get through it. You had that block on *Soldier's Dilemma* and it ended up being your best book."

"This feels—different."

"But why? Why? Eric, don't do this to me, please. I'm sorry but I can't—I don't think I can handle it right now. You just have to believe in yourself. You've hung on for so long, this book is going to be the one, you'll see."

He could not meet her gaze. His tenderness had shrunk into a hard dry pellet of shame.

"It's just a bad time," he said quietly. "I'll get through it."

"Darling, I need you to be in this with me."

"I am. I will be."

Though her face was wet and her eyelids swollen and she spoke of need, she was back in control. Power had shifted, found its level.

Before her, he had disciplined himself in austerity through half-hearted involvements, depending on no one, wanting no one dependent on him—but all the while he was afraid of being unfit for love. So from the beginning with Jane he was surprised to find how wonderfully intimacy suited him, how it released his energy and eased the burden of self. What he had been before now seemed callow, insular. Marriage gave him the subject of other human beings.

Jane was the sanest person he knew, but she had an acute imagination of disaster. Her father, a self-employed fire-alarm installer, had gone bankrupt when a system failed to work and a warehouse burned down. Their house was lost, her parents' marriage nearly ended, and for two years her father disappeared into part-time jobs. "Everything could go in a blink," she once told Eric, and threw her energy into making sure it didn't.

One after another his first three books appeared, and he and Jane waited together for something to happen. They didn't tell each other what it was (they didn't exactly know). They didn't even tell each other they were waiting. But something was bound to happen, soon, bringing the recognition that had eluded him and with it peace of mind. He came to sense that the marriage—not its survival, but its vitality—depended on this something. Without it they would grow old like a childless couple, the disappointment would always gnaw. It was what she expected of him and he of himself, part of an unspoken bargain.

And as years and books went by and they continued to wait, he began to feel that he was letting them both down. The waiting ceased to be something they did together; it became his separate vigil. When they did discuss his work, they no longer talked much about ideas, worrying instead over the mechanics of his career—contracts, contacts. But he resisted doing the small practical things that might help. The something would happen or it would not. He was becoming the kind of man who, in a deepening hurt, regarded pain as the only reliable sign of virtue.

Lovemaking remained a sure thing for them, the charge of attraction always mutual and strong. But when Jane became obsessed with getting pregnant, Eric, who had always wanted children with her, took it as an expression of discontent. She was saying that time was running out, for him as well as her. Then pregnancy itself seemed to drain her away from him. Money became an issue, they stopped making love, and he was left to solve his problems by himself.

He had long since lost the ability to manage alone.

Jane found the remote and turned the sitcom off. "What about the baby room?" She had shed her mood and plunged into the future.

"I'm going out to Lincoln tomorrow. Rachel's guy won't let anyone hire him until they've met his crew and seen his work."

She squeezed his hand.

six

When the first frozen rain announces winter, and the ground hardens and the blood slows and drivers test their brakes, all that keeps the city in circulation is money. Money pulls a man out of a warm bed into a cold room, pastes a smile on the chapped face of a woman behind a counter, stirs the dormant spirit of four o'clock in the afternoon. At the low ebb of the day and the year, when nothing else starts bodies in motion, money becomes the primum mobile, the hidden principle of vitality and connection. Visible, aging dollar bills pass from hand to hand and link 10,000 unsuspecting strangers like shared genes or the germs of disease. Money is both desire and necessity. It buoys and sinks like water. All across its surface millions of heads bob up and go under, while below the entangled limbs support and drag. But the same vast indivisible body of water surrounds the floating, the sinking, and the drowned. The pressure this body imposes grows by one atmosphere for every thirty-three feet of depth, but it is always the same pressure and never lets up.

At the last minute a stockbroker decides to work out at the gym before going down to put a deposit on a new car, which makes the salesman who needs one more sale for his monthly bonus wait at the lot past seven o'clock, leaving his girlfriend to sit by herself at a table in the restaurant where they were going to decide whether or not to stay together. Money is the relationship no one can leave, the community that remains when all the others decay, scatter, disappear. Money keeps us from being merely individuals. Everyone is compromised and no one is alone.

Joe stood before the broad oak door of Number 27. It was a big elegant house midway down a dim street of similar houses, lighted bay windows giving glimpses of bookcases and chandeliers, drawn shades upstairs. Although the street was only a few blocks from Central Square, this neighborhood felt like another city. There were no cars or people. As he walked past in his dead white man's clothes, the windows stared him down.

Three days had taken him all over the city, and at the end he was exactly where he had started. The staff and guests at Rainbow House treated him with special friendliness because he came from Africa, but it was beginning to make Joe feel he would never get out of the place. Soon he would be one of the regulars who knew the rules by heart, slouched at dinner, slept in their clothes, dawdled in the morning, were first in line outside the door at night, and dreaded going back into the lottery. The poet had disappeared, maybe to France. Kevin, the ex-con, was gone too, leaving the impression of some potentially lucrative business he had to attend to. Joe felt stranded.

He made a point of going out every morning, showered and shaved, with at least one appointment scheduled. Today he had four. In the morning there was a restaurant on Beacon Hill that needed a busboy. At 11:00 the place was empty, and the only light was daylight filtered through the grimy streetfront window. The advertisement had mentioned fine Italian cuisine, but the dining room smelled of fried grease. The manager, a fat chain-smoker, sat Joe down at a table with a white tablecloth and asked him what restaurant experience he'd had in Africa.

Joe made up a hotel in a capital city, with a European management that trained him to arrange table settings for the foreign businessmen who ate there. He discovered that making things up was easier than telling the truth, which always felt like signing a confession. His new voice was deeper than the old one, and richer, and as he listened to its strange and wonderful sounds he began to think of a shy, elegant, skillful young African, full of promise, and he noticed that his slender hands were gesturing excitedly. The manager drew on the cigarette and breathed smoke.

Joe was so engrossed in his story that he was slow to notice what was happening in the kitchen. Voices were raised—two men were quarreling. Before long they were screaming curses. The manager sat slumped with his back to the kitchen door while his breathing became labored. Sweat broke out on his forehead. The fold of fat over his collar began to shake. Then he exploded out of his chair and heaved through the swinging door.

Now three voices were screaming. It seemed that one of the men had used the other's shirt to wipe off the griddle.

Left alone in the dining room, Joe realized that this restaurant would smell of grease every day, and every day men would scream. The telephone started to ring but no one came out to answer it. He escaped through the front door into daylight.

At his next appointment, a recycling yard by the harbor, the supervisor read Joe's current address and didn't even give him a chance to talk about Africans' natural talent at recycling.

The third was back in Cambridge, a big busy French-style fast-food restaurant in the middle of Harvard Square. The workers in berets and blue aprons, taking orders and making sandwiches behind the counter, came in every color. Joe felt that he would fit right in here. He sat at a small marble table across from a young white man with bad skin named Greg Kircher. Kircher's tie was tucked between his shirt buttons; his nametag said "Management trainee." At the next table a noisy chess game was going on. Three tables away sat Harold, the white whiskers from Rainbow House, drinking coffee and staring into space. Joe kept his face hidden, afraid that Harold would wave to him and blow the interview.

"What does the word 'reliable' mean to you?" Kircher read from a clipboard.

"Always there," Joe said. "Steady like an ox. As good as his word."

Kircher dropped his head and ran his finger down the clipboard.

"What will you do to promote teamwork here?"

There were a lot of questions, and in answering them Joe corrected his mistake from the Italian restaurant. It wasn't enough for him to like this new person, this Joe Amouzou; he had to make Greg Kircher like him too. He tried to hold Kircher's eyes, but the management trainee never looked up from his clipboard. He was always getting ready for the next question, as if he was the one taking the test. When Joe asked what "interactive management style" meant, Kircher explained the term by repeating it three times.

He ran his finger down to the last question and looked up. "Can I see your green card?"

There was nothing Kircher could do for Joe. As soon as Joe obtained a green card he hoped that Joe would come back because he seemed like the kind of person who knew how to work as a team.

Joe wandered down Massachusetts Avenue toward Central Square. It was already dark. He had permission from Rainbow House to come in late, but he thought about skipping his last appointment, which was at seven o'clock. He hadn't even begun to consider all the problems that he was going to be in for. Once you lied you had to tell more lies. He would have to be quick on his feet. As himself he could have just taken out his passport.

His hundred dollars had turned out to be only ninety at the bank. He had about seventy left and it would go fast. Nothing was free, everything was expensive. He had asked a couple of day laborers at Rainbow House about the Big Dig and they had laughed in his face. Mr. DeSouza had told him that no one was going to pick him out of the crowd—he had to sell himself.

The memory of his foster parents' dinner table kept coming into his head. He was asking his mother for potatoes, and she was sliding the steaming bowl toward him. He didn't know if this ever really happened, but it gave him a strong sad feeling. He was standing at an intersection near Central Square. People passed him on the sidewalk and he knew that you had to make your way alone. If he went back to Rainbow House, jobless, the smell of dirty feet in the dormitory, another night of spaghetti and tomato sauce, he might end up dead in an alley.

He pictured himself walking on to Rainbow House—easy to see. He tried to picture himself turning left to his last appointment—

harder. He kept disappearing, like a ghost. Then he had an idea: It wasn't he who would go down that street, but Joe Amouzou. And suddenly he saw it clear, a man striding toward an address, and he began to walk and fit his strides to that man's.

The door of Number 27 opened to his knock. On either side of the entry hall, four men were sitting on wicker benches. One of them, a large man with a red beard, had let Joe in without getting up.

"Is this for the construction job?" Joe asked.

"Can't you tell?" the red beard shot back, his laugh exposing a mouthful of brown teeth. Somebody else snorted. Joe hesitated at the threshold and had a partial view of the house—a broad staircase with a rich, dark, curving rail, a hardwood floor gleaming under tracklights.

He stepped inside and took a place on one of the benches. The men, brooding and massive in steel-toed boots and dusty jeans, surveyed him.

"What's he doing, giving head?" The man opposite Joe had a thick brush of mustache and a pale, hard face. "Doesn't this guy have a fucking office or something?"

"I didn't even see a truck," the red beard said.

"It's in the driveway." The man who said this had gray hair and a soft voice. "Newburg Construction Corp. I hear he's got a lot of work."

"I heard the guy was into coke," a dark-haired man muttered in a Spanish accent.

"Dealing?" the brush mustache said. "That's how he got a fucking place like this."

They all looked toward the staircase and fell silent. Somebody sighed. The gray-haired man put his face in his broad, veiny hands and kneaded his eyes as if he meant to gouge them out.

"This sucks," the brush mustache said. "I don't have time to sit around waiting for some asshole to connect with me."

The older man stopped massaging his face and looked up. His fingers had left deep grooves, as if the flesh was modeling clay. "I find that there's plenty of time for things like job interviews when you're unemployed."

"That's what he told me on the phone, this asshole—he wants to see if we'll connect."

"If he wants to connect, who am I to stop him?"

"Two-thirds of the guys in my local are out," the red beard said.

"I got you all beat," the Spanish accent said. "I ain't even a laborer. I was doing rough and finish eight years. This is a comedown."

"Go home, you're overqualified," the red beard said. Someone laughed sarcastically. "How many guys you think answered this ad?"

"Fifty. A hundred."

"Is he going to connect with every fucking one of them?" The brush mustache seemed about to get up and leave. Instead he looked across at Joe. A blue anger was burning in his eyes. "You in Local 151, Jackson?"

"I come from—"

"Make no difference," the Spanish accent said, "this is non-union. We all lining up to be scabs. Make my kids real proud."

"I'm just asking. He looks a little young to me. Doesn't he look a little young to you?"

"I'd trade places," the gray-haired man said.

Another man came around the corner shaking his head. "Next batter." He walked straight out of the house. The brush mustache jumped to his feet. He patted his short black hair and glanced at the others. None of them looked back. He said something to himself, then disappeared around the corner with his heavy boots echoing across the floor.

Half an hour later Joe was sitting alone when the gray-haired man returned, hands buried in his coat pockets, his clay face furrowed and pale. The others had come back silent or cursing, but he winked at Joe. "OK, kid, maybe you'll connect."

The door closed heavily. The house was silent. Joe walked horse-like in his workboots over the bright blond floor. A few paintings were hung along a spotless wall. There were no chairs or children's toys or anything else in the hall, and Joe felt as if he was in a museum. One of the paintings was of a naked woman lying on a bed. Her arm was thrown back behind her head, and the pink of her nipples looked so lifelike that Joe instinctively glanced away and felt his cheeks flush. He stole another look. Her face wasn't a happy face. She wasn't flirting or teasing or even enjoying her nakedness— it seemed like an ordeal. Aroused and confused, Joe had a notion that someone was watching him watch this woman and that it was part of the interview.

He pictured the coke-dealing boss lying in bed, being rubbed by naked women with pink nipples. Joe willed down his hard-on. That would be the first thing Jim Newburg would look for; he would point it out to the naked women, they would all have a laugh, and the interview would be over.

The room at the end of the hall was long and dark. There wasn't a single piece of furniture anywhere, except a low glass table in the middle of the floor, surrounded by cushions on a straw mat. On one of the cushions a man was sitting Indian style, the way Joe was taught to sit in kindergarten during story time. The man's back was straight and his shoulders sloped in a sportshirt open at the neck. Curly blond hair was disappearing beyond his forehead. He held a teacup and saucer in his lap.

Newburg seemed to say, "Ah."

The mat had to be crossed, but it looked fragile. Joe stopped, unlaced his boots, and then carried them in stocking feet to the table.

Newburg, watching, smiled. He set down his teacup to shake Joe's hand. The grip was surprisingly strong and rough-skinned. Joe lowered himself onto a cushion, avoiding one that still showed the sunken impression of someone else's bottom as if it might bring bad luck. He sat Indian style and tried to keep his back straight.

"Jim Newburg. And you are—" Newburg glanced at a sheet of paper on the coffee table: He did this by extending his neck, turtle-like, without moving his head or shoulders. The hairline made his head look too big for his small, neat body, like a wizard's. "Joe Amouzou. Tea?"

On the glass table there were five or six teacups half-full of leafy brown liquid. Newburg lifted the pot and poured into a clean cup as thin as an eggshell. In the silence, the chink and slosh were excruciating. Joe picked up the cup and it rattled against the saucer.

"What I'd like, Joe, is for you to tell me about yourself. Then you'll hear a few things about me and the kind of work I do and we'll see if we connect. So far tonight I haven't felt it. But tell me where you're from."

"Africa."

Joe described the town in the hills, the work he did cutting and planing and hammering forest timber into furniture, and somehow lying brought the smell of Amouzou's workshop to his nostrils, and he had to set down the teacup so that he wouldn't break it in the rush of energy.

Newburg never took his eyes off Joe. When he sipped, only his arm and lips moved. The rest of his body remained completely still, as if he were wearing a steel brace under his shirt. Joe searched the pale blue surface of Newburg's eyes but had no idea what impression he was making.

"How long have you been here, Joe?"

"Three days."

He knew the next question and still had no answer. "Why did you come to America?"

"Politics," Joe said vaguely.

Newburg tilted his head a couple of degrees to indicate a question. Joe took a breath and went for broke.

"In my hometown there were killings. I lost my family. My mother, my father, my children, my wife. They are all dead. They wanted to kill me, too."

On an inspiration, he unbuttoned his sleeve and rolled it up. The wound had hardened and grayed as it healed in the cold, but it was still vivid.

"It is a miracle I am alive."

"Why, why would they kill your family?"

"Because—"

Blocked, Joe picked up his teacup. He saw Amouzou with his knees propped up in the tomb. He saw the bread lady's son, clutching the skirts of the strange woman at the border bridge. He started to speak and had to clear his throat.

"Because I healed the sick. And I cared for the orphans. And I buried the dead no one else would bury. And when evil enters people's hearts, the good ones must suffer."

Jim Newburg closed his eyes. He kept them closed for some time. Joe rolled down his sleeve and waited. Maybe the business with the cut had been too much.

When Newburg's eyes opened they were moist.

"I've known other trauma survivors, Joe, but not with your grace, your peace. . . ." Newburg bit his lip and shook his head. "What can I say except to respond to your courage by being honest with you and telling you about me."

Somewhere in the room a clock was ticking. Newburg's face was drawn and blue-veined.

"In the eighties—I don't know how much this is going to mean to you as an African—but the eighties were bad for a lot of people here. I got into prefab condos, mass production. My partner and I were building units on spec on every square foot of empty lot in this city. I made a lot of fast money, and I developed a serious cocaine habit. I felt like I could take the nail gun and frame up a whole development by myself. When my wife left me for my partner, the bottom fell out.

"I went into recovery and contracted with myself to only do jobs that permit 100 percent respect for the space, the materials, and the people. Now I'm doing even better than in the eighties because there's balance, there's harmony."

Newburg's face appeared to be losing blood. His voice was thinning, winding itself taut like wire on a crank.

"Look, Joe, I'm a people person and you were right the minute you respected the Javanese mat. You probably don't know much about residential renovation. If I was just looking for a body, I could hire any of the guys I've seen tonight." Joe glanced at the sunken cushion and the cups of undrunk tea. "They'll show up on time, they'll do what I tell them, they'll only cheat me a little. They'd probably work for less than I pay, because some of them are desperate and that's sad. There are a lot of desperate people in this country and some of them own their own trucks. But let me tell you about the men I've seen tonight.

"When I talk about respecting the wood, they look at me like I'm crazy. They can't think past money. It's punch in and paycheck. The light has gone out of their souls. I don't blame them, I blame America, but there's no way they could work on my crew. On some level they would know it was wrong. But I get a very different energy from you. A totally different energy. Because you're African."

"Yes."

"So I don't have to explain that shelter is sacred."

"No."

"Or that excellence and success are a total relationship between you and the world."

"No. Yes." Newburg waited for something more. "You mean neutral buoyancy."

The pale eyes lit up. "*Yes.*"

Newburg's vocal cords were going to snap. If he sneezed or coughed, the bloodless dome of his head would fly off his body.

"See, what I do is very special." The crank was about to turn one more time. Then Newburg's shoulders dropped. He set down his teacup. He was finished. "Have you ever used a belt sander?"

"No."

It wasn't true—Amouzou had an electric sander in his shop. But Joe knew not to say so, not to mention the BBC, or the truck stop where men drank shots of White Horse, or the rap lyrics the boys in his cooperative recited. He would give Newburg the Africa Newburg wanted.

"Never mind, you'll learn in a minute. Can you start tomorrow?"

"I do not have the green card." By now Joe knew how to go on. Knowing made him feel wise and powerful. "Your government is giving me difficulties. I asked for political asylum—"

Newburg held up his palm. "Rules that are designed to crush the human spirit we have a duty to ignore."

On their way to the front door, Joe couldn't help glancing at the naked woman on the wall.

"My wife," Newburg said. "She was a beautiful person. We're still very good friends."

At the door Newburg took a wad of cash from his pocket and peeled off five twenties.

"We call this earnest money. Where are you staying, Joe?"

"Rainbow House."

Newburg shook his head. "No, that's, that's—not going to last. You don't belong there. I'll arrange something."

He said that Joe should come by at 7:00 tomorrow morning and they would drive out together to Lincoln, where his crew was finishing up a really innovative job.

Newburg started to close the door. "Joe, do you—as an African, do I seem like one of the good ones to you? After what I told you about the eighties. Do I?"

Joe squeezed Newburg's arm, in the warm African way. "Before tonight I had nothing, Jim. You have given me a second life."

He smiled. No Halloween mask stretched across his face; it wasn't skin and jawbone but himself, the sweet boy, the smile that used to light up the faces of grown-ups, and Jim Newburg seemed to bask in the sun's radiance.

Joe walked up the street breathing cold air. The big houses reached out to embrace him. He imagined people inside watching him as he passed. *There's that African Jim Newburg just hired. Jim says he has a totally different energy.* He remembered the sunken cushion in the living room and realized that it had been him once, too—no light in his soul, never getting anywhere and not knowing why, like trying to run under water, or in the dream where you can't move your legs.

In San Francisco, in another life, after his foster parents were killed and Joe moved up to the city, he saw a movie one night. At the time he was working at a chicken restaurant, without a plan, drifting. It was an evening of thick fog and he had to get out of his room so he would stop thinking about his foster parents. He went by himself to a theater in the Tenderloin.

The movie turned out to be in black and white. It was about a black woman in New York and her three lovers. Everyone else in the theater seemed to know it already, and Joe felt anxious to react the way the audience reacted, laughing when they laughed; and he was ashamed.

But the movie began to work on him. Soon he forgot the people around him and lost himself in the people on the screen. They were beautiful and always said smart and funny things, and yet they were no older than he was. One of the woman's lovers was more serious than the others. He declared his love passionately, and she loved him too, and at the end when she refused him, he tried to hurt her because there was nothing else for him. He was her true lover.

Joe began to see himself in this man—not himself as he was, for he didn't have the words or assurance, but as he could be. He wanted to be part of the woman's world, and her lovers'. He didn't want to be ordinary anymore. As the ending approached, he dreaded the house lights coming on.

He left the theater and walked the foggy streets back to the apartment he shared with two other guys. As he undressed for bed, the sight of his orange work uniform draped over a chair startled him. He wanted to change everything about himself: his voice, his name, his face. He felt ignorant, and dull, and unloved. He felt crippled by the home in which he'd been raised. Then he asked his foster mother to forgive him. "You're special because you're you," she always said, and whenever he got angry or frustrated she asked him to smile for her and not break her heart. Home had been the world, and though there was never enough money it was a safe, sound world, and he never forgot the earlier years when he lived from night to night in each house. After the car accident, he felt everything had been taken away.

But they had misled their sweet boy. A life wasn't something you were born with or that was given to you, but something you had to find for yourself, make for yourself. No one had ever told him that. But everyone else seemed to know already.

A little later, when Joe met the film students in the Mission, they were like the characters in the movie—his age, in their early twenties, but college graduates from families with money, white and black, taking classes at an art school. They thought Joe had grown up a gangbanger in Oakland and he decided to let them think it, his silences suggesting a hard-won reserve of street pain and passion. He grew his pencil-line mustache, and two of the girls slept with him. He was given parts in a movie they were making, as cop, junkie, and pimp. They said he was a natural. And for a while, San Francisco became a movie screen. Then things went wrong and he lost what he'd discovered that night in the fog.

A clouded half-moon hung over Central Square. Joe walked toward it along a chain-link fence behind which steel beams rose up out of a hole. There were blue signs on the fence. One of them said: "You Could Be Anyone." In Jim Newburg's living room, ahead of fifty more qualified men, he had been picked. He had a hundred new dollars in his pocket, and a job. He went back to Rainbow House like a free man.

seven

"I'm very good at what I do," Jim Newburg said behind the wheel of his Toyota pickup. He said it as a matter of earnest self-assessment, which was how he said everything. "That was one thing the drug didn't get to."

"That must be rewarding," Eric said, "to know that."

"It is. There's an interface between centeredness and success. I'm expanding, just hired a wonderful helper from Africa, a magical person. I think you'll really respond to him as an artist, Eric."

They had driven out of the city on Route 2, and by the time they turned off for Lincoln, Eric knew all of the contractor's secrets. He had read somewhere that in the eighteenth century people observed a distinction between public and private life, so that reserve between strangers was normal: one language for the square, one for the home. People didn't feel phony for holding something back, didn't become less authentically themselves. But being contemporary, Newburg was compelled to report on every kind of disease, sordidness, addiction—arranging personal history into a parable of fall and redemption that he carried around for quick display like a driver's license. This new idea of truth and human connection left Eric, who would have been at home in the eighteenth century, feeling embarrassed, strangely weightless, and hopelessly repressed.

Off the highway, Lincoln's open acreage spread before them like real countryside. He hadn't been out of the city in months, and he stopped listening to Newburg and loosed his thoughts across a marshy field over which a pair of Canada geese were gliding in a milky sky. The maples and birches were stripped bare. He imagined walking through piles of leaves, kicking them up and grabbing armfuls. He had somehow missed fall this year—at some point in the middle of the new book his runs along the Charles had stopped. The river had always been one of his great pleasures, the giant sycamores following its curves, the mallards burying their heads in mud for worms after a rain. He should get back to it.

But all the land out here was private, he suddenly realized, even the ponds and some of the roads. Lincoln was less a town than a group of contiguous estates. At the end of winding gravel drives, lawyers and software executives were hidden behind stands of spruce. Coming out here for dinner at the Silvers' was inconceivable.

In the semicircular drive a Dumpster the size of a small barge signaled construction work. "She's still at acupuncture," Newburg murmured as the engine rattled and died in the cold. He pocketed his keys and looked at Eric. "It's better if I'm here when Missy gets back."

From outside, the Standish house spoke of sober, gray-shingled New England prosperity. Beyond the cast-fiberglass front door, all was postmodern aggression. A low tapered hallway designed for dogs led out into a towering atrium hacked out of the second floor and attic. Forty feet overhead, wall planes and roof lines were colliding at a dozen angles, like a shattered Cubist cityscape. Winter light seeped from rhomboid skylights. The cathedral ceiling effected a gradual fragmentation rising into the white purity of madness. Eric could hardly bear to look up. It was like staring at the sun.

Newburg was at his side. "When I saw the plans I said, 'I was born to build this space.'"

In one corner stood a marble igloo that Eric determined to be a fireplace. "Is this the living room?"

Newburg nodded. Far below the light source, his eyes seemed drained of color. "All I do is help express people's vision of themselves."

Eric glanced up into the shrieking void. "What if they don't like themselves?"

"Those are the ones I avoid." From a lacquered table by the

staircase, Newburg picked up a piece of jade carved in the shape of a crouching lion. "Chinese, Eric, Ming dynasty. These people have *money*. But the thing about Missy and Ted is, it hasn't killed their vision."

"Jim, our budget's pretty tight—so is our time. The job might be too small for you."

"You're creating space for a new life, Eric." Newburg set the Ming jade down. "I'd be honored to be a part of that."

The walls were answering Eric's psychic dissonance with a high-pitched scream. On the second floor someone was drilling. He followed Newburg upstairs, where an orange extension cord marked a trail into the master bedroom and through an inner door to the bathroom.

Black and white wall tiles were patterned in a 3-D perspective, Escher-like; in opposing mirrors the shapes receded infinitely. The two men appeared single file a hundred men deep. An illusion of vast space in a small room (he was catching on), so that at first he didn't notice the pair of legs in blue jeans sticking out from under the sink.

"Frank," said Newburg, "say hi to Eric Barnes."

Frank groaned, began to withdraw his upper body, and hit his head on the bottom of the vanity. He swore under his breath. Then, as if reconsidering, he swore again very loud. Horizontally he was much too tall for the room and lay twisted up in extension cords and the tails of several power tools like Laocoön coiled in snakes. At last his face emerged, freckled, sad-eyed.

"How's it going?" Eric asked.

"I don't know anymore."

Newburg said, "You're almost done, Frank."

"No, I'm going to die in here. I must have been a corrupt plumber in a former life. I can't make a move, right, because everything's perfect. It's my tomb." He picked up the drill, put it to his head, and pulled the trigger. The slender bit whirled into his silvering hair. "Watch it, that grout's setting up."

"Eric's going to have some work done. Not a bathroom, Frank."

"She'll never let us go. I am convinced—" Frank caught himself and stared up with a strange smile. "She wants us around forever. Really! We're the queen's own workmen. This whole job—did you see the place?" Frank looked to Eric for sanity and sympathy, and with his nod Eric tried to convey both. "It's like a huge makeover. She doesn't want it to stop. Did you tell him about the closet we built and had to tear it out because her stepladder didn't fit?"

"Missy can be very demanding."

"Demanding! I'd like to—I lie here and think about the chop saw, or the table saw—"

"Cool it, Frank," Newburg said sharply.

Downstairs, a door closed. Frank disappeared under the vanity. A voice sang out, "Jim?"

"In here!"

Missy swung into the bathroom brimming with such confidence that it suddenly became very crowded. She gave Eric her hand and an appraising look, as if to challenge his right to be here and seduce him at the same time. Missy had mastered the art of youthfulness with strategic makeup and a skirt that showed her legs to good effect.

"And where is Carpenter Frank? Oh my God, there you are, like the Wicked Witch of the East under Dorothy's house. Just kidding, I know that's my part." She planted her hands on her hips. "Well, it really looks like I'm going to get my house back this millennium. You guys are great, but you just don't know when to leave. Aren't they great?" This was addressed to Eric. "I wake up thinking: *See-through front door!*—and Jim makes it happen. Behind schedule and over budget, but so was Michelangelo."

Eric said, "Do you sub-contract novels, Jim?"

Newburg was distracted. "Careful, Missy, the grout's wet." He eased her off the tile wall.

"Grout?" She brushed the padded shoulder of her black jacket, then leaned forward to inspect the tile. "Is it going to dry this color?"

It was astonishing how fast the mood in the bathroom changed. All the zest drained from Missy's face and it became a mask of eyeliner and lipstick. Newburg looked at the floor, where Frank's legs lay paralyzed.

Missy said, "Come out of there, Frank."

Frank emerged, speechless. He had left his drill under the vanity.

"Look at this color."

"It's Antique White, Missy." Frank was looking to Eric. "We agreed on Antique White."

"This is *beige*. It's practically *brown*."

"I showed you the sample. We talked about Bright White and you said too harsh."

"Oh that's great, it's *my* fault. As if I know what the hell Antique White is—it sounded like ivory, marble, something Greek. There's nothing besides Bright White and Antique White?"

Frank was sitting with his head at the height of a three-year-old's. It was terrible to hear him mutter, "Colonial White."

"Colonial White! I can't believe it. After six months you don't know I'm Colonial White? Does this crap look like me?" She dug her nail into a joint and came away with grout crumbs. "You're going to redo it."

"There's no more time for extras, Missy," Newburg said in the voice that had told Frank to cool it. "One way or another, in five days we're out of here."

Until this moment, Eric had wondered how Jim Newburg managed to get anything built. But he had just heard the voice of a contractor with a bottom line. The necessary, invisible element was will.

Missy started to lean against the wall again, then jerked away as if the grout were electrified. She moved to the toilet, a narrow ellipsoid bowl with a German brand name, put the cover down, and sat with her stockinged knees together and her face in her hands. She was crying softly.

"Why is it so hard to get what you want?" Frank was immobilized and Newburg unyielding, so she turned her streaking eyes to the only man in the bathroom who might answer. "I know I'm a difficult bitch. But I just want this house to be right. No one knows what it means to me. Ted doesn't have a clue. Is it so much to ask?"

Eric thought of Zachary. In the middle of the funhouse was a girl who'd exhausted herself playing and screaming and just wanted to be told it's bedtime. Money and therapy unleashed the ego to an awesome power, its purest state, that of a toddler. Eric knew exactly why Frank couldn't speak; he felt the same way himself.

Missy looked up. "Joe will understand." She rose from the toilet. "Joe understands everything. Where's Joe?"

Newburg followed her out. Eric trailed behind, leaving Frank on the bathroom floor. He imagined Frank taking his drill to tile and marble and Antique White grout and destroying his perfect tomb.

In the gallery along the atrium Missy was opening a door. A white cloud enveloped her. The burring inside the room stopped; a moment later a tall, lean figure appeared. He was wearing a dust mask and holding an electric sander. Fine dust coated his hair and caked his work clothes. Except for red-rimmed brown eyes, he was white from head to toe.

"Oh God, Joe, you should see yourself." Missy wheeled around. "*That's* how I want my grout. African White!"

Joe lifted his mask. In the middle of his face a brown oval appeared. Missy touched his forearm experimentally, then wiped it. Her fingertips left a streak as if they had smeared him with chocolate. Just when Eric expected Joe to snatch his arm away, he smiled.

Eric was prepared to dislike anyone identified as "a magical person." But he took in Joe's quiet eyes, the reserve in his powdered posture, the way he accepted Missy without submitting to her, tangled in neither extension cords nor stifled feelings, the only one who stood free from the madness of the house. Most of all, Eric took in the smile. It told him that life couldn't possibly be so hard as to kill all pleasure and joy. He had the oddest sensation that his life was about to change.

The smile died, the eyes shifted away—Eric had been staring. The African lowered his mask and retreated into the dust storm.

"I don't trust a guy who tells you he's good at what he does," Jane said.

"That's how people talk these days. It's the new honesty."

"And he's over our budget. And the other guy's bid came in lower."

"You can't price Newburg's kind of skill."

"Well, you seem set on them."

"I am. It's my study."

The day before the crew started, Eric came to life like a broken machine that had been kicked. He wrote pages and pages, and at one point he was surprised to find himself strongly moved. He worked into the early darkness; around six he suddenly put his hands in his lap and rested his forehead on the desk. When he looked up he saw that it had begun to snow. Large wet flakes blew slanting past the barred window, but the storm dissipated.

He spent the evening taking his study apart. He was determined to do the job efficiently and without sentiment, but soon he became distracted by odd things that fell into his hands. Sitting on a cardboard box, he pored over broken-spined college books whose margins were covered with his own feverish notes. "Mortality lays down its hand into his full life. What to do? Just live?" Pages and pages were filled like this. Such desire and energy, such naive faith! He remembered the mildewy basement room where he'd sat one cold midnight in the grip of a paragraph from Kierkegaard's *Either/Or* that had seemed to explain everything.

Then he turned to the books that had sustained him in his early writing. These needed no scribbles; the grayed edges of their pages spoke eloquently of the frequent hunger with which his fingers had opened them for inspiration. And the bound galleys of books he'd reviewed, piles of promotional literature falling out. The little volume of poetry Jane gave him on their first Christmas. And the copies of his own books, each cover still carrying traces of pride and hope.

After the books were boxed up, he took out the files that held his manuscripts and for an hour he leafed randomly through the smudged typescripts. He was dismayed by the posturings of his early style and at the same time awed by his feats of devotion—the ludicrous ideas passed on like genetic defects through countless drafts, deformed children that still evoked tenderness and worry.

He threw some copies out and packed the rest away. Now memory was charged and everything resonated, even the stray pink paper clips from student papers behind his desk, fortune-cookie slips, lists of things to do with a quarter of the items checked off, dried-up pens he never threw away, phone messages for Jane he wrote down years ago. He dismantled the bookshelves, furred in dust, and took down his pictures of Jane (sun-splashed in Oaxaca was his favorite), and he moved out his furniture and crammed everything into the gasometer closet out in the hall.

By 11:00 the study was bare. The walls were pocked with holes from shelf standards, dustballs lurked in corners, pennies under the baseboard heaters. Jane appeared in the doorway. Her arm slipped around his waist and he put his over her shoulder, and they stood for a time without saying anything.

"It's sad this way," she finally said. "Doesn't it make you sad?"

He had learned the new limits of her tolerance. "I've already forgotten what it looked like."

"It looked like you. I'm so used to seeing you sitting there." The words affected him like a soft kiss on his neck. He pulled her close. "It's not the end, it's the beginning," she said. "And in ten weeks there'll be a light blue carpet and a cute little critter in a crib right there." When he didn't answer she asked, "How did it go today?"

"Better. Maybe I need a gun to my head."

"Good!" Her arm tightened around his waist. "Read me something."

So they sat on their bed, and he read the day's pages and Jane listened, as they used to do. When he finished she said, "Wonderful, love. It's sad and beautiful—I've never heard you sound this way. Where did you get that scene with the Moorish slave boy?"

"Funny thing, this African on Newburg's crew. Suddenly there he was in the book, telling my syphilitic playwright how he used to hunt bush pigs with his brothers before some men stole him away to London."

"Makes me want to cry."

Jane took his hand. Her eyes were shining, her lips full. She kissed him with an intensity for which he wasn't prepared. He realized that she wanted to make love, after so long, still wanted him.

They were awkward undressing each other, almost like new lovers, but when she said, "Hope we remember how," they both laughed and the strangeness lifted. They remembered. He was careful to caress her belly, worrying that she might fear herself less desirable, trying to include this new body with its new being as the price of keeping her. But it was Jane who brought his hands to her breasts, and their tender fullness was exciting, and it was she who moved on to the touches and rhythms that had long been their way. He delighted in the pleasures she took, they thrilled him more than his own. At the end he couldn't help saying, "I've missed you," and she nodded and stroked his hair and they lay together in the dark. For the first time in weeks he had no trouble falling asleep.

The crew arrived at 7:30 in the morning. Before the clients were out of the house, the room that for so long had been silent with the effort to imagine scenes and characters came alive with the rattle of electric saws and the smash of hammers breaking walls.

Eric spent the day teaching and seeing students. In the late afternoon he took his laptop to write at Widener Libary, but yesterday's momentum had deserted him.

At home that evening he found a note from Jim Newburg. During demolition they had uncovered a badly rusted waste pipe. Replacement was going to raise costs a thousand dollars—more if the line to the sewer main was gone and the front of the house had to be dug up. But Newburg thought that this might be the key to the rat problem.

With the note crumpled in his hand, Eric went into the study. It had been destroyed. Instead of walls there was aged wood striped with plaster and lath marks. From the gaping ceiling hung coils of ancient wiring. Black grime coated the floor. The air was sharp with the peppery smell of plaster dust. And here was the rotten pipe, exposed behind the bathroom wall, five feet from where his desk had stood. Brown and flaking with corrosion, it had the massive, crumbling aspect of an archeological find. Apparently, it had had enough.

He searched for his little rat, and among wood splinters and chunks of plaster he found the body curled around a ball of congealed grease, like a child hugging a beach ball. It was much smaller than he'd imagined.

In one day the crew had stripped away the euphemisms and reduced his study to its essentials: wood, metal, dust, a furred corpse. The sight was sobering. He had no idea where they were going to find another thousand dollars.

His first thought was to borrow from Jerry and Rachel. He was certain that they would do it, would say it was nothing—that it would *be* nothing. But every day Jane would have to work alongside a woman to whom she owed money. The Silvers would have them to dinner in Lincoln, and graciously accept the gift bottle of wine, and refrain from saying, "But you still owe us money." Later, in bed, Jerry and Rachel would ask each other why Eric's writing didn't earn enough to pay the bills.

What would Paul Duffy do? He would turn out something for *Edge*. It would take him about a day and it would be snappy and hip. If Eric tried, it would take weeks and come out cheap and nasty. Anyway, that wasn't who Jane had married. She had married, she always told him, a "serious" writer, who would get what he deserved the serious way.

His parents were in no position to lend him money. His father was a retired pharmacist. Five years ago his mother's breast cancer had soaked up their small savings. And to ask his parents for help would prove them right.

They had never understood why he was pursuing this life. To them it was folly, an invitation to a crash. His farmer grandfather had a motto: "A fool eats his seed grain." The wise expected little from life. Hope was dangerous, disappointment the common run of things. Deep down, Eric shared this view—it had been bred in his bones. Yet he resented it wildly, like inherited shortness. As a boy he liked to get away to the lake downhill from the lumberyard where he spent hours alone or with friends, looking for critters, later getting high. He had grown up feeling (it shamed him to remember) contempt for his father's job, his Lions Club membership, his position on the school board, his narrow uncommunicative ways. Writing and the city gave Eric an escape.

But recently he had begun to sense how deeply he'd absorbed the prairie skepticism about big dreams. He had begun to see how much the pharmacy and the Lions Club mattered; how badly a husband and father needed tokens of recognition in his family's eyes. Eric had never given his father that, and now he regretted it.

He was standing in the middle of the demolished study, staring at the rotten pipe. It should have been exposed long ago, a memento mori as he wrote, a goad to production. Its ugliness made him alert to some danger. He thought about his own child. He saw himself at fifty-five, soft and defeated, faced with a teenager's contempt. He saw himself trying to explain why the phone never rang for him.

How had it happened that books, his access to the world of feeling, to life, had left him numb with panic?

Eric found his flashlight and lowered himself through the trap door in the rear entryway. He hadn't been in the crawl space since the rat problem compelled him to lay traps. He crawled under the floor joists and his light caught glintings of glass, decaying lumber. His knees were getting wet with mud. There was a cold, close smell. And here was the waste pipe—covered with larvae-like bubbles, pockets of escaped gas. He pressed a finger to the cast iron. It gave slightly. Q.E.D.

He turned toward the trap door's square of light and felt his hand sink into something sticky. He jerked away, but the thing came with him. Flailing, he felt a plastic corner and then the thing fell against his thighs. His flashlight found it: a shallow tray of yellowish glue. In its middle lay a rat at least eight inches long, face down in the glue, nearly skeletal, with tufts of wiry fur on the back. Death by suffocation, after a struggle. Bugs had come to feed and met their death too, on the way in or out. Some ate, then died, like the little rat in his wall.

In his haste to get out he slammed his forehead against the pipe.

"What did you go down there for?" Jane asked that night as she examined his bruise at the kitchen table, where he was nursing a beer.

"We have to face the things that are real."

"My husband's becoming a very odd man."

"Look, I have a plan. I've decided to go to New York and see Ann. I'm going to renegotiate the contract." He ignored the startled look on Jane's face. "I've got to make something happen. In Lincoln, you have no idea, this woman just snaps her fingers and it's done." He saw Frank lying mute on Missy's bathroom floor. "Only people who have money can say it doesn't matter."

Jane was silent, the silence of worry, calculation.

"You've never cared about money."

"That's right." He took a hard pull of beer. "I act as if I just have to hold up my end and good things will come."

"Good things will come. Good things came yesterday."

Yesterday seemed like months ago. "Don't you see, Jane? That kind of thinking *put* me in this trap."

She was stung. "What do you mean 'trap'?"

"This is how the world works. And I'm as corrupt as anyone. Last week I encouraged a student just because she's attractive. It was gratuitous praise—she's a lousy writer. When she gets her grade she'll be disappointed."

"Eric, what are you talking about?" Jane was gazing into his face as if in search of a feature that had deserted it. "This comes from that Paul Duffy. He did something weird to you. You never used to talk this way."

"I've been an earnest little shithead, haven't I?"

"Eric," Jane said quietly.

"What do you think of my plan?"

"I need to hear more about it."

"I'm going to ask for more money. Five thousand more. Half

up front and half on delivery. Ann's a big shot now, she can do these things. It's not like when she was at Hermes. NWC is a major corporation."

"How can you change the contract?"

"I'll send her what I've done so far, spend a week getting it together. She'll read it, see it's good. Ann knows the advance is too low. She keeps talking about needing a breakthrough book. This is the only way."

Jane ran her fingers through her bangs. The practical muscle was emerging in her cheek. "I think you should run it by your agent. Let him handle it."

"I'm not important enough for him to spend capital with NWC. People have to get things for themselves."

"Eric, be reasonable. You've never done a negotiation. You're not the type to play hardball. It might backfire."

"Jane, you be reasonable." Her skepticism goaded him. "Look— what do you want me to do? You tell me not to write for *Edge*, not to go to New York, not to ask for more money. But you keep telling me we need money! And we do, we've got a baby on the way and a pipe full of shit that's about to explode. What's the kid going to say at school when they compare what their daddies do? 'Mine used to get dicked around by New World Communications, but now he doesn't do anything.' I'm not going to have my kid saying that."

"Our child will love and respect you whatever you do."

"I have to make something happen. It can't go on like this."

"Why can't you just keep writing?" When he didn't answer Jane pressed: "You'll antagonize Ann. You're taking a risk at a time when we can't afford to."

Eric had a knuckle between his teeth. "I have to do something."

At the sound of his thin, strained voice, Jane stopped arguing.

"Why do you have to go all the way down?" she said at length, low and somber.

"To make it count. And I hate the phone, I forget what to say."

"You'll tell her—"

"I happen to be coming down. Let's get together."

"To talk about?"

"The book. And I'm sending the first half ahead of time."

"What about the book?"

"She can find out when I get there."

"Are you afraid she'd tell you not to bother coming?"

"Jane, it's pretty clear you are."

"I am, a little," she said, meeting his eyes with a gentle, decisive nod. "Ann's a businesswoman. I'm trying to think of it from her end. Ask for some of the advance now but don't try to renegotiate the amount."

"You don't have much confidence in the book."

"How can I? Other than last night you haven't shown it to me."

Last night his work had gone well and they had made love. Tonight she was rejecting everything he said. He could keep all sorts of things from Jane but his essential self remained in view, and she knew it better than to have faith in his plan. But he would despise himself if he backed down now. So would she. And perhaps, if he pulled this off, he could regain his rightful place in her heart.

eight

The project to which Paula had committed herself at the staff meeting in order to save her job was the kind of thing she excelled at: solo foraging, problem solving, detail work. If she were living her life entirely in her own grain (who did?), she would be a research assistant to a professor who specialized in Italian opera, major league baseball, and extreme states of mind. It was just as well she hadn't hooked up with this perfect job, because it would have left her by herself for entire days and nights and handed things over to the persistent suspicion that life would be easy without other people in it.

Harvard was all most outsiders knew of Cambridge, but Paula rarely went there. To her, the city's true and human essence lay in Central Square—its discount shops, foreign restaurants, secondhand music stores, social services, hawkers and idlers and unstable energy around subway entrances and bus stops. Inside Harvard Yard's spiked iron gates she expected at any moment to be carded and expelled. She turned censorious around the self-conscious girls tossing their hair and the boys who knew they would inherit the earth. She invented buried traumas and perversions that would erupt just when these kids thought they were safe, during graduation week, or ten years from now over lunch at the Harvard Club.

But she liked the main reading room of Widener Library. It was vast but cozy, and most of the people here didn't look like students. Directly across from her sat a graying pink-faced man in a turtleneck, sniffling and clearing his throat as he peered down through reading glasses at the *Boston Globe*. His pained stiffness suggested a hard-fought battle for self-respect. Down the big oak table, a man in his coat had an atlas open to a map of Bosnia, and he kept re-arranging index cards into little stacks with some private meaning. Opposite him, an aging beauty with a long delicate neck and her hair in a bun was filling up a notebook with an air of discreet but intense passion. Some of them might have been homeless, washing in the big marble bathrooms downstairs and bedding down in corners of the stacks after the library closed at ten. Some looked like potential clients of hers. All pursuing obscure missions and lonely obsessions—the marginal, semi-intellectual crust that formed along the edges of a great university.

Paula, on her own mission, brought an armful of heavy volumes to her chair and began leafing through lists of charitable foundations. There turned out to be amazing numbers of them, and they handed out hundreds of millions of dollars. Given that libraries and schools all over the state were cutting back, cities going bankrupt, water mains bursting, her own clients seeing their checks nibbled away by the cost of living or eliminated wholesale—given that the staff of the Problem Place took turns buying milk for coffee—it was a shock to discover so much money stashed away, just out of reach.

But only a few foundations gave grants for mental health. Those that did doled out $25,000 or $30,000; some went as high as $50,000. But their number was narrowed down by region and then further by pet cause—racial issues, eating disorders. . . . The potential sources turned out to be very few. Dozens of starved social service agencies would be competing for the available cash. These days all the money was in private hands. It was like a hundred years ago, when Andrew Carnegie was all that stood between the poor and T.B. T.B. was back too, one of her clients had it. Paula's spirits flagged. She had no knowledge of costs and revenues at the Problem Place—she should have made Fine show her the books. Why wasn't his salary public knowledge? She knew that he lived in a big house in Brookline and drove an Audi. How could anyone who worked with poor people drive an Audi? How the hell much money was he making?

She stared at the foundation names she'd written on a scrap of paper. She couldn't begin to imagine how she was going to get them to give her some money. It was an alien world, she had no connections in it. Distracted, she found herself looking around.

One table down, a man hunched massively over a tiny paperback. He read with labored purposefulness, stroking his heavy black beard. Now and then his head jerked up as if he had heard a noise, always in the same direction. But there was no noise. Maybe he was delusional. Following the line of his sight, Paula saw that the distracting object was an Asian woman at the far corner of his table. The woman didn't notice. With her bright red lips she looked pretty and breakable—he would crush her like a bear. Paula could have diagrammed the line of observation. Fantasy had its own physics. This was what men did. Paula sometimes caught them looking at her, their faces somber with the intensity of all that hard mental work. More creepy than flattering. But now Paula felt the safe thrill of witnessing a crime unfold. This man's every glance begged the Asian woman to look at him. Such longing for a total stranger!

The woman had looked—the shock of seeing her come to life registered along the man's entire body, and he hunched farther over the paperback as if he wanted to squeeze the whole of his bulk inside it. At the other end of the magnetic line, the Asian woman was exerting an immense effort to undo her awareness. She sat stricken and absolutely still with her finger on a line of text. If she didn't move a muscle she might become invisible. Both of them were desperate to disappear. And in his determination not to glance again, the man looked up and locked eyes with Paula.

Instinctively, she smiled. The smile told him that she had seen everything. His head fell as if under a blow. Paula went back to her research.

When she looked up again there was a hum of tension in the room, like just before a thundershower. The seated bodies had assumed postures of hyperalertness. Force fields of desire crisscrossed the tables in every direction.

Paula found herself gazing several tables down at a man in a flannel shirt. A laptop computer was propped open before him and plugged into an outlet in the floor. He had dark blond hair and sideburns; she couldn't make out his features. His unbuttoned collar exposed his neck and a wedge of chest, and she had an impression of the hollow formed by his collarbone. She watched him closely. He was typing at good speed, occasionally checking a stack of papers. A hard worker, undistracted. Maybe a young professor, dressing down. She imagined a confident face.

Here was someone thoroughly engaged in life. The fingers were moving because the work needed to be done, because this was what made the world. Unlike Paula herself, who was capable of focusing on anything but her own work.

What if he were to get up from the laptop and walk down the aisle toward the giant Webster's on its wooden stand. That would take him right past her seat. What if she said something like, "Working hard?" He'd be surprised—but would recover, self-assured, "Enough for today." And "What about coffee?" Her cheeks grew warm, her heart beat richly as if it was happening. The new cafe in Central would be empty, and under the table his knee grazed hers and his hand was on her thigh and she kissed his collarbone. . . .

He was smiling at her, with one side of his mouth, an unflustered grown-up smile. Her own was frozen and idiotic. A few moments later their eyes met again: This time he looked less relaxed.

Paula gathered the volumes, returned them to their shelves, and went back to collect her things. It was almost 5:00 and the fluorescent ceiling panels were brightening. It was time to go back to the Problem Place. The afternoon had dissolved in pointless daydreams. Wrapping herself in the coat and scarf, she was overcome with disgust at the waste of time, the loss of purpose, her dry winter skin and sudden mindless needs.

As Paula left the reading room, the man was closing up his laptop. Turning on the stairway landing, she saw his green parka starting down.

Oh God, had he read her mind? He was still behind her on the second flight of stairs. But he seemed to be walking at his own pace, thinking his own thoughts. Down the tunnel the distance was lengthening. She would never see him again. Her pace slowed as she approached the inspection desk. The elderly attendant ran his hand through the chambers of her bag. The man was close behind now: ten feet, five feet. She wouldn't turn to look. Beyond two sets of doors she saw Christmas lights, Harvard Square rush hour, darkness and rain.

Her umbrella was upstairs in the reading room, lying beneath her chair. She should turn around and go back—embarrassed smile, "Forgot something." Or not even explain, he didn't care. But she found herself passing through the inner door and then the outer, under the stone awning, facing the raw rain. He was right behind her. He was passing her.

With a whoosh his umbrella opened, a couple of its spokes were broken.

"I thought it was cold enough to snow."

He said this so off-handedly that she couldn't tell if he was talking to her or himself. She stood between the library and the rain, unable to make a move.

"Don't you have an umbrella?"

To her. She took the cue to look up at his face. It was not the face she had expected to see. It was friendly, and there were lines of fatigue around his eyes. No trace of arrogance—if anything, a little sad. A nice-looking face. He was smiling the same lopsided smile that had given her a shock in the reading room.

Paula said, "I left it at work."

"Look"—the crippled umbrella moved over her head—"I'll walk you as far as you're going my way, but then self-interest takes over."

"I'm going toward Central."

"So am I."

And they went out into the rain together.

After they had negotiated the cars and the crossing of Mass. Avenue: "Are you a student?" he asked.

"No." She added, "No Harvard affiliation."

"Me neither."

Paula found herself relieved. They threaded past pedestrians and traffic, and he was working hard to keep them both from getting soaked. Occasionally her shoulder brushed his arm. Paula was trying to find the rhythm of his stride and at the same time avoid rubbing against his body without making him give her too much of the umbrella.

"I hardly ever go to Widener," he said.

"Me neither."

"Libraries are weird places." Paula tensed. Was he teasing her? Had she been found out? "I'm trying to find a place where I can get some work done," he went on.

She almost gave herself away by saying that he seemed to be getting a lot done. "What kind of work?"

"Writing," he said quickly and without clarification.

She was determined not to be intimidated. "You're a writer?"

"When I answer yes it sounds like I'm lying."

"Are you lying?"

"Not technically."

"I'll bet you're famous." This was the way to talk to him: with irony, as if she had his number. It made her seem knowing and equal.

"Afraid not. But I'm not above trying. Tell me what you do."

"Wait a minute. What's it like being a writer?"

"Bouts of megalomania alternating with despair."

She made up her mind to dislike him. Arrogance took all sorts of forms and false modesty was one of her least favorite. Cambridge was full of men like this—he was a cliché. Up ahead was a bus stop for the Number 1. She would tell him thanks for the umbrella, hope you win the Nobel, bye. A neat little cut.

"I'll bet it's a great life," she said. "You drink espresso in Harvard Square and collect characters. Most people would trade jobs with you in a second."

"They might end up regretting it."

Here was the bus stop. With a hiss the Number 1 was bearing down behind them. But Paula's trained ear had picked up a sound in his voice, the sound of candor. He had been straight with her from

the start; she was the one playing games, including with herself—
because she liked him. He was kind and attentive, without flirting.
He seemed to like talking to her. Whenever she glanced his way he
was looking at her—a casual look, but it penetrated. His very open-
ness made him hard to read, and reading people was essential to
Paula's well-being. Failing to, she felt exposed and endangered.

"What makes you do it?"

"Don't know what else to do. Look, let's not ruin what's left of
our walk. I don't even know your name."

"Paula."

His was Eric. It fell into the category of male names she liked—a
fourth-grade crush. They had passed the bus stop.

"What do you do, he asked again."

"I'm a social worker. Adult psychotherapy. Very mundane."

"I'll bet it isn't."

"No?"

"Are people's minds ever mundane?"

Since this was exactly how Paula felt, it startled her to hear him
say it. She composed herself by putting him on the defensive. "Have
you ever been to see one?"

"No. Doesn't mean I shouldn't. In Iowa where I come from it
means you're crazy."

"People assume I'm looking for early warning signs."

"You don't seem that way to me."

Paula blushed with pleasure at the compliment, and shame at
having fished for it.

"What are they like?" Eric continued.

"My clients? Oh, the men—easily humiliated."

"Really." He sounded interested. "What humiliates them?"

"Life. It's a never-ending slight."

"The women are healthier? They don't get humiliated?"

"Of course they do. But they don't put their self-esteem on the
line all the time. They take it out on themselves."

Glib, cheap treachery against Gladys and Earl and the others,
but Paula didn't care; she felt smart and intriguing to this man. Eric.

"The men with secure jobs," he said, "that must help."

"Who's got one nowadays? Anyway, they don't *feel* secure."

He was silent, thinking. The rain fell all around them.

"Do you dislike the men?"

"They're human."

"Can you help them?"

She started to answer, and then stopped herself for fear of disappointing him with her uncertainty. "Some of them learn to talk about it."

"But does that change things?"

"Change starts with talking."

"I mean, people win and lose all the time. It's American. Maybe we can't do anything about it."

"My clients are generally poor. They already know they've lost." She didn't mean to sound self-righteous. Why couldn't she sound like herself? "But some of them stop seeing everything in terms of winning and losing."

"Ah."

He fell silent again. She was sorry, afraid she'd snuffed out his interest. They were halfway to Central Square and her trousers were wet up to the knees. She knew that he was soaking because she was getting most of the umbrella and the broken spokes were over his head. And she was pretty sure he'd gone out of his way for her.

Across the avenue stood the row of stores where Steve Lorenz had his loft; a light was on. The sight buoyed Paula. Steve never asked her questions like this. It had been the right thing, ending it.

"Why don't you work at home?"

"We're having construction done."

"Oh." Paula stared at the rain-spattered sidewalk. "What's your wife's name?"

"Jane Juneau. She works at a foundation on the other side of Harvard Square."

By way of reply, Paula couldn't make a sound. Not only the revelation but its casualness stunned her, as if it had no significance for her, as if she'd been making this whole thing up. Was this how he talked to every woman on a rainy night? She should have gotten on the bus. Furious and heartsick, she resolved to say nothing more than was absolutely required the rest of the way.

But soon his questions had her talking about herself again, almost against her will. He made her feel as though her job was the most interesting thing in the world, far more valuable than what he did. Her answers suggested more certainty about her curative powers than she ever felt, because she didn't think she could afford to let him down. The work she did for other people was, she sensed, her hold on him. She found that she wanted to keep it.

The Problem Place's sign appeared up the street. Another permanent good-bye. She stopped and turned. "This is where I get off." Within the small shelter of the umbrella, he stood very close. "Thanks for the umbrella. Next time I'll have to remember mine."

"Put a note on it. I guess if you forget it that wouldn't do any good."

They laughed at the conundrum and his laugh made his face seem youthful, except his eyes, which were green like his parka and still sad. Above the upturned collar he was looking at her in a new way. Then he glanced down at the pavement, and Paula felt that her eyes were possessed of some power.

"Good luck with your work," she said. "Wherever you can get it done."

"I hope I didn't complain too much."

"You didn't complain at all."

"Good. It's an anxious time. I'm going to see my publisher in New York next week."

Impulsively Paula said, "I'm from New York."

"You don't seem like a New Yorker."

She considered the range of irrelevant replies and discarded them all. "I'm going down on the 20th to spend Christmas with my mother."

"We'll overlap. I stay with a friend downtown."

"My mother lives on West Fourth."

"Why don't we meet for coffee in the Village?"

Paula's teeth were beginning to chatter. An instinct told her that if she asked him to run off with her tonight he would throw away everything and do it. But he hadn't tried to hide his wife. That meant coffee was safe; the wife ceased to matter, and Paula contrived to forget her. She agreed through clenched molars.

Paula had one evening session and she sat through it in a fever of empathy and impatience, dispensing remarkable insights but desperate for the girl to leave. Alone, she went back over the encounter every step of the way, from Widener on. The familiar unvacuumed air of the Problem Place calmed her, and she broke things down as if she were preparing to present this man—Eric—to her colleagues. There was maybe a slight tendency toward manipulation there. Narcissistic (he was a writer) and lacking a fully developed sense of boundaries. The type who didn't always know what he was doing. As for her own role, declining coffee would actually have made things weirder than otherwise, like pretending they hadn't seen each other in the reading room. She had responded to his tone, which made the whole episode seem the most natural thing in the world. If they both kept an eye on appropriateness there couldn't be any harm. In a sense it didn't matter what he was doing as long as she knew what she was doing, and she decided that she was allowing herself to bask in a little needed warmth. In her world view the distinction between thought and action meant everything. And although by professional standards coffee on Bleecker Street probably qualified as an action, it was not, she felt certain, an inappropriate one. This wasn't a client; they were both grown-ups. She knew as much about boundaries as anyone.

It was a strong presentation, and yet a feeling remained that she couldn't shake. She didn't know the clinical term for it, but she was acquainted with the feeling itself. It led you to make slight omissions at staff presentations. It was fluttery and unruly. She associated it with fervent daydreams and unbearable waits. It promised happiness and unhappiness on a large scale, and it dismantled defenses in nothing flat. Paula recognized it with elation and dread.

As she was getting ready to go home, Peter Fine invited himself into her office and took a seat in the clients' chair.

"Are they all gone?" he asked. Paula nodded. "But they'll be back. Because they need us. The more we give the more they need." Fine was picking at the dark hairs of his sculpted beard. "They'd drink our blood if we let them. So the question is: How do you disinfect?"

Fine's pudgy, knowing presence made her feel found out.

"Disinfect?"

"How do you—" His teddy-bear eyes searched skyward and encountered the low ceiling tiles. On one there was a yellow water stain in the shape of Florida. Fine became angry. "How the hell do you keep them from making themselves the last person you'll ever heal?"

"To tell you the truth, Peter, I don't think I've ever 'healed' anyone."

"Paula." His smile was masterful. "Do you think there's anything about your clinical experience I don't know? Do you think I don't know what goes on in this little room? Look at your eyes. You're giving them everything, aren't you? Yes you are. Your life blood."

Paula was shaking her head, but she was two seconds from tears. Fine was a genius at profound fakery. He used to talk to her like this, before she spurned him. Now she would have to sit still for it.

"And for what? So the state can give you the finger? So you can collect your little fee in this miserable excuse of an office? Paula, you deserve Persian rugs and bookcases. That misogynistic liar Freud had Persian rugs and bookcases, why not you? Why not me? We deserve *better*."

"Oh, sure."

"It's offensive that our funding's been cut off, but I see it as a positive. The government has become toxic. Only organizations that break free of public money are going to make it."

"Well, Peter, there seems to be a lot of private money out there."

Fine smiled and winked, as if they were flirting. "Bless you,

Paula. I'm sure you'll help us get our share of it." He narrowed his gaze. "Christ, you're aglow. I've never seen you look so alive."

As he raised himself out of the clients' chair and started for the door, she avoided his eyes.

"One way I disinfect, Paula, are these Wednesday groups I meet with. There's a lot of anger out there, a lot of grief, but a lot of positives, too. It's amazing! They want to change everything—totally ordinary, average people. But there was a leadership vacuum. I think the organization benefits from my input."

"What kind of organization is it?"

"It's called 'The Community.' So far, it's all been word of mouth, everyone brings in three friends. But we're looking at new ways to grow the membership." Fine had a surprise. "We're the ones doing those signs, you know. There's a meeting here tomorrow night."

"I was wondering who did the signs."

"We need to move past the signs. There's an exciting energy that needs to be channeled. Honestly, I've been quite depressed this year. Worn out. Very deep doubts about my life's work. But that's completely changed. You're ready for this too, Paula. I look at you and I can tell."

"It sounds like a political group."

"What's politics but the psyche writ large? You change your mind, you change the world." He had stopped in the doorway to survey her. "We all need something bigger in our lives than just ourselves. You too, Paula Voorhees."

Paula smiled. The Community sounded like just the right thing for Fine. As for her, she was in love and she didn't need anything.

It astonished her to be thinking this.

"Thanks, Peter, but I get nervous in large groups."

"We're all so goddam alone." Fine eyed her nakedly. "It's more than we can stand sometimes."

nine

Outside Penn Station Eric looked up and down the rain-washed street. A construction canopy hid the block to his left, and at the other end a building's corner obscured the street sign. There were no skyscrapers in view to orient him. He walked half a block under the scaffolding and discovered that he was at Eighth and Thirty-third—moving west when he needed to go east. He started the other way but found himself caught in the press of a lunchtime crowd and forced off the curb. At once his right foot sank up to the ankle in standing rainwater. He jerked his leg out, but something pushed him from behind, back into the gutter. "I'm moving!" he cried and wheeled around. The something was a stump of a woman, almost a dwarf. Beneath her black brows the eyes were not to be found; they had traveled into their sockets like cartoon slits of the dead. The hand that had applied pressure to the small of his back was gripping a long white stick. Even sightless, the woman's face expressed the most vivid contempt.

"Come on, come on, make up your mind."

As Eric crossed Manhattan, one shoe squished and a wet chill seeped into his thin winter skin.

He found standing room by the window of a fast-food pasta place on Madison and sipped coffee, trying to dry his foot over a heating grate. The early train had put him in New York with an hour to kill before his one o'clock appointment. He had left home in too much haste to have breakfast and only managed to get down half a stale bagel on Amtrak. But he didn't want to spoil his appetite for lunch with Ann, so he didn't eat. Next to him, two men were talking about technology sales in a vocabulary he couldn't follow. He picked up an abandoned *Daily News* and began reading an article about management problems on the New Jersey Nets. Everyone in the restaurant seemed to be shouting.

He had always relished a couple of days in the city's huge furious life. He used to meet Ann Jenkins downtown, where Hermes Books had its dusky little offices off Union Square. The ancient elevator had a sliding gate and was operated with wordless formality by a white-haired black man who had probably sent up Dos Passos and Berryman. The fifth floor was book-cramped and dark, but its dust smelled of promise. In a rubber-banded brown paper bag, he had carried up the manuscript of his first book, the one he wrote in Oaxaca: a murder story about a boy and a disturbed Vietnam veteran, set in the Iowa he knew so well, an homage to the landscape of his boyhood. The package had weight—the heft of a finished book. He handed it over to Ann, and she scrutinized him under arched brows. "Is it good?" He answered, as earnest and proud as a favorite schoolboy, that he thought so.

Ann did too. She took him for a celebratory lunch to a Japanese restaurant. He was a newcomer—anything was possible. But the blank slate was about to be written on.

Death in a Small Place appeared just before Christmas and got lost in the rush. The reviews were favorable, but they came in too late to generate any momentum. He now had a track record and it said: good writer, disappointing first book. Still, each time he came down Ann took him to the Japanese restaurant for lunch.

The second book was about the 1832 Black Hawk War along the Mississippi, and one federal soldier's crisis of conscience over the death of an Indian prisoner. Shortly before the book came out, Hermes was swallowed, digested, and dissolved by New World Communications, which had vast holdings in electronic media. Ann survived the layoffs and moved to the NWC building in midtown. Eric had an ominous feeling as his new book edged noiselessly toward publication and then appeared still bearing the old winged sandal of Hermes, like an expired date on a supermarket perishable.

Soldier's Dilemma was his best book and did remarkably well given the circumstances of its birth. But no one at NWC seemed to have heard of it.

Ann convinced her new bosses to include him among the authors she brought from Hermes; for that he was grateful. But their relationship underwent a change. Now they never spoke unless he called, and she always told him how busy she was. After three years her new assistant still didn't recognize him on the phone (the young woman at Hermes had made him the audience for an unhappy love story). He noticed that Ann no longer passed him morsels of publishing gossip, or used the confiding tone that privileged him with a future in which she had a proprietary interest. He had counted on spending his whole writing life at Hermes, and when that idea fell through he didn't sit down to plan a different future. Ann never told him to come to New York and meet his new publisher, and it wasn't his nature to sell himself to NWC. So the trips stopped.

His third book was about an American couple living in Mexico in the 1930s, their marriage threatened by the arrival of a German painter who might be a Nazi agent. It marked a conscious break from the first two—the prose more impressionistic, the subject turning from individuals in isolation to their relationships. An imperfect but necessary book. NWC was bought by TX Media, the entertainment giant headquartered in Dallas. *Freytag* came and went without a trace.

Eric's coffee was lukewarm and he was deep into an article about the New York school board when he looked at his watch. He was five minutes late.

Struggling through the crowd of pasta eaters he came out onto Madison Avenue, temporarily lost. He determined which way was east and started to walk, but he had gotten the order of the avenues wrong. Third wasn't the next one down—first there was Park, and then Lexington! He broke into a jog and the overnight shoulder bag banged against his hip. The heating grate had not dried his foot. In the cold, in his parka, he was sweating.

By the time he reached the glass tower at Third and Fifty-sixth,

Eric was faint from hunger. In the lobby, NWC's steel global logo gleamed on a soaring wall of polished granite. He'd had a plan, what was it? Something to do with more money—turning things around—the details were lost. He saw the approach of his confused reflection in the elevator doors.

"Hey, buddy, where you going?"

No elderly lift operator, just a meaty young man in a security jacket, telling him to sign in. It was 1:17. The middle elevator went to the twelfth floor. It ascended in smooth silence. At the eleventh it stopped and a man and woman got on chatting.

"Lucy figured four hundred thousand. She thought Roberto was asleep at the wheel."

"Not Roberto. Hey—I'm sick of Chez Vous. Let's eat someplace new tomorrow."

At the twelfth floor they preceded him out onto a powder-blue carpet. Eric approached the reception desk. A blond in a ruffled white blouse and red jacket was on the phone. He tried to stifle his panting, leaned forward to speak, straightened again, then blurted out: "I have an appointment—"

The receptionist cupped the receiver. "I'll be with you in a moment, sir." She took in the overnight bag, the parka, the band of perspiration on his forehead and lip. She was pretty and hard, her eyes heavily mascaraed.

He waited. The reception area was circular, and all along the curved wall were the glossy jackets of NWC's recent publishing events, under glass like rare butterflies of bright and varied hues: self-help, personal finance, popular fiction, political exposé. His right foot felt shrunken with wet and cold, but it was the only part of his body that had any sensation.

He was announced, but Ann was in the middle of something. There followed another wait. Finally she came striding down the hall, reading a sheet of fax paper through bifocals.

Before he could begin his apology she looked up and said, "God, I'm sorry, Eric. It's an insane day, one of my authors is being a complete prima donna. What a breath of fresh air to see a nice guy like you. Come on in."

He followed along the hall, everything cool shades of blue and silver. Ann's office overflowed with books and papers.

"You've got me on a terrible day, Eric. My God, what's the occasion? I don't think I've ever seen you in a tie. You must be down for something important." Her brows knitted sympathetically. "You look tired. Are you taking care of yourself?"

"It's just seasonal. I was running," he said illogically. The visitor's chair was occupied by someone else's manuscript. "We could do it tomorrow."

"I'm going to California tomorrow. Can you believe this crap?" She waved the fax at him. "My millionaire computer visionary got fifty things wrong, didn't return calls, we were staring at lawsuits, destroyed the galleys, now he's having a nervous breakdown and needs me to go over *Virtual Communities* with him in *person.*"

Ann laughed in disgust, removed her bifocals, and rocked back against the window. Behind her, the peaks of midtown floated in a charcoal sky. She was angular, shoulders square in a padded plaid jacket, gray hair cropped very short. She was fiftyish and divorced. In Eric's experience, her owlish eyes and masculine voice expressed only two moods: wry affection or irritable impatience. Today she was making an effort to move from the second to the first.

"Eric, how are you? It's been much too long. Sit down, move that aside."

He hesitated before the poundage of prose in the chair.

"Aren't we going for lunch?"

"Lunch? I've got about six free minutes today and you're getting them. Sorry, I wish I had more time."

He cleared the chair and sat down. The drop in altitude made his head dizzy. "Maybe there was a misunderstanding."

"You said you'd come by at 1:00. I don't remember lunch."

"I mean, it was really to see you that I came down."

"Jesus, the tie's for me?" She squinted and cocked her head. "I thought you were coming down for something else. You should have been clearer. I would have told you a different week."

Ann was capping and uncapping her pen in a gesture he knew from the sins of others. His little plan had already squandered a portion of her goodwill.

"Did you have a chance to read—"

"Some of it. When am I going to have the whole thing?"

"I'm getting there. Right now, you know, with Jane almost due, the house is a wreck with a construction crew."

"This doesn't sound good. When's your deadline? Christ, I think it was about three months ago."

"I just need another month or so."

Ann shot him a skeptical look. "Is that realistic? You're about to become a father."

Her phone rang and she picked it up. "OK, I'll take it." Then, in a smoother voice: "Roberto, I didn't think you'd have the chutzpah to call after what you pulled."

By the time Ann got off the phone, two of Eric's six minutes were gone. Time to come clean. But he backed in slowly.

"I wanted to talk about the advance. I'd like to have a quarter now instead of half on delivery. On the basis of what I sent you."

Ann regarded him with a kind of fixed blankness. "Are you saying you want to renegotiate?"

"Is this a renegotiation?" he said mildly.

"We shouldn't even be having this conversation. I assume you've talked to your agent?"

"No." She widened her eyes to express dismay. "I thought I should do it myself."

"Bad idea. It sounds to me like you're saying, A, you're going to be even later than we thought, and B, you want some of the money now."

"You've got over half the manuscript, Ann." His damp foot ached, and now a little piece of flesh under one eye was beginning to twitch. Ann noticed and looked away. "And we're talking about barely—"

"What would it look like if I went to Bob Chafee with a request like this?"

"You've got some clout here."

"Oh, you think so?" Her lips tightened to two pale lines. "I'm already dealing with some frankly very skeptical people."

"How late is *Virtual Communities*?" he said rashly.

"So I need two writers to carry? Eric, your situation here depends on mine. I'm being frank. And these people get rid of editors who don't produce like—oh, you're the writer, you think of the metaphor."

He actually tried, as if a brilliant enough one would win her over. Like—like dead cows—

"Anyway, NWC has too much invested in the computer book."

"And if you had more invested in me? Another five thousand?"

"Why?" Ann shook her head, open-mouthed, and looked toward the bookshelves for a witness to this unreasonableness. "Do you want to see your sales history?"

"They never had a chance, Ann, they were just thrown out there. Hermes was being eaten. . . ."

His face was burning, his throat thick with chronologies, explanations, too many to be named. Jane had said: Consider Ann's position—but he hadn't, because it was inside this granite, steel and glass, implacable fortress. The power was all in here, not up in his demolished study; and so he had assumed Ann could do anything. In another minute he would crawl out empty-handed, Jane's view of his limitations utterly confirmed.

"OK, I have to show you something." Ann turned to her keyboard and typed instructions into the computer, reluctantly at first, but her mouth soon set in the same frown of concentration with which she used to line-edit his manuscripts. "Here, look." She swiveled the monitor toward Eric, and a blue screen crowded with figures swung into view. "This column is plant cost on each of your books. This is printing, paper, and binding on runs from three thousand to five thousand. This column reflects marketing—there was a small ad budget on the first one, see? OK, here are the advances.

The reason you see them decreasing is because of the numbers I'm about to show you."

Ann hit a key and the screen scrolled down.

"Here are gross sales, but 25 percent goes for general overhead. This is what's left, including subsidiary rights on hard-soft deals. So here's total revenue . . . and here's total cost. Do you see? Even number two didn't break even, but we'll call it a wash. But look at number three. NWC took a thirteen-thousand-dollar loss. The total balance over an eight-year period is minus more than sixteen thousand. The industry standard is 15 percent on investment." Ann sat back and crossed her arms. "This is your sales history, Eric. I don't see how you can say you haven't had a chance."

He tried to read the numbers on the screen but they were a blur. Minus signs appeared all over the place. His eyes throbbed as if the flu was coming on. Ann didn't look well either, her complexion was mottled, her face rather grave. There was no triumph in it. He had compelled her to show him the truth, and like a patient confronted with bad test results, he didn't have to understand the details to grasp the essential point. For years he had been waiting for something to happen. Now Ann was telling him that the something had already happened and here it was. It had come and gone.

She turned the monitor away. They sat in silence.

"If there'd been advertising—"

"There's advertising when there's a reason to think it would generate a return."

"It's a Catch-22, Ann." His voice rose. "You can't tell me the company has gone to bat for me."

"Eric, this conversation doesn't seem very productive to me."

"Maybe we should have had it a long time ago."

"Maybe we should have."

They stared across the crowded desk at each other, all good feeling burned away, a desperate client and an angry professional.

Eric subdued his voice. "Without a bigger advance, Ann, do you really believe this book is going to do what it has to?"

She closed her eyes and rubbed them under her bifocals. "There's absolutely no chance of that. There isn't even a chance of moving up a quarter of it."

"Do you think it's going to do what it has to?"

"What do you mean, has to?"

"You know what I mean. NWC wants a breakthrough. How can I possibly do that without—"

"Breakthrough? Who said that?"

"You did. You've said it several times. And it's true. You've just shown me it's true."

"You just write a good book. That's your job. No one's talking about a breakthrough. That's a nonexistent concept."

He caught himself about to look down from her eyes and resisted.

"I know how the market works, Ann. It needs to be fed. You don't have forever."

The phone rang again. "Tell him I'm at lunch," Ann said and hung up. "I don't like fighting with you, Eric. We never used to talk this way."

"No, we didn't. Things have changed."

"Why?"

"Things changed when you came here." She glowered, but he made himself go on. "Ann, do you really think you can work for NWC and TX Media and run out to computerland and not lose something on quality? Because that sounds like having it both ways."

She was furious. "I don't have time for this."

"Ann, be honest, what's there to lose? I see the position you're in. You have to survive and answer for quarterly reports in Dallas, so you spend your time on projects you despise. This isn't how you saw yourself when you started out. You got into this business because you love books."

She was staring at a point just above his head as if to restrain her temper. Her silence told him that he had struck a truth.

"I sure as hell didn't see myself this way," he went on. "I thought if I wrote good books the rest would take care of itself. These last ten years I thought I was building a future. You've just shown me those three books are a weight around my neck and they're going to take me down."

"This has always been a business. It was a business when Shakespeare was around. If books are to be published, someone has to make money."

"The system is winner-take-all. What kind of work can get done?" He no longer knew what he was trying to persuade her of. "Are you happy with this situation?"

"That's irrelevant. No one promised me anything. Or you. And you're wrong, I'm always looking for good literary fiction. And Eric," Ann said, engaging him with her large, steady, intelligent eyes, "if the stuff you sent me had been stronger, I'd be more inclined to go to bat for you. I think we both recognize it's not up to your best."

Even in anger Ann looked sorry for the blow she'd inflicted.

"I don't think it's bad."

"It's not bad. It's competent. It isn't very sparky. That's a bad word, but you know."

He knew. He had used every ounce of energy simply to fill up the required pages. Now Ann was having trouble looking him in the eye.

"You want to be honest. If I went to Bob Chafee and Lucy Baumgarten with your request, they'd probably say, 'Let's use the fact that he's late to get out of the contract.' They'd say, 'He's unhappy, we're unhappy, the book's unhappy—let's divorce.' At the very least it would kill any chance of NWC signing another book of yours. I've spent capital just keeping you here, Eric. But I can't carry you forever. You need to start thinking about other publishers, and given what the market's like, probably other sources of income. I'm sorry to be so discouraging, but there it is. What I wanted was for us to talk about how to spruce up the book instead of all this other crap."

He was staring at the pattern of her jacket lapel.

"I'm sort of on the chopping block."

Ann winced, looked away, and then leaned forward. "I think we could still save this book."

"It sounds like it won't matter."

"Of course it matters. I have a few ideas." Ann looked at her watch. She had given him much more than six minutes. "It needs a new title. *The Insubstantial Pageant* is going to scare people off. I was thinking, what about *Passionate Bards?*"

He didn't answer.

"Well, we need *something*. Think about it. The problem is, there's never been a target market for your work. I know you probably hate that term, but it's a reality out there. I can't tell Sales, 'Here's another really good book'—they need a handle. OK, call it a break-out if you want, breakthrough, whatever. I think we should pitch this as an Elizabethan romantic comedy. But it needs to be livelier and funnier."

With professional economy, Ann sketched out her ideas for revision. Eric listened as carefully as possible. If he rejected what she was telling him she would cut him loose in an instant. He tried inwardly to conjure the mood of romantic comedy. That would be fine with him. He longed for it—but it stood on the other side of an unscalable wall. And his book was going to fail anyway. It was earmarked for failure. He wanted to tell Ann, "You know *Passionate Bards* can't save me." She liked him, that was all, and had been seized by a moment's kindness.

But he listened and nodded and even jotted down a few notes on a piece of NWC stationery.

"That's the best I can do." Ann was finished. Her mood had changed—talking as an editor had eased the tension out of her voice. She took off her glasses and smiled at him, a little sadly, as if she had caught an echo of their old days at Hermes. "I know what you can do, Eric. I haven't lost faith in you." He couldn't speak. "But please consider these changes. My fall books didn't do what they were supposed to and I'm walking around here on eggshells. There's plenty of room on that chopping block."

"I certainly don't want to become a liability. You know I'm

reliable, Ann. You've seen how I work. These last few months have been hard." He cleared his throat. "Really, I feel like I'm trying to get air and something keeps pushing me down. On some level I must have known this was going on here. I was hoping for a vote of confidence. That was all I came down for, really."

Ann covered her eyes with a hand and pinched the tear ducts between her thumb and finger.

"Eric, NWC can't hand out money for that."

As he stood up, his vision seemed to grow dark. Ann walked him out. In the hallway they ran into a tall, silver-haired, humorless-looking man in a double-breasted suit. He started in with Ann.

"What's with the computer thing?"

"I'm flying out tomorrow to let him know if he doesn't cooperate we'll sic the lawyers on him."

This was Bob Chafee, Ann's boss. Chafee had been responsible for dissolving Hermes into NWC—at the time of the takeover there was a story that he'd given one longtime editor two hours to clear his office. Standing by, Eric observed Ann's manner toughen; her accent left midtown and crossed the East River into Brooklyn. Chafee glanced at Eric once or twice, but Ann didn't introduce them.

"Do you have any names?" she asked at the elevator.

For a moment Eric thought she was talking about his book again.

"Possibly Emma or Fred."

"Nice. So you don't know if it's a boy or a girl."

"Jane doesn't want to form any ideas before it's born."

"That makes sense. Back in the Bronze Age when I had my kids, no one ever knew and no one was the worse for it."

His mind was blank. Ann went on about epidurals and obstetricians, and then she suddenly said: "Give my best to your wife. Best of luck to both of you, Eric. Hey, give *yourself* a vote of confidence." The elevator had arrived.

Inside, Eric turned to see Ann's smile die as she moved away. He descended to the granite lobby.

Out on the sidewalk, he began walking south. It wasn't yet 2:30.

A weak sun was struggling to shine. The abbreviated meeting gave him some free time, but he had no use for it.

At the corner of Fifty-fifth, a man was sitting on a piece of wet cardboard against the wall of an automatic teller machine, his head bowed under the monkish hood of a sweatshirt. A hand-lettered sign said: "Help the homeless living with AIDS." People passed within a few inches without looking. An hour ago Eric had been one of them. Now he saw. On a patch of pavement a man was breathing out his life; a few feet away another was punching in his bank code, a woman was tugging at her leashed dog, a man was coming out of an unsuccessful meeting. Only a chain of circumstances had prevented each of them from ending up on the piece of cardboard—a life of accidents.

As he dropped a handful of coins into the cup, this insight touched him with grief.

He walked aimlessly in the direction of downtown. His eye sockets ached. New York was in full pre-Christmas ripeness. Amid the lighted displays there was a growing afternoon frenzy as people left work early and shoppers rushed the stores. He went into one and bought a scarf for Jane, feeling as if he owed her something. What would he tell her? Officially there was little, yet he couldn't shake the feeling that somewhere along the way he had taken a wrong step, lost his chance, every possibility now closed.

Near Union Square, he saw the face under his umbrella and it brought him to a standstill. The eyes were dark and vivid and they were looking back at him. That night he hadn't known what the impulse meant. Now he clung to the thought of seeing her again as if for life itself.

ten

On every visit since Paula had moved away from New York, her hometown seemed dirtier, scarier, more demon-driven. On every block she saw ten people who looked more dissociated than Earl. She was offended by the profusion of homeless, the blackmail of boys in the subway, the birdlike preenings in the Village, the lavish window displays along Fifth Avenue, the spirit of brutal dedication to self. Most of all she disliked her own sanctimony. But give me Boston, she thought on visits home, give me people too inhibited to vomit on the train. Give me minor-league egomaniacs like Fine and middling casualties like Gladys Dill. Give me ordinary squalor and cruelty.

It was different at Christmas. New York at Christmas tapped directly into the source of all childhood memory, and the city transformed itself into the immense dreamscape amusement park it had been when she was younger: the lights on the tree at Rockefeller Center, the skating rink, the Salvation Army bell ringers outside Macy's, the cooking smells at her mother's, the Dickens novel next to her bed. She was swamped in the Christmas emotions of excitement and generosity and tender pity.

The complication, as always, was her mother. Paula had decided to move away when she was twenty-five, at the end of her mother's brief flirtation with local politics. Fed up with spotty garbage collection and the encroachment of dealers and squatters, her mother, casting about for a new existence, decided late one night under the spell of wine, music, and monologue to launch an independent candidacy for the city council. Paula, inured to such inspirations, watched with some astonishment as a campaign team was assembled. The man who sold capicola and mozzarella became the campaign manager; her chief fund-raiser was her third ex-husband's sister, with whom she remained on good terms; Paula herself was secretary-treasurer. Her mother's boundless energy was set loose upon the district. They pounded on doors, stuffed envelopes, bothered people on the phone. At a $10-a-head fund-raiser, she sang Puccini and Kurt Weill. For a few weeks her apartment filled with campaign paraphernalia and the thrill of the horserace.

Only after the landslide defeat did Paula understand that her mother had really expected a coalition of Italian Americans, opera lovers, divorcées, and personal acquaintances to put her over the top. She studied her 3 percent of the electorate and decided that close friends had betrayed her. The leftover signs and leaflets turned poisonous, the red wine flowed, and Paula—who was living down the block and wasting her time working at a bookstore—felt trapped, desperate to get out, all the way out. She had never imagined herself other than in the close company of her mother, Sancho Panza to her mother's Quixote. Meanwhile, what she was missing out on was life. Moving to another part of the city wouldn't do. She had to leave.

It wasn't easy, because her mother threatened to die. Not to take her own life, but there was an unmistakable suggestion that Paula's departure would remove her only motivation for continuing to breathe—in the middle of some night her heart would stop. Paula faltered, tormented. She was accepted by Boston University's School of Social Work. This was, she knew, the crossroads. Both their lives were in her hands and she could only save one. She steeled herself and made her bid for freedom.

Once Paula moved to Boston two things happened, or failed to happen. Her mother did not die, and freedom did not come. Along with phone lines and railroad tracks, a net of a thousand invisible knots of feeling still entangled them, under such tension that her mother only had to twitch—a syllable on the phone—and Paula felt pain.

When Paula arrived at her mother's apartment, she found a week's dishes lying in the kitchen sink, reeking of dirty water. The rest of the apartment was a mess of discarded clothes and old newspapers. Her mother, who took pains with her appearance as if every new day were a new booking, had begun to decay. Her skin had no shine, her unbraided hair needed washing, and in a shapeless, clinging dress her arms and thighs looked shrunken.

Paula spent the evening washing dishes, doing laundry, tidying. Her mother sat with a wineglass at the kitchen table and talked nonstop. This state—her mother improvising an aria of the emotions, Paula doing the business she was born to do, listening, her own emotions withdrawn into a corner—was so familiar that she was slow to notice how much wine her mother was consuming. When Paula suggested giving it a rest her mother agreed, but half an hour later she was still talking and had poured herself another glass.

The next day they picked out a dwarfish tree at a nursery in Central Park. The outing turned into one of their adventures, her mother making friends with a skeptical Kazakh cabbie who didn't believe the tree would fit in his trunk, mother and daughter giggling like best friends all the way back downtown. In the evening they transformed the tree into the madly bejeweled little creature that annually struck Paula with its resemblance to her mother. By now the decorations were ancient things—painted slabs of hardened dough Paula had baked in third grade, fragments of Styrofoam in the shape of bells and stars, dismembered Santa Clauses. *La Traviata* was going full blast on the CD player Paula had given her last Christmas, and her mother paused now and then to accompany it, wineglass in one hand, the other resting on her fallen breast. She looked like a flamboyant bird trying to fly out of an oil spill.

Paula wanted to do some talking herself. She wanted to tell her mother about an absurd arrangement she had made to see a married man tomorrow. She wanted them to laugh about it, and for her mother to say something ironic about the human talent for folly. That would never happen. In tonight's mood her mother would declare: *Love is all that matters.* Another night, another mood: *They'll take your heart and throw it in the dirt.*

"Mama, let's finish the tree and go to bed. I'm tired."

"*Andiamo a letto dopo la morte di Violetta.*"

It augured badly that she was lapsing into Italian. "Violetta takes two more hours to die. Come on. You're going to be in a bad mood tomorrow."

"Stop treating me like a *child*," her mother snarled, baring Chianti-stained teeth. Paula was composing an answer when someone knocked at the door. The sound turned her mother's face into a mask of vengeful glee.

"It's that idiotic man, that little *finocchio* who lives upstairs." She stalked to the door and flung it open.

"Mama, let me—"

"What do *you* want?" her mother sneered into the face of the *finocchio.* He was a small man in his fifties, wearing a red velvet jacket, obvious hair plugs, and a half-suppressed flinch.

"Mrs. Luti, I must ask—"

"*Va via,* go away, we don't want you here. Can't you see my daughter and I are celebrating Christmas? *Via!* Shoo!"

With brisk hand movements, her mother tried to whisk the man away. He held his ground, summoning the courage to pull back his cuff and demonstrate the time. "The hour is very late, the music—"

"Jealous!" she mocked. "Jealous I have my family here and yours refuses you!"

With all his might the little man reiterated his complaint. Above the crushed richness of the jacket his face was pale and unwholesome, his lips pink, some hairless soil creature disturbed from its burrow. Paula saw in him the type who turned other people into sadists. She went to the CD player and switched off Maria Callas midvowel. In the dead silence there was a cry of pain like a wounded animal's.

"That's enough, Mama. We're going to bed now." Her mother's body slumped against the doorjamb. Paula told the man, "Sorry we disturbed you, good night."

When she touched her mother's shoulder, Mrs. Luti swung around. "How can you do this to me?"

"Mama, enough."

"Disloyal!"

"Every night," the man told Paula, his smile inviting her to share his fascinated distaste. "Every night she does this."

Paula wheeled on him. "What the hell do you know about it?" Her fury drove him backward. His ego was exposed, a naked writhing grub, she could squish it if she wanted to. The power was thrilling and horrible. She turned away. "Leave us alone."

He scurried down the hall.

Paula's mother sat at the kitchen table, tiny and hunched, with caved-in eyes, an old woman. "You betrayed me to my enemy."

"You were rude to him. Cruel."

"That man is more important than Verdi? He is afraid of life, he never leaves the building, why do you take his side against me?"

She reached to remove the paper-towel stopper from the wine. "You've had enough."

Defeated and indignant, her mother whimpered, "Yes, take away every delight in my life." But she let go of the bottle.

"You don't seem delighted to me."

"How can I? First you go away." Paula hardened herself. "I accept, in this country everyone lives for himself. Then you take away my music because it doesn't please this *finocchio* for whom love is a man's bottom. Now I cannot even drink—"

"Go ahead and ruin your life, I don't care."

Paula remembered leaving the super's wife in the Dumpster. That time she hadn't been bluffing. Her mother unplugged the Chianti—the discarded paper towel looked like a bloody piece of evidence—and brought the glass to her lips, watching her daughter as a child would, wondering if she could get away with it or even wanted to.

"Look at this place!" Paula engaged the argument with dread, knowing in advance all its twists and torments and the hangover it would inflict on her. "You're not taking care of yourself. And you drink too much. I'm here to say you have a problem."

"I will not sacrifice my *gusto di vivere* to this puritanical country!"

"What *gusto di vivere*? You wait for that pathetic man to come downstairs so you can terrify him. What a relationship!"

"Leave me alone," her mother said, "go back to your crazies."

"At least they know they need help."

"Who voted you for the world's savior? If I am unhappy that is my business."

"It doesn't have to be like this." Paula became gentler. "You can do something about it. I'll help you."

"I'm too old for help."

Her mother's lips were set in a manner that no one but Paula could know meant grudging surrender.

As Paula looked up a Manhattan rehab center and called the emergency number to ask about procedure, her blood quickened. She would gather books and articles and talk to professionals and hurl herself into this project with competent zeal. It was, in a sense, the most natural thing in the world. Her mother had spent most of her life looking for someone to relieve her of her own rash forays into self-reliance. Several men having failed at the job, her daughter was the sole surviving candidate.

Paula lay in her childhood bed with the door open and listened to her mother's troubled breathing in the next room. She had made her bid for freedom but freedom hadn't come, and perhaps she never wanted it. Who did vote her the world's savior? What was in it for *her*? She had just arranged the day tomorrow so that it would be impossible to see Eric Barnes—and it was her habit and training to regard such acts as deliberate.

Her body would take revenge on her. An organ vital to her survival would go rancid from disuse and stop functioning. She would die; her mother would have to take care of herself and so would her clients. Her mind was conspiring to screw things up and kill her. It was the enemy within, the sand in the engine. The rest of her was simple, healthy, wanted love.

eleven

"Sorry I'm late." Ray Laing climbed onto a barstool at Eric's table. "I was detained by group cunnilingus with three Third World supermodels."

"Which left one mouth free."

"Not for your married schlong."

"I believe the Bible exempts fellatio from adultery."

"Mr. Quiet Desperation visits Babylon, melts like butter."

Ray's jaw was flecked with shaving cuts, as if he'd turned his gibes on his own face. Though the Coke-bottle glasses helped disguise his emotions, Eric knew from a rubbery mock smile that Ray was glad to see him.

They had met in New York during the eighties at a party given by a mutual friend. Slouching in oversized antique clothes, hair damp-combed, Ray had run a finger along the host's bookshelf and pronounced judgment like an automatic rifle: "Fraud. Fraud. Fraud fraud fraud." His pose was that he saw through everyone, and he was going to expose America's corruption in high places like *Rolling Stone* and the *New Yorker* with a signature style of acerbic detachment. His lacerations of New York's young media stars would be so mordantly brilliant that they would have to admit him into their ranks.

Ray had a way of making the person he was talking to feel that the two of them were the only uncorrupted people in the room and probably the world. Eric, basically apolitical, far from self-confident, and lacking a pose of his own, had been impressed. A long-distance friendship was struck up, and he crashed at Ray's

136

whenever publishing business brought him down. For a decade Ray had been hustling articles in small left-of-center magazines for just enough money to keep him in a walk-up studio.

"Tell me about NWC," Ray said.

"Later."

"Come on, I want to know how things are done in the big leagues."

On the way down from midtown, Eric had been looking forward to soaking his aches in the hot bath of Ray's outrage. Ray, in fact, was the only person he knew who might understand what had happened to him today. But now he only wanted to talk about the face under his umbrella.

"The short version is, a deal's a deal."

Ray shook his head in disgust. "Writers like you are a front at NWC."

"How've you been, Ray?"

"It's like the mob with their family restaurants while they run drug and hooker rings in back. They deal celebrity best-sellers, *Kiss My Ass* by Nancy Reagan, and they put you in the window under a sign that says 'home-cooked literature.'"

"My editor says they subsidize people like me with the other stuff."

"Freeloading off the taxpayers, bringing little baby books into the world that you can't afford. Well, we're gonna cut you off! Get out of the wagon and help pull!"

Eric felt oddly implicated. "Ann still looks for good fiction."

"Yeah, well, I hope you told her where to put it."

"I don't have much leverage, Ray."

"So you had to sit there and swallow spit."

Ray's outrage was not a personalized bath. More like a tap he could turn on and off or redirect. Eric had no stomach for this fight. He said, "What happened with that article you were doing for *New York*? That developer who was cheating on his taxes with immigrant labor."

"It wasn't for *New York*." Ray shifted on his stool. "Well, they killed it, the frauds. The *Voice* might run a mutilated version. Nothing'll happen to the sleazebag, of course."

Or you, Eric thought. Perhaps after a decade it was becoming clear that the city's leading magazines didn't require Ray's brand of perceptual rigor.

A waitress came to the table and took their order. The motif in the Rat's Tale was black and industrial, painted ductwork and piping. Its patrons also seemed metallic.

The only food on the menu was nachos. The platter arrived orange and glossy; the cheese coating seemed to have been sprayed with polyurethane. Eric, without food since his Amtrak bagel, ate rapidly and soon began to feel sick.

"When something like today happens," Ray said, "doesn't it make you feel like those angry white guys who walk into their ex-workplace with an automatic? Ann Jenkins—*bam bam bam*, what a surprise. Lucy Baumgarten, Bob Chafee in his big old office—*bam*!"

"No, what I think is why didn't I see the train coming? Why didn't somebody point it out?"

Ray shook his head. "It'd be better if you got even with an automatic. *Non carborandum illegitimi sunt*, know what I mean?"

"Don't let the bastards get you down."

"Instead of feeling sorry for yourself."

"I've always thought self-pity was morally superior to mass murder."

"Your problem is, you're part of that world. You don't want to change it. You just want to make it."

In a stronger frame of mind, Eric would have pointed out that Ray himself obviously nursed certain ambitions that wouldn't heal. But Eric was still holding out for fraternal bonding.

"It's the world we have to live in, Ray. Can we afford to blow it away?"

"Don't tell me life is a compromise."

"Isn't it? Where's the line between integrity and stupidity? Today Ann Jenkins had some suggestions for my book. To make it more marketable." Against his better judgment, Eric found himself wading into the debacle. "It's not the book I wanted to write, I doubt I'd do it well—but if I don't try, NWC's going to get rid of me. I'm at the end of the road there." He was trying to address the place in Ray that knew something about how much it took to get by. "What do you think I should do?"

"If you can ask that question," Ray said, "you shouldn't be coming to me for an answer."

"I'd like your opinion."

"What do you want me to say? Life's unfair?"

"I already knew that. This is a genuine dilemma. Should I do what she says?"

He hoped that Ray wouldn't think he was condescending; the question had involved an attempt to disarm with flattery.

Ray said, "You can't hit it big in commercial publishing without some sleazing."

"I don't want to hit it big, Ray. I want to stay in the game."

"No one forced you into it. This is a luxury."

"Yes, I chose it. But now it's the work I do. And recognition, it's something everyone needs. I don't mean fame. Recognition, isn't it basic?"

"I don't hand out moral indulgences."

Eric leaned back and drank his beer. Something had gone wrong with Ray. The past decade, a carnival of Dickensian scandals and scoundrels, had come and gone without catapulting him into the front rank of moralists to whom the indignant looked for piquant phrasing. His malice, once mirthful, had become rancorous. Pickled in the vinegar of New York, his progressive politics amounted to things and people he hated. Maybe Ray had been stoking himself for this night on each of Eric's visits, points on a trajectory that must have looked boundlessly upward.

There appeared to be only one honest man left in Ray's world.

"You can't make a principle of living without rewards," Eric said, "and then be pissed off because there aren't any rewards."

"Why the hell not?" A girl with two studs in her nostril turned from the bar to look at Ray. "Do you have any idea what I put up with on a daily basis? The Unabomber got instant editorial attention while I wait months with my thumb up my ass. It's harder now than when I was starting out. They want to marginalize independent voices like me. I'm telling you—it messes with your head."

Ray searched the crowded darkness for a waitress.

"I'm sorry it went like this," Eric finally said. Ray looked suspicious. "I hoped we'd talk as friends."

"We're still friends. But no one really gives a shit about anyone except themselves."

The aperçu seemed to cheer Ray up. It was the sort of thing he used to say at parties, reminding Eric of the freelance dissident he once found provocative. Such a waste, because his life could have been a fulfilling one in a city that made room for exceptions to big-time success, or in New York as lived by another man. But Ray couldn't accept that this marginal existence was the real one, the one to which he ought to commit himself with passion. He hadn't married, never stayed with the same woman for long, lately didn't seem to see any at all—living at half-capacity. Eric had sought advice in the wrong place.

It struck him how alone he was. Neither of his parents had ever been much good in a crisis—his mother too anxious, his father too remote—but in his hometown there had been several men who would hear him out and administer common sense. In college there had been his roommates. He had lost touch with all of them, hadn't visited home in two years. Slowly the circle had shrunk to marriage and work. His only confidante was his wife, the last person he wanted to tell about Ann's bad news.

Much unfinished business awaited him in Boston. Jane was still pregnant, they still needed money, the house was in ruins and so was his career. And somehow he had to go on pulling this book out of himself. The difficulties rose like a wave, so large and daunting that he could only close his eyes and wish it away. In the moment of wishing it away, he thought of Joe, Newburg's African. Joe, who had given him a day's good pages, who was free, whose smile opened a glimpse of possibility—a life that knew nothing of this day.

It was after 11:00 when they came out of the Rat's Tale. Sheets of newspaper blew along the sidewalk on a wind from the river. Houston Street had a deserted weeknight menace.

Ray said, "It's been over a year since I slept with anyone."

Eric tried to think of a suitable reply. "I guess everyone's pretty paranoid these days."

"Sometimes I wonder about myself."

Eric froze. What was Ray about to tell him? "How do you mean?"

"Could I still live with someone? Would a woman still want me?"

"Ray, why wouldn't they?"

"I can go a whole day without talking to anyone. Maybe I've become unfit."

"The demographics are on your side. We know tons of single women in Boston. Every one of them would give you their phone number."

"Even if they would, which I don't know, phone numbers, demographics—I'm talking about companionship. What you've got."

"Men in my situation are supposed to envy men in yours."

Ray was shaking his head drunkenly from side to side. "Married people forget what it's like."

"You called me Mr. Quiet Desperation."

"Quiet desperation is living alone in your thirties."

Eric wondered why they couldn't have talked this way before. He reached and put an arm around Ray's shoulders, but he felt Ray stiffen, and after a few moments he removed it.

Jane would be asleep but he had promised to call her.

"Did I wake you up?"

"Where are you?" She sounded disoriented.

"At Ray's."

"The phone scared me."

"You doing OK?"

"Some jerks were fighting outside and I was going to call the police but I didn't, but the police came anyway."

"Are the jerks gone?"

"I don't like sleeping alone. Did you drink with Ray?"

Jane disapproved of Ray. The New York visits were too much like bachelorhood. "Not much. He drank some."

"Did you two bring home some little number?"

"She's struggling with my zipper as we speak." Eric took off his shoe and peeled away the damp wool sock. His foot had the white shrunken look of a bandaged wound. Flu appeared to be seeping from it through his body. "Actually, it's depressing here. Picture the lodgings of an aging bachelor with pee-stained underwear."

"What happened with Ann?"

He had made up his mind not to conceal, not to go down that road—to report the whole conversation, the sales history, the chopping block, the sense of doom that had come over him as he walked downtown. But Jane's voice, so familiar, so practical even half-asleep, checked him. What he described for her was a businesslike meeting in which Ann had refused to change the terms of the contract.

There was a silence on her end and it annoyed him. By the bedside lamp, he saw her face tightening in a worried frown. She was deciding whether to tell him that she had known this would happen.

"Say something," he told her.

"We'll talk when you get home."

"I did my best, Jane. Ann was unmoved by our family situation."

"What did you tell her?" she asked warily.

"That we're struggling parents-to-be who need money right away."

"Eric, why did you say that?"

"Why shouldn't I? Those people need to know the human consequences of their neglect."

She sighed. "Well, you'll just have to finish the book."

The book was a blue screen covered with minus signs. Being told that he just had to finish it roused a mutinous feeling. He almost said it was too late.

"When are you getting in?" Jane said. "We have to figure things out about the baby room. They're about to start building the diaper cabinet."

"Oh. The diaper cabinet." For an instant he was going to laugh. Then he remembered what he was doing tomorrow, and his despair suddenly lifted. "I'm taking an afternoon train. I have a couple of appointments first."

Ray came into the room as he was putting the receiver down. Eric looked up with a guilty start.

"How's your wife?"

"Sleepy," Eric said. "Pregnant. I look at Jane's stomach and think: The end of life as an individual."

Ray shrugged. "Normal male anxiety. In a marriage you can be honest about everything."

"Some things you can't."

"Like what?"

Eric was thinking: What happens if I tell you? Is it the first slip, then all the others? Will you inform my wife to avenge your disappointments? But he felt a compulsion to tell, to gauge its reality — to make it more real.

"I met this person the other evening. I spent a total of twenty minutes with her. I didn't think anything was happening."

"An infatuation."

"Maybe."

"It's like a buzz — enjoy it till it wears off."

"I'm seeing her tomorrow on Bleecker Street."

Ray was throwing cushions on the floor. "Eric, I'm not worried. You're not the type to follow through on something like this."

It felt like the deepest cut yet. "I'm not so sure of that."

Ray stopped unfolding a blanket. He was squinting in some peculiar pain. "Tell this person you can't see her again."

"And spend the next forty years walking away from life?"

"Pure shit." Ray snapped the blanket over the cushions. "You have a good thing. I'd change places in a second, you bastard. Don't fuck it up."

The cafe on Bleecker was almost empty. Eric sat nursing a cappuccino. She was half an hour late, and what alarmed him was that the thought of going back to Boston without seeing her was too bleak to face. How could that happen after one rainy walk? She was becoming a phantom, an invention. But he kept sitting beyond his self-allotted five minutes, trying to summon her face as if then Paula herself would finally show up. He thought: *dark eyes, cheekbones,* but the words didn't materialize into her eyes, her cheekbones. Her absence was somehow connected to this fact. The waitress kept giving him skeptical looks.

Dark hair rushed past the window. A moment later the cafe door opened. He decided to trick himself: It was someone else. He lowered his head into a book.

The person was coming toward his table. At the last second he looked up and the trick rewarded him: Paula, out of breath, brushing hair from her face, apologizing.

"I was afraid you'd already left," she gasped.

"I was afraid you weren't coming."

"I didn't want you to think I forgot. My mother got sick. I'm really sorry."

"Oh, I'm sorry."

He had forgotten the way her hair waved and was parted on the side, cut short so that her neck showed. She was darker than he remembered, like a Syrian. More than just breathless—a little panicked. His own fingers were trembling on the book.

"Here, sit down."

"I really shouldn't. I have to get back." She stared, wide-eyed. He realized that she was waiting for him to insist.

"Please. I'll be very disappointed."

"Just for a few minutes."

When she had sat down and ordered, he asked, "What happened?"

"I had to take her to the hospital," Paula said vaguely.

"Is she going to be OK?"

"Oh, I think so. I think she will."

"Good. Good." They were mired in polite hysteria. "You can't seem to get away from patients."

"What?"

"Well, your mother."

"Oh." Her eyes wandered away. "I guess not."

"Is something wrong?"

She shook her head. She spooned sugar into her coffee and seemed to compose herself. He watched her, trying to figure out who this phantom woman was. Not so calm and sharp as that night outside Widener—more skittish, elusive.

"You had a meeting with your publisher?" she asked.

"Oh. Yeah."

"And?"

He began to tell her, and found himself pouring out everything that he hadn't told Jane, that he couldn't tell Jane. He saw that the effect was not to bore or repel Paula but to make her forget whatever was troubling her. She listened closely and plied him for details. "Your right foot? Oh, it's already terrible." When he came to the moment when Ann turned her monitor toward him, Paula flinched as if someone were forcing a picture of corpses on her. But she was able to hear everything. She made him want to rise courageously above a great and unmerited wrong.

"She suggested those changes because she felt bad." Paula shook her head. "She knew she shouldn't be doing this to you."

When her head shook, the hair grazed her neck. She had a lovely, slender neck. "It's sort of built into the profession," he said.

"Not just yours. Next month I'm losing my staff job—I'm going to be freelance like you. It must be terrifying, having no security. I don't know how you've survived."

"Well," he said, "I guess I'm not alone."

"It's happening all over the place."

And her eyes, those dark pools—he wanted to dive down and swim in them.

"I've thought about this idea of the breakthrough book," he said. "This might interest you, because of your work. I keep asking myself what it means. Change the voice? Sales, new readership? Get on the map? No, what you have to break through is yourself. You almost have to become someone else."

She immediately nodded, then she said, "How is that?"

"Because you're not enough. I recently turned thirty-eight. At thirty-eight you see the limits. I'm not going to be a pro basketball player or a genius. My voice will always be Iowa flat. No, it's OK, the point is I accept these things. My nose will always have this little twist. My hairline won't reverse course. I might be attractive to women, but never charismatic. When I'm angry, I'll always become quiet. My signature has stopped deteriorating at a loop and a squiggle."

Paula laughed. He could see that she was enjoying his list, registering each quality and weighing it against the evidence at hand. Candor was his ally with her.

"And my sentences will always sound the way they do. All these things are fixed, maybe genetic. You learn to live with them, it's necessary for happiness. At my age I'm supposed to be settling in. Now they want me to shed my old skin and break through."

"Are you getting sick?"

His forehead quivered. She might as well have reached across and touched him.

"I feel fine." He wanted to kiss her neck, know the feel of her skin where it disappeared into her blouse. "It's a wonderful relief telling you this stuff. I can see how good you are."

"I'm not on the job right now." Paula blushed and abruptly stood up. "I have to get back to my mother." The panic was returning to her eyes. "Maybe we could continue this in Cambridge."

"That might be possible."

He told her that his favorite pastime, even in winter, was walking along the river. She agreed, but the afternoon she suggested wasn't until after New Year's. At the last she seemed to be protecting herself. To Eric it seemed a hopelessly long time—he could hardly stand to let her go.

The sun was setting over New Jersey when his train emerged from the tunnel. He had found a window seat on the right side so he could watch the coastline above New Haven; but it was the shortest day of the year and the sky would be dark by then. He had a stack of student papers out but didn't even try to work. Queens slipped by, thousands of blocks of row houses jammed together, and then over the bridge into the industrial upper Bronx, with gas tanks and ruined factories and the distant towers of Co-op City.

His throat tingled, his eyelids and lower back ached, he was shivering lightly. These days the flu wasn't the same as it used to be; it knocked you out for weeks.

He drew the illness around him like a blanket and let the rhythm of the train lull him. His New York disaster and his New York flu had freed him, and he closed his eyes. He and Paula were lying in a sun-drenched bed. The sight of her body released within him something sweet and long unused. He murmured her name. The light was African, the warmth of the morning. But when he moved his hands to touch her, the body dissolved.

Night fell, New York receded. The train sped along an embankment, mile after mile of garbage, spiky graffiti under bridges. This was where bodies turned up. Outside Pelham, a hobo in a ski cap was pushing a shopping cart over gravel in the ten feet of berth between the embankment and the tracks. Then the tracks rose up to overlook boarded factories and collapsed wooden houses. Bridgeport appeared in yellow vaporous light. The brick projects ran one after another at right angles to the track. Men were working under car hoods in floodlit parking lots while others stood by with bottles and radios. The silhouette of a Catholic church. Eric imagined rats in the shadows. The train seemed to be passing through his crawl space. Flu was working its way into his muscles, dissolving the solid enclosure of his body. Far ahead he made out the ghostly chutes and towers and pinprick lights of United Illuminating.

After New Haven he slept, anticipating feverish freedom. But he dreamed of hot, damp caves, an ancient pipe, the threat of violence, an obscurely doomed mission.

He woke up hollow and frightened as the train lurched to a stop. They were in South Station. On his tray the papers lay unmarked. He was home, with nothing to show for the trip.

Standing to gather his bag, he remembered the panhandler on Fifty-fifth Street—how the crowd moved past without seeing. He had thought of something important then, much bigger than his own problems. He had to get back to that. The whole subway ride to Central Square, he struggled to remember what it was.

love

twelve

The glimpse of a woman lighting a cigarette in her doorway at 6:00 in the evening, the face of a man checking his watch at the top of the subway stairs, are the romance of the city. Where everyone is a stranger, longing haunts the streets. Around each corner waits a new chance for a flowering, and a loss, and this is never more true than on a winter evening, when people are going back to their cells, daylight has been withdrawn and the blue half-light of dusk makes every face a mystery. The same city that reminds them of being separate individuals makes them conscious of what lies beyond themselves. They seek that extension everywhere they go, and so love and the city are bound up together. When love fails, when private happiness is elusive, the city is what stands in for the object of desire, inspiring the strange passion of strangers.

Earlier that fall, when a few leaves were still flaming red and brown, an organizer arrived in Cambridge with a new idea for empowering the citizens of a small city. He wanted to avoid traditional institutions, with their bureaucratic meddling and inertia. The political parties, neighborhood associations, churches, unions, all were fatally weakened by the forces of contemporary life that dissolve bonds everywhere: television, parenthood, computers, overwork, fatigue, disbelief. The only way to unleash buried energy was to find a language for each separate person, to become the group in which each person could discover the extension of his or her self and through which larger problems could then be solved. The new ground for organizing was private life; the point of entry, private feelings.

The organizer began a series of conversations with citizens, and these quickly led to two breakthroughs. A marketing strategist from a small software company came up with the notion of posting signs around the city—their provocative and anonymous riddles would not only generate buzz, but also prepare people for the group's emergence and its campaigns to come. The slogans would sprinkle ideas like seeds, or spices, to germinate in the public psyche and arouse it. Most of the signs were brainstormed over three successive late nights, then released in timed intervals throughout November.

The second breakthrough came when the organizer approached the executive director of the Problem Place, who offered to transform his Wednesday evening therapy group into recruitment meetings that would retain the original therapeutic structure. The organizer immediately saw in this a way to reach people outside formal insitutions. And the results were so successful, the numbers of friends and friends of friends wanting to participate so large, that the meetings were soon expanded to two nights a week. By word of mouth in a small city, The Community began to stir civic love.

Joe was working under the house with a drop light, bent over on his knees, driving a short-handled shovel into the dirt where the waste pipe went underground. Water was filling around the shovel blade, gray, with a sewage smell that reminded him of the African town. In places the mud caved in on itself, not all the way but down into a lower hole. He had a feeling of being suspended on a bed of mud over deep waters. If he dug hard enough he would break all the way through and see the dark shapes of big fish pass underneath. This pipe ran out to the sewer main under the street and on down to the pumping station by the river. Then it flowed out through the harbor into the ocean, where tides and currents took it across to the west coast of Africa. Africa was what lay at the other end of the pipe they were going to replace.

Now and then, under the noise of tools and voices just above his head, Joe heard something moving across the mud. The rats kept their distance. The first time down here alone, he hadn't liked being cut off from the others. The rats frightened him, the work was hard and dirty, and when he came back up he put on a silent air of suffering an insult. So it was strange to find himself looking forward to being sent under again. Down here the years fell away and he remembered old things—he kept thinking of the time a boy in fifth grade asked him if it was because Joe's parents weren't his *real* parents that his dungarees were always too short, and he hit the boy and made his nose bleed, and the boy hit him and bloodied his lip, and somehow the sight of blood made them friends again. He went home and proudly showed his bloody shirt to his foster mother. But she said, "We're all God's children," and sent him to his room without dinner, making him pray for Jesus to forgive his sin of pride and anger. And though he prayed fervently, he didn't understand why she had been unhappy with him. He told Jesus he'd never make her unhappy again. He climbed under the corduroy bedspread and waited for his door to open, telling himself that if he held his breath another five seconds she would come in. His eyes were starting to close when he saw the crack of light run across the floor. She came over to his bed, and he pictured an angry frown on her face and shut his eyes as if he were asleep. He felt her lean over the bed and kiss his forehead. "Can I get a smile, sweet boy?" Then everything was all right again; he could stay.

What Joe liked best about the crawl space was that he could stop being Amouzou. Down here his breathing relaxed, he didn't have to think about his accent or worry that someone was about to spring a question he couldn't answer. There weren't many places like this left. He wasn't staying at Rainbow House anymore—Newburg had helped him get a room at the YMCA, on the other side of Central Square from the shelter, next to the post office. Joe had heard it was impossible to get a room there unless you were insane or had AIDS, but Newburg knew someone who knew someone, and he advanced Joe two weeks' pay. Newburg was funny about money—he offered any kind of advance, but Joe hadn't been raised above five dollars an hour. The Y charged ninety-five dollars a week and his wages even under the table only came to about two hundred, so there wasn't much left over after he paid his rent. Still, the people at the Y let him know he was lucky, and he thought so too. It was like getting into Rainbow House on his first night.

At the end of the day, Joe was exhausted and sometimes he fell fast asleep at nine o'clock in his work clothes. Everyone at the Y left everyone else alone unless someone had a problem with you. But the room was very small and bare and underheated. It made him lonely, and he spent most of his time there asleep.

It was always the African who came out of the room in the morning, who climbed up through the trap door.

Newburg said, "Joe here has solved the riddle of the rats."

Eric Barnes looked at Joe. "You're going to take my rats away from me too?"

Joe laughed. He didn't know the right answer.

Eric had gone away to New York and come back sick. His voice was hoarse, his eyes glassy and bloodshot, and whenever a power tool stopped they heard him coughing in another room. He hadn't left the house all day. No one could figure out what Eric Barnes did. His presence made Joe nervous. The first time they met, at Missy's house, Joe had caught Eric looking at him in a way that set off a warning in his head. The look said: I understand. It said: I know who you are and I understand. It made Joe want to tell him everything. Right there and then he knew he had to avoid Eric Barnes.

"Your rats are coming up from the sewer through holes in the waste pipe," Newburg said. "Vintage World War II—'victory pipe,' some substandard alloy. It had a life of half a century."

"My dad laid about two miles of it," Dennis, the plumber, said. "I see this happening all over the city."

Eric said, "'Victory pipe.' That's appropriate."

He laughed and started coughing and it turned into a fit. When he bent over double, Frank patted him on the back. "Hey Eric, stay away from New York this time of year."

"I'm fine. Is this hard to fix?"

"Not with big Dennis on the team."

Dennis rested his Sawzall on its swordfish nose. "Dennis" was stitched on his shirt pocket—carpenters didn't wear uniforms, but for some reason plumbers did. "I don't work with rats."

"Dennis," Frank said, "when you go down there with your big tool and start cutting that big pipe, there won't be a rodent between here and the river. You'll be their worst nightmare, Dennis the Rat Man."

"They carry the plague. A whole tribe of Indians in Arizona died just from breathing ratshit." Dennis glanced at Joe and the heavy flesh around his jaws tightened. "Anyway, do we know this for sure? Maybe indoor plumbing's kind of a novelty for him."

Everyone looked at Joe.

"That's a stereotype," Newburg said. "This is what we have plumbers for, Dennis. Every plumber I've known is part rat anyway."

"*That's* a stereotype." Dennis rubbed his broken-vesseled nose and picked up the Sawzall. "And I'm offended by it."

Newburg started to apologize but was drowned out by the shriek of motorized blade on metal pipe.

"Is this going to cost much extra?" Eric shouted, moving away from the noise.

"We'll see how far down the rot goes," Newburg said.

"That sounds ominously symbolic."

"Eric, in every house there's a hidden evil that could undermine the whole structure. Carpenter ants, rotten sills, cracked foundation. Here it's rats and old plumbing. The thing is to catch it early, eliminate it, and restore the house to goodness."

"No wonder I'm dreaming about you all." Eric smiled at Joe. The look again. Alarming strings of words uncoiled in Joe's chest.

He escaped to the trap door. As he lowered himself down the hole, Newburg appeared above him.

"There's something important I want you to be a part of tonight."

It was in the basement of an old brick building, just around the corner from Rainbow House. On the way from the Y, Joe noticed blue signs on lampposts and stoplight boxes. These weren't like the other blue signs he saw around the city because nothing was written on them except black arrows pointing him exactly in the direction he needed to go—a trail of breadcrumbs. He was playing with the thought that someone had posted the signs for him.

A blue sign with an arrow was taped to the basement door. Above it were the words "The Problem Place."

He knew the name. They used to mention it at Rainbow House. Kevin the ex-con told the poet: "Why don't you take your problems to the Problem Place?" It was where mental cases went.

Joe hesitated at the door. What something important? He imagined a roomful of people in white coats. They would ask him questions and write his answers on clipboards but he wouldn't get to see what they wrote. And his voice might give out or he might make a mistake, forget what his mother's name was supposed to be, or else they might just know. Know the way Eric Barnes knew.

"Do you know who I am?" Joe said aloud. The sound of his voice startled him. He wanted to hear it again. "In Africa, I was a magician." It was a strong voice. It couldn't be hurt. He opened the door.

Inside, more signs with arrows led him down a hall. He turned left into a small crowded room. Men and women were sitting around a table, chairs jammed against the walls. There were maybe twenty of them, and their expressions reminded Joe of people in church. The man who was speaking stopped. Frozen in the doorway, Joe spotted Jim Newburg motioning to an empty chair beside him.

Everyone watched while he struggled along the wall. When he sat down, Newburg lightly touched his arm.

"Go ahead, Bill," a man at the head of the table said. "We're with you."

Bill had a squashed face with a shaggy mustache drooping across its middle. "I'm not used to talking in public," he muttered in a growly voice.

"You're doing beautifully. We're just human beings here." The man at the head of the table had his legs crossed in his chair, shoes

off. He was plump, with a dark curving beard and brown eyes lit up
by secrets. The eyes shifted to Joe, and the man slipped him a smile
and a wink. Joe felt that this must be the man people took their
problems to.

"I guess I lost my confidence when I got laid off." Bill addressed
his clasped hands on the table. "I know it was downsizing and a
hundred other guys went with me, but I felt responsible. Like if I'd
been faster on the ADI project."

"I hear you," someone said.

Bill looked up. "I was good at what I did. I submitted like fifty-
four resumes to every software company in Eastern Mass. Most of
them didn't even answer. I try to keep busy. But I get kind of discouraged. I know I shouldn't but my wife wants to know how she's
supposed to pay the mortgage and what do I tell my daughters?
They keep asking why daddy's home all day." Bill's growl was coming loose. "I don't want to bellyache too much."

"You're not bellyaching," said the man with secrets in his eyes.
"This is real pain we're talking about, real lives. Go ahead, get
angry."

Bill didn't get angry. His face crumpled until there was nothing
but forehead and mustache. A woman put her hand on his arm and
then his shoulders began to shake, but no sound came out.

"I hate feeling like a failure," Bill croaked into a knuckle.

"No!"

"Who says that?"

"You're the one *been* failed."

"Blaming the victim!"

"Do you see, people," said the man with secrets in his eyes,
"what pain and grief do in this society? They isolate us. We think
it's our fault, that we're alone and no one else can help. That's why
we need The Community. We *have* to tell our stories. The people
closest to us don't want to hear them. But these stories save lives."

Everyone was nodding. Joe nodded with them. The words
stirred him; he thought of his own life and whether there was a
story in it that could save him.

My mother told me to wait by the ticket counter. She said she was going to the ladies' room. She was crying and she gave me some money to hold. I waited for a long time. A man gave me candy but I wouldn't go with him. Someone from the bus company brought a policeman. I didn't know where I lived. She never came back from the ladies' room.

The woman who had touched Bill's arm was talking now. She had straw-colored hair and a dry chapped face, and she said, "Things just go from bad to worse with me." She told them about her son who stole from her, her deadbeat ex-husband, her impossible water bills, her weekly migraines. Yet a warm color was filling her cheeks and she even laughed once or twice. Joe couldn't tell if the story saved her, but it made her happier.

Four years, seven houses. The second to last said I wet the bed too damn much. I kept waiting for her to show up at the door, but I forgot what her face looked like.

They were going around the table, one by one, moving toward Joe. There was a black man wearing a coat and tie and a neat gray mustache—he was retired from the school system and complained about the youngsters in Reeboks who made him afraid to go out at night to his social club on the street where he'd lived all his life. An Indian waiter with cropped hair had been burned out of his apartment by a fire; he was terrified of ending up in Rainbow House if his co-worker at Bombay Delight kicked him out of his room. A man in a plain white shirt said, "I haven't been present for most of my life," and that was all.

Whenever a story ended, a black man in denim overalls, with a rigid, unsmiling jaw scarred from old acne, got up and went to a flip chart propped up in the corner. In blue Magic Marker he wrote down words about what had been said: "displaced workers," "health insurance," "parenting," "insecurity," "water rates," "anger." At the top of the chart was the word "Problems."

This was the Problem Place. They were two people away from Joe.

The last ones kept me. But they died. I stole, I almost killed someone. Amouzou got killed because of me. I came here and started lying.

The man with the Magic Marker, what could he write about the bus station, or the fight in fourth grade, or how the corduroy bedspread felt so sad, or the movie in the Tenderloin, or everything that happened in Africa? It didn't make sense, telling wouldn't save him, they wouldn't care, they'd be crawling over the table to get out the door.

"Now, let's talk about what you people can *do* about these problems," the man with the Magic Marker said. "Because you are *not* powerless."

Joe exhaled. They had forgotten him.

"I'm hearing that a lot of us feel abandoned by our government, our employers, and our communities," the man said. "So how do your issues interconnect? Where is the power? What resources do you have? And then what action to take."

The radiator hissed. The man with secrets in his eyes leaned forward.

"I think one or two people haven't told their stories." The eyes cut over to Joe. "Ed here is sort of Mr. Action. I'm Mr. Talk. We go together," he said with a little laugh. "But first you have to talk. Change starts right here."

Mr. Talk patted his sweater vest.

Mr. Action said, "All right, I don't believe we've heard from the young fellow yet."

Blood pounded in Joe's ears. His tongue was thick and dry like a hunk of jerky. They were all looking at him.

"Tell them about Africa," Newburg whispered.

"I am going to tell you about Africa," Joe said, and at the sound of his strange new voice he became calm. It claimed the attention of everyone in the room.

"There was a man in Africa by the name of Amouzou. This Amouzou worked as a carpenter, making chairs for the people of the town. But they did not like Amouzou. During the day they quarreled over his fees, they spat at him, cursed him, threw stones at his three-legged dog, they called him Monkey-Head. But at night these same people brought him gifts of roosters and gin and put their problems in his hands. At night in this town, Amouzou was the Problem Place."

There was a ripple of laughter, then the room fell silent again. They were listening closely. Encouraged, Joe went on.

"After the sun went down, this despised man could turn his spirit into any living thing—a snake, a tree, a girl, an ancestor. To Americans this will not seem possible, but believe me, in the African darkness these things happen. At night people came from their houses, and he took the sickness out of their bodies with the power of his spirit, and he healed them."

Joe glanced at Mr. Talk. The eyes with secrets were wide open.

"A little girl was brought to Amouzou half-dead with jaundice. Her mother and father were at the end of hope. The clinic with all its injections and pills could do nothing. Death had come for their dear little girl." Joe heard his voice riding the cadences, gathering intensity. The things it was saying exhilarated him. His whole life had been moving toward this moment. "But Amouzou—he held up his hand and stopped death. He took the jaundice into his own body, and his own spirit possessed this girl and filled her with life and gave her back to her beloved parents. He refused their gifts of thanks. That little girl lives today because of him. He was stronger even than death."

Suddenly the crowd was outside Joe's house, his boys holding machetes. He tripped, stopped, and checked to see if Mr. Talk noticed. The eyes had filled with tears, like a child's.

Joe began speaking quickly to get away from the memory.

"But one day a government man who was jealous of Amouzou's power and goodness—he told the people of this town that Amouzou's magic had killed another man. That Amouzou was wicked. These people were ignorant, and because it was a government man they believed him." Mr. Talk groaned. "And Amouzou ran from that town with *nothing*. His family all were killed." Someone slapped the table. The woman with the chapped face shook her head. "Yes, all killed. He had to leave. His last money went for the ticket. America was his only hope. Amouzou's only hope was you."

They stared at him. Their faces seemed very distant. Joe felt that he was gazing down on them from a great height. His body was inflating, his own words blowing him up, it was time to stop or he would burst.

"Tonight that man is sitting before you. My life saved. Delivered by God's grace from the hands of my enemies. They took everything from me except my spirit. It is alive tonight in this room to thank God for each of you because you saved my life."

Joe laid his hands upon the table to show that he was finished.

"Amazing."

Mr. Talk wiped his eyes and repeated himself. The others were leaning forward, as if there might be more. Then their expressions changed. They began to smile at him. "Beautiful accent," someone said. In their faces Joe saw his foster mother after he'd fought with the other boy, when she came in and said good night and he opened his eyes and gave her his smile. He gave it to them now. *This* was the story that could save his life, the one he told them, the one he was making even in this moment.

They loved him.

Mr. Action stood and went to the chart. He filled up a new column called "Resources," with everything from tax revenue to the people in the room. Then he started a third column called "Strategies" and filled it with everything from the blue signs to a public meeting. He began to draw lines between problems, resources, and strategies, showing how everything could be connected with everything else, health insurance with house parties, anger with phone trees, until his chart looked like a map of global routes in an airline magazine and "the people in this room" was the main hub. This little meeting, Mr. Action said, and the other little meetings The Community had been holding with other little groups, were the start of something much bigger than any one person or group.

"The Community will provide you with very real skills," Mr.

Action said. "You will learn to talk to public officials, where to find key information. Personal growth and leadership skills are a very big part of what we do. But we need a project, and as facilitators, Peter and I want to propose one to you. A few blocks from here there's a building going up that the city doesn't know what the hell to do with. You know the one I'm talking about?" Around the table there were grunts. "People call it Building X because it doesn't have a name yet, an identity. We have information that the city is in discussion with members of the state legislature and Entertainment Management Enterprises of Orlando, Florida, to explore the possibility of leasing this building for slot machines and low-stakes blackjack. In plain English, the city wants to put a casino in Central Square."

The room was buzzing with voices.

"There would be jobs," Bill said.

"There would be jobs," Mr. Action echoed. The pits in his jaw seemed like rivets holding it together. "True. What kind of jobs? Low-skill, low-wage service sector exploitation jobs for a few of our brothers and sisters. A few of us would catch the crumbs and the rest of us would be losers." He began drawing Xs on the air with his Magic Marker. "The casual gamblers would lose and the addictive gamblers would lose big. Local entertainments would lose. But what we would all lose is our soul as a community, because all you have to do is get on a bus to Atlantic City or drive right down 95 to the Mashantucket Pequot reservation to see how casinos turn a community into a jungle. We are becoming a Casino Society. That's what The Community is *against*. It would tear us apart, not make us whole."

"Amen," someone said.

Bill stared at his hands.

"So we propose making Building X The Community's first campaign. It's visible, it's real. There's media interest. Naming that building will empower you people and everyone in The Community."

"What do we want to do with it?" asked the woman with the chapped face.

"What would you do with it?"

"Day care."

"Employment counseling."

"Just bringing folks together."

Mr. Action wrote these down on a new page of his flip chart.

"You could do your therapy there," the woman said to Joe. He was afraid they had forgotten him. "A lot of people would be interested."

Others agreed. Mr. Action wrote down "African medicine."

"Before we all leave. . . ." At the end of the table, Mr. Talk uncrossed his legs and sat up in the chair. "I think every one of us feels the spirit that entered this room with our African friend." He paused for everyone to feel the spirit that had entered the room. A few people closed their eyes. "This wonderful night world where we can be anything we want—it's like a dream, like childhood. Healing by taking each other's sickness into our body—wonderful! Powerful! To me that's what The Community is all about. In the day world—why do we call it 'the real world'?—where Bill's a computer professional and Sheila works for the cable company, we throw stones at three-legged dogs and call each other Monkey-Head. We honk in traffic, dysfunction with our loved ones, and hate ourselves. Why can't we connect the day world to this wonderful African night world? Tonight we began."

On Joe's way out someone touched his shoulder.

"You were incredible." Mr. Talk was winking. By his side Newburg nodded gravely, the veins blue in his head. "Jim told me about you, but my mindset was too Western. You raised the awareness level for everyone. You put them right where I wanted them."

The secrets in Mr. Talk's eyes said: Eric Barnes *doesn't* understand. You are not that boy who wants to tell him that other story. You are the words you spoke tonight, buried inside you all these years in a concrete tomb. I'm the one who understands.

"No problem," Joe said.

"The Community is very fluid. I want you to stay in touch through Jim."

They shook hands. On the release Joe snapped Mr. Talk's middle finger with his own finger and thumb, in the African way.

Mr. Talk giggled. "What was that?"

"In old times they cut off the middle finger of slaves. This is how we Africans shake hands. To show we are free."

Mr. Talk was delighted.

In Central Square the rockers and dealers were out in force. The cold air made Joe feel high. He didn't want to go back to the Y yet, to lie on his cot in the chilly little room and listen to the drunk next door argue with himself. The excitement of the evening would be over, as if it had never been real. He no longer wanted to be alone— there had to be other people around for him to be Amouzou. When he was alone it would stop.

He crossed Mass. Avenue. On the other side there was a bar called Benny's Lounge. He had passed it a dozen times. The marquee listed the same band every night of the week. He went through the door and was swallowed up in smoke and noise.

In the far corner a group of musicians in studded jackets and sunglasses played loud electric blues. The place was half-empty—a few couples were dancing and some men were sitting by themselves at the bar. Christmas decorations were strung above the mirror. Joe ordered a beer and turned toward the music.

A woman slipped onto the stool next to his. He caught a glimpse of long brown hair, a loose sweater, slender legs sheathed in black jeans.

"Big Al's a little off tonight."

He turned, expecting a girl his age. Her body was blade-thin, but the smile gathered folds around her cheeks and under her chin.

"I never heard him before."

"You must be from somewhere else."

"San Francisco," Joe heard himself say. To his surprise, it was his own voice.

"Christ. And you're spending the winter here for your health?"

"Something like that."

"Something like that?" Her skin was beige, she might have been part Mexican or Indian. Her tired eyes were locked on his, flirting over the rim of her glass. "Got a girlfriend here?"

"No girlfriend."

"Nobody to make your Christmas merry?"

"I lost my job in San Francisco, so I came here."

"I lost my job—in San Francisco," the woman sang and laughed vacantly. "Why'd you lose your job in San Francisco?"

"Stealing."

He was trying something out. He wanted to know if the magic could cross over with him.

"You're bad." She mimed disapproval. "And you got caught? You needed someone to teach you. My name's Patty. Now you tell me yours."

"It's—Eric."

"Hey! My favorite name."

He ordered another beer for himself and a vodka tonic for Patty. She lit a cigarette. As she swiveled from the bar to face him, her knee pressed against his thigh. His body was getting warm. It would be easy to make it happen, and he wanted her even though she might be a little old and nothing was real.

"Have you heard of The Community?" he asked.

"Which one?"

"I mean—this one. It's some kind of organization, people with problems. The blue signs."

"The blue signs." She blew an amused plume of smoke upward. "I love it."

"That's what I came out here for. They needed leadership."

"Well you're the man, Eric."

It was working. He could change shape back and forth and the magic was still there. So it wasn't just Amouzou—it was him. He felt higher than he'd ever been in his life.

"That's what Mr.—the number one guy told me. I was just there tonight. Building X is going to be our first campaign."

"Go for it, Eric!" She raised her glass to toast him. "Where you lead I will follow."

Joe clinked glasses and swallowed his beer. It was just the right thing, stopping in this bar. A celebration. Christmas was in two days. He was glad for the company. After tonight, she would disappear and he would go back to being Amouzou. "The Community is very fluid. It's going to make things happen for people here."

"Don't look at me, I operate on my own."

"In the day world."

Patty shut one eye and gave him a look. "I do my best work at night."

"I'm talking about another awareness level."

"I used to be into that. Didn't work out. Whereabouts you staying, Frisco?"

Joe started to tell her when he remembered that they didn't allow guests at the Y. All residents had to be buzzed in by the deskman. The policy was very strict because of theft and drunken rowdiness under the old management.

It angered him not to have a place to take her. It was a comedown, as bad as Rainbow House. And he had less than a hundred dollars left.

Desire kept bubbling up like fizzy water in a capped bottle.

"Something wrong?" Patty asked.

"At the Y."

"Hey, classy guy." She laughed in a way that struck him as unpleasant. "I can deal with it."

"But they don't—"

"Look, it's easy. J.B.'s working the desk tonight. Just slip him a ten." Patty stubbed out her cigarette and slid off the barstool. She seemed impatient now, no longer looking at him. "Onward, Christian soldiers. Or is that the Salvation Army?"

Joe paid for their drinks. That and the ten for the deskman wouldn't leave him much more than seventy dollars till New Year's. He wondered how much Patty was going to ask for, or if it was up to him. Money was flying out of his hands. The whole thing was starting to go sour. But it was too late.

"I just want to freshen up a little," Patty told him.

Joe went into the box of a men's room. The walls were covered with ridges of hardened adhesive where the tiles had fallen off, and between the zigzags messages had been scrawled. "Brown Bomber Sucking Crew" made him hesitate before unzipping, as if someone was present with him, like at Logan. Standing over the toilet, he looked away from the bowl and noticed a machine by the sink that sold aspirin and condoms. Back in his room he had some condoms from his travels, but they were at least a year old and probably no good anymore. After flushing with his foot, he found some quarters and bought a three-pack.

The last woman he'd been with was Esther, the waitress at the Good Luck bar. One day Amouzou had said, "Esther would like to make your acquaintance," and that night at the bar Joe invited her back with him. She told him to go home and wait; she had to wash at her auntie's after work. He was dozing on his bed when he heard the knock. She had put on her best dead white man's dress for him. Soon it came off, and in the darkness she felt so soft and they hardly spoke except when she told him that African girls did not make love with their mouths. Afterward, Esther went home to her auntie's without asking him for money. She never asked for anything, but sometimes Joe gave her gifts of perfume and pirated music tapes. On Sundays, when everyone else was at church, they went to the river beyond the cemetery and soaped each other's bodies.

One day her auntie told Joe that a man with a dozen cattle and thirty goats was going to marry Esther unless Joe could match him. The nights in his bed when there was no time or money stopped. He saw her sometimes in the market—a married woman, with a baby coming, couldn't work at the Good Luck bar—and when they greeted each other there was a look in her eye, though nothing ever happened again and Joe felt no jealousy, only nostalgia.

Esther was dead, he suddenly realized. She was from Amouzou's tribe. And the baby inside her, too. But not the man with a dozen cattle and thirty goats. How could he have forgotten that Esther was dead? Joe put his hand to the ridged wall—he was getting dizzy. All of a sudden everything seemed low and sad. He tried to wash his hands but the sink didn't work. In the mirror, his own face surprised him. He didn't know what he expected but it was still him, confused and a little angry, as if someone had played a trick.

On his way out of the bathroom, Joe's back was pounded hard from the blind side. He wheeled and confronted a blue knit cap and a doughy, stubbled grin.

"Hey hey hey! I thought it was you."

Joe pretended not to know who it was.

"Come on—we did time at Rainbow House." Kevin locked Joe's hand in a crushing shake, which twisted into the soul brother's. He was drunk and excited. "How you doing? Remember that bullshit artist who said he was a poet? And frigging Kool-Aid every night? I was thinking: Jesus, get me back to Walpole. But hey, we're free now, right?"

"Right."

"How you like this fucking country?"

"Oh, it is fine." The accent sounded clumsy.

"Got a job yet? Yeah? Well fuck you." Kevin's laugh sounded like a machine gun: *uh-uh-uh-uh*. Even when he laughed his eyes were flat, like a lizard's. "I'm trying to go straight, right—I can't get a job wiping asses and this is my own fucking country. Got a ball and chain, know what I mean?"

In another minute Patty would come out of the bathroom, expecting Eric from Frisco. And that would be the end of the game. Joe took a step away. "You have to tell them?"

"It's on every form. You try to lie, it's like—" Kevin pulled a frown as he pretended to read a sheet of paper. "'What have you been doing the past year, Mr. Fitzgerald?' And I was kind of famous when it went down. The student paper called me the Flyswatter cause that was the name of the first club I took off, the Fly. A lot of students were on my side, it was like a Robin Hood thing. They thought the clubs were elitist or sexist or something, *uh-uh-uh-uh*. Where you staying?"

"YMCA."

"Why you little fuck. I tried to get a room but they told me there's a pisser waiting list, so I'm fucking mooching off my buddy in East Cambridge. How'd you do that?"

The door to the ladies' room opened and Patty appeared. Joe walked toward her, too fast for Kevin to stop him.

"Hey, I'll look for you at the Y!" Kevin called after him. "I need to talk to you. I got an offer to make."

Ten dollars got Joe and Patty buzzed into the residential quarters. But she wasn't interested in Eric from Frisco anymore. It was over very fast, and then she wanted more money than he could afford. The compromise made for ill will on both sides. Alone, Joe fought off an empty feeling and told himself that he still had Amouzou, Mr. Talk, and The Community. He shouldn't have let that go even for a moment; he wouldn't do it again.

thirteen

Christmas came and then New Year's, dark and bitter, too cold for snow. The river was edged with pale gray ice; the water looked as black and heavy as oil. Paula was walking with Eric Barnes over the footpath's frozen mud, past dead yellow grass, bare oaks and birches, willows suspended over the water in stark, lugubrious poses. The wind was blowing into their faces. All day there had been bright sunlight, and now the sky was glowing in pink streaks where the sunset caught tufts of cloud. Behind them the city had disappeared around the curve of the river, submerged in dusk.

"Look at that black duck," she said. "Why doesn't he get the hell out of here?"

"That black duck," Eric told her, "is a merganser. Beautiful head, isn't it? They're deep divers. Look, there he goes. In a minute he'll come up way over there."

"Where did you learn about ducks?"

"When I was a kid in Iowa I spent a lot of time at a lake near our house."

"Who are your parents, Scott and Helen Nearing?"

"My parents are what politicians call Mr. and Mrs. America. My dad was a pharmacist. Disappointed?"

"It sounds like paradise to me."

"Anyway, I've had ten years to study this river. I used to run it every evening."

"Why did you stop?"

"I don't know. I shouldn't have." He looked at the river. "But in the summer, once you get past the next bridge, it reminds me a little of Iowa. The banks are so lush, you forget there's buildings or cars. Last summer there was this explosion of carp, they were jumping all along the banks. The river turned amber. People were out fishing every day."

While he told her about the river in summertime, she watched him and listened to the pleasure in his voice. The subject of mergansers and carp made him seem boyish. He wasn't cinematically handsome, but there was something about his face's imperfections—the slight curve of the nose, the lopsided smile—that invited entry.

"I didn't see you as the Huck Finn type."

"No?"

"I saw you as more the indoor bookish type." It was a kind of flirting. And why not? The river, the trees, the distance from the city made her feel free, as if words carried no responsibilities out here. "Are you healthy enough for this walk?" He had broken down into a coughing fit.

"I got a bit of a flu in New York—you were right. I can't smell anything, but given what they're digging up under my house it's OK."

They were passed by a bundled jogger wreathed in frosty breaths. Paula said, "I wish somebody had told me about ducks when I was growing up."

"How's your mother doing?"

"She's an alcoholic." Paula wanted him to know everything. "I intervened, as we say. I checked her into a rehab clinic."

Her last view had come four days after Christmas: her mother a loose-haired little woman in a bathrobe, older and smaller than Paula had ever seen her, like a child handed over to an orphanage, confused, braving a smile in the marble lobby as she waved and waved until her daughter, whose heart was breaking, disappeared from sight.

He said, "You take very good care of her."

"Her life hasn't been easy."

"It would have been harder without you."

Tears started in Paula's cold-stung eyes. "Wine was one of her reliable pleasures, Eric. She's fifty-eight. Do we really know what's best for other people?"

"You probably saved her life."

What a luxury it would be to have this kind of conversation all the time. To have his intelligence and care affirming her.

"I've helped, but—"

"You can't be your mother's shrink."

She looked at him. "No." She wanted to say: How did you know?

They were crossing the Eliot Bridge at a sharp turn of the river. From here they would start back. The sun was dying over Watertown in a final radiance of purple and red.

"What I want to know," he said after a moment, "is whether it's easier to help other people than yourself."

"You ask a lot of questions. You should be a therapist."

"How else can I get to know you?"

Paula turned to look over the low brick wall at the water so he wouldn't see the anxious pleasure she knew was blooming across her cheeks.

"Most people don't understand how therapy works." She tried to flatten her voice. "It's very slow. Small insights, small changes— you see how things could be done differently. Fifty percent is acceptance of what you can't change. Right now they're telling my mother one day at a time. It isn't her style. She'd rather rummage in the closet for a new self."

"I'm with your mother." They were coming down into the parking lot of a boat club, where a man in a tuxedo was unloading a catering delivery van. Paula thought of his tuxedo as a self hanging in a closet. "Total transformation! No compromise! Let's walk over here."

She followed Eric out of the parking lot and watched him walk onto a wooden pier that jutted low over the river. He was hugging its perimeter, right at the edge of the boards just above ice and cold water, arms extended like a tightrope walker.

"This is America," he called to her. "You're as big as your dreams. One day at a time is for wimps and Europeans."

She laughed. "You sound like my boss. He always talks about liberation and . . . reinvention."

"Sure. That's Emerson."

"Well my boss is a jerk and so was Emerson, and *you* don't believe it."

"Certainly I do."

"'After thirty, men wake up sad every morning'—that's Emerson too, what about that?"

He nearly lost his balance. Recovering, he looked up and grinned. "Bad time for a quote."

"Be careful," Paula told him. Where did that come from, why did she say it? She was giddy and scared and didn't want him to stop. "There's another merganser."

He turned to see.

"He pretends to be looking at the sky just before he goes down. Maybe to fool the fish." Eric came down off the pier to her side and touched her shoulder. "If Emerson said that, he's a wimp too."

On Memorial Drive the outbound traffic was thickening with rush hour. They were heading back into the city where night had already fallen. A wind blew off the river onto their backs, a blast from the Canadian Arctic. Paula shivered. She felt they were running out of time.

"I'm going to make a confession that I think you'll understand," Eric said quietly, under the noise of cars. Paula's heartbeat quickened. "When I was in New York, I realized something. I want in and I want out and I can't do either. So I'm stuck."

She turned to him, looking for a sign. "What's in and what's out?"

"In is four children and a Volvo in Lincoln, and Christmas cards from my publisher. Out—" But out momentarily stumped him. His eyes, red and watery with flu, were looking in the distance toward the sharp, wintry lights of the Prudential Tower. "Out might be something like going to live in Africa."

Her heart sank. This wasn't what she wanted to hear. Out was just as much a fantasy as in.

"Do you have to go all the way to Africa for out?"

"I have a friend who's trying to do it in New York, but he can't. Emersonian freedom is too tough there."

"Of course he can't. Everyone compromises. In, out, they're just words."

"Words are necessary."

"Can't you . . . tinker?"

"When America was young, there was room for tinkering. These days we live with more constraints. It's all or nothing."

His abstractions were making her impatient. She wanted to yank him back to here, now, to her. She wished there was another pier for him to walk along—this time she would follow him.

"What about your book? In, or out?"

"The book . . . is dead. You're the first person I've said that to." He sounded relieved.

"How did it die?"

"Neglect." He buried his hands in the pockets of his parka.

"Maybe its death is the revenge of out on in."

Eric snapped a look at her. His mouth fell open as if he'd been hit. His skin had no color, like ice.

She tried to talk her way out of it, but nothing she said would ease the stunned expression from his face. She felt sorry, and powerful—not as sorry as powerful, because now she knew she could get to this man, to the very bottom of him. If she could take him down, she could bring him back up. The surge of confidence thrilled her.

"I have this client, Earl, who farts his way through every job interview. He doesn't know why he does it." She was babbling.

"One of your humiliated men? The Will-to-fail Club? Sign me up, I'll be a cliché."

"That isn't what I mean."

"The problem with you therapists," he said, pointing a gloved finger at her, "is everything is everyone's own fault. Did your parents die in a plane crash? You wanted it to happen. Lose your job? What'd you go and do that for? There's no such thing as circum-

CENTRAL SQUARE | 175

stances. The only thing that's real is the mind. It's like Christian Science. It's a great racket, too. No wonder all the shrinks can afford to live in Newton."

"I live in Union Square," Paula retorted, "where there's plenty of circumstances. I see circumstances at my job every day. I see a woman who's been abused from age six, her check is going to be cut off, her little boy has asthma, her boyfriend yells at her whenever someone looks at him the wrong way—talk to Gladys about circumstances. She'd love to reinvent herself."

"What can be done for her?" he asked.

"You could write her a check for a thousand dollars."

"I would, if I didn't need five thousand myself."

"Gladys can't even imagine your privileges."

"Well, one of my privileges is some expensive rot under the house."

It was the easiest thing in the world, pulling rank with him. Look to your own advantages. Why were they quarreling? Beyond the line of giant sycamores, the Harvard bridge came into view. Student joggers, more cars: Freedom and privacy were gone. The little outing was coming to an end and something was blocking Paula from speaking truly—everything came out twisted.

"I don't know your situation," she admitted.

"As Emerson said, my situation is waking up every morning to convince yourself that it's worth it. In the face of all evidence, that you aren't wasting your life. No one else will—the telephone won't. Your wife won't." He spoke as if describing how a piece of machinery operated. "I don't know how to explain what happens when you look in yourself for certain resources and don't find them."

"You don't have to explain yourself, Eric."

"Oh no, I do, Paula. So do you. Are you happy?"

"I'm happy enough." It was pathetic to have to say it. "Are you?"

"Basically, I'm a responsible person. I deal with the contractor, I return student papers on time, I rarely forget to pay my credit card, I always put the toilet seat back down. I'm not complacent enough to mistake that for happiness."

Paula said, "You don't know everything about my life."

"I know what you tell me. And it sounds like you're strung out on a high wire and on call twenty-four hours a day."

"I can't control when my mother gets sick."

"Maybe all she wants is for you to have some joy."

They were at the bridge and Paula's cheeks were burning—he could get to her too. What was she feeling, what did she want? What if the light turned green and she said good-bye forever? Back to her apartment, bottled pasta sauce in the refrigerator. . . .

"Do you have time for one more bridge?" he asked.

"The footbridge isn't on my way." Perversely she tried to harden herself.

"Look, you got to hurt my feelings ten minutes ago. Now we're even."

The light changed. Instead of answering, she started across in his direction, neck-deep in a pout she didn't understand or want. It wasn't real. The real thing was this sparkle in the cold evening air, at the edges of perception. In the grip of falseness she longed to break free, to give in.

They left the asphalt path and crossed the frozen ground to regain the riverbank. Two ducks were floating beyond the ice. Paula had to say something or she would drown in regret.

"Those are ducks, right?"

"Those are ducks. Mr. and Mrs. Mallard. Said to mate for life, though that might be human sentimentality."

"Which is the male?"

"With the green head. The more beautiful."

"Hah. Is that—that's not another, is it?"

Fifteen or twenty feet downstream from the mallards something shone black on the water's surface. The ducks seemed to take no notice of it.

"I believe that's what's known as a rock."

"No it isn't. It's moving."

The something was swimming parallel to the bank. Its body barely disturbed the surface, flat and sleek, its nose straining forward.

"My God," she said, "it's a beaver, or—"

"It's a rat."

"It's huge!"

"It is a big fucking rat." He was moving down the slope. "You are a big fucking rat!"

The rat, as if it had heard and intended to respond, glided over to the bank, its ratness coming into full view: the sharp extended nose, the little pointed ears pressed back by the water like a swimming dog's, the fat haunches, the naked tail. Its back was missing tufts of hair and pink skin showed. It passed from water to ice to ground with amazing smoothness, its glide ending in a waddle on little feet, the body all wet and shiny, a foot long and dragging a ropelike tail.

He approached the animal.

"Eric, be careful, they bite."

A corrugated drainpipe came out of the ground here, its mouth emptied into the river where plastic wrappers were floating. On the bank there was more trash, bottles, dirty clothing left by homeless people who spent days and nights here. The rat began scratching in the garbage.

"You dirty sonofabitch," Eric said. He had stopped ten feet short. "Do you have to fuck up my river too? Is this where you've been coming from? Why don't you walk down the street and go in the front door? Try it. I'll crush you in a glue trap."

He took a step forward. The rat looked up and reared on its hind legs, the wet fur aroused. Eric stepped back and bumped into Paula. The animal opened its mouth to hiss, and the hiss became a scream that exposed long teeth and inflamed eyes. Paula clutched Eric's arm.

"Get back in the water!" he ordered.

"Why don't we leave it alone."

The rat held its ground and screamed again.

"Eric, please!"

Reluctantly he allowed her to guide him back toward the path. To her astonishment his eyes shone with tears.

"You two have a history?"

"They've had the run of my house for a year."

"I didn't know they got so big."

"Look at all this garbage. The picturesque Charles."

She wanted to caress his face, where the feelings were exposed and live like cut wires, and cover it with kisses. "Should I have let you two duke it out?"

Now he was embarrassed. "Your reaction was normal."

"But if you have a relationship, I shouldn't have gotten in the way."

"Don't analyze me and the rat." He began laughing. "You leave us alone. You're not getting me and the rat on your couch."

Paula flashed on her cubicle, a couples session—the rat triumphant, having just torn Eric to pieces, and she rising out of her chair with a baseball bat and clubbing it to a pulpy mess. Now she was laughing, and all of a sudden she saw that her gloved hand had somehow ended up in his. She looked up at him in surprise and the look made him laugh more and then they were laughing together, there by the river as joggers and cars went past.

"Paula. This can't be the last time I see you, can it?"

A burst of air forced itself from her chest. Sensation had become extraordinarily clear. The stoplight was dazzling, the green of his parka looked tropical, her heart beat inside her coat like a little animal, a living thing—herself, her own aliveness, more than she could bear.

It took her a moment to remember her own phone number. With stiff, trembling fingers she scrawled it on the back of a bank receipt. He didn't offer his, and she didn't ask for it.

It was like living continually in a state of high alert. Without warning, her stomach would turn over. And the blood—she didn't know it had such a life, racing around like a dog off its leash. The lungs under pressure, constricted. Her whole body in an uproar.

That night she finally had a good purpose for her insomnia. She replayed their walk by the river until it faded from overuse. His face was blurry, but now and then it materialized as in life, those green sad webbed eyes, tender, passionate. Humiliating fantasies bloomed.

All the while, Paula kept hearing a familiar voice. It was calm and level, though sometimes its tone grew slightly contemptuous. It was, she came to realize, the voice of a therapist she had gone to see six years ago when she was trying to leave New York. The woman's office was in the basement of a brownstone on the Upper West Side, and every Thursday afternoon Paula rode the Broadway local uptown, sick with desperation. Mrs. Anderson (she insisted on being called this; Paula was Miss Voorhees) pondered her from a leather armchair. The light over West Seventy-eighth Street slanted in so narrowly that as the session deepened Mrs. Anderson became a disembodied voice, calm, level, saying: "Is it me you want to kill, or your mother? Or both of us?" Mrs. Anderson wore dress suits or pressed slacks, her styled hair was going gray, her bearing was formal, the furniture tasteful, but in her world view human beings were savage killers. It was Paula's task to convince her that going to Boston was neither murder nor suicide. But none of her reasons— work, personal growth, New York fatigue, filial independence— impressed Mrs. Anderson. Paula understood the point. She was supposed to talk the decision completely through; without talk, leaving would be flight, all her repetition compulsions following her intact to Boston. But Paula was frantic to get out of the city—it was summer, her mother irascible after the election defeat, garbage ripening in the streets, the subway full of rank and leering men— and the longer she went uptown to face implacable Mrs. Anderson, the more impossible getting out became. She had wandered into a mind system where going to Boston equaled death. She thought she was going crazy.

One day in mid-August Paula shocked herself by informing the voice that this session would be their last. Mrs. Anderson told her she was choosing death over life, sent Paula away with a curse on her head. And although the handshake was businesslike, with polite smiles on both sides, Paula went out into the sticky afternoon feeling doomed.

The feeling lifted; she moved to Boston. But she never forgot Mrs. Anderson and the calm and level voice. It spoke to Paula in moments of confusion or high emotion, insinuating that her premature termination was the cause of her unhappiness (unto death), coming down like tempered steel in the clang of whatever Paula didn't want to know about herself.

Now the voice was telling Paula that married men often became dissatisfied with their lives, especially in a crisis, released their dissatisfaction extramaritally, then returned to the fold with their penises between their legs. It was also common for the third party to imagine that she was the exception, that she had the power to make such a man happy and in doing so also save her own life. This too was delusional, for such a woman was nothing more than the screen on which the man projected his fantasy of the fulfillment that eluded him in real life.

And there was more: Choosing to fall in love with a married man displayed an unconscious aversion to an authentic relationship. Such a woman was compelled to sabotage every possibility of exiting her own aloneness, to which she was addicted. Far from breaking out of an old trap, she was being herself to the hilt. If such a woman was a therapist, it only proved the truism that she could help everyone except herself, see everything and remain blind.

This, Paula was given to know, was the long-awaited curse. It had followed her to Boston after all: The curse was her self.

I know all this, she thought, it's my bread and butter. They don't have anything on me. For so long she had been passing through her days with the thought: *Oh God, send me some love.* Now that it had been sent, should she hand it a Kleenex and talk it out of the office?

Her mind tossed and turned while her body boiled. Under the spell, she overflowed with restless energy. Not knowing what else to do, she poured it into her sessions. When Gladys Dill came in the next morning, Paula knew from her slumped face that things were bad.

"You're depressed today," Paula said at once. Taken aback, Gladys shrugged. "What happened to depress you?"

Gladys started into the litany of chaos and fecklessness, the gas company, Michael's acting out, the job training program she'd dropped out of because day care cost too much. "It's like the littlest thing going to start him off," she said. "He's drinking hard again."

"Has he hit you?"

"Saturday night. And I'm waiting for it again. Could be today, could be tomorrow."

"How is that, waiting for it?"

Gladys looked down at her lap, and up in tears. "I'm so mad at him. He got no *right* doing me like this. If I was a man I'd kick his butt, but I got to take it because. . . ."

Paula leaned forward. She had just had a startling insight. Change happened through action. Talk prepared the action, but then it had to be done. It was so simple. In her excitement she wanted to take Gladys's hand and share this with her.

"Gladys. He doesn't have a right and you don't have to take it. You can get a restraining order."

Gladys stared at her in astonishment.

"James ain't no criminal."

"Battery? That's not a crime?"

Gladys said, almost inaudibly, "Where would I live?"

"He's the one who'd have to leave. He can't come within a hundred feet of you or the house."

Gladys seemed to be picturing James maintaining a distance of a hundred feet. She looked doubtful.

"He'd come back and be so riled up he'd kill me. He *hates* the police."

"Then you're trapped, you're his hostage."

"What can I do?"

Paula made it up as she went along. "Next time you feel threatened, even if he's just yelling at you, tell him that it is unacceptable, and that if he continues to abuse you, you will leave. He has to hear that and believe it because otherwise you're totally powerless and he can brutalize you any way he wants. This is good for James, too. *He* can't stop himself, so you have to lay it down."

"If I leave he'll die. Or kill me."

"He has to know you're a human being!" Paula's face flamed. Why hadn't she said this long ago? "Some things are unacceptable. But you need to do a few things first. Call the police. Not for a re-straining order, OK, but to let them know you might need their help. If you have trouble, call them again and they'll be ready to come right out. Also let your neighbors know, the ones you trust. You've tried to do this by yourself, Gladys, and it's too hard, you need help. And the last thing is, you can call me. You've got the emergency number. If you ever feel at risk, I want you to promise you'll call me. All right?"

Gladys picked at the skin around a bitten-down fingernail. Paula was suddenly stricken with the thought that she'd simply been per-forming for herself—riding her own mood somewhere. None of it had anything to do with the woman sitting here. Then Gladys let her finger go and looked her in the eye.

"Unacceptable," she said as if trying to memorize it. "Right?"

Paula wrote up her notes half-blind with tears.

That afternoon Paula went over the Problem Place's records and discovered that Peter Fine was doing almost no therapeutic work at all. He never seemed to be around, and his salary was over $80,000. At last year's fund-raiser, needlessly catered by Pasta Basta, they had netted barely half the goal. And the cuts in state funding were even more draconian than Fine had suggested. It was gross mis-management. Why didn't the board know these things?

The staff now practiced on a fee basis, and two clinicians had been cut—Philip, and a young MSW who never had a clue about Fine's games. The survivors had to see six clients a day to equal their old pay.

Sparked by passion, a pure, uncomplicated loathing of Fine took possession of Paula. She embraced it happily. He was the corrup-tion that floated to the top of every organization, every boss who took credit for his subordinates' work, put a company car to per-sonal use, flattered the powerful and exploited the weak. His ego was a primal creature driven by an appalling hunger, all the deadlier for being clothed in pudgy softness and positive feelings. And he had failed to take care of his staff. Writing up a new grant proposal between sessions and paperwork, Paula felt as if she were running the Problem Place all by herself.

Half the foundations she sounded had turned out to specialize in the wrong things. She had submitted applications to others, but she sensed that hundreds of nonprofits in Boston and all over the country were lined up ahead of her for money to feed the hungry and shelter the homeless, eliminate prejudice, save afflicted children, develop new food sources. Her proposals were articulate and heartfelt, strengthened by examples from her own caseload, but something was missing. There was nothing very special or hopeful in this work; on paper it looked like sheer maintenance of chronic cases. And these days the long-term mental health of the wretched had come to seem like a luxury. Shouldn't they be disarmed, detoxed, fed, housed, job-trained, and employed first?

Paula knew the argument. On some days she even agreed with it. But at the moment what she needed was a grant.

Three days after her walk along the river with Eric, she was waiting for Fran to vacate the cubicle when Fine came out of his office and into the hallway. As she turned to give his sweater-vested plumpness passage, their eyes met. He looked rapt, like a businessman about to close a deal or a suitor with a marriage proposal out. He flashed a nervous smile. Paula was the Cassandra at his war.

"Hello, Paula," he said cautiously.

"Peter. How's the world out there?"

"Interesting. Very powerful. But you're against all that, aren't you."

"What makes you say that?"

"You think political action is frivolous."

"Not if it does some good."

Fine regarded her with distrustful eagerness. "Something new is going on. Something very exciting."

"You mean, like a trend?"

"A spirit." He smiled meaningfully. "The spirit of something that's been missing in our lives."

She decided not to ask what it was. He held out for about five seconds.

"People out there are longing for community."

She hated the word. It sounded like *nurture, mucus*. It was soft and slimy and coercive. "How can you tell?"

"I've learned more in these groups than in eighteen years of practice. See, we've focused too much on personal change." He was gone, set free from the basement clinic, already addressing a vast audience. "Therapy isolates us, just like the family, the market, technology. You do years of therapy, you find out lots of stuff about yourself—then what? You're still depressed. Because you're still not living in the world. So, bring them together. Mend society and the self at the same time because, *it's the same process*. An unbreakable circle. This is what's new. This is where mass therapy has a place. It should *not* be done in private."

He looked angrily at the closed door of Paula's session room.

"You should not be waiting for someone to come out of there. That's the sickness, right there. It's Freud's bad joke on us. We have a new member, an African, who took about five minutes to clean my head of all that Germanic pseudorationalism they fuck you up with in grad school. He is fantastic. In Africa the healer is a central figure in the community, a teacher. He instructs the people in their infinitude. They change shape. Spirits fuse. No one analyzes guilt and early bowel movements. I've rethought everything."

The shine in his teddy-bear eyes repelled her. "Is this political action, Peter, or self-actualization? Are you sure they go together?"

"Paula, what is going on in your soul?"

"I mean, what is this group actually doing?"

"For starters, we're going to take back that new building on the other side of the Square. We're going to let this city know who owns it."

"It must be gratifying."

"I know you feel contempt."

"You've got to stop assuming things."

"But you might consider that you have your own issues to deal with."

The word fell on her anger like gasoline. "Ah, Peter, it's just one cliché after another."

"Defensive contempt, Paula. Defending from what?"

The door opened. Fran came out with her arm around a grossly overweight young woman, who was crying. Fran looked radiant with triumph.

"Infinitude," Paula said as the cubicle enclosed her. In five minutes she had Earl; then she could go home and check her messages for Eric's call.

fourteen

Eric felt as if he was standing still in a gale. The house swam in plaster dust and sawdust, and his New York flu had turned into one of those colds that hung around all winter, irritating his eyes, closing off his sinuses, muffling the world like a sack dropped over his head. Inwardly, he had gone numb. When the carpenters' hands grew numb or their tool blades blunted, that was when they hurt themselves. He feared acting in this state, like picking up a chisel and gashing himself just for sensation.

All around him life was moving forward. Jane's belly swelled hugely, impossibly. New walls rose and were buttoned up in board, a parade of subcontractors—plumbers, electricians—fitted the baby room with systems of gut and nerve, and under the subfloor a drill's wheeze or man's curse reminded him that they were working down there, in the gloomy brilliance of drop lights, like miners or grave robbers. They emerged through the trap door wiping their knees and palms, complaining of rat noises and a cold stench that Eric couldn't smell.

Their savings were almost gone. What remained of the work would drain away the rest. If there were complications at the hospital, their health plan would leave them with a heavy portion of the bill. Then Jane was going to take eight weeks' maternity leave, unpaid—from the Whitset, with its millions. And the expenses that would start flowing the moment of birth, and only increase in pressure and volume through infancy, childhood, adolescence—beyond imagining.

On his return from New York, Eric had forced himself back to his book. Between Christmas and New Year's he had worked long hours, first in the bedroom until the construction noise became intolerable, then at Widener. He gathered the pages, fragments of some vast and crumbling text written in a language he didn't know, and tried to transform them into a romantic comedy called *Passionate Bards*. He strained his fluey imagination to squeeze out a few drops of the wit that Ann wanted, indulging the notion that the highest form of integrity was selling out.

Soon, though, he remembered that NWC had already written him off. Whatever part he had played in his failure, whatever the reasons, they were going to get rid of him anyway. Ann had given herself an out: Do this impossible thing and there might be a slim chance. So if he kept working beyond any rational purpose, it was in the spirit of someone knowingly violating himself and taking a perverse satisfaction in seeing the job well done.

In the first week of the New Year, with Paula along the river, he set down the load of his book. At once he felt lighter, more hopeful, even a little manic, and as long as he was with her the sensation remained. Later that night, at home, all the years of work, years of wanting what wasn't coming, wasn't available, released themselves in his bones. Exhausted, he went to bed. His sense of loss and shame was so great that only the thought of Paula made it tolerable. There was no question of practical alternatives—another publisher, another book—because he had given it up for her, and without her he would have to carry his work on to its appointed doom.

And yet nothing happened. Life went on as before. He never told Jane the details about New York and she didn't ask for them. "Ann was discouraging," he said, and she replied, "Don't be discouraged too easily," and he said nothing more. Now that the renovation was moving at full speed, walling them off from the world, Jane seemed content, and her contentment made him feel they were strangers living alongside each other—talking about the news on the radio, the Silvers' move, the birth classes that were about to start. They didn't argue. They were pleasant and respectful. But all the energy of their marriage was gone. It amazed him that Jane didn't feel it too.

Maybe she did and expected nothing more, wanted nothing more. Their kisses were brief and open-eyed, and their night of lovemaking had not been repeated. She no longer pressed him for enthusiasm about the baby; it was her concern. As long as the construction was going on and his share of the money coming in, he owed her nothing. It was terrible to see how easily they lived together this way, how comfortably.

He tried to examine his situation as if it were someone else's. It looked like this: pregnant wife, conjugal estrangement, failed career, other woman. In this light, his longings struck him as contemptible. Yet when he thought of Paula, he didn't feel contemptible at all. In his wallet he still had the bank receipt with her number, like a secret key, and sometimes he touched his back pocket as if he were giving her a private signal. Alone, he studied the receipt, coaxed from it the image of her face, which was bound up with the clean, cold smell of evening and the river, the merganser's elegant neck.

The impulse that made him take her hand had shocked him. It had felt like life itself, moving through him. Yet even in that moment, a voice in his head—a dry, severe compound of Iowa maleness—told him that eventually he would have to subdue himself to circumstances. Most of the time he lived by that maxim. His one revolt had been his decision to write, and now it mocked him. Falling into an affair would be a far greater revolt, and yet he also knew that the moment with Paula by the river was the best thing about him—cheerful, loving, generous in spirit. When he called the number on the bank receipt, this hidden self and the official one would fuse.

"Jim, no, please," Frank said. "Don't start on your group."

"I won't proselytize," Newburg said. "I'll just point out that you're part of a community whether you like it or not."

The crew—minus Joe, who always seemed to vanish in thin air at the end of the day—had invited the client to join them for beers in Frank's crowded apartment in North Cambridge. Eric had been grateful to be asked, and surprised. Class stood between him and the crew—despite their steady jobs and his money squeeze. He was college educated, reproducing late, hiring labor to create a suitable environment for his baby.

"What group?" Eric asked.

"You know," Frank told him, winking, "the blue signs."

Newburg said, "It's way beyond the signs."

"I'd like to hear, Jim," Eric said.

In Newburg's account, The Community sounded like a cross between a block watch, a nonviolent militia, and a twelve-step group. And yet they had vast ambitions, a sense of historical destiny. By his second porter, Eric found it all absurd and intriguing.

"Joe, your African laborer?"

"Joe, our African laborer," Newburg said, "is a shaman—a magician. He mesmerized everybody in the room."

"What did he say?"

"He just talked about . . . changing shape. In Africa he had these spiritual powers. He made everybody in the room feel that if we come together, the possibilities are endless."

"Personally," Frank said, "I think there's something not quite solid about young Joe. He'll catch me looking at him and jump out of his skin. My theory is he got himself in trouble back home— poked the chief's daughter—and came here as a stowaway on one of those Liberian-registered freighters."

"He won't talk to me either," Eric said. "I don't think he likes me. I thought he was different with you."

"You're both wrong," Newburg said. "The problem is our own isolation. We need to be more connected."

"I've got all the connections I can handle." Frank waved his bottle at the noise of three children in the next room. "The Community isn't going to feed my kids, Jim. The bottom line is if I don't do it I'm fucked and so's my family."

"You were fucked until Jim hired you," said Dennis, the plumber. "Didn't you collect benefits most of last year, Frank? I mean, be honest, the taxpayers bailed you."

"Being unemployed wasn't Frank's fault," Newburg said. "We're conditioned to think we have to do it alone. Believe me, it's a cocaine mindset. Instead of looking at someone and saying: Hey, that could've been me. He's my responsibility."

Driving home, Eric found that he was drunk and elated. Beyond his windshield Central Square loomed in the cheap chiaroscuro of streetlights. The spirit of Newburg's African laborer presided over the Square. Eric had locked himself away from it in a room with rats and his dead imagination. The walls were built of words that weighed like bricks. Soon they would be mortared with baby shit, and tons of dynamite wouldn't blast them.

The revenge of out on in. She was shrewd, she saw straight through him. On the other side of the walls, she was waiting in Central Square.

By the time he got home, he knew what he was going to do. He wouldn't have to go all the way to Africa and a clay road by a river, because Africa had come to him. He would write about Joe, the magician, hero to The Community. Somehow, the way to Paula went through Joe.

On Massachusetts Avenue, near a discount liquor store where a roving band of drunks was often encamped, the Harp & Plume guarded its modest fame against the gentrification and decay that closed in from Harvard and Central Squares. Its clientele was neither monied professionals nor downbound boozers, but a self-consciously bohemian crowd of hippies-turned-architects, middle-aged freelancers, divorced soccer fans, and unemployed wits. In asking Paul Duffy to meet him at the Harp, Eric recognized something of Jerry Silver's secondhand attitude: He liked the idea more than the sticky, oaken place itself. He had chosen it because this meeting was personally risky. He would need a distraction, and the subject of their mutual friend provided one.

Eric wasn't surprised to be kept waiting. But when the Napoleonic overcoat and excited crimson face breezed through the street door, Duffy came over to his table in a profusion of apparently sincere apology.

"Eric, how's the life?"

"Except for my annual winter cold, I've been great. You?"

"Great. Things are great."

Eric tried to gauge Duffy's appetite for humiliation. He appeared to have come without malice.

"Are you still with Heather?"

Duffy feigned horror. "Heather? Oh no. No no no. Heather was dangerous. Needy feminist. Weirdness in the sack—wouldn't permit penetration, said sex was 'sacred.' No, I didn't see Heather again after that night at Jerry's." With a flick of the fingers Heather vanished.

Eric saw no point in delaying. "I'd appreciate it if you'd speak to your friend at *Edge* for me."

"You have something?"

"An idea. I think it's sort of current."

"Great. I'll tell Feloni we're friends and that I admire your work."

Eric thanked him. He hadn't dreamed of getting off so easily.

"I hope it's not too serious."

"Oh no."

"You have to understand, George Feloni is not a literary man. He has zero power at *Edge* without Charles McGarry. McGarry has to sign off on everything. When you write for them, three or four illiterates have a perfect right to fuck up your prose before it sees print. Italics, underline, all caps—there is not a premium on quality writing."

"Got it." Eric wouldn't let himself be faced down.

"And your cooperation will be rewarded to the tune of a dollar fifty a word plus expenses. For a midsized piece that's a lot of candy. But if it doesn't work out, their kill fee's only 10 percent."

"Fine."

"So you finished your novel?"

"I've . . . put it aside for now."

"Well, pick it up again. We can't lose a fine craftsman."

"I think we're dealing with your market and Zeitgeist."

Duffy laughed. "Oh no! They got you too."

Eric made a move for his coat and was finally snagged by the look he'd been expecting.

"Just curious. Did your wife change her mind about *Edge*?"

The tired euphemisms shuffled through Eric's mind. He discarded them; Duffy wouldn't be fooled. "We need the money."

But this wasn't the whole truth either.

"Jerry's out in Lincoln missing this place." Duffy scanned the premises as he stood up. "A real sentimentalist, isn't he?"

"How do you mean?"

"Jerry likes it here," Duffy said, "because it's a losers' bar."

Edge was undergoing a heavily publicized identity crisis. For years it had cornered the Boston market in sophisticated consumption; but declining ad revenues, changing demographics, and aggressive competition that outslicked *Edge*'s legendary slickness had forced the monthly to make a bold play for a new seriousness. The cover slogan would be changed from "The Best Revenge" to "The Way We Live Now." The barrier between high and pop culture would be assaulted on every side. The front of the magazine would feature short profiles of newsmakers, artists, idea men, change agents, all photographed in casualwear.

It was an opportune moment for a new writer to come in with a pitch. And to his great surprise, Eric was invited one bitterly cold afternoon for a chat with George Feloni.

Edge had moved from its Beacon Hill brownstone to a new granite-and-glass palace on Boylston Street. In the atrium a Hispanic worker was scrubbing the rim of a fountain. A security guard took Eric's name. In the elevator he was beset by the notion that an instinct for self-sabotage was compelling him to repeat his afternoon at NWC. But this time he was shown quickly and courteously past a framed poster announcing "The New *Edge*: The Way We Live Now" and down to Feloni's large, neat office.

The senior editor was on the phone. He gestured for Eric to sit. Feloni's handsome face, with its aquiline nose, was deeply tanned, his thick black hair going impressively gray. His suit was European-cut, ash-colored and pink-striped. A scarlet handkerchief that matched his tie dangled from the double-breasted pocket. In the middle of Boston winter, Feloni was the picture of Mediterranean health and elegance.

"At his desk. Something writerly, an Underwood or whatever. But get Santa Fe in there." The office was perched high above Back Bay, but Feloni's heavy nasal voice lingered in East Boston. "No Indians outside, that's way too obvious. Look, big picture: white guy writer, sensitive but rugged. Think Harrison Ford, Costner. Fax it. Later." Hanging up, he engaged Eric man-to-man in a sardonic smile. "Photographers—zero sense of originality."

Eric shook his head to express agreement, ironic amusement, whatever was called for. Feloni didn't seem to intend any irony.

"It's my pleasure, Eric. A rec from Paul is money in the bank. That guy is pure writer, from his cranium to his phallus." Feloni leaned back and put his fingertips together. "Let me hear you talk about yourself. Describe yourself as writer."

The dropped article was troubling, not just grammatically but morally. Yet as Eric set about to describe himself "as writer," he realized that it was a con game and his only responsibility was to play it well. After all, he had no track record with George Feloni. There would be no more torments over working in his own grain.

The thought was liberating. He launched into his self-presentation with great creative energy. Yet the writer he described wasn't wholesale invention or fantasy collage. Given limitless choice, he chose to be recognizably himself, but himself as he wanted to be, his best self, his highest aspirations. And the portrait so stirred him that he suddenly felt sadness come on, wondering what had stood between this vision and flesh, why it seemed possible only in the context of a fraud.

As Feloni listened his eyes wandered sideways. He seemed to be trying to fit Eric-Barnes-as-writer into writing-as-he-knew-it, which meant into *Edge*. There was some apparent difficulty that augured trouble. A paradox—you didn't want a track record, but you needed a handle.

Feloni was nodding without conviction. "Sort of a . . . sort of Midwestern Faulkneresque."

In desperation Eric reached into the depths of his career and fished from the jacket of his second novel a wet, decaying blurb. "James McWhirter said my work deals with ordinary lives caught in the tides of history."

Feloni's nod began to take on more vigor. He looked happier. He was smiling. "Good. That's good. OK. Now tell me what you want to do for the new *Edge*."

Eric kept his pitch simple: He would write about a new grassroots movement that combined citizen anger and alienation with psychic healing. His background research suggested that this movement spoke to the isolation of contemporary Americans, the longing for a larger, common purpose. The article would focus on an African magician who had captured the movement's imagination.

Halfway through, Feloni's attention disintegrated. He pulled out his handkerchief and began wrapping and unwrapping his left fist, like a boxer. Something had gone wrong. Eric had set out to be witty and hip, but he'd gotten caught up in what he was saying and talked himself into sincerity. He'd forgotten Duffy's warning, and his voice rose as he described how Joe's smile gave people the sense that they could transform their lives. By the end Feloni was punching his right palm in slow motion.

"So you want to write about this community." Eric nodded. "And the idea is . . . community. The common—communal. The community, right?" Eric nodded again. "What's this about a magician?"

"Actually, it's interesting—he's working days on a construction crew in my house. There's a sort of Bruce Wayne/Batman quality," Eric said hopefully. "Hidden powers. On the surface you wouldn't know."

Feloni was unwrapping his fist. "Why do we care about this?"

Eric lunged. "Because it says something about the way we live now. Something funny and serious and uniquely American."

Feloni didn't answer at once. He was folding his handkerchief back into his breast pocket. "It could be a go. As you know, we're transitioning into something new. Fax me a written proposal. If it's for us, you'll get a contract in a few days."

Eric realized that Feloni had no idea what the new seriousness of *Edge* meant. He would have to check with Charles McGarry, his rumpled and seersuckered boss—utterly mangling the proposal. Feloni's standing was shaky. He dressed too well, his office was too orderly, his eyes never smiled, he'd been too eager to meet this unknown. Eric recognized a guy on the way down when he saw one.

"Let me just suggest," Feloni said as Eric started to get up. His voice was louder, reasserting control. "I've seen pieces like this go down in flames when they're not reader-friendly. I want people to open the magazine and say: *This* is the one piece I've got to read. The lead should grab their shirt. Give it spin. Know what I mean?"

Eric started to nod, then he said, "I'm not sure."

Feloni was impatient. "Spin. Some juice. Have fun with it, be droll. Don't sound better than our readers—that's arrogance. The bottom line is: The reader's always right."

"I can't believe you didn't tell me this," Jane said.

"I'm telling you now. I just told you. I've been trying to tell you for weeks."

Eric and Jane were driving home from birth class at Brigham and Women's Hospital. With other couples, they had watched a video that promised a birthing experience suitable to their needs, and then he had practiced saying "Push" over her prone body, with her knees up. Afterward they had all held hands in a circle and visualized healthy babies.

"That you were going to drop it?"

"You weren't listening. You were too distracted."

The windshield was fogging up and the fan was turned on high, so that both of them had to raise their voices. Eric scraped the frost with his fingernails, showering ice over the dashboard, then rubbed the glass with the heel of his hand. He was trying to maneuver through the streets of Mission Hill, which were badly lit, unfamiliar, and unsafe.

"Would you stop and pay attention for a second?" Jane shouted. "'Future Mom and Dad Killed on Way Home from Baby Class.'"

She reached across the dashboard, her belly pressed against the gear shift, and wiped the glass with awkward furious circles of her palm. Their hands collided. He refused to give ground; she jerked hers away.

"What is wrong with you?" He didn't answer. "I fail to understand you, Eric. You're walking away from it?"

"I'm doing what any responsible father-to-be would do. You ought to be delighted."

"That you're abandoning years of work?"

He switched from defrost to heat and turned the fan down. In a few minutes the car would overheat; he would adjust toward cool, then switch back to defrost and turn the fan on high again.

"Those months of research? All that hard work?"

"It's an act of sanity."

Jane turned away, exasperated. She turned back. "OK, take a break from it. A month or two. Finish after the baby comes."

"What do you propose we do for money in the meantime?"

"Frankly, that's not what worries me most. I don't like to see you quit."

The word rubbed a deep place in him that was still raw. "Last month, money was all you worried about."

"I was worried, who wouldn't be? It wasn't all. This is far worse."

"It's not a scandal, Jane. Things don't work out—it happens. I don't know why you're being so alarmist."

"What about full-time status at the college? You used to talk about that a lot. Now it's going to be impossible."

"I might even be let go."

He knew that his casualness seemed perverse and was driving her away.

"Eric, you sacrificed a lot to be a serious writer. And frankly, I did too. For some reason you're not admitting it but this is catastrophe. For you and us. You know that, don't you?"

He took a breath and swallowed. "Jane, I don't think you know what it's like to work day in and day out when you know you're going to fail. To watch years go wasted. I'm not going to explain myself."

"Why?" She was critical, unyielding. "Why are you going to fail?"

"Because Ann Jenkins says so."

Jane sat back impatiently. "That's your paranoia talking. Ann wouldn't say that. She's too practical."

They were approaching a line of cars at a red light. He waited until the last moment, then hit the brakes hard.

"Listen to me, Jane. When you don't earn, they throw you out. Ann made it very clear that this is what I count for at NWC." His thumb and index finger formed an O. "She told me to start looking for other work. They're getting rid of me."

"I don't believe it. You said she asked you to make some changes."

"They were impossible."

"What were the changes?" He refused to answer. "Why can't you try to do the book the way Ann wants? Maybe the changes would improve it. They wouldn't just get rid of you if you really tried."

"You're not hearing me, Jane. They already have, and I'm not going to give them an excuse by fucking it up Ann's way. I can't be what I'm not."

"Why can't you compromise?"

"You won't let me! I've been trying—you don't know." He had planned to command her assent without asking for it. But he never imagined the tone of her response, and this challenge in the flesh was undermining him. "Look what's happened! I'm someone I'm not, I want out before it suffocates me."

"This is just wild talk. Tomorrow you'll be reasonable again, then we'll discuss it."

He slammed his fist against the steering wheel. "You cannot understand me!"

"You're right, that's true." His loss of control only made her calmer. "Eric, has it occurred to you that this is terrible timing? We're supposed to be settling down as a family. Instead everything's going to pieces."

"I told you. I've signed a contract with *Edge* for five thousand dollars."

"What do I tell our friends?"

"You tell them whatever the hell you want."

"Just yesterday Rachel asked about your work. Next time what do I say? 'Oh, Eric's not doing that anymore'?"

The road was a blur of headlights. Imagining the two women gossiping about him, in the soft secure hush of the Whitset Foundation, he had to grip the wheel so that he wouldn't reach across and choke her. "Would that embarrass you? Your husband isn't the success you bargained for? Is it going to be hard to face your friends?"

"Do you blame me for being unhappy about this?"

"I blame you for wanting impossible things of me." Knowing that this was barely half-fair only inflamed his desire to wreck everything, make her see and regret. He wanted to force the confrontation onto the elemental level where his fury and despair might have some release. "I blame you. Rachel! The Silvers have no idea what this book cost me."

Jane made a noise of impatience; it came close to contempt. "I'll be honest, Eric. You could be tougher. I'm sorry if that hurts you. My father once held down *three* jobs. That's pressure. Yes, you've had more than your share of bad luck. But you make certain choices, you tough them out. Instead of giving up and going to write for a sleazy place like *Edge*, which is very hard for me to understand. It sounds to me like a great way not to face your situation."

"I've faced my situation long enough. In fact, I've had my face right in it. I've had the taste of it in my mouth."

"It won't work out. *Edge* won't take what you write."

"*Edge* is reinventing itself. Which is every American's right, including mine."

"What do you care about this ridiculous group anyway? And this African on the crew? They don't mean anything to you."

His new project threatened her—he exulted in the knowledge. "How do you know what they mean to me? They mean a lot."

"It must be humiliating, Eric. You used to be better than *Edge*."

He could hardly see. The windshield was fogging up again—he had forgotten the defroster. They were along the river now, on the approach to Storrow Drive, preparing to join it on a sharp blind curve, and instead of slowing down he was speeding into the merge. Out of darkness and fog a car blew past with its horn blaring.

"Jesus!" Jane screamed.

He grabbed the window handle and rolled it down. A blast of cold air hit his face as he leaned out into the night.

"Fucking sonofabitch!"

"Eric! It was your fault."

"Everything is."

At home he retreated to the baby room out of mindless habit, like a bear looking for its old ground where a highway has been built. Lying on the plywood floor, he tried to lose himself in a nineteenth-century novel, but in an hour he only managed two paragraphs. He could hear Jane putting dishes away. Through the wall he felt her unhappiness, which she was fighting off with small tasks. He saw the look on her face: lips set, emotion showing only in the color of her cheeks. Her head would be bent to the work, bangs falling across her eyes so that no one could peer in. He knew these things better than his own features. Every muscle of her face had become the repository of a thousand memories, eliciting from him the involuntary reflex of years. And what did she feel? Defiance? Regret?

It was a stand-off. Neither of them would speak first for fear of seeming to admit wrong and show weakness. Both of them hating it, ready to be kind and tender as soon as the other gave in, but refusing to be the one.

What finally drove him out of the study was a fear that he was doing this on purpose, willing himself to feel coldness in order to be given a pretext.

He went to the refrigerator and was confronted with the difficulty of finding something simple to eat. Jane sat at the table with a book.

"Do you want something?" he asked without turning around.

"No."

The overture deserved more. He resolved to say nothing else. He found a hunk of cheese wrapped in plastic, cut away the mold and sliced it on the countertop, and began popping crackers and cheese in his mouth. She continued reading, her back turned.

He could stand here for hours and she wouldn't turn around.

"Have you decided I'm unfit for conversation?"

She moved slowly to face him, closing her book. He saw the title: *We're Pregnant*. On the cover sat the usual smiling, blue-eyed wonder. A humiliating jealousy stabbed him. Instead of brooding about their marriage like him, she had been staring at the picture of a lover who was arranging to come and stay for a long time. And for this lover, Jane felt unconditional love. She wouldn't demand that this lover be someone he couldn't. Instead of pointing out every imperfection and failing, she would accept and love them all. The lover had turned her against her husband.

"Don't be so melodramatic," she said.

Something hard and callous began to grow in him. He welcomed it. He didn't want anything to soften it—he knew that even now a kind word from her would melt him.

"You are incapable of focusing on our marriage," he said.

"And you are incapable of focusing on the fact that we're about to have a baby."

"Which is more important?"

He had never seen such open dislike in her face. "I don't see how you can ask that."

"And I should shut up and be a good soldier."

"Eric—" Anger flashed in her eyes, and his heartbeat answered it. She turned back to her book. "You can do whatever you want."

He went back into his former study. He tried reading for another hour, with the same success, until he heard her getting ready for bed. By the time he looked in, the light was out. He made out the shape of Jane's body lying far over on her side of the bed. He closed the door and went down the hall into the living room. He picked up the phone and took out the crumpled bank receipt from his wallet. He looked at the faint scrawled number, although he knew it by heart.

He could still put the phone back. He could stop himself right now from invading her life. She was going about her nightly routine, brushing her hair, listening to music. And he wanted to be part of it. He wondered how much happiness anyone had a right to expect.

"Hello?"

"Paula, it's Eric." He kept his voice low. "Did I wake you up?"

"No, I was reading."

Her voice was tense. The sound of it stirred his desire—not just for her, but for peace and rest.

"How's your cold?" she asked.

"My head's full of cotton, but aside from that. . . ."

There was a silence on her end. He began to worry.

"Paula?"

"Still here."

"I was waiting for you to analyze my cold."

"Well, what don't you want to experience?"

"Sometimes snot is just snot."

He heard the music of her nervous laughter. "And sometimes it's not."

"Rats, sewage, hammers, drills. Everything and everyone, including me." He hesitated. "Except the sound of your voice."

When she didn't answer he thought he'd gone too far.

"Good," she finally said.

"And you?"

"Am I glad to hear my voice?"

"You know."

Another pause. "I was waiting. It's been ten days."

"I've had to figure some things out."

The smallness and self-loathing of an hour ago fell away as if they were someone else's, an impostor's, not this person who was hungry for contact, for the richness with which intimacy filled the blood.

They made plans to meet on Thursday evening.

"Shall I come to your apartment?" He hoped he wasn't being presumptuous.

"It's kind of a dump. And my neighbor's a snoop. A friend gave me her keys to feed her cats while she's at her fiancé's. We could meet there." She told him where the place was, sounding as if the idea had just occurred to her. But he could tell that she had planned it, and this delighted him. Then she hurried off the phone; he hardly had a chance to say good-bye.

He sat still until his heartbeat slowed. Then he went into the bedroom, undressed, climbed under the covers, and tried to fall asleep without wishing Jane good night for the first time in their lives.

fifteen

Missy Standish opened the door in a green spandex workout suit, then disappeared. Joe had the house to himself. Newburg's punch list took him from room to room like a treasure hunt. He installed glass knobs on cabinet doors, polished the table where the Chinese lion carved in green stone lay, touched up paint on the window trim above the sink that looked out on a frozen pond. A length of time had been written beside each task. When he checked himself against the clock, he found that he was ahead of his boss's schedule.

The strange thing was that some of the tasks didn't need doing. The bathroom doorstop was already in place. Holes were predrilled for the brass toilet-paper holder, so installing it took five minutes against Newburg's fifteen. The whole downstairs was the same: sills that didn't need cleaning, weatherstripping already lining the sashes, touch-up spots he couldn't find. He was far out in front of the timetable and it made him uneasy, like noticing there's no one else on the road going in your direction.

He followed the list upstairs, his hammer dangling from the nail belt like a sword. Silence poured down from the cathedral ceiling. Looking up, he noticed that the highest skylight was streaked with white and gray birdshit. Maybe no one would ever clean it off.

The last room on the list was the master bedroom. The door was ajar. He knocked lightly twice: no answer. He stepped inside.

The shades were drawn, the room was dark. Missy was lying on the king-size bed, one arm flung over her eyes. Joe imagined her naked, and the painting in Newburg's hall came back to him. But Missy's spandex sparkled in the light from the doorway.

She murmured something.

"Sorry," he said, retreating.

"Joe." A command. He stopped in the doorway. "Do you have work in here?"

"The closet hardware."

She sighed, and her bound, flattened breasts filled and emptied. Her legs were bare from midthigh, the knees dimpled. "Go ahead."

By the closet light, he installed locksets and magnetic stops. No one had predrilled these holes. Wool-smelling garments draped his head and made it difficult to work.

He cleaned up and packed his toolbox and started to leave.

"Joe."

She had lifted her arm, dampness shone on her cheeks.

"Are you all right, Missy?"

"I'm very depressed."

He waited.

"Why?"

She laughed wetly and sniffled. "Why, these men ask, even the African. There is no why here, Joe."

Something made him feel that she had prepared these words, as if she were the last item on his punch list. There was a smell of set-up in the room. He moved toward the door.

"Actually, Joe, there are a few whys." Missy struggled up against her pillows. "Since you ask—and your concern is touching and appreciated. Ted doesn't ask anymore. There's a why: Ted. I bet one thing African women don't suffer from is sexual neglect. Their men haven't been completely feminized by absent fathers, they don't divert their libidos into really fascinating things like Microsoft Windows. There's something to be said for basic human needs. Once Africa gets indoor plumbing, you'll learn all about sexual dysfunction."

The room was growing lighter. Missy's eyes were puffy and smeared with mascara, but talking seemed to calm her.

"Another why is this backache in the face of which both my chiropractor and acupuncturist are helpless. I'm sure my depression seems utterly trivial to you. My hot-shit therapist thinks I invent needs to get the attention I missed as a child. I can't stop Africa's bleeding, Joe, do you hold that against me?"

"Of course not."

"Thank you." She patted the comforter. "Come on. I don't bite, I just gnaw. I'm about to tell you the biggest why of all and I don't want to shout to be heard."

As soon as Joe sat down he felt himself sink into the comforter and mattress as if into sand or swamp. Sliding toward the center of the bed, his back encountered something solid: Missy's leg.

"I'm depressed because of you! You're like the last soldier to pull out and I'm the sixteen-year-old girl, *la jolie jeune fille française* whose life was so exciting with foreign troops around, dancing every night to Glenn Miller and the Inkspots. But now they're gone and it's back to her boring life and her boyfriend the agronomy student. Instead of a new me, I get the world's funkiest, priciest cage. I'll bet you came here for freedom and all that bull, but it's a *trap*. So boo-hoo for Mrs. Ted Standish. Do you have any idea what I'm talking about?"

She lay there, spangled green, hair spread across the pillow. Everything about her seemed soft, boneless, the flesh on her face, the breasts and thighs, as if she were part of the bed and only her voice was solid. Her voice was a rope that she had tied around his waist. He wished the lights were on. If the lights were on he could get out.

"Please get me the box of Kleenex on top of the toilet."

Joe struggled off the bed. When he returned with the box, Missy was sitting up straight, brushing hair from her face. She wiped her cheeks and blew her nose. "Jim told me all about you. Don't be modest, this case is way too urgent. He said back in Africa you healed people."

Joe knew it was going to be all right.

"Yes. It is true."

"Heal me! Can't you? You have a lot of power because you don't say much. The rest of us yammer away—it's our weakness."

There had been a night when he ran a malarial fever and Amouzou had boiled up foraged leaves in a brew thickened with ground root and bushrat lungs. The magician chanted a prayer, cut Joe's shoulders with a razor, invoked the ancestors, cursed the evil eye, and sent him home. By morning his fever was down, but then it spiked again. One of the cuts had gone septic and he had to be given antibiotics at the clinic.

"I must prepare in your kitchen."

"Thank you, Joe," she whispered.

Downstairs, he rummaged through the new maple cabinets. Randomly he grabbed oregano, grated ginger, and peppermint tea, which he steeped together in hot water, spiked with amaretto from the liquor cabinet. He poured the mixture into a National Public Radio mug. It smelled nothing like Amouzou's forest broth. On the other hand, it didn't matter. If Missy thought he had the power, then he did. That was what Amouzou always said: Their minds, it happens in their minds. In Missy's mind, Joe was going to heal her.

He was staring through the kitchen window at the frozen pond. What if he had the power after all—*really* had it? What if the power was a ghost that had left the body in the tomb and gone into his, because he had given the body burial, because he was the only one who didn't want Amouzou to be killed?

Then he wouldn't have to worry about being found out. He wouldn't even be lying, only about details. What if it *were* true? He could take this whole thing to a higher level. He could go upstairs and heal Missy. He could heal anyone—the people from The Community, anyone.

The excitement of this discovery almost made Joe spill the cure. It must be the cure because the power was inside him. In his blood and breath.

Missy was sitting cross-legged on the bed.

"I'm thrilled," she said. "I await your instructions."

Joe sank into the comforter, careful to keep the mug steady. It was burning his knuckles but the pain didn't even feel like pain now.

"First close your eyes."

Missy closed them and smiled. "I love it."

"Tell me the names of your grandfathers."

Her sightless face frowned. "Really? On my mother's side he was a crazy old inventor, and on my father's side he worked for Aetna. They're both dead."

"Say their names."

"Jack Fogarty and Crawford Tilden."

"Say Grandfather Jack and Grandfather Crawford."

"Grandfather Jack and Grandfather Crawford." She giggled. "Sorry, I haven't thought about them in years."

"Be among us."

"Oh!" Missy was delighted. "Be among us."

"You've neglected them, Missy."

"God, can you tell?"

"Of course." Her spirit was a little creature cupped in his hands—he could stroke it, or crush it. The power was an awesome thing and he felt humbled. He promised Amouzou that he would only do good with it. "They give you life and strength, but they need to be cared for." She didn't answer. "You mustn't think so much of yourself."

Her mouth opened to object. "I'm so sick of myself!"

"Because your spirit is empty, like a drum that cannot talk."

Amouzou would have her now, take possession, shout a command, and Missy would fall on the bed, snapping her jaws like a crocodile or snorting like a bush pig.

Joe didn't think he could do that. That was Amouzou and Africa. There was a limit to the power here and he would stay inside the limit because it was working, he felt it working.

"You live in a beautiful house. You spent your husband's money to make it more beautiful. But your drum is silent. Why?"

"This is very hard for me, Joe."

"You wanted to be healed."

"I know," she murmured.

"Repeat what I say: My house is hollow without love."

"My house is hollow without love."

"I will not feel sorry for myself."

In the middle of repeating it, Missy's voice broke.

"Instead I will love."

"Instead I will love."

"You are living for yourself. At your age, an African woman has eight or nine children. You have none."

"Children—oh God. Ted says he wants them. Joe, I'm afraid I'll be a lousy mother. I'm afraid I'll go crazy here alone with them, feeling totally suicidal with *Sesame Street* on."

"Call on your ancestors for help."

She took a breath. "Grandfather Jack . . . Grandfather Crawford . . . help me. I know I'm selfish. Make me a better person. Bring us children. Make me a good mother. I really would like to care about other people. Show me how. I'm sorry for neglecting you."

When he brought the mug to her face, Missy opened her eyes. "Oh!" She inhaled the vapors. He might have put in too much ginger. "I didn't expect that."

"How is your back, Missy?"

She stared at him. "I can't feel it! Oh my God—you *are* a magician."

Joe was so grateful that he had to stifle a laugh. "Yes."

She accepted the mug in both hands, cradling it, sipping deeply, and came up coughing. "Sorry, I'm so blasphemous." She cleared her throat. "It tastes like Africa, like trees in Africa. Pure and clean and healthy."

"How do you feel now?"

"Like firing my therapist."

The way she said this alarmed him. It was her other voice, the one that had tied the rope around his waist. She reached for his hand and stroked the length of it with her fingertips.

"You're great with a sander." She lifted his hand to her lips, but instead of kissing the palm she took his middle finger in her mouth. "My turn to heal you."

She eased him down and he sank deep into the bed, watching as she undressed him. She made a game of it, changing pace, pulling the springy hairs around his navel, raising her eyebrows. He was naked; she was still wearing her workout suit.

She went away and he lay smelling her shampooed hair on the pillow, as if part of her had stayed behind. He was struggling now to hold onto the calm, strong Joe, the Joe who had healed her, because the rope was pulling him down.

When Missy came back, her spandex was gone. But she didn't act modest or coy—her nakedness was a fact, without meaning for him; she was a woman walking naked through her own house. She took hold of him. "Good boy." She began fitting a condom over him as if she were dressing a child. "No offense, but you're from the hot zone."

Her body was soft but hard at the joints, and as she rode him her grimaces turned ugly. She wasn't aware of being observed; her pleasures were all private, even when she brought his hands to her breasts. She came quickly, before he was able to, and then she rolled off and looked at her watch.

"Jim should be here in ten minutes." She kneeled above him and a smile played on her lips. "You knew I hand-fed that list to him."

"I knew," Joe lied.

"God, what a cliché!" She took his penis with the condom on it in her hand. "Workman slash housewife? White black sex thing? Come on, you've heard of that stuff in Africa."

Joe was still struggling when he felt a dream-weakness come over him. His muscles turned to liquid; it was like feeling himself die. She'd had the power all along. Not him—her. He wanted to take her hand away but he didn't have the strength.

"Hey, what's this? I thought you came. God, how selfish—guess you'll have to come back and have it cured another time. Well, look, I'm not going to send you out like this."

She peeled off the condom and began stroking him, but he went lifeless in her hand. The chafing only dulled sensation.

"Mm mm mm." She pretended to be cross, like a mother. "Look at this. That's what you get for coming to America."

His mouth tasted sour, and the nerves along the back of his

neck burned. He wanted to cover himself but he was afraid to move. He lay absolutely still. If he moved a muscle, he would smash something.

This was the point of bringing him to her house, into her room: to show that he was still nothing but Joe.

"OK." She released him. "Any time you want to finish this, you know where to find me."

Joe went into the bathroom and ran water in the sink. He doused his face and tried to wash his groin, keeping his eyes from the mirrors because the sight of a hundred Joes would sicken him and he would have to break them all.

When he went back into the bedroom, Missy had her robe on. While he was dressing the doorbell rang.

"Your ride. Hey, why so pale and wan, fond lover?"

Joe shook his head.

"Did I hurt you?"

He looked away.

"Come here, sweet love."

Stepping toward her, Joe detached from himself the way characters in movies sometimes step out of their own bodies—a transparent image leaving the original—so that now he was watching himself stand by the bed. What he saw was the African man he had become, but now he, Joe, had no claim on that man's victories. It was just a body standing there, its spirit poured out.

It wasn't him but the African she pulled down into a tender kiss, the African she called sweet love again, the African who left the room carrying his toolbox and descended the stairs.

At the bottom of the stairs, on the polished black table, the Chinese lion crouched in green stone. Joe stopped on the last stair and reached down to cover it with his hand. The surface was smooth and cool. Touching it calmed him. The power had to have gone somewhere—maybe it had gone into the lion. He lifted it, felt its heaviness, imagined it in his coat pocket.

When Joe lived in San Francisco, there was a man who decided to destroy him. His name was Clark, and he managed the Kinko's where Joe worked. Clark was a friend of a girl in the film group who'd found Joe the job. He had a fat pink neck. From day one, Clark's little eyes said he wasn't fooled by Joe's new pencil-line mustache and Oakland cool. "So you were down with the gang, Joe?" Clark said. "Did you, like, kill anybody?" He called Joe "J.G.," for Junior Godfather, and Joe imagined shoving Clark's head into the paper feeder, saw the retrieval tray filling with color copies, the same flattened face fifty, a hundred times, each one pink and laughing.

When the film group started making their next movie, Joe wasn't cast. One day Clark slipped Joe a note: He had done a background check and discovered that Joe was from the peninsula, had two dead foster parents and a G.E.D. At the end of the day, Joe waited for Clark in the stockroom and jumped him, wrestling his fat body to the floor. Clark's eyes had become big, the terror in them felt so gratifying that Joe found his hand in a fist above his head and knew if he started he wouldn't stop. He ran out of the stockroom, leaving Clark on the floor screaming threats. He went to the register, wanting the feel of money in his hands. He took everything.

That night, from the grave, his foster mother scolded him. He told her that she didn't understand, he couldn't just return the money and pray to Jesus. Jesus hadn't spoken to him since his foster parents' death. Jesus hadn't protected him from a man of no account who decided to wipe him out for fun. Within a week, Joe was flying to Africa to plant trees for an organization that didn't require previous experience. He clutched the bills in his pocket as hard as he'd held the money his mother gave him in the bus station.

The green lion was still in his hand. At the end of the hall, Jim Newburg stood outlined in winter sunlight on the other side of the front door. It was cast fiberglass, translucent from the inside; from outside it was opaque. Joe opened his toolbox and put the green lion inside.

That night, a man in a blue knit cap was leaning on the front counter in the lobby of the Y, talking to the deskman. Joe had somehow known that Kevin would be here.

"Hey hey hey! Just the guy I wanted to see. Still working, huh?"

"Still."

"Some guys got all the luck. I was hoping you'd show. I want to make an offer." Kevin looked at the deskman, a light-skinned black man with plump cheeks and sleepy eyes. "I'm just going up for a few minutes, J.B. Don't call the cops or nothing, *uh-uh-uh-uh.*"

To Joe's surprise, J.B. buzzed them into the residents' quarters.

"The common room is on the second floor," Joe said.

"No can do. This is private. Got to be your room. 318, right?"

"How did—"

"J.B. and I used to be associates."

Joe had a corner room with two windows—one looked along an alley toward the traffic on Mass. Avenue, the other gave out onto a rooftop jogging track that no one used in the winter. The room was no wider than the length of a metal bed against the wall. There was a table and chair and an alcove where Joe's things hung from a rod, and nothing else. Kevin sat on the chair, not taking off his knit cap.

Joe noticed that his own hands were covered with gypsum from hanging sheetrock at Eric Barnes's house, the chalk like some residue he had carried from Missy's bedroom, dead matter from the body that had drowned in her comforter.

"What is the offer?" he said.

"Hey, slow down. Let's partake of a little American-style hospitality."

Kevin took off his baseball jacket and pulled out a quart bottle of malt liquor. His sweatshirt sleeves were cut short and Joe saw that his build was powerful. On his pale veiny forearm a tattoo said "Flyswatter," with a picture of a flyswatter; on his bicep there was a terrified insect.

They took turns sipping warm froth. When Kevin bent his elbow to drink, Joe noticed that the fly on his bicep was swatted.

"Where'd you say you're from?"

"Africa."

"Like, South Africa? The Belgian Condo?"

"Near there."

"Listen, I want to tell you something 'cause you're my friend and you don't know how it is here. Maybe you got a job already but there's something you need to understand. This country shits on people like us. You heard about America the beautiful land of the free home of the brave, right? Sooner or later it's going to shit on you. I'm a natural born citizen and I can't *pay* to work. It's *fucked*."

Kevin set the bottle on the floor. His thigh was jiggling, his eyes shifting around the room.

"I had it explained to me in the can by this very sharp lifer from Brockton who had a lot of time to work things out. Pretty recently, America canceled all the rules except for rich people and mongrels. As a result you got two things: You got people shitting on other people in new ways that are totally legal, and you got mongrels on top. When there's no rules the mongrels win, every time. Because they're naturally more vicious. You take J.B. down at the desk, how you think he got that job? A pureblood like me or you, we try to go straight we get fucked. That's what's happening to this country, people shitting on other people in totally legal ways and rich people and mongrels coming out on top."

Kevin took a deep swallow from the malt liquor. His voice had a rattling metallic sound like a hammer hitting a piece of aluminum. Joe found it pleasurable. It warmed and dulled him like malt liquor.

"That's why you and me need a partnership and a plan. I've already got the plan. Want to hear it?"

Joe nodded.

Kevin's plan was for Joe to recruit a well-spoken woman from the local African community who would enter their partnership on a short-term basis. Kevin would bring access to quality forging equipment—the woman would be provided with a false driver's license, counterfeit death certificate, and photograph of a black child. Dressed in traditional costume, she would go door to door in the affluent Huron Avenue–West Cambridge area—where shitting on people was an art form as long as it didn't happen face to face—and solicit contributions for a tombstone to place on the grave of her daughter, who had recently died of a brain tumor. As her managers, Kevin and Joe would equally divide 80 percent of the earnings. After two weeks, they would shut down the operation. Kevin stressed the ingenuity of his plan. Being liberals, it would be impossible for residents of that neighborhood to refuse this woman. Even if they were suspicious, they would rather pay her off with ten or twenty dollars than spend the rest of the night feeling like cold-hearted racists.

"I don't know anyone," Joe said.

"Come on. A good-looking guy like you must be banging some nice African lady. Don't tell me you're against doing shit like this?"

He wasn't, but a second African con seemed foolhardy. Because a con was all it had been. And the one most conned was himself. He should have guarded the magic better. He had given his smile away too easily, he wouldn't smile anymore. Other people had everything; he had nothing but the magic, and Missy had done something to it.

"What about another plan?"

"OK. Good. Because listen, these high-tech companies in Kendall, they're all doing it. And you see these fucking CEOs, some of them ain't even thirty and they're millionaires driving a Lexus. I'd like to feed every one of them to my buddies in Walpole."

Joe stopped hearing what Kevin said and let the hammer blows work on him. He felt that he himself was made of metal, and the hard flatness of his stomach wall felt cool like the green lion. Kevin was right: They would all do it if he let them, Mr. Talk, Mr. Action, The Community, all of them. They could steal the African any time they wanted, but it was only a transparent image that had stepped toward Missy's bed. From now on Joe would keep himself in this metal casing and not come out again.

"My old man worked in a shoe factory in Haverhill—they sent the jobs down to Guatemala or something. This is survival. You totally happy here? Nothing pisses you off? The attitude toward African people?"

Joe said, "Some things."

"Like what?"

Joe closed his eyes. He saw Eric Barnes's face. Eric Barnes pissed him off. Why?

Because his face said: I know, tell me, it will be all right, it's what you have to do.

"I'm working at a house in Cambridgeport. The man is a writer. They're rich."

"Fucking writers. What the fuck do they *do*? They don't make anything anyone needs, why should they get rich? Jesus, it's enough to make you violent. Could you get a set of keys?"

"I don't think so. And the window has bars. But I can take off the nuts and washers. Then someone outside can pull the bolts."

"Sounds like you had some experience back in Africa."

Joe opened up his toolbox. Of course when the magic deserted him it hadn't gone into the green lion—only into money now. It was no accident that the ex-con had shown up with his angry rattling voice just when he was needed. Everything had a purpose.

Kevin inspected the lion with an air of authority. He was smiling, but his eyes were still a lizard's. "Jade. Beautiful. I have a lot of experience moving items like this." He slipped the lion into the pocket of his baseball jacket. "Listen, everything we do is fifty-fifty, even though I bring the logistics and expertise, because that's just who I am. The thing is, my role has to be behind the scenes 'cause of my record."

"I don't do violence," Joe suddenly said.

"That's cool. I'm not against it on principle, but the return is pretty low considering the investment." Kevin put on his baseball jacket, and the lion weighted down one side. "I'll be in touch with another plan. Here's where I'm staying, my fucking cousin's number, if you think of anything else. I guarantee you won't regret it."

They shook hands as partners and soul brothers.

sixteen

On the day Paula had arranged to meet Eric Barnes, Gladys Dill missed her appointment. It was also the day of the winter's first storm, and as the city outside turned white, she imagined Gladys falling heavily on the sidewalk, blindsided in an intersection, her beige coat invisible in the blizzard, lying in a heap as the snow covered her. Fifteen minutes into what would have been the session, Paula called Gladys's home, as she always did when a client failed to show. No answer. She checked her voice mail—no new messages. Gladys had never missed before. At the rock bottom of depression she dragged herself here.

In the middle of the morning, Earl came in grinning.

"I dreamed about you. Want to hear it?"

Paula tilted her head to an attentive angle, dreading his dream.

"I said do you want to hear it?"

"OK."

"Look, if you don't want to I don't give a fuck."

"What was your dream, Earl?"

He stared through fat-squeezed eyes. "You and me, in here. You've fired me from therapy. I say you can't because we signed a contract. Then you go for the door but it's locked from the outside. You're stuck with me and I've got nothing to lose and you're scared shitless that I'm going to do something. And it pisses me off that you're scared, so I start faking punches, jabs. You're on the floor begging, drooling. And I'm telling you, 'It's not an action yet, you can't call security, this is just my feeling.'" Earl sat back and smiled. "How about that? Pretty good, huh?"

Her eyes were on the Cape Cod picture. It had become Gladys's head in a pool of blood.

"Pretty good."

All day the snow kept falling, and all day the clients kept coming. Paula resented having her attention drawn away from the panic at hand. After every session, she went through the drill of checking her voice mail and calling Gladys. In the early afternoon, she left her blind room and went out to reception in the unlikely event that Gladys had fallen asleep, or had arrived late and was waiting to be noticed in her quiet protesting way. Paula stopped to watch the storm through the wire mesh of the basement door.

There was nothing cozy in the white silence outside; the wind-whipped drifts piling on the concrete steps looked threatening. If the sky had been clear today she could have controlled herself, but the snow and Gladys and her rendezvous with Eric this evening got mixed up into one single impending disaster that was somehow all her fault.

There was a message on her voice mail from a client who had to cancel because of a court appearance. The rest of the afternoon was empty. The next voice mail would be from Gladys: *You're the one who got me into this, how can you leave me, you coward?*

Around 3:30 Paula found herself under siege from one of Fran's monologues about the psychic benefits of her women's support group. Paula's heartbeat suddenly went out of control. She couldn't sit another minute. Interrupting Fran midword to apologize, she bolted from the room and ran down to reception. Through the door she looked at the snowfall. It was coming down harder than ever; a six-inch ridge lay on the bottom step. The sun already seemed to have gone down.

Paula went into the closet and took her coat.

Where was she going? She couldn't go to Gladys's. There were rules about that, and they existed for a reason. There were rules not to be friends with the clients. The work had to be conducted in a hermetically sealed environment—fifty minutes, same hour every week, a windowless room—even a window let in contamination.

Outside in the snow she would be out of her element, she might find anything. She might find Gladys dead.

Her stomach knotted. *You* made her do that. You wanted to throw yourself headlong into life. Instead you threw Gladys, and now she's dead, James killed her.

The reception intern was watching Paula out of the corner of an eye. Paula smiled frantically, replaced her coat, and went back into the cubicle.

There was a staff meeting at 4:00. She could spend the rest of the afternoon in the warm safety of the Problem Place. She hated the warmth, the safety. It was like a fortified bunker down here. She could taste what it would be like to sit through the meeting, breathing the headachy air, having to impress Fine with an update on her fruitless search for grant money, then the bus home. It was Thursday—the night she camped out in front of the TV. She saw herself as a creature of habit, obedient, crippled, afraid of life, talking endlessly about feelings while a poor woman lay bleeding to death.

She knew now that she had to go. She would go find Gladys because it was the voice of her old frightened self telling her not to. And she had stopped being that person, by the river with the night air sparkling around her.

She checked her voice mail again. She dialed Gladys's number. She let it ring ten times, and then she hung up, left the cubicle, put on her coat, and slipped outside without a word to the reception intern or anyone. They would tell her she was crazy.

On the street it was already twilight. Headlights appeared dull yellow in the storm, utility vehicles clambered along with wheels and blades rattling in a spray of snow and sand. There was no distinction between streets and sidewalks, and Paula walked in a lane of slow traffic past half-buried parked cars, crossing over without intersections or lights, climbing mounds of plowed snow. Watching where her boots stepped, she only noticed other people when they were right alongside her. Once she broke into a half-jog, squeaking and slipping on the compacted snow. She was hatless, and her eyelashes fused and glittered. She heard her own quick breathing.

Paula had rarely been through Gladys's neighborhood. You never heard about it. It didn't seem like part of the city, didn't even have a name—it was just called Area 4 in the crime reports. Columbia Street was a notorious drug bazaar, with at least a couple of shootings and a child killed in traffic every year. No one she knew lived here or went here, except clients. This afternoon Area 4 was almost empty. A man clutching a package came out of a *groceria*. A mother trudged up the deep sidewalk and screamed at a child she was pulling by its little mittened hand. In the middle of Columbia Street, two men were working under the hood of a truck. Street numbers were missing, or hidden, or impossible to make out in the snow. The address Paula wanted wasn't materializing where it should be; between a badly leaning triple-decker and a boarded-up cottage with no front steps there was just a hole, a narrow, empty space.

The foolishness of her mission began to burn on her frozen cheeks. She was a meddling white woman with no business coming here. She imagined someone in a tenement window laughing at her jerky movements back and forth in the snow.

The hole turned out to be an alley. She followed it down and came out into an asphalted courtyard where cars were parked in front of row houses that had been concealed behind the triple-decker. There were two dozen of them, all the doors were brown, and their numbers were in the single and double digits—not at all what she was looking for. She had entered some kind of separate development, a housing project with its own system of numbers. How was she going to find Gladys in here? She would have to knock on every door and humiliate herself in the face of angry project dwellers.

There was a squat outbuilding in the near corner of the yard, hardly more than a trailer. "Office" it said over the door. The word gave her heart. She approached and brushed the snow from her hair.

No one answered her knock. She let herself in.

The room was tropical, a steambath. Imitation-wood panels seemed to be melting off the walls, wafers of tile drooped from the ceiling. Somewhere a heat source was blasting away. Everything looked makeshift and flimsy, including the skinny white woman in sweatpants and T-shirt who stood with her back turned.

"I was five days late last month—so what. Do your job, Cooper, I've got water all over my floor."

She was making odd stiff-armed gestures at a crewcut, sour-faced young man in shirt sleeves, who was rocking back in his chair behind a metal desk buried under papers.

"You are a sliver up my ass, Sheila."

"I hope it hurts like hell."

"Your toilet is not a priority one. There's a storm outside, or have you been unconscious all day? What'd you throw down, left-overs?" Laughing, Cooper glanced at Paula. He sat forward. His face rearranged itself. "May I help you?"

Sheila turned around to look.

"I'm trying—"

"Cooper," Sheila said, "I'm standing right here making you miserable until somebody fixes my toilet."

"Sheila, as soon as Luis becomes available I will send him over."

Sheila glanced savagely at Paula on her way out.

Cooper shook his head and chuckled, in the manner of a long-suffering public servant confronted with the folly of his clientele. "A normal day at Columbia Gardens." Sweat bubbled above his lip, heat was pounding out of an electric space heater. Paula's arrival had occasioned delight. "Please sit down, if I'd known a visitor was coming—"

"I'm looking for a tenant named Gladys Dill. Is this where she lives?"

Cooper's smile faded. "Gladys Dill." He made a show of searching his memory, then nodded slowly. "A Gladys Dill lives here. May I ask who is looking for her?"

She read him at a glance: somebody's nephew, unfit for anything except presiding over a toilet. Naturally he wanted to detain this interesting visitor. Paula introduced herself vaguely as a social worker.

"So you serve the poor like me. And you saw for yourself the thanks we get. Dave Cooper, project manager."

"Which apartment does Gladys live in?"

"Gladys Dill." With self-important fussiness, the project manager retrieved a sheet from his desk drawer and ran his finger over it. "Gladys Dill lives in Number 7. May I ask what you'd like to see her about?"

Paula was beginning to sweat under her coat. "I'm just checking in. She's sick today. Have you seen her?" Cooper shook his head. On the verge of leaving, she decided to press him. "Do you know of any recent problems with the man she lives with?"

Cooper leaned back and threw up his hands. Dark stains circled his armpits. "Anything humans do to each other, it goes on at Columbia Gardens. These people have no sense of responsibility or community. When you give people everything, they don't take care of it. They leave trash around, they block up the toilets with rice, anything. These days no one cares about anyone else, everyone's out for themselves. It starts to lower you to their level, then you think: Hey, I'm the professional here. But it's hard to maintain your ideals."

Her appearance had embarrassed Cooper, for he was in the shit now himself. He tried to delay her but she escaped from the heat back into snow. Someone was coming up the office steps—a Hispanic woman, short-cropped hair, a face of bone-deep fatigue bracing for another round of war.

Number 7 shared a flight of steps with Number 5: It was the upper-story unit. All the blinds in both units were drawn, but there was light in a small upstairs window. Without letting herself think, Paula pushed the buzzer. From within she heard no sound. In the gathering dark the building's asphalt shingles looked like the loose scales of a disease. There wasn't any porch roof and the snow was falling on her head and coat. She buzzed again and then wondered if the buzzer was broken. She knocked, softly at first, not wanting to sound rude, but the silence drove her to stronger knocking, until the hollow-core door rattled on its hinges. Suddenly, from high up within, she heard a door open.

There were footsteps inside. They took minutes to descend. Anything humans did to each other they did here. How could she stop them? Paula stood blindly behind the windowless front door. Then it opened.

"James?"

He was a big man and his shrunken long johns made him look bigger. One hand on the doorknob, he blinked with glazed eyes into the storm.

"James? Is Gladys here?"

James's face betrayed no expression. Drunk.

"I'm her—I'm a friend of hers, James. Is she home?"

She didn't know if he heard a word she said—beyond drunk, as if he were coming out of a dream. But he made an effort to gather himself, straightening up.

"Gladys ain't here."

"Do you know where she is?"

His eyes had focused enough to avoid Paula's. Why didn't he slam the door in her face? "At her therapist."

"Really?" She had to be careful, because now she knew that Gladys was upstairs and something was wrong. She became very calm, willing her entire being into gaining entry. "There must be some mistake, because I'm her therapist. James, is Gladys in trouble? Was there an accident?"

"She's asleep."

"But there's been an accident, hasn't there? I'd like to see her. Can I?"

His body had once been muscular, now thickened in the belly and thighs. Paula remembered that he had been a minor-league baseball player, begun to drink, worked at a garage. This wasn't the cruel face she had visualized while Gladys recited the litany of wrongs. He looked puzzled and resentful and a little scared, as if trying to answer an unfounded accusation. And still he didn't shut the door. The initiative was hers, in his front door.

"We can still help her, James. But if she's had an accident and we don't help her then you might lose her."

She took a step forward and put her foot on the threshold. Instead of pushing her out, he backed into the hall and the door opened wider.

"You can't come in," James said feebly.

"We both care about Gladys, don't we? I do, and I know you do." She was talking without thought, riding an instinct, fearless. "And if she needs help—neither of us wants something bad to happen to her." James looked at the floor. "So let's make sure nothing does."

Paula stepped inside. She began to climb the high leaning stairs. At the top, there was dull light where the apartment door stood open. She waited to be ordered back down. Behind and below her she heard the front door close.

The living room was small and carpeted. On the TV set there were family portraits, and sports trophies on a shelf. She had been braced for stench, cockroaches, a toilet overflowing filth—and yet the tidy ordinariness of the place made her heart sink. The family pictures, the shut-in smell of deodorizer, the matching lace curtains that had begun to yellow, all told her that Gladys's life was being lived here, that there was nothing temporary or fixable about it. Gladys would not get out, nothing would change. All Paula's calculations had been wrong.

James appeared in the room. Paula went deeper into the apartment, down a narrow linoleum hallway, past an open door with a glimpse of unwashed dishes in a kitchen sink, then another open door, an unmade bed.

The room smelled of rubbing alcohol. Gladys lay with her eyes closed and the covers drawn up to her neck. What Paula first took for the pillow case or sheet turned out to be a piece of white gauze, raggedly cut and Scotch-taped across her right cheek. Blood had soaked through the gauze and more blood had run under the bandage and dried on her jaw. A chair was pulled up to the bedside. Next to it was a table on which stood a glass and an open bottle of vodka, surrounded by a litter of bloodied cotton balls.

James had been drinking and cleaning the wound from the same bottle. Got drunk, beat her up, nursed her, got drunk. In some order.

Gladys seemed to be sleeping, although for an instant Paula thought she was dead. But approaching the bed she saw that Gladys was watching her out of her left eye; the right eye was swollen shut in a pocket of gleaming skin. The open eye was void of expression. Somewhere in the room an old R&B song was playing on a badly tuned radio.

"What happened, Gladys, my God, are you all right?"

Paula sat in the chair. The eye followed her, watching. The rest of Gladys's face was lifeless as meat, but the one-eyed stare suggested harsh skepticism. When Paula reached to touch Gladys's shoulder, a crust of snow fell from her sleeve onto the covers.

Fresh blood was welling under the bandage, and a trickle rolled toward Gladys's ear. The gauze was soaked through with bright new blood.

James was standing in the doorway, fingers playing with the button of his thermal undershirt. He was unwilling to enter his own bedroom.

"I need to look under the bandage." Paula took his silence for permission to undo his work. The Scotch tape peeled away easily, but when she held the corner of gauze between her thumb and finger and began delicately to pull back, the wound came with it. Gladys opened her mouth and uttered a wild shout of pain, and Paula withdrew so fast she nearly fell backward in the chair. "Sorry, sorry." Gladys's one eye filled and rolled upward to appeal to heaven or the ceiling for mercy. "I just need to look," Paula pleaded, more and more aware of her own recklessness. Gladys lay rigid as she peeled back the other piece of tape. On this side there wasn't so much dried blood and the gauze gaped open from Gladys's cheek.

The flesh was torn in a cut that ran diagonally under the swollen eye. Not a long cut, but Paula saw at once that it went very deep. It was still bleeding.

"I'm going to help you," she whispered. "Don't worry." Gladys stared back.

Paula replaced the bloody, useless swatch of gauze with James's tape. Then she walked over and touched his arm lightly for him to follow her into the hall. He obeyed, keeping a distance.

She didn't look at James, because what she wanted to feel was pure hatred and she was afraid that his face would talk her out of it. For once she wanted nothing more complicated than a villain, she craved evil. But even his posture, leaning away from her like a sullen boy waiting for his punishment, seemed pathetic. To her chagrin, the hatred wouldn't flow.

"She needs to go to the hospital," she told him severely. "Did you cut her with a knife?"

Her first mistake. James stiffened in outrage. "You think I'd *cut* Gladys?"

"Then what happened?" She braced for him to throw her down the stairs. What made her think he owed her an explanation?

"We had a fight. She provoked me."

"What did she say?" Paula made herself ask.

"I didn't mean to catch her with my ring. It was an accident. I just meant to slap her."

"What did she say, James?" Paula pressed him. "How did she provoke you?"

"Threatening me, saying she was leaving. That she was going to leave me if. . . ."

Paula cringed, as if the fist were coming at her. "If you hit her again?"

"Something like that," he murmured. From Paula's chest a groan was wrenched free. James seemed to take it as an expression of disdain. "She shouldn't of." He became indignant. "What is that, leave me? I can't make it without Gladys, she knows that. Why did she say a thing like that?"

So hit *my* face, cut *me*. *I'm* the one you want.

Help Gladys, she told herself.

"Where's Michael?"

"At her sister."

"I'm going to call an ambulance, James. She needs to go to the hospital."

"I fixed it, I'm taking care of her. She don't need a hospital."

"That wound is still bleeding. She could go into shock, it could get infected. She needs to be sewn up, and her bones need to be checked for fractures." She knew the power was hers. James or Gladys would never dream of going into someone else's house like this. The arrogance of education, profession, skin. "I know you tried to fix her. Because you didn't want to hurt her like that, did you? You don't want to lose her."

In the dark hallway she couldn't tell the effect of her words.

"I love Gladys." His voice was thick with self-pity and shame.

"You love her and you don't want to lose her."

"I don't want no police involvement."

"I'm calling an ambulance. She might die, James. She might leave you by dying."

She knew by his breathing that he wouldn't stop her.

There was a phone on the floor in the bedroom. Paula informed 911 of a domestic violence case that required emergency assistance at Number 7, Columbia Gardens.

"Do you need police assistance?"

James was back in the doorway.

"Yes, please."

The police arrived first, big and jangling, heedless. When they twisted James's arms back to cuff him, Gladys rose in the bed.

"James!"

James bowed his head and slumped under the cops' control. Once he was cuffed, they handled him with rough contempt. "Guess what, bitch?" one of them told him. "You're going to jail."

As James was led away, Paula and a woman officer had to restrain Gladys. Her cries became howls. "Why did you do that? It wasn't none of your business. Why did you do that?"

"What he did to you wasn't right," Paula answered lamely.

When the EMTs bustled into the apartment they were trailed by Cooper, the project manager. He had put on an air of responsible authority, but Paula knew that he was enjoying the crisis. As the EMTs struggled under the heavy load of Gladys on their stretcher, Cooper's eyes met Paula's and his lips flickered: See? You're in the shit just as deep as me.

Paula rode in back with the EMT. Once she tried to take Gladys's hand and Gladys yanked it away.

In triage at Cambridge Hospital, a woman in street clothes inspected the wound and immediately declared Gladys a Grade 2, which meant that she had to be seen within fifteen minutes. A nurse walked her into the E.R. Paula was sent back through the sliding doors into the lounge, where she sat with a pair of Hispanic parents, whose little son was sniffling between them, and a pretty young black woman who sat by herself. In the corner of the room a television was on, a local news reporter was shouting over the noise of a snowplow.

Once, when Paula was knocked off her bicycle and fractured her wrist, she was taken to Mt. Auburn Hospital, down on the river. She never told the EMT; it was where people like her went. The public hospital was for Area 4, Columbia Gardens, for Gladys. This wasn't remarkable, everyone knew it. Her expedition was coming to an end. Soon she would be returned to herself.

"Would you come, please?"

The nurse, a big-boned, harassed-looking woman with blond hair, was addressing Paula.

"She won't say anything," she told Paula on their way through the brightness of the emergency room. "They come in looking like that and they forget how to talk. We need some basic information."

Outside the suture room Paula gave Gladys's name, address, and approximate age, while the nurse scribbled on a chart. All she knew of Gladys's medical history was depression, addiction, and high blood pressure. She had probably violated confidentiality, but she was desperate to seem competent, to be of use.

"What's your relation to her?" the nurse asked suddenly.

"I'm Gladys's therapist."

Pen poised over her chart, the nurse nodded in some private confirmation of Paula's role in the foolishness.

"Did you expect something like this to happen?"

"I—" Paula dropped her head. "He's been abusive before."

The suture room was empty at 6:00 on a Thursday evening, except for Gladys and the policewoman, who was squatting by her bed when the nurse pulled back the curtain.

"We can't get a restraining order if you won't talk to us." Seeing the nurse and Paula, she stood up. "I told her about the Victims of Violence program here at the hospital, but . . ."

"It's up to them," the nurse said. "They have to want to help themselves."

They stood around the bed: nurse, cop, and therapist, three white women in social services, two in uniform, trying to help a black woman, who gazed mutely at the curtain beyond them. The wound was exposed, a red angry gash, staring like another eye.

"The doctor will be here very soon," the nurse told Gladys, "and he'll sew you up."

The nurse went about her business with swabs and ice pack and chart. Her job was Gladys's face. Paula and the policewoman went out into the hall.

"Talk to me about her situation."

Paula recounted the varieties of abuse. She tried to describe the particular quality of Gladys's courage and fear, the trap she was caught in. The officer was nodding, growing impatient. It was impossible to convey the nature of their sessions, the hints and shadows, the starts and stops, the love and the infinitesimally slow progress, so that it would fit on a police report.

She didn't mention their last session, the breakthrough session, the plan for Gladys to change her life.

"Are they going to charge him?" she asked.

"Don't you think they should?"

Paula started to weigh the problem of James's anger, its relation to his shame—but with a woman like this you had to know your mind. "In the long run, it would be better for her."

"In the short run, he ought to be locked up," the cop said. "But it's going to be tough to press charges if she doesn't cooperate."

"What about a restraining order?"

"She has to file a complaint. You're her therapist, maybe you can work on it with her."

The cop looked to be Paula's age, dark and stout and ponytailed. By her accent she was a native of the city, a daughter of the working class, and for Paula's occupation she seemed to hold a reserve of irony, maybe even contempt. The radio on her hip was crackling. Like the nurse, she had other business. Sew up a wound, lock up a boyfriend. If they don't talk, move on to the next one. The mind, Paula's business, exasperated these women, its mysteries only got in the way of their work. Paula had taken pride in being able to unlock Gladys's secrets. She had seen her through moods in the face of which these women would be helpless. Most people would rather deal with the criminal or with dying than the mental states that were Paula's daily work. But just now she wanted to trade in the session room for the E.R., her progress notes for a chart and swab, her Kleenex box for a police report and a pair of cuffs.

"We'll call if we need more information." The policewoman's wide blue hips, adorned with radio, baton, cuffs, and gun, pivoted and swung out of the emergency room.

Paula returned to the lounge. But she wasn't ready for it to be over, to be confronted with herself. She went back into triage and won permission to wait outside the suture room. She stood by the door the way James had stood in his own bedroom door, guilty, superfluous. Nurses and doctors passed in the hall. A doctor came out of the suture room; his nametag said Holtzman and he wore a Garfield button on the front of his white coat. Paula moved toward him, but she was at a loss for something to say.

"Yes?"

"Is she . . ."

"I've sewn her up. We'll keep her overnight and watch that eye."

He was bearded, kind, busy. She would have served gladly as his nurse. Fine should have been this man. She wanted the doctor to linger. He must have something wise to tell her. That she had done all she could, hadn't caused it, couldn't have stopped it. That she might have saved Gladys's life today. What she wanted was for him to reach over and touch her face.

"Is there a fracture?" she asked.

"X rays came out negative." He was slipping away down the hall.

"Could you tell me about Victims of Violence?"

"A little legal advice," he said, "and a lot of therapy."

Dr. Holtzman disappeared around the corner. By the nurses' station, a resident and a woman in scrubs were looking at Paula with vague curiosity. The big-boned nurse came out of suture. "Go home, honey, there's nothing you can do here. She's going to be OK. Go do something fun. *I've* gotta work till three in the morning."

Then Paula remembered. It was 6:30. She was already half an hour late, he was waiting in the snow—but the stab of guilt had nothing to do with that. It was the frivolity of having a date with a man, a married man, while Gladys lay in there. She walked out of the hospital into the cold night and her face was blazing. Her tears filled her with shame. It was shameful to be human with these useless feelings, to feel these things and do nothing, to charge in and smash things up. She started walking without knowing where she was going, wanting the snow to cover her, hide her, make her cold and hard and pure.

seventeen

After teaching his class Eric went into the subway at Park Street, where the man in the token booth gestured for him to brush the snow off his hair. The storm made it possible again for strangers to address one another. On the train there was an atmosphere of pleasant hysteria, as if an invading army with a benign reputation had reached the outskirts of the city.

In Central Square the streets had fallen magically silent. He helped a black businessman push his plowed-in car and felt a surge of fellowship at the man's effusive thanks. He wanted to look for other people to dig out or push. The snow was bringing the city together, like a holiday or a national tragedy. Everyone had to shovel, every car had its lights and wipers on, the whiteness covered everyone equally, created the same hazards everywhere and the same soft beauty. People looked like figures in a dream.

Outside the building he paced the sidewalk, following his own footprints in the fresh snow. She was late—but she always was. He turned his face to the streetlamp where the snow fell glittering in the light, a silver shower. Paula was bringing the snow, she was there every minute.

Half an hour passed. Jane would be home by now. He'd told her he had appointments at school, and she'd said fine. His pocketed hands were beginning to throb, and his nose seemed to be swelling into a grotesque bulb. Every passing car and all the people watching him from lighted windows knew from his nose exactly what he was doing here—a foolish man with a pregnant wife at home, on an adulterous errand, the result of a misunderstanding with a woman who had come to her senses. He would stand here all night as his nose grew bigger and bigger.

But Jane no longer cared what he did. How could you cheat on someone who had already withdrawn her love? He told himself the storm was making Paula late. He waited long past the hour, until there was nothing but his pacing and the passing cars and the snow. When it fell less thickly, he was confronted with the thought of going home.

He looked up and she was standing on the sidewalk ten feet away, as if she had been watching him for a long time.

"Paula."

"I always seem to make you wait."

"Well, you're here."

He wasn't sure of it. Her stillness made him think of a deer on a trail—if he moved she would bolt, or simply vanish in the snow the way she had appeared. She was staring ominously. She had come to deliver a rebuke and then leave.

"It's a blizzard," he observed.

"You must be freezing. I'm sorry." Her eyes, neither hard nor vacant, looked frantic, although her voice was low.

"I didn't know if I had the right address," he lied.

"This is it. Second floor."

He looked up: The windows were dark, the way was clear.

"Something happened," she said.

"Ah."

"I almost didn't come."

He hesitated, unable to judge her mood. "I'm glad you did."

Paula burst into tears. She buried her face in her gloves. When he came to her side and touched her, she shuddered and the sobs shook her body. He stood gallantly and absurdly with his bulky parka arm around her shoulders.

"I've got to go," she said into her hands.

"What happened?"

She looked at him. "Oh God, I screwed up."

"Tell me."

She shook her head, but she was frozen to the spot. Eric saw what he had to do. He switched to the imperative, taking control, persuading her inside where they could warm up. She didn't refuse, she obeyed like an automaton. Her eyes were red and beautiful and frantic.

Her friend's place looked like a thousand other overpriced condos inhabited by single professionals: kitchenette with an aerobics schedule under a refrigerator magnet, matching furniture set in the living room, halogen lamp, framed Monet, oak-veneer bookcase with CDs and tapes. No clothes were strewn across the futon, no books lay open on the coffee table, just an arrangement of magazines—the *New Yorker*, *Mirabella*, *Edge*—like a doctor's waiting room. When Eric searched the cabinets for teabags, he found little more than stacks of canned cat food. A smell of Kitty Litter emanated from a corner of the room. The atmosphere of tidy loneliness was oppressive.

He heated water and Paula fed the two fearful cats, and these tasks created a suggestion of domesticity that hung in the air like a provocative smile. She took off her coat and draped it over a chair. He realized he had never seen her without it. She was small, fine-boned, the skin of her arms olive-colored and smooth. Her arms and hips moved with unconscious grace.

They drank herbal tea out of cartoon cat mugs.

"Sara's a cat person," Paula said, and they both laughed tensely. "She thinks they'll be jealous of her fiancé, so she sleeps at his place in the burbs. But she's afraid they'll be depressed here without her. At least they have each other."

"And there's always cat therapy."

"One of the doctors at Cambridge Hospital wears a Garfield button."

Something in her voice made him alert. "Paula, what the hell happened?"

Her eyes on the steaming mug of tea, she told him in a monotone; and by contrast her story took on the quality of high drama. The more she spoke of sad and frightening things, the happier he became. Imagining her going out into the storm, into the projects, small and brave, he felt himself falling in love with her, felt it happening physically in his bones and blood. He had to keep himself from reaching to touch her face.

"You didn't screw up."

"I had no business going there. I could get de-licensed or something. It was out of bounds."

Most of her pulled off a passable imitation of every woman he knew—the low neutral voice, the self-sufficient posture. But her eyes gave everything away, fears and longings. Most people wouldn't look into her dark eyes for long; they wouldn't want to be reminded of their own smallness.

"Well, I think the world of you for doing it."

"One hundred percent guilt-driven. Thinking of myself. I was afraid I got her in trouble and I was right."

"Everyone thinks of themselves. It doesn't mean you don't care about her."

"So I had to go fix it. Life and death in my hands. I must see her! Open up, James, I know she's in there! Starring Susan Sarandon! Two thumbs up!" Her hands were simulating brilliant klieg lights. "Now Gladys'll drop out of treatment."

"I doubt that. On some level it might help."

"No." She shook her head but her eyes searched his. *Go on. Persuade me.*

He savored the taste of power. "Maybe he'll think before hitting her again. Maybe it'll get through to her that she matters, like your mother. You're so hard on yourself."

Paula became quiet. Her head was down, and he thought she was crying again. He wanted to tell her about the magical sensation of the snow, but he didn't speak, her presence was still fragile.

When she looked up there was a smile on her lips—she hadn't been crying. And when she spoke her voice sounded lighter, almost playful.

"I was about to get on my bus. It came by when I was walking here. I didn't care if you were standing in the snow. I wanted you to be cold."

"Why?"

"I blamed you. I never would have gone out there if it hadn't been for you."

Taken aback, he said, "I don't get it."

"I was furious."

"Why did you blame me?"

She shook her head. She was still smiling. He began to understand: Her day had not been so different from his.

"But you didn't get on the bus."

"Because I knew you'd know what to say."

Her hand was on the table. He reached for it. Slender and cold, it turned everything inside him soft and hot. When it answered his touch he felt so weak he was afraid of slipping out of the chair.

Paula said, "What's happening, Eric?"

"You know what's happening. We both know."

Her answer was almost a whisper. "Yes."

Her lips were warmer than her hands. It wasn't her passion that surprised him—he had sensed this about her—but his own. He heard the whimpers of some grateful animal and realized they were his. Where did you come from? he wanted to ask her. Who are you? But there was no time for questions, she was moving ahead of him, unashamed in the delights she took.

The bedroom was as embarrassed by their conduct as the rest of the apartment. The cats, startled off the pillows, fled, leaving behind a stuffed tabby and, on the bedstand, an ovulation test kit called OvuQuick, with a picture of a baby on the box. The sight jolted him. Its aspect was sour, frowning. It seemed to say: You can't act this way, this isn't what sex is about, sex is serious business, it's about responsibility.

Paula was laughing. "That's the last thing I want." She turned the box away and pulled him down onto the the flower-patterned comforter, not disturbing the sheets.

For a time she was so full of play and laughter that he began to fear he'd become a trifle. Then she took his face in her hands and told him with her eyes that it was him—he was the one. Shed of his clothes, he became aware of the belt of fat above his hips, the winter whiteness of his legs. His body had always been an imperfect vehicle of desire, and through her eyes he recognized a decade's aging that marriage had let him ignore.

Soon he forgot to be conscious of himself and the alien room. The smoothness of her skin was a miracle. It wasn't enough to touch, he wanted to possess and be wrapped in it, could hardly take in all the sweetness of her small body. With her there was no need to hold himself back, whatever he offered she took, the only limits were those of flesh. Pleasure never carried him away from her, she was always there, and he said her name again and again. He trailed kisses along her neck, her collarbone, her nipples, heard her sighs, felt her hands moving through his hair. She brought him onto her, guiding him. He wanted to slow everything down, hated for this to be ending so soon, but he couldn't stop each moment from melting into the next and so he clung to her shoulders and felt her heart fluttering like a bird against his chest.

When it began to happen, he almost cried in protest. It started quietly like a rumor far away somewhere in the middle of the earth, something that didn't involve him, but it gained speed as it raced upward from the floor and bed, into his body, surging through him. It was stronger than anything he had ever felt. It shook him like a creature without bones, in a spasm of helpless nerves. At the last so much feeling seemed dangerous, his life too frail to hold it, he would have to shut it off or be broken apart.

They lay entangled on the comforter in the intimate darkness.

"The cats will tell on us," she said.

"You don't already regret this?"

"That word," she told him, "shouldn't get anywhere near this bed." Wrists together, huddling against his chest, she seemed to fold her body inside his. "It's so strange, Eric. I feel new."

"My name sounds different when you say it, like someone else's. Someone I'd like to be."

He felt dampness on his arm.

"Sorry," she said. "I get a little sad when I'm happy."

"I love your sadness and your happiness, and what you did for Gladys, and your laugh, and your eyes. I love saying your name when no one's around."

She breathed into his neck. "This is the only cure."

He was trying to imagine her life, its trivial dailiness. He knew nothing about her. How could he feel this way about a stranger? Turning toward the window, he saw that it had stopped snowing. The sight dismayed him.

"When it's spring and I'm lonely," she said, "I like to go to Mt. Auburn Cemetery. Have you ever seen the azaleas there? I'll take you this spring, Mr. Merganser. If it ever comes."

"I'd like that."

He was thinking that this condition they were in now, this intimacy and peace, couldn't withstand the world outside the window. He had no plans for the spring. There was no future. There was this room, this moment, her warm breath on his neck. And he was afraid to move. What he wanted was for it not to change, not to end, to lie here with her forever. Yet something had already ended, they were separate beings again. The snow's stopping told him that the world outside the window was their enemy. They were not on the side of life. The image came of them buried side by side under a blanket of snow amid the azaleas in Mt. Auburn Cemetery.

He resolved to ignore it. He settled his arm across her warm breasts and kissed her hair. "I don't think of you as lonely."

She turned toward him and her mouth found his. "It's the basic state. Everything else is to get over it. My work. Yours, too, isn't it?"

"It started that way."

"But . . . ?"

"Circumstances plus me." He wanted to say: Plus you. But it

would probably frighten her, so he said, "I'm more interested in The Community, this magician."

She raised her head and her hair brushed his chest. "The African shaman?"

"You know him?"

"My boss won't shut up about him. My boss is using him."

"Maybe he's using your boss."

"Let me tell you something about The Community," she said sharply. "People with money and privilege can walk away whenever they want. The others get hurt. It's dangerous to mess with other people's lives. They're hungry, they have fantasies. These people are looking for love. It doesn't come on that scale."

He wondered if she was warning him not to do the same thing to her.

She said, "Why do you want to go prying into this African?"

"I envy him," he said at once, surprising himself.

"Why?"

"I don't know. He . . . claims to change shapes. Whatever that means. I almost feel," he laughed at himself, "like he made you possible." She narrowed her eyes. He felt a danger of revealing too much. He would gape open and she would see through to the defeated man who had taken to indulging strange whims, fantasizing freedoms and powers a grown-up shouldn't want. "And I want to know why he's been stealing from me. You know he's working at my house."

"Has he been stealing?"

"Yesterday afternoon I saw him pocket the fixtures for the new sink. Do you want to know how I felt? Excited. I wanted to see if he would get away with it. I felt like an accomplice. Bizarre, isn't it? Of course, part of me reacted like a violated homeowner. But I didn't stop him."

"And you want to know why he did it. Well, I'm not into that 'to understand all is to forgive all' crap. Some people should just be shown the door."

"Your patient's boyfriend?"

"If it was in my power to show James the door, I would. What, do you think all shrinks are made of mush? There's such a thing as evil."

She fell silent. A complicated and intense creature, battling evil single-handed, vulnerable.

"Do you think this is evil?"

"This?" She turned her face to his and made a sound of disbelief. "Eric, this is the best thing in my life."

"If you hadn't said that, I'd be lost." He drew her closer, smelling her hair. "Honest fact about myself: I need your approval."

"Why?"

"Because I feel like pulling my life up by the roots for you."

Her silence became the silence of thought.

A car slid by on the street.

"What's your wife like?"

Jane was present, a full moon through the window, a cat watching them in the dark. He tried to attune his answer to the tone of the question, off-handed and curious.

"Taller than you. Very competent, strong-willed, knows her own mind."

Nothing about the years of intimate knowledge in a shared bed, the world's insults through which they took each other's side, her tenderness, the geography of her face. Impossible to describe the person you were married to; but his feeble attempt was itself an act of betrayal, worse than what had been done in this bed, which somehow didn't trouble him.

She was waiting for more.

"I don't know what else to say."

"Because you don't know why I asked. And you're afraid I'll get upset."

"You have every right to ask."

"It isn't a matter of rights. I just have a certain image of her and I want to know if it's correct."

"But it's like trying to describe your parents, your own face."

"Is she beautiful?"

He saw Jane's face, the practical muscle in her cheek. "People tend to call her handsome."

"What else? I won't get mad."

She's pregnant. It was the first thing Jane would say about herself. He didn't dare; he would have to tell her, but not yet.

"She's from a working-class family. That gives her a sense of disaster but also a sense of purpose. She'd be impressed with you. She's self-critical about working for a rich institution."

"It's important work. Charitable foundations are a lifeline."

It occurred to him that they were talking about Jane as if she forced no conflicts on either of them, like a friend they both admired. Paula fell silent again. Her body was beginning to resist a little, it no longer fit along his, her knee was drilling into his calf and her chin pressed awkwardly at one of his ribs. This was how it happened—tension, evasion of things they both knew, silence, sliding between their bodies like a transparent membrane. When he tried to adjust along the length of her she said, "What time is it?"

"It's—Jesus."

Almost 9:00: They'd been lying together for over an hour. Without speaking, they got dressed and Paula straightened the covers. Eric was already beginning to miss her. Under his clothes, the smell of her was on him like a secret and it would be all he had until next time.

The living room looked like a shrine to dispiritment, but Paula hurried straight through to open the front door, looked both ways, and waved him on. "Coast is clear!" On the way out she brushed the hair from his face and took his hand, a confirmation of what they had done. They said good-bye on the sidewalk and her eyes met his. She was waiting for a sign. It was the look of a lover, direct, without interest in the rest of the world. It made claims. He wanted them.

"We'd better do this again on Monday," he said. "I don't want the cats to get depressed."

Jane was reading *We're Pregnant* in front of the television when Eric came in. His face was hot with blood and fear. She emerged from the book and looked up, and on a page in his mind's eye a single printed word appeared: *adultery*. It couldn't be undone.

He had prepared a story, but he also felt certain that it wouldn't matter for she would smell the deed on him and spot it in his eyes.

"Sorry," he said.

"I was worried."

"I had conferences."

"How were they?"

"Fine."

He had to look away. His gaze fell on a pale childhood scar on her left thumb. How well he knew that scar—but he'd forgotten it, left it out of his description. This seemed worse than anything.

Jane returned to her book, her affair. The details of his lie didn't interest her. He kept them to himself, letting the mutual silence stand for amnesty.

eighteen

Within three days the snow had become a burden to everyone except children. Since few people were civic-minded enough to shovel sidewalks, footprints carved out narrow gorges between ridges of snow leading to mountain passes that blocked intersections. Five days after the storm, a brief warming began to thaw the mounds. That night a deep freeze coated everything in ice, taking down morning commuters all over the city. Then it snowed again, lightly, just enough to hide the ice underfoot. People took to walking experimentally, as if they were learning on wobbly yearling legs. Every now and then, a man with a briefcase would break into a flailing jig. Then it warmed, then rained, then froze again.

Within a week the streets were lined with tortured shapes of blackened rock-hard snow. Within ten days curbs had become icy fjords. By mid-February the winter was like a war whose causes no one could remember and whose end would never come—trench warfare, a war of attrition.

There was a Central Square face. Visitors noticed it, along with the city's brick sidewalks and bad driving, its quaintness and its meanness. Although most outsiders associated the city with learning and elegance and tradition, the Central Square face was without refinement—and yet you saw it as often at the tables of Widener Library as anywhere else. It originated in the city's weather and its history of entrenched social classes and neighborhood suspicions, but it crossed these boundaries to take on something of a citywide, year-round character. In color it was reddish gray, more gray than red, like a tomato in an advanced state of rot. There was no trace of soft living or spiritual transcendence in the fixed downward stare of hard eyes, the pocked snout, the mass of grooved, gravity-ravaged flesh. It was an angry face, but not the anger of liberated, free-floating rage. The face was making a supreme effort to keep the anger under control. Everything—all wants and disappointments—was held within. The suffering was silent. And this effort disfigured emotions, which found expression only in the features of someone bracing to go out into another cold morning, trapped under the low ceiling of a winter sky, confined with an ill-tempered spouse. It had learned to endure limits.

By February, everyone in the city had this face.

Snow everywhere, turning to ice, to slush, to pointless mounds of exhaust-fouled crud. And people turning to general nastiness and misery, nostrils raw, backs itchy, desires imprisoned in frozen blocks. The struggle for a legal parking space (the main source of civic conflict even during the warm months) took on a desperate ferocity after the storm, as if the meager rations of a city under siege had suddenly been cut in half. Longtime neighbors with shared political views came to blows. Busybodies reported nonshovelers on the city's hotline.

Just outside Central Square, Building X seemed to be the only thing in the city that was still growing. All through the winter, even after the storm, it continued up to its fourth story, developing steel bones and a skin of poured concrete. The city, paralyzed by cold and politics, hadn't officially decided what to do with the building, but the need for revenue was such that the project could not be slowed or stopped. City Hall was laboring under complex and intense pressures. The gambling idea, which had advanced from bingo, slots, and video poker to the full range of casino offerings, was gaining followers inspired by the Indians' huge successes. A coalition of large property owners, developers, lawyers, and civic boosters foresaw business opportunity, lower taxes, and a long-sought solution for Central Square's chronic shabbiness. They were joined by hard-core betting addicts and a handful of MIT number crunchers who anticipated calculating their way to personal fortunes. The pro-casino lobby sang the siren song of jobs: The computer industry was downsizing, the gas company was outsourcing, Biotech only employed a handful of Ph.D.s, the candy factory in East Cambridge had closed, the universities were under hiring freezes, the hospitals were merging, social services and nonprofits had no money, state government was cut to the bone. Cambridge could no longer afford its pose of high-minded truth-seeking and liberal good taste. The city had to acknowledge that it was part of the United States of America. And if the country was going to be saved, it was going to be saved at a profit. Out with the sherry-drinking department chair and the Brattle Square guitarist; in with the dealer, the croupier, the out-of-state speculator, the suburban amateur. Even smoking would be permitted.

Rainbow House, which had a policy of turning away the high and intoxicated in order to shelter the clean and sober, was lobbying for Building X to be deeded as a fifty-bed wet shelter and detox clinic. The need was visible in the zoned-out streetkids sprawled in the Harvard Square pit, and the roving bands of tangle-bearded men who shared pints by the river and punched one another bloody in parking lots. As for drugs, they were already being bought and sold in large quantity in Central Square and Area 4. Better to have the addicts sleeping indoors where they could be monitored for treatment and wouldn't jump the citizenry.

But the neighborhood's tolerance extended about as far as its front yards and steps, where puking, pissing, fighting, and passing out would overwhelm the most entrenched altruism. Neighbors claimed that drunks and addicts would converge on Central Square from all over the metropolitan area. Rainbow House's old-fashioned appeals to Christian charity and progressive social conscience only inflamed opposition to its plan. All the while Building X continued to grow, even as its purpose remained a mystery.

In the middle of winter this was the community.

But The Community was in the grip of spring. It tended a vision in which sidewalks were gladly shoveled, men and women spoke their feelings without rancor, and the struggle for bread and position didn't turn citizens into enemies.

By now its name was known all over the city. Its evening group meetings, first through word of mouth, then advertised on kiosks, local-access cable, and computer bulletin boards, had become legendary; the winter-long effort to recruit people from all backgrounds had paid off in publicity and remarkable numbers, without quite losing the original teal-colored mystique. The local weekly had run a long and sympathetic article, featuring an interview with The Community's leaders. The organizer said that the group was thousands of drops of water whose power depended on bonding to one another. The Community had shown that it could touch individual lives; now those lives had to be brought together in a common cause. Building X had become the key. The leaders called for a public meeting to discuss its fate, at the end of February, inside the unfinished building itself.

In a city of 100,000 talkers, rumor of Joe's healing powers had spread rapidly across a broad spectrum, although only a few people actually made the pilgrimage to the Central Square YMCA, paid off J.B. the deskman, and ascended to Room 318. A Harvard secretary wanted to quit smoking. A gay chiropractor was in love with a patient and worried that he would destroy his practice. A graphic designer kept dreaming about her own murder. Several people sought divinations of the lottery. A woman from Columbia Street didn't know how to make peace with a sister in Roxbury to whom she owed money she couldn't pay.

Joe's method with all of them was the same. He put on the wax suit and adapted Amouzou's techniques as closely as possible: turned out the ceiling light and left on a table lamp, asked a few questions, made tea on his forbidden hotplate, brought out Amouzou's wooden figure, and inside the hollow skull mixed a potion like the one he'd invented in Missy Standish's kitchen. Like Amouzou, he let them pay what they wanted, and the chiropractor alone matched half Joe's weekly wages. "You've really helped. I still don't know what I'm going to do but you've made me feel better about myself."

All the while, in the corner of the room, Missy was saying: "What's wrong, sweet love?"

Newburg had asked him about the green lion. Joe had been on his way back with bagels and coffee for the crew when his boss met him in the hallway by the trap door.

"Missy thought you might have seen it."

Off guard, Joe almost said: I'm the one. Behind that utterance, the rest of the truth would pour out.

"No, Jim, I didn't see it."

"She wondered if you're even now?"

The voice sounded unsure, but the blue eyes knew. Joe wanted to put his hand on Newburg's arm like the night he was hired. It wouldn't be the same. Newburg would never ask, "Am I one of the good ones?" again.

"I don't know what she means, Jim."

In his room at the Y, wind rattled the panes and the baseboard radiator never produced enough heat to keep Joe warm. No matter how tightly he wrapped himself in his blanket, he shivered at night and had trouble falling asleep.

He spent little, taking his meals at the cheapest joints in Central Square, pizza, Ethiopian, sometimes missing dinner if he was too tired after work. By now he had saved over 300 dollars from his job, his treatments, and the stealing gig with Kevin. The ex-con had visited again and given Joe the sixty dollars that he said was 50 percent of the green lion. He told Joe that something very big was coming up at the end of the month. "The Community is our opportunity," Kevin kept saying. On the night of the meeting at Building X, houses all over the neighborhood would be empty—there wouldn't even be kids or baby-sitters, The Community was going to arrange child care on the premises. So it was important for Joe to get the writer's house in Cambridgeport ready, and any other houses that he was working at. It was going to be so big that Kevin was bringing in some of his old associates from Dorchester. This time there was no malt liquor and Kevin was not so brotherly; he kept stealing looks around the room and didn't stay long. After he was gone, Joe kneeled beside the cot and asked his foster mother to understand that there was no magic left except money.

All his life it had been hard for him to save anything; now money piled up. He stored it in his backpack in the alcove, keeping careful track of the amount, afraid that if he carried it outside he might be robbed in Central Square by one of Kevin's associates. Some day the money would all be spent and then the magic would be over.

At the Y most people didn't speak when you saw them in the hall or bathroom, and the men on other floors might as well have been living in other cities. He heard scraps of rumor: 308 killed his wife in 1967, 331 owed the Y hundreds of dollars in rent. There was an obese old man, at the end of the hall in 303, who had lived here for something like thirty-five years. He always kept baked beans warm in a Crock-Pot and you could drop by any time, and in exchange people did his laundry because he had gotten too heavy to go out. Someone said he hadn't left the third floor since the seventies. The residents here were like the regulars at Rainbow House, a step or two higher up the ladder. You even had to spend the night here—a housekeeper checked your bed every day and if it wasn't slept in the night before she notified the director. The Y was like a prison you volunteered for.

Joe didn't decorate his room, and other than clients he never had another woman up after Patty. His mind crowded with visions of escape. Where? What's wrong, sweet love, sweet boy?

One evening the poet appeared at Joe's door, clutching his briefcase. His beard had grown where beards don't grow, up to the hollows under his eyes. His showerless smell filled the little room.

What he wanted was Joe's assistance with a poem he had written in a fever one morning in the main reading room of Widener Library. It was a miracle: He had been made the vessel for one of the very greatest poems of the century. But there was a problem. No one would want it, because it had been written by him. His enemies and detractors covered the literary world.

The sheet of paper he pulled out of his briefcase was corrugated, as if it had gotten wet and dried out. At the top was written: "My Life As a Maggot." The poem wasn't long, but Joe couldn't get past the first lines. Sentences changed directions and never finished. And there were lines like "Poor Tom's a-wanking in the men's room" that made no sense.

"What do you think? Early Eliot, Lowell, Soyinka?"

"Because I'm not from this culture—"

"You have to help me," the poet told him.

"What can I do?"

"What can't you do?" The bearded face approached, and Joe recoiled. "You're the Black Pimpernel, African Prometheus, Equatorial Faust. Don't you see? I'm a used Kleenex, everyone in this city has blown his nose, wiped his ass, or come on me. When it dries they can't get rid of me, I'm glued to them by their own living ooze. We're so bloody weary of each other. 'Computer Programmer, Divorced, Libertarian, Crashing Bore Inside Two Minutes.' You, sir, have the benefit of coming from the ends of the earth. The possibilities!"

The poet snapped his fingers in Joe's face.

"What do you want me to do?"

"Put your John Hancock on this piece of immortality!" The poet snatched the wrinkled sheet and waved it. "Our leading magazines shall fight over it like the snarling dogs they are. Anthologies, college reading lists, popular spinoffs. At a strategic point we'll leak the truth to the *Times* and literary scandal shall forever link our names. What do you say?"

Joe looked at the poem again. "It doesn't make sense." He tried to give it back, but the poet pushed it on him again.

"Read it carefully." The poet smiled. "It's about you."

"You're crazy."

"Of course I am."

"You're the maggot, not me."

"Me. You. Man's inhumanity to man."

When you went crazy, did you know it was happening? But if you were crazy, how would you know? Sometimes Joe would look at himself in the bathroom mirror, trying to catch signs in the size of his pupils, the shape of his smile. In Africa being crazy meant being possessed by another person's spirit. In Africa he would already be crazy. And here was the poet like a messenger from God come to tell him: What you've become is me. A maggot.

Joe tore the poem to pieces.

"What are you doing?" the poet cried. "That's my only copy!"

Joe immediately regretted it. He didn't understand how one moment the poet could have the power of God and the next be on his hands and knees grabbing at scraps of paper.

"Once in a lifetime. It could have changed everything."

Joe's apologies were useless. The poet rushed from the room, his coattail flying, fragments of poem fluttering from his clutches to the floor like confetti.

Joe waited for the visitor who would come in and rip away his mask and set him free. In Africa when a dancer in the masquerade did too much evil, casting curses and harming the innocent, someone in the audience came near and pulled off the mask to show his face. Then the evil power was gone, he was just a human being again. But what if the dancer was harming himself? Who would know, who would stop him? He would have to pull the mask off himself.

From his rectangle of window over Mass. Avenue, he looked out at the city: daggers of ice from the gutters, snow spilled like milk over the shingled slopes of rooftops, the muffled traffic of Central Square below, the charcoal glow of afternoon light disappearing from the sky.

The view never changed, and the fixed shape of the window frame made him feel as if he were looking at a picture of a city. There was no way to get inside it. Others were free to travel between the picture and his room, but he, who had all the freedom in the world, could not. The picture was real. Joe was the wooden figure with the hollow skull: It had strange powers but it never spoke.

It was as if he had begun dreaming a dream and at first everything was new and gave him heart. Then the dream became frightening and it wouldn't stop, but he couldn't get out of it or wake up.

He was bound up in lies, a mummy of lies. He had put on his lies like someone else's clothes and now his arms and legs were pinned. He couldn't lift his hand to feel where the lies began, to unravel them and free himself. He couldn't ask for help. The world went about its business and occasionally stopped to look through the eye holes, but when Joe tried to convey with his eyes the desperate situation he was in, the lookers only smiled as if he was telling them good news. When he opened his mouth, the muffled noises he made delighted them. Then he wanted to strike out, to hit, but he couldn't move his arms.

If he told them he wasn't Amouzou, who should he say he was? Who would that other person be?

He was saving his money so that he could leave. When he had enough, he would take his backpack and go somewhere new. Winter persisted, and he waited for something to cut him loose.

Three evenings after the poet's visit, someone else knocked on Joe's door. No one had an appointment, J.B. hadn't left a message.

Eric Barnes was standing in the doorway.

"Sorry to drop by like this. Do you have a minute?"

Joe's instinct was to shut the door, but before he knew it his visitor was inside. Eric took in the little lime green room and lost his smile.

"Did you want a treatment?" Joe asked.

"Treatment? Oh no." Eric seated himself in the chair. "Honestly, I'm not quite sure why I'm here."

Joe sat on the cot opposite. The presence in his room made it hard to breathe. Joe's mouth was dry. He had always known this man would be the one.

"What are the treaments? What do people want you to do?"

Joe folded his arms across his chest. He would make Eric Barnes finish it.

Eric looked around the room and sat back in the chair.

"Look, I'm not doing this very well. What I came for is this. I'm writing about The Community, as part of my work, and I wanted to talk to you. At the house, there never seems to be a chance. Tell me about yourself."

Eric Barnes wanted to write about him. This terrified Joe, but he couldn't help being flattered. And what he still saw in this man's face was: Tell me, I understand.

"Where did you learn your trade?"

"My grandfather chose me."

"Not your father?"

"My parents died when I was little. I was raised by my grand-parents."

"How did he choose you?"

"He—when you are born they know. They see signs. They knew I was special."

"What kinds of signs? I'm curious."

"Signs . . . I don't know. I was a baby." Joe closed his eyes. He was losing altitude. "Why are you asking this?"

"No, I'm just trying to understand. I have to admit, Joe, the first time I saw you at Missy's . . . I wanted to trade places."

Joe laughed abruptly. "You looked at me like you knew me from before."

"Did I?" Eric lost his color, glanced around the room, and leaned forward. "What exactly do you mean by changing shape? How does it happen? Maybe I do want a treatment."

"If I told you everything? Are you going to write it?"

"Not if it's privileged information. Absolutely not."

"That's what it is. Privileged."

Mr. DeSouza asked a lot of questions too, and when he saw the truth in a silver bag he thought: That's all? That's all you are? Eric Barnes was going to think exactly the same thing.

"See, Joe, people like me look at you, an African, the shape-shifting, and we think you might be able to change our shape, metaphorically anyway, and it almost doesn't matter who you are."

"If it doesn't matter, what do you want from me?"

Eric winced and the lines came out around his eyes like glass fracturing. "What made you leave Africa?"

"They said I stole some things."

A bubble of air in Joe's chest collapsed.

"What did you—what did they say you stole?"

"Things."

"Did you steal them?"

"I needed them. I had to save someone's life."

"And did you?"

"He died." More air, Joe drew it into his lungs. "Then they said I killed him, so I had to leave."

"Jim told me your whole family was killed."

"He misunderstood."

Eric scratched his eyebrow, confused. "Did you . . . kill the man?"

"No!" Amouzou was squatting in the shower. Joe gave him the bread lady's son, and Amouzou took him in his arms and stroked his head and the little boy stopped crying. "No."

"Look, I have to tell you something." Joe shivered, although there was no draft. "I saw you take some things from the job site. Sink fixtures. I don't know if 'steal' is the right word. Did you take them?"

Joe's head was moving. Yes. I am the one.

"Look, I don't care about your reasons, but it has to stop." A new voice, louder, in command. "It can't continue. If I told Jim, he'd fire you. Are you in trouble? Money?" Softer. "How much do you need? I don't want you to have to steal, for Christ's sake, coming here as a refugee. Tell me what I can do. Say something."

"I am in trouble."

"What kind of trouble?"

Don't you know? I thought you were the one. Joe had hidden himself so well, in such an un-thought-of hiding place, it was like hide-and-seek when he was a boy and he had to make a noise, cough or bump a chair, pretending it was an accident, so that someone would find him before everyone got tired of the game and went home, leaving him alone.

Eric said, "I thought maybe the theft had to do with being a witch doctor. I guess that term's offensive by now. It's like in Africa—you have to steal for your healing work?"

Joe despaired of explaining. "The magic doesn't work anymore."

Eric stared.

"The people who've come to see you—it hasn't worked with them?" Joe shook his head. "Do they know that?"

"They keep coming."

"Maybe they get something out of it anyway." Joe didn't answer. "I still don't understand. This is the trouble you're in?"

There was a game Joe used to play with his foster parents called "Who am I?" They were allowed twenty questions and no matter who he thought up, twenty was always enough. Eric Barnes could be given twenty thousand and it wouldn't be enough. The room had dwindled to the glow of the table lamp in whose circle were only himself and a stranger. Joe stood up, weightless, not moving under his own power, Amouzou's ghost inside him one last time. He went to the closet, which was dark, so that he had to feel inside the backpack. In a dream, his hand identified one object after another— soap dish, foot powder bottle, all worn smooth from long use like stones under the flow of water. The wax suit. The wooden figure, the corked skull. He touched his own arm, the healed scar. All that Africa had left him, and his hand said good-bye to each thing. The Community too, the faces of love around the table, the night already a dim memory. Another moment and it would be over, tears were going to come, sorrow and relief.

When Joe had what he wanted, he walked back to the cot. Everything was slowing down. Eric was watching his face as if the answer lay there. Joe held out his hand and followed the other man's eyes downward.

Eric stared for a long time. He still didn't understand. He looked up at Joe, down again. The eagle on the passport was faint, a ghost. Eric took the booklet as if he had never seen such a thing, opened it delicately from the back, and turned its pages one at a time. At the moment he reached the last page, which was the first, the long-ago snapshot from San Francisco whose twin lay in a tomb in Africa, Joe touched the ground and felt what Eric Barnes felt, received in his own body the same shock, saw as if for the first time his own face in a flare of light before the room went dark.

nineteen

It was a small city, and Paula only needed a few inquiries to learn that the foundation where Jane Juneau worked was called the Whitset. Eric's wife always entered her mind with a disconcerting jolt, like the thought of death. *Oh, yeah. You.* But whenever Paula tried to think her way through the moral dilemma of this other human being, no solution announced itself—like death. So her thoughts always came to an inconclusive end, and the wife slipped from her mind.

But Paula had struck out finding a grant, and necessity gave her the idea of a meeting on professional terms. She imagined his wife dressed in the high-necked Laura Ashley armor of a Cambridge professional. Blond, politically correct, proprietary. A stare to freeze the blood. "Let me get this straight. You want my husband *and* a grant?"

The moral dilemma remained theoretical. What Paula felt was that she needed to meet Jane Juneau. She needed to know who she was up against.

So she sent a proposal to the Whitset Foundation, and within a few days she was summoned for an interview.

The building was near Harvard Square, on a quiet street lined with clapboard Victorian houses. A gaunt gentleman in tweed and L.L. Bean boots came out of one and avoided eye contact. Two women in full-length skirts shared subdued laughter under a neo-classical portico. It was a Henry James novel with Saabs. By the time she found the Whitset's bronze plaque on a brownstone set back from the street by a winter garden, Paula was acutely conscious

255

of her denim skirt, her half-baked upbringing, her ill-planned adult-hood, her blank future.

She was damned if she would grovel, though. Give me the money or don't, but I'm not going to do a song and dance.

The reception room was soft and hushed, with a mauve carpet and ornate moldings. At the desk sat a young black woman wearing a kente scarf, earnest and correct.

"Can I help you?"

"I have an interview about a grant proposal." Paula heard the "and I don't give a fuck" in her voice; in this setting it sounded incredibly vulgar. "Paula Voorhees, from the Problem Place."

The receptionist picked up her telephone and announced Paula without evident disapproval or condescension. "She'll be right out."

A moment later, a woman came in from the hallway. She was neither blond nor Laura Ashley. She was short and dumpy, in jeans and a shapeless Andean sweater, with frizzy salt and pepper hair. She looked forty and sleep-deprived, and she made Paula think of the mother of her best friend in third grade. Braced for a sexual rival, she was confronted with peanut butter and jelly sandwiches.

"Nice to meet you, Paula, I'm Rachel Silver. Come on back, Jane's in the conference room. She's a bit incapacitated," the woman added.

Was Jane handicapped? Paula smiled grimly and followed Rachel Silver down the hallway, feeling as if she were looking through the wrong end of a telescope. Then they were in a vast chandeliered room, high French windows letting in overcast light, a fresh and perfect paint job, a long and polished table, at the far end of which sat a woman with her arms folded over the file spread before her.

"Jane, this is Paula Voorhees from the Problem Place."

Jane looked up from the folder and said hello. Her lack of curiosity was total and devastating. "I won't get up," she said with a cryptic smile, "but please sit down."

As she stumbled toward her seat, Paula tried not to stare. She had an impression of handsome pallor, longish brownish hair with bangs, a blazer over a billowy dress. An encumbrance in the way she sat forward, as if she was determined to overcome a disability by intelligence and will.

"Let me start," Jane said, "by saying we were very impressed with this. Especially your case descriptions. We found them very moving."

A businesslike woman. There would be no chitchat.

"We hadn't heard of your clinic," Rachel said. "And we haven't given grants in mental health before."

"With all the cutbacks," Paula offered, "there must be lots of demand."

Jane said, "We always have room for worthy proposals."

She didn't appear to be handicapped. Paula wanted to establish a bond, exchange a word or look that acknowledged what humanly united them. But the "we" was institutional. Not just these two women, who already outnumbered her, but a tax-exempt entity with an endowment of millions. Paula felt that she represented nothing but her own compromised motives. She was here to ask something for herself alone, an outrageous thing, unlikely to be given. She had come for his wife's permission.

They were waiting for her pitch.

Paula took a breath and began. In unison, the two women assumed the role of attentive audience, and as Jane unfolded her arms and sat back, the distinctive mound of a pregnancy rolled into view.

Paula stopped midsentence. Her heart sank so fast it took her breath away. She recovered, but sadness was already spreading through her blood like hemlock. She had no chance against this; and as she went on, the Problem Place got bound up with her own hopeless desire until the two were the same thing and the clinic became a doomed enterprise. Jane listened, magisterial. Her womb told Paula: Yes, we're a family.

"What happened to your state funding?" Jane asked.

"We were considered a nonessential social service."

"You didn't have any legislators in your corner?"

"I don't think our director did much lobbying."

"There's still AIDS money. Do you counsel AIDS patients?"

"Some."

"You could have asked for AIDS money from Public Health."

I give up, Paula thought. He's yours.

"Not that our decision would be affected," Jane said quickly, as if noticing her desolation. "It just helps us assess the need."

"You do incredibly important work," Rachel added. "And we know it's only going to get tougher out there. However this turns out, we really wish you the best."

This was her cue. The interview was over. Rachel stood up and Paula obediently followed. Jane extended her hand and gave Paula's a soft, warm, consoling press of flesh.

"When are you due?" Paula asked in a clotted voice.

Jane lost her smile. "End of February."

"Boy?" Paula pressed, determined to carry defeat all the way to annihilation. "Girl?"

"We don't know. We'll see."

Again: we. Another institution, the family. A lowly individual could not find a knife-width's crack in its wall. Yet as she went out into the elegant wintry silence, she realized that this expectant mother hadn't been brimming with joy.

Paula had promised to meet Sara Simon for coffee. As she walked back to the Problem Place, she tried whipping herself into a righteous fury. *Coward, deceiver, bastard, jerk.* Too weak to tell! Maybe he didn't want to be a father, maybe that was where she came in. Feeling her anger die, she desperately fanned it. By now she was walking along Mass. Avenue exactly where he'd held an umbrella over her head. Harvard's prosperity was fading into the shops of mid-Cambridge. Nearing her own turf, she had a notion that the marriage was crumbling. She caught herself, went back over the facts, laid them out and inspected each one. Here was betrayal, here was danger, here was a socially sanctioned unit that closed its door and hung up the phone on the likes of her. In a calm and level voice she would tell him why she couldn't see him again. Solve your problems with your wife and have your baby.

In this way Paula counseled herself, and by the time she reached the Problem Place her misery was unendurable. There was no talking cure for what ailed her.

"As if life isn't disappointing enough," Sara said, "now my periods are disappointing."

The new cafe was intended to bring an air of Left Bank to Central Square, but patrons who looked like potential clients of the Problem Place harbored stacks of ill-used reading material, their saucers puddled with hours-old coffee.

The caffeine was reacting badly on Paula's nerves, which jangled inside her dry winter skin. It was painful to hold her eyes steady on Sara. "Isn't it a little soon to worry about that?"

"Number 1, the whole point of worrying is to do it early and often. Number 2, I'm thirty-seven next month."

"You've only been trying—"

"Clearly you're unfamiliar with the recent data on male infertility. There's an estrogen-like chemical in the atmosphere. It's like some feminist mad scientist lost control of an experiment. And I could be malfunctioning in any number of ways. We're engineered to reproduce at eighteen, like these teenagers who look at a guy and get pregnant, God damn them all."

"What does Lewis say?"

"What does Lewis say about anything? Not much. Basically, it hurts his pride. To which I respond: Deal with it. They give you a fun magazine and you do what you've been doing since you were thirteen, only you catch it in a cup and it's for a good cause."

"I can see why he'd think it's a little dehumanizing." Paula's pleasure in pushing Sara's buttons made her feel guilty, and guilt made her angry. She was a mess, on a high wire, spinning. "Let's not talk about it."

"Why don't you just take my side?"

"OK, I'm on your side."

"I want you to think it, not just agree to it."

"And if Lewis agrees to jerk off into a cup, does he have to like it too?"

Sara raised her cappuccino. "Very deft analysis. What a controlling bitch I am. You would be too if your world seemed this out of control."

"How do you know it doesn't?" Paula snapped.

"At least you're getting certain satisfactions out of life."

"What do you mean?"

A smile arranged itself on Sara's face. "I knew something was wrong because my tabby was out of place. But what clinched it was a faint circular stain on the comforter at approximately crotch level."

Paula considered issuing a flat denial. But the blood flow to her cheeks had already given her away. It was like the dream of being naked in public.

"I should have asked. I'm sorry. It happened three times and it won't happen again."

"Why be sorry? Do I know him?"

"No."

"Tell me about him." Sara set down her cup and leaned forward. "Come on, we'll compare notes."

I wish I could trust you, Paula thought. She had no friend like that. Her mother was the closest thing; but her mother was far away, being forced to make lists of people she had wronged. Paula imagined telling. The sunlight in her window the morning after the storm. The new power she felt in her own body. The hollow of his neck. The fits of anxiety. This afternoon's discovery.

"What's the matter?" Sara was looking at her with concern.

"Hmm?"

"Are you crying?"

"No. Am I?" Paula touched her face and her fingers came away wet. "Jesus, that's weird." She dabbed her cheek with a coffee-stained napkin. She pushed her cappuccino away. "I'm a little run-down these days."

Sara reached to touch her hand. "What's wrong?"

The world had no time for anyone else's trouble and it was a million to one that the person you told was the one who could make herself you for the instant it took to see. But she had to tell someone. Certain she was making a mistake, Paula began to talk. It was sheer indiscretion. She wasn't to be trusted with her own secret.

She didn't apologize or fudge, putting it in the most straightforward terms possible, even what she had just learned about his wife. And her words had an extraordinary effect. Sara was forgetting herself.

"Oh my God, Paula," Sara moaned. "You're in love with him, this is so serious." Paula's heart began to open. "Oh, no no no no no. This is so bad, don't you see? I don't care about him, he shouldn't be doing it, but you are in extreme danger and as your friend I have to tell you that you *must stop it now*. Don't get angry. This is suicidal. I've seen friends—it ends badly, Paula, that's the rule, it's like a law of physics. He'll spend five years telling you he's about to leave his wife and by the time you realize he's a jerk you're my age and you have to grab some also-ran at a singles party and tell him to masturbate into a cup."

A patchy-bearded man scraping sugar out of his demitasse turned to look. Paula said, "Please lower your voice."

"Promise me you'll stop it. I can tell you don't like this, but I have to go on record and say I object, for your sake as your friend I object."

"I didn't ask for your approval."

"I know you're angry."

What a mistake to confide in Sara! She made it all seem so crude and shabby and *doomed*.

"What do you do with love? Watch TV till it goes away? Have it surgically removed?"

"I don't act as if there aren't consequences," Sara said coldly.

"And pretty soon there's nothing in your life but consequences. What did you say—marriage is like real estate?"

"You don't worry about breaking up a family?"

Paula trembled. "Of course I do." No one was going to grand-stand with her. She made herself look directly into Sara's eyes, ex-pecting smug disapproval. But Sara appeared stricken. She was in the presence of something strange and frightening and she wanted it to stop. The sight of the comforter had devastated her. The heedless waste, the irrefutable evidence. What else could that stain be but love?

Now Paula had to call him, because they had planned to meet at Sara's over the weekend. But calling him wasn't permitted, and the imposed silence drove her wild with resentment and seemed to bear out Sara's warning. The whole situation was designed to fling hu-miliation in her face, the endless obsessing, the passivity that made her both clutching and fatalistic. She refused to become the kind of woman who whined or threatened for more attention, she knew it would repel him as much as her. But the alternative was helpless-ness, which was intolerable. When the evening went by without a call from Eric she started muttering out loud: "Forget it, I'm not sit-ting still for this shit." But home from work the next night she ran for the answering machine—its red light was blinking.

The message was from the rehab clinic: Her mother was refusing to cooperate unless they let her listen to opera on her Walkman at mealtimes, which were supposed to be communal. Paula almost laughed at the thought of their solemn efforts to get her mother to share in group. But when she called and her mother came on the line, Paula pleaded, "Mama, don't fight them, please stick with the program."

In the middle of the week an envelope arrived with no return ad-dress. It was a computer printout, which made what he wrote seem more intimate, like a passionate stare in a business meeting. He was a writer after all, and the blockage of his work had given way and words came pouring out, tender, funny, never mawkish, honest in the way he seemed that night in the rain outside Widener. Even when he wrote of her body and its delights, a subject Paula was not disposed to read about, she found herself becoming excited. Written proof of the happiness she knew how to give him.

Did he know that he hadn't signed the printout? There was "I love you" but no name, as if he'd forgotten or had been in a hurry. The blank space at the end left her fighting off vertigo. She urged reason on herself, reread the letter, sucking all the sweet juice from its phrases until she was calm.

But she couldn't write back, and it grated.

Through it all she had to work. Gladys came back, as Eric had predicted. She showed up for her appointment stitched and sullen, like a mistreated dog with no other home.

"James got released. They didn't bring no charges."

Paula made herself start probing. "What's that like?"

"He's back at work and he's being good—I ain't ever seen him this good. Michael's asthma's worse."

"I'm not surprised. He must be extremely upset." Gladys didn't answer. Paula had no idea how to bring that wild afternoon into the session room, and Gladys wasn't going to help. It was present anyway, a contaminant. "Gladys, do you think this therapy was damaged by what happened? Would you rather see someone else here?"

Gladys looked at the door and shrugged. Her lip was curled slightly as if to say, "You're probably no worse than them." She looked back at Paula. "Not really. Uh-uh."

The stitched swelling reminded Paula of the missing lens, the silence around it overpowered the session room. Trauma was buried deep in the flesh. Months of painstaking surgery would be required to extract it. Meanwhile, the mystique of Paula's authority was lost. Therapist and client had seen each other naked, both of them helplessly stuck.

Watching Gladys retreat down the hall, Paula felt that the only thing of value in her own life was the secret she was carrying. It alone had color and savor, everything else was bland necessity. And as she waited for the next fragment of the world's suffering to shuffle into her office and resume its confession without end, she wondered why her triviality didn't disgust her.

She decided to call Eric at home, braced to hang up like a criminal if his wife answered. But if he answered and fussed at her, then she would tell him what it was like, the waiting and the doubt, she would let him know what this was doing to her. He answered: a little surprised, not irritated, sorry for what Paula had gone through with Sara, eager to see her. He would drive over to the Narconia tomorrow afternoon, a Saturday. In the background she heard workmen.

"I went to see the magician the other night."

The radiator was clanking and the bedroom smelled of stale steam. Through bamboo blinds, a pale sun was struggling in. Eric lay alongside Paula, propped on an elbow.

"Did he cure you?"

"No, but you were right about him. He's a fake."

"A fake magician?"

"You can't tell anyone, I promised him. He's not even African, Paula. He's American."

She didn't feel the least bit curious. As soon as the lovemaking had stopped and he had withdrawn from her body and begun to talk of other things, she had fallen into nameless melancholy. Now it was quickening into panic.

"How disappointing."

"It was, at first. It was like having a really interesting dream end. But then I had a different reaction."

"What was it?" she made herself ask.

"I was intrigued. Why did he do it? And it occurred to me: He's a kind of magician after all. Because he's conning everyone. He's like an escape artist. This is what shape-shifting really means. I tried to explain it but he didn't want to hear. He asked me to leave."

On the ceiling above the mattress there was an ugly yellow stain. Water damage. She hadn't noticed it before; it must have happened the day of the radiator flood.

"But imagine that kind of freedom." His voice grew loud with the excitement of his ideas. "People toil away for years, and this guy makes it overnight by taking on a new identity. It's like he figured his way inside the mechanism of success. It's changing people's perceptions, getting them to see you in a different way. And it's a hell of a dilemma, because it's privileged, but this stuff would be perfect for my article." He was tapping his finger on the mattress. "I could write something interesting about the American Joe."

"Could you just do that, expose him?" Her severity took her by surprise. "I can see why you made him angry."

"You can?"

Why didn't he know that she was feeling this despair? A lover would know. Why didn't his fingers sense it through the skin of her back, why didn't he shut up about this crap and tell her what she was desperate to hear? The thought that his love wasn't equal to hers oppressed her.

"Think what he's going through." She tried to make her voice toneless. "If it was so easy to change, nothing would mean anything and life would be totally bleak and depressing. You're talking about a fantasy. What's real is choosing and sticking with it."

"You're sad," he said, touching her cheek.

She kissed his fingers. "Thanks." She laughed inwardly at the non sequitur.

"And I'm going on about nothing. Darling, what's made you sad?"

"I'm not." She wasn't. Not now. Hungry for more, she asked, "Do you wish my body was different? More filled out, here and here?"

"Tits and ass have a short shelf life. This shape of yours"— running his hand down her shoulder, into the hollow of her waist, up along the soft curve of her hip—"is perfectly perfect and edible."

A warm tide of pleasure washed over her. "If you didn't like my body would you tell me?"

"But I love it." He hesitated. "People should be honest."

"Wrong answer. If people were honest all the time it would be total chaos and no one would be able to stand anyone and the crime rate would go up. Never tell a woman what you really think if it's bad news."

Would he confess to his wife, just to be honest? Paula had become aware of a weak strain in his character, a dutifulness that tended toward fatalism; a self-fulfilling conviction that life was bound to disappoint. He was not hard enough. He was not one of the winners. Some people knew what they wanted and got it without second thoughts or self-sabotage. She knew people like that and he was not one. His wife was, Paula had seen it in her face. And right now Jane wanted a father. Pregnancy made some women hapless cows but Jane was a lioness. If Eric told his wife, Paula would lose. She was certain of it.

"Do you think your wife's noticed anything?"

She felt his caress on her waist slow down. "I don't think so. She's distracted." He paused, and she could almost hear him holding his breath.

"Because she's pregnant?"

His hand froze. "How did you know?"

"Accident. I went by the Whitset rattling my tin cup and realized this was the woman."

"I wish I could say I would've told you," Eric said. "But it felt like that would be the end."

For a while they didn't speak. Paula wished that she'd never mentioned his wife, never seen her. The only hope was to go on pretending there was no wife.

Suddenly, he chuckled harshly. "Did I come up?"

"Of course not."

"What was it like?"

"Scary. I liked her. She's very impressive. But I have the feeling they won't give us a grant."

"They might." He was trying to sound natural; she had rattled him badly. "They're rich. And very into the local community."

"How would we all get along without that word?"

He reached for her hand and stroked it until she became peaceful.

In her shower, where for years she'd washed herself alone, he took the soap and the coarse sponge to places she'd never reached, between her shoulder blades and in the small of her back, lovingly over every inch of her body.

He suggested taking advantage of the clearing sky. They drove out of Somerville into Cambridge and down to the river, where they parked and set out on foot.

It was difficult going. The paths were buried under a crust of frozen snow crisscrossed with deep footprints. The effort of walking side by side required concentration and there was little talk. After they crossed to the Boston side, he took her hand and they walked together like any couple. A thin disc of sun hung low over the city. The February trees stood twisted in the pallid light; in an oak a flock of crows was cawing at the empty air. The river was frozen now from bank to bank, a white curve, and Paula saw no ducks. When he reminded her about the merganser it made her sad because it no longer felt the same. The memory of that other walk weighed on her, and she fought the sensation that a circle was closing. On the Cambridge side, they let their hands drop.

He drove her home. The afternoon was dying behind Prospect Hill as they crossed the bridge over a scrap-metal yard and descended into Union Square.

"What's going to happen to us, Eric?"

"I don't know," he said, as if he'd been thinking the same thing.

"Do you worry about it?"

"Of course I do."

"Something worries me." Turning into Union Square, he glanced at her and waited. But what she was about to say scared her and for a moment she couldn't go on. "That one day you'll wake up and think: That was a nice dream but now I'm myself again. Like this African magician who turns out to be American. That this is just situational, your book, your wife's pregnancy, and—"

"This isn't someone else." He turned from the windshield and she saw a look on his face that she'd never seen before. It was the look she'd felt on her own, lying in her bed two hours ago, waiting

for him to rescue her. "This is me, more than anywhere, with anyone." He reached for her hand. "Don't ever forget that—and don't
let me."

She went into the Narconia alone. She found that she was shivering uncontrollably. As she fumbled with her keys, Mary's door
opened.

"Hello, dear." Mary grinned past her myopically down the hall.
"Did he leave?"

"He left."

"He seems like such a nice man."

"Yes," Paula said. "He is."

central square

twenty

"Who's Paula?"

Jane's hospital drama had just broken for a commercial. Eric was in the middle of a comment on a student paper. As he looked up, his pen staggered off course into the margin. There was a bitter smile on Jane's face.

"Or is it Pauladotbak?"

It was a moment before he understood. He had forgotten to delete the backup file.

"You went into my computer?"

"That's right." Her eyes warned him not to protest. "For some strange reason I felt like I might have been ignoring your problems. I wanted to see whether we could rescue your book." She laughed faintly. "It seems you've been occupied with other things."

He saw Jane staring at the screen, scrolling down in disbelief through pages of betrayal. He saw her doubling over in pain, clutching her womb. His last letter had been brief and informational, and he wondered if that was the one in the file. Behind the pounding in his temples he was disturbed to recognize a feeling of relief, the roller coaster finally settling back at its gate.

"What was there?"

The question enraged her.

"You bastard, you—bastard! What was there? You mean what's the damage? Oh Jesus, Eric."

"I'm sorry," he said.

"What?"

"I'm sorry."

"For what? What are you sorry for?"

Her eyes were fastened on his like talons, waiting, harboring their fury. Her rights had become limitless.

Although he purged his voice of abjection and invented nothing, in the telling his love affair took on the quality of a sordid and mindless folly. Somehow he had expected confession to cauterize the wound he'd inflicted; instead, she lost all her color and began shaking her head as if in sync with some mechanical inner noise.

"I can't believe it, Eric. I can't believe it's true."

"It's true."

She put her face in her hands. The hospital drama was back on, a surgeon was barking orders. Eric reached for the remote control beside Jane's thigh, and she recoiled against the arm of the couch as though he were going to touch her. He aimed the remote at the television set, but her reaction so unnerved him that instead of turning it off he changed the channel. A nature show came on, wild boar were trying to mate.

"For God's sake turn it off!"

"Sorry."

The word was a reflex, a flinch. He would have to find a better one, which might encompass responsibility and remorse and a remnant of dignity.

"Please leave me alone," she said into her hands. "I'm not going to let you see me like this. I hate you for making me do this."

In the kitchen he washed their dinner dishes, then went into the baby room. The new carpet was covered in drop cloths, and all the woodwork was washed in a pale coat of primer. The painters had left their brushes and buckets in a corner of the room by the diaper cabinet. He picked up a brush and began to apply a coat of semi-gloss to the cabinet, working by a drop light, making sure to brush out drips and bristle marks. He soon fell into a rhythm of dipping and stroking and brushing out, forgetting everything, completely intent on giving the diaper cabinet a perfectly even coat as if it would be subjected to the most exacting scrutiny.

"We're paying the painters to do that." Jane was standing in the door.

"I thought I'd get a head start."

"That's wonderful, Eric."

Her face was chalky and her eyes red, but she was no longer crying. One hand lay on the dropped oval of her belly, fingers spread in absentminded motherly care. The sight brought Eric a stab of self-loathing. He stood up with the paintbrush in his hand.

"I want some answers," she told him.

He waited.

"Exactly how many times have you lied to me? Count them. Tell me every one, including tonight."

Jane was panting slightly, with large shining eyes. The hunger in her face made him think of the moment in lovemaking when she was too aroused to hold back but almost resented needing him to bring her off. Hurt pride was intolerable, it tortured her. She had come in here for relief.

With the smell of paint in his nostrils, he tried to recall his transgressions. His affair had required little deceit because he had numbed himself to the fear of detection and Jane had had her own preoccupations, and perhaps because after all these years she had trusted him.

"Who is she? How did you meet her?"

"I—no." He tried to firm himself. "I'll tell you anything about me but let's leave her out of it."

"Oh, you're such a fucking gentleman. What a good guy. Who you fuck doesn't matter to your wife." It was shocking to hear her talk like this. Jane despised obscenity. "Do you love her?" she demanded with outrage and dread.

"No."

Paula had said no one needed to know everything. They were lying in her bed when she said it, he was stroking her hip. He already missed her. He had just betrayed her, too.

"Is she some young slut you scraped off the sidewalk?"

"Not that either."

"Have you picked up a disease?"

From the doorway, she blasted him with questions. He was still holding the wet paintbrush, as if he were about to go back to work, to show his goodwill, as if putting it down would mean he was re-signed to his own rancidness. His answers all inflamed her, and her color grew high as she regained her mastery. When she greeted one of his explanations with a sarcastic laugh, he rebelled inwardly but didn't object, imagining her anger as something finite like acid—better to drain it all out at once, scald and corrode and be done.

"You'd never have told me, you coward."

"It wouldn't have gone on long." He saw Paula's eyes, startled, wounded, already turning away from him.

"And you'd have come and said, 'Sweetie, I've been fucking Paula So-and-so but it's over'?"

"I would have found a way to tell you."

"I don't believe you. Prove it."

"How can I?"

They sat on the drop cloths past midnight, in this room that had been his study, surrounded by new wood and fresh paint.

"That book nearly killed me." He was remembering the despera-tion that had come over him in early winter. Old resentments rose to his tongue. "You told me not to be discouraged—everything was crumbling in my hands and I was in it alone, Jane."

"So I made you do it." She barked a laugh. "Did the baby, too?"

"You just wanted the book to be finished. Do you deny that?"

"How dare you try to put this on me? You chose it!"

At some point his mind stopped working and he forgot what they were arguing about, aware only of the exhaustion behind his eyes and Jane's drilling, probing him for some clue that continually eluded her as the night dragged on and was finally unavailable, be-cause what she wanted was for the thing not to have been done. And what he wanted was expiation, which wasn't coming either. So they clutched like two boxers in the late rounds, Jane bloodying him but unable to knock him out and unwilling to call a draw.

They ended up crying in an embrace, as if consoling each other over a death or a fire that had consumed their past.

"Let's try to sleep," he said gently. The paintbrush was caked and dry, ruined.

Eric brought a blanket and pillow into the living room and lay down on the couch. In spite of his fatigue, he couldn't sleep. There were no blinds and the streetlight dazzled him. He listened to the intermittent cars passing and the middle of the night shouts of a drunk, and once, holding his breath, he heard Jane sobbing in the bedroom. If he went to comfort her she would send him away. She would rediscover the enormity of his deed and the cycle would start over, rage, remorse, explanation, disbelief. He pressed the pillow over his head and for some reason thought of the picture in Joe's passport. To pull off a thing like that, you had to be free. He himself had tried to work a sort of magic and defy the limits, and it had failed. He was neither magician nor trickster, but a hopeless creature of the day world.

Just after falling asleep, he woke up. Jane was running water in the bathroom. It was morning. His lower back was a knot of pain from the couch; in the throbbing behind his eyes recollection came. He waited until she was out before getting up to use the toilet. They encountered each other in the kitchen—she was dressed for work, eating a bowl of cereal standing up; he still wore last night's incriminating clothes, licked with white paint. The practical muscle stood out in her cheek, and the sight of it told him the overnight reconciliation he'd dared to hope for wasn't coming. She didn't greet him.

"This is the way it's going to be. I don't want you to be here when I get home. Pack a bag, take what you need. You'll have to find someone to stay with. I suppose you could go to a hotel, but we can't afford more than a few nights. I'd like you to be out of the house for at least the next two weeks."

She spoke with cool authority. He longed for last night's melodrama. "And then?"

"I don't know. I need to decide whether I'll ever be able to trust you or even like you enough to live with you again." She waved her cereal spoon at him. "And you need to figure out what the hell you want, whether you really even want to be married. But listen to me." Her eyes flashed. "If you ever go to see that person again, we're totally through. Do you understand me, Eric? I'm not going to track you with an electronic bracelet. Do you think you're capable of being honest?"

He bridled at her contempt, and nodded. "When will we talk?"

"When I'm ready I'll call you. Leave a note where you're staying. I have to go to work. Someone has to earn a living around here."

She gathered her bag, her coat, her scarf.

"Jane—"

She turned on him and her eyes shone with the distress she was trying to contain. "Well?"

But what he wanted was beyond words and wouldn't be given, not now, not here.

The prospect of leaving shook him, as if he were being dispossessed of clothes, lodging, past, future, everything. Where would he go? He could stay with Ray in New York for a few days, and sink to the bottom, with the beer cans and pee-stained underwear. New York frightened him, he'd be lost there. He needed to stay nearby.

He had already begun the process of severing his connection to whatever force had made him take Paula's hand by the river. In a matter of time he would feel it draining out. The source of every sensation, alertness in the blood, the cold grip of fear on his testicles, life itself, would run dry and leave him alone. Whenever the face under his umbrella came near, confused and reproachful, he willed it away.

At last he phoned Jerry Silver's law firm. A receptionist passed him to a secretary who, after putting him on hold for several minutes, connected him with Jerry.

"You don't need to explain yourself to me, Eric. Drive out right now. Geneva can let you in."

"Maybe you should OK it with Rachel." Jane would already have told Rachel at the Whitset; they would be bonding in womanly outrage.

"Get out. She'll feel the same. You're our old friend and you've had some bad luck." Jerry's kindness and moral vagueness made it difficult to speak. "It's a misunderstanding, I'm sure it is."

"Jerry, I can't tell you—"

"Get out. We'd love to have you. We've been meaning to show you guys the new house but it just seems like there's never any time."

For the second time this winter, Eric found himself in Lincoln. A couple of miles down the road from Missy Standish, the Silvers had established their new life: a snow-covered parcel of land, a stand of spruce and a giant old oak, a sloping lawn with a redwood playset for Zachary. The house itself was all electronic-eye alarms and climate controls and intercoms that kept the family in perpetual touch with itself no matter which room its members were in, even the bathroom. A West Indian housekeeper and a Danish au pair had become part of the ensemble. The world was banished beyond the trees, but telephones, fax, and modem allowed an instant buzz of communication with the law firm, the Whitset Foundation, and all other integrated nodes. The house was a self-contained nesting system, a temple to the nuclear family. The Silvers had found true expression here.

Eric spent the afternoon reading in the living room. The floor's high polish, and the gathered drapes, and the stillness outside made his troubles seem almost unreal. It was difficult to believe that anything unpleasant was happening anywhere.

When Rachel came home, she showed him nothing but hospitality. It was extremely common, she told him, for this to occur during pregnancy; she knew a number of cases. Hearing that he conformed to standard male psychology made Eric want to tell her that Paula was rare and so was what he felt for her.

At dinner Eric's subdued mood drove Jerry to higher than usual spirits, he regaled the table with his adventures on the Web and plans for a summer garden. Eric tried hard to show interest.

"It'll sort out," Jerry suddenly said.

"It won't be quite as easy as that," Rachel said. "It takes a lot of work, after something like this."

"Call me sentimental. You two belong together. Wait till the baby comes, you'll see."

Eric saw Rachel flash Jerry a look and realized they had fought over his staying with them.

Zach had already eaten with the au pair. In the new Lincoln order he was more out of sight, a better-regulated child. It was only after dinner, when the Silvers lapsed into their evening routines—a fire going in the living room, Rachel with a book in the big arm-chair, Jerry and Zach playing on the Persian rug—that Eric knew how alien his presence was. The flicker of Rachel's eyes over the top of her novel told him that he blighted the harmony of the house, that Jerry was weak enough for the crime to threaten contagion.

Eric sat at the other end of the room and tried to read the news-paper. But he found himself unable to keep his eyes off father and son at play on the rug. Legs spread, Jerry pitched a Nerf ball to Zach, who grasped, knocked it away, and ambled after it. Then Zach tried to toss it back with a stiff, erratic arm. As often as not, the ball slid backward off his fingers; but each time, Zach recovered it and earnestly set about to make a proper throw. Once, when the ball sailed from his hand miraculously straight into his father's six feet away, Jerry roared cheers and Zach beamed and clapped his hands, a perfect little display of pride and delight.

Three months had transformed Zach from an unpleasant mess of manipulation and appetite into a little boy. His face was no longer thick and stupefied from the indulgence of every urge. Its shape was molded by striving, the tongue stuck out, the eyes sought approval. Eric wanted to clutch him, feel his little bones and hot child's breath. He had never imagined a son, a companion, only the voracious blob that had stolen his wife.

In the guest bedroom he fell asleep feeling cheated out of every-thing that could have brought him happiness, yet sensing that some-thing was wrong with this version of his misfortunes.

"Take a look at this."

Silver tossed a magazine across the kitchen table. Rachel was up-stairs putting Zach down. Eric had lingered in the city after his class, taking dinner at a fast-food place in Central Square before driving back to Lincoln. He was trying to stay out of the Silvers' house as much as possible.

The magazine was the inaugural issue of the new *Edge*. On the cover, below "The Way We Live Now," a sextet of young men in suits was sitting around a poker table in a plush book-lined room that suggested a private club. It was a parody of the card-playing dogs cartoon. Among the vaguely familiar-looking faces—caught in moments of shock, malice, delight—was Paul Duffy's, pink and turning to grin at the reader. He was about to pull an ace of spades from under the table. Below his hand the title said: "The New Culture Winners."

After a suitable interval, Eric returned it. "Good for him."

Jerry was outraged. "I can't believe Paul stooped to this!"

"Hell, I might have done the same."

That night with Duffy at the Silvers' old house, Eric's existence seemed to have been under dispute; now he couldn't remember what it was about. He had an instinct to protect himself. An old bruise was about to be bumped, a dying fire stirred, a desire that wouldn't leave him alone. Jerry didn't understand, he lived in Lincoln and worked on State Street, outrage cost him nothing.

"Can I ask you a personal question, Eric?"

Eric tensed for the bump. At this point, there were no good personal questions.

"Rachel said you stopped working on your book." Jerry was looking at his hands on the kitchen table. "I mean, you've been so successful."

The thought of explaining exhausted Eric. How could he make Jerry sit at his desk back in those darkening afternoons of late fall and early winter, his powers of work failing, the feeling of going under? There were things he himself didn't understand. He suspected (he'd begun turning this over, in the restless thoughts brought on by loss of his routine) that he had a secret longing for oblivion, that some inner necessity had compelled him to seek ruin as methodically as others pursued their careers. How could he explain that to Jerry?

"I lost my nerve." There was pleasure in being hard on himself, and it drove him to exaggerate. "What I've found," he said, engaging Jerry's unwilling eyes, "is that Duffy was right about one thing: The world is what it is. What matters is your character. We think what matters is whether this or that thing works out. No, that's just circumstances. The truth is, I'd be a better father than writer—I know that sounds ironic now. But it would have been my real talent."

Jerry said, "Not would have been. Will be."

"You're a good friend, Jerry."

"You'd do it for me."

"It wouldn't happen to you."

"No?" Jerry lowered his voice, as if the intercom mounted on the wall were broadcasting to the rest of the house. "You don't think I go stir crazy out here?"

"You seem happy. You all do."

"The other night Rachel was at a meeting and I popped my Cambridge home video in the VCR. I was taking lots of tape those weeks before we moved—that pulse you get in Central Square with all the crazies, the girls around Harvard, inside the Harp. It was like I was watching the highlights of my life as a man." Jerry smiled sheepishly. "Believe it or not, I got a little jealous when I heard what happened with you."

Eric shook his head. "Rachel's going to blame me and kick me out."

"You know what she said last night? 'Eric's face has changed. When a person looks like that you have to forgive him.'"

This unexpected piece of kindness left him temporarily speechless.

"She didn't happen to tell you anything Jane said today?"

"No—sorry. But you know what? Zach came in while the tape was still on and said, 'Daddy sad.' The little guy came over and put his arms around me. I started bawling like a baby."

"No need to be jealous."

Silver laughed from his chest and rolled his eyes. "It's not exactly the same thrill, is it?"

"Jerry, I wish I could tell you about this person. You might have the wrong idea. She's—wonderful." Eric was picturing Paula rushing out into the storm. "She's a social worker, she really cares about them. She has this patient named Gladys Dill. I'm not explaining well."

"You must be going through hell." Silver reached over and put a hand on his shoulder. "Are you OK for money?"

"Sure." Eric felt himself flush. "I can always pick up a couple more classes."

"It's not a big deal."

"Jerry, you've done a lot and I'm grateful."

He had thought once that a few thousand dollars drawn on Silver's account might change everything. At the time that amount of money had seemed the difference between success and failure.

In the mornings he woke up before dawn, momentarily lost. Then he dressed quickly, laid out the breakfast table, and made coffee. After breakfast he washed the dishes, although both Silvers insisted it was Geneva's job. As soon as possible he got out of the house and drove into the city. All day his face felt unwashed and his teeth unbrushed, he never seemed to be wearing his own clothes. The new routine left him outdoors much of the time, and the cold he'd never gotten rid of grew worse.

He didn't know how to spend his days. Teaching and holding extra office hours, inventing little tasks, didn't begin to fill the time he suddenly had to himself. He had lost his purpose. It had been his books, and then it had been Paula, and now he was floating.

He kept ending up in Central Square, and at least once a day he passed the building where she worked, hoping for a chance encounter that would keep to the letter of Jane's warning. But Paula never appeared.

He called her apartment twice from pay phones and twice got her answering machine. The first time he hung up; the second time he was about to tell her what had happened when the sound of her recorded voice stopped him. Telling her would mean the end.

"It's me. Where are you? I'll call back." A truck was braking past in hydraulic wheezes.

He tried to throw himself into his article. Joe was one person he was still allowed to see, but he didn't know what to do about Joe. The secret that had fallen into his hands seemed like a precious thing, and he still harbored a hope of bartering it for some modest achievement that might salvage his lost vocation. Yet he also felt that as long as Joe's secret stayed secret, and Joe went on being the magician that he wasn't, there was hope for something much better: renewal.

One morning, Eric stood outside a chain-link fence and watched workers pour the fourth-floor slab of Building X. On their lunch break, they let him walk around the site in a hard hat and he studied every detail with the care he had put into his own renovation. People he was beginning to recognize as Central Square regulars hung out by the fence, stamping their feet in the cold and nursing cups of coffee while pigeons pecked along the sidewalk. He approached and asked what they thought of The Community.

Some of them quoted the signs and then either burst out laughing or speculated at length on their meaning. Others talked about the big rally that was going to happen in Building X, just a few days away.

"What about this young African?" Eric asked. "Why do you think he's caught on with people?"

"They say he gets inside you," one man said, "changes your shape or something, fixes your problems. It's an African thing. We can do that over there."

"Now what the hell do you mean?" an old-timer with an eye patch asked the other man. "You got one shape and that's the one God gave you. And you ain't any more African than this white fellow here."

"Damn, Reuben, you been totally brainwashed."

Eric asked, "Has anyone here been to see him?"

No one had.

"I'm waiting to see what this Community thing can do for *me*," the old-timer said. "So far I ain't seen anything. You with the paper?"

Eric jotted down what they said, and people noticed and came over to join in. Soon there was a crowd, white and black, and a loud argument about African magic and the merits of a casino in Central Square. The women held little children by the hand; most of the men appeared to have nothing to do, some even seemed homeless, and the talk went on and on. Eric wondered if any of these people were Paula's clients. Listening, he felt closer to her.

In Central Square he lost his immunity. Strangers addressed him freely, teenagers muttered drug offers, every handbill found him. Work and marriage had identified and also concealed him, like clothing. Who was he? There had been a socially and legally sanctioned answer: Eric Barnes, husband of Jane Juneau, writer, resident of Cambridgeport, voter in Ward 5, Precinct 2. Without these, he was his individual self—compelled to account for himself with anyone who happened to glance his way. When a drunk accosted him in front of Woolworth's and launched into an incoherent speech, Eric didn't move on, he had nowhere to move on to. He listened and tried to make sense, until a wigged and lipsticked old woman passing by said, "Can't you see he's crazy?"

This was his community. It had been his community all along.

"Don't blow it," Ray had told him.

Sometimes he was tempted to return home and spy through a window, fearing that Jane would have turned the house against him in drawn shades and locked doors. She was always scared to be alone at night. He thought of feigning a break-in while she was at work to make her see she couldn't live without him. Sometimes she decided on a course of action and pursued it even if she wasn't sure she wanted to, *because* she wasn't sure, rigid with ambivalence.

He imagined turning into one of the Central Square regulars. His green parka would become a familiar emblem of decay to the people heading for the subway after work. Shopkeepers would glare when they saw him coming, Indian waiters would threaten to call the police if he didn't leave, but the new coffee house would let him sit all afternoon. He would sleep in the trees behind the little park on Western Avenue, an easy mark for drunks and punks. The police would kick him awake and tell him to get moving. Jane—her pregnancy somehow gone—would see him on the street the day he reached bottom. At first she wouldn't know him through the dirt and sunburn and bloody cuts. Then she would run to hug him, stroke his knotted hair. "Forgive me," he would say, and she would say, "Forgive me."

Or: "Never."

At times as he stood waiting for the light to change and gazed at the people across the intersection and hoped there was no one he knew, he felt like a victim of some flagrant injustice. And at times his regret throbbed like a cold headache and he beat his fists against his skull to make it go away.

One unusually warm February evening, Eric found himself across the street from the building whose basement housed the Problem Place. It was sunset, and the sky was on fire. The brick façade was bathed in red light, the shadow across the basement door was blue and cool. The intensity of color suggested Paula's presence inside.

Without looking for traffic, he started across the street.

But he was forbidden to see her. How petty of Jane! A ban on happiness!

He had a feeling of being watched. She's inside, he told himself. Go. It's what you want.

The door gave when he pulled. But to his dismay the front room was empty. The lights were out. It was almost 6:00, the office was closed, they had all gone home.

At the end of the hall he noticed light spilling from an open door. Maybe she was alone, working late. Waiting for him. The hallway was papered with signs for prenatal care, AIDS testing, trauma-survivor groups. This was where she helped Gladys and the others.

A voice came from the lighted room. Not hers, a man's voice. Eric turned into the doorway.

A dozen people were sitting around a table, but no Paula. No one noticed him because they were listening to the man whose voice Eric had heard.

"... techno-consumerism has us all in its thrall. No one gets off. The unholy trinity of the nineties: God the bottom line, Christ productivity, the Holy Ghost downsizing. Every one of us is a believer. If you disagree you are cast aside like trash. It's a coercive, totalitarian faith."

This was Paula's boss. This was The Community.

But Paula had gone home. She didn't believe in The Community, and she loathed this pudgy man with his stocking feet drawn up in the chair and a gleam in his eyes.

Eric stood frozen in the doorway.

"Welcome, friend." From the end of the table Peter Fine was waving him in. "Whatever you're looking for, you've found it."

Someone edged aside and pulled out an empty chair. Eric thought he might have seen a few of these people around Central Square. They seemed glad to make room for him. In the welcome there was something of the unanimous bonhomie of a prayer group or a meeting of alcoholics.

He sat between a woman with frosted hair and a weak-chinned man who smelled of mothballs. Eric decided that he would listen for a little while, then excuse himself and look for Paula in Union Square.

"Tell us who you are," Fine said.

"Eric Barnes." It was like arriving at a new school midyear.

"Anything else?" Fine's smile said that he was only asking for the group's benefit, that he already knew every one of Eric Barnes's secrets. "What brings you here?"

"What are your issues?" a red-faced woman across the table asked. She was wearing a "Somerville High" sweatshirt. "We all had to name our issues. Mine are my teenager and the crap he listens to and the crap they put on TV. I'm a single mother," she added.

People were nodding. They wanted to hear his issues.

"I'm not sure I have any."

Guffaws and headshaking.

"Everybody has issues," the single mother said.

"Or is everything absolutely and splendidly perfect with you, Eric Barnes?" Fine was teasing, between old friends. "Are you content with the world? Maybe you don't think anyone here can help."

"They helped me," the single mother said. "I didn't even know what a frigging community was, we didn't have them when I was growing up. There was your family and your parish and your crowd at school. None of them's giving me any help now. These people here make you feel like a human being, I'm telling you, just knowing you're not the only one with problems."

The thing to do, as writer, with a contract for an article about this very group onto which he had fortuitously stumbled, was to guard his privacy, bait them with a few questions in the manner of a spy, and commit the choicest bits to memory. A droll portrait was already in evidence along the lines of *Edge*'s house style.

But he didn't want to spy on them. The woman across the table was challenging him with an angry smile. Traces of eyeliner suggested that in spite of the ordeal of motherhood she hadn't given up on her looks, never beautiful, now wrinkling. He'd been such a solitary of late. They didn't know him, wouldn't judge him, just wanted to hear his story. They were all waiting.

He began to talk about his work, his early ambitions; how the years had made writing not easier but harder, like walking in sand; how it sometimes seemed he'd woken up at thirty-eight to find he'd overslept his alarm; his crisis in November with the setting back of the clocks; how NWC had lost faith in him long before he knew about it; the relief and shame of failure; the stubbornly persistent desire to make something of worth and be recognized for it.

"That Ann let you down," the single mother said. "They all did. They were screwing you all along."

"I share some of the blame." Why was he saying these things to complete strangers? Because . . . they were strangers. Paula would mock him, but maybe this was her talking cure. "My wife says I could have been tougher. And the last time I saw Ann, she showed me all the chances they've given me."

"Now don't go blaming yourself. That's just what they want you to do. And your wife should *support* you."

"She has her own worries."

"Mine left after I was downsized." The man with the weak chin at Eric's side said this. "Human Resources told me it was an efficiency decision. Every time I looked in the mirror I saw inefficiency. I hated my face."

"I'm sorry about your wife. I wish I could say I was downsized."

"You were. You didn't bring in enough profit and they got rid of you. That's what downsizing means."

Eric turned to the man, feeling he had just been given an entirely new view of himself—a little degrading, and profoundly comforting.

"I didn't see it like that. I felt like it was my responsibility."

"Egotism," Fine declared from the head of the table. "You're flat on your back and still think you're omnipotent. You want all the credit for your pain. But these people won't let you have it. They've learned where the pain comes from."

The single mother across the table said, not unkindly, "You're no different than anyone else here. Maybe that's one of your issues."

"Maybe it is," Eric said.

Fine leaned forward. "Stop taking credit for every tragedy in your life and then other people can help you, Eric Barnes. We're glad you came tonight, whoever you were looking for."

Fine smiled on him. The single mother's eyes glittered with benevolence. She was the sort of woman—working-class, a hard face and voice, a narrow life of drudgery and temper—who would have seemed alien had he bumped carts with her in the supermarket. Jesus, he thought, I'm already a recruit. But he was glad they had made him name his issues. He felt hopeful, he didn't know why or for what. If he'd known about these people in this basement room, things might not have turned out the way they had.

Fine was moving on. "Everyone, please be there Friday night. How the city decides this issue is going to tell us whether we live in a city of human beings."

"Anyone who wants to volunteer, we'll need marshals, people to deal with the media, help with parking cars, anyone who knows about sound and lighting systems." A black man in overalls at Fine's side—Eric hadn't noticed him—was talking. "We'll provide child care on the second floor—kids are part of The Community. Also, we've got a problem. One of our scheduled speakers disappeared on us. Our African brother—some of you probably know him. He's gone. If you hear of his whereabouts, let Peter or me know."

The meeting broke up. One by one they came over to Eric and gave him a hug. The single mother, who smelled of cigarettes, planted a kiss on his cheek.

Out on the street the sun had long since set, and the unseasonal warmth was dissipating in a chilly wind from the river. Eric watched the strangers who had just embraced him go their separate ways, some disappearing down subway holes, others making for the bus shelters or groping in their pockets for car keys. They all drew in their shoulders and ducked their heads into the wind. This was the way most people walked on the street, especially in winter, an unconscious shrinking, almost self-abasement. It was like watching them return to their old lives.

His first instinct was to go home and tell Jane that the blue signs weren't from a weird cult, but from their neighbors. He had always regarded his neighbors as agents of litter and graffiti and crime, and now they had induced him to undress and show his wounds. But Jane would take it as more eccentric rebellion. There wasn't room in their house for The Community, so it hardly mattered that he wasn't allowed to go home.

He could return to Lincoln, and watch Jerry bond with Zach before bedtime, and talk to Rachel about The Community and Building X, in which she had expressed the detached interest of a recent emigrant. But to scuttle back to the warm safety of their computer-controlled house would reduce the experience to a titillating urban anecdote.

An hour ago the façade of the Problem Place was ablaze and he had gone inside like a free man to find Paula. But he had come out encumbered with other people, almost a whole city, and now all he could think of was the complications. By a kind of double book-keeping, he had kept alive the incompatible hopes that his wife would accept him back and he would not have to snuff out his passion for Paula.

He went to the pay phone outside the post office and dialed Paula's number. Her answering machine again.

"Paula, where are you? Jane found out. I want to talk to you but I can't find you. I even went to your office tonight. Where are you? I'll keep trying to reach you. I—I'll try again."

He hung up and immediately looked around as if someone might have overheard. Half a block down was the YMCA. And Joe had disappeared.

"Defaulted on his rent." The deskman swiveled his head from a televised basketball game to confront Eric. His tie and collar garroted his neck and squeezed the flesh up under his chin, which rendered his face somnolent. "Mr. Amouzou was evicted."

"He didn't say where he was going?"

"Maybe back to Africa."

"Not if he couldn't pay his rent." The deskman returned to the basketball game. Eric wanted to seize the necktie and throttle some fear into his face. "He may be in trouble. He has nowhere to go."

The answer came, and he ran out before the deskman could move his head again.

Hurrying through Central Square, he passed solitary women refusing eye contact at bus stops, knots of hooded young men. The commercial day was over, the Square had emptied out, anyone left was looking for trouble or fair game. By streetlight the sidewalk appeared liver-spotted, strewn with cigarette butts and used lottery tickets. He had always made it a point of honor not to avoid the Square after dark, but tonight he felt vulnerable. He had lost the rationale of a homeowning citizen returning a video or buying a gallon of milk. His errand was complex, uncertain, probably rash.

The rainbow was lit but there was no one outside. The sign's childishness had a sinister aspect, like a doll in a horror movie. Had the place shut down? Eric approached. People had to fall a long way to reach this place. Behind the door he imagined bodies clumped together like worms. He imagined hands reaching to pull him down into dampness and filth.

His second knock admitted him into a dark room, an entryway at the bottom of a stairwell. Walls of tile trapped the cold air. The light was murky, underwater light. Among a dozen human figures floating in amber he spotted Joe sitting on the steps. Elbows on the backpack between his knees, head bowed, his long slender hands were spread over the top of his skull in the posture of a grieving peasant.

Aware of a presence, Joe looked up. Whatever had gone wrong was apparently made worse by the sight of Eric. Joe lowered his head as if Eric were a hallucination.

"How did you find me?"

"I remembered you stayed here."

Joe laughed tonelessly. "Back where I started."

"What happened?"

It was a long time before Joe answered.

"My money."

Someone had gotten into his room and stolen it. All the money he'd saved from work, all the money from his treatments. He was left with the sixteen dollars in his pocket.

"Do you know who did it?"

"I met him here. A criminal. Maybe he got a key from J.B." Joe put a hand over his eyes. "That money was all I had."

"You didn't ask Jim to advance you something?"

Joe shrugged, the hand covering his eyes. "I don't want to ask him that."

Somewhere in the entryway there was a noise of eating, people sucking strands of noodle. An empty paper plate lay on the step below Joe. Eric felt superfluous and irritating.

"What are you going to do?"

"I was going to leave. The money was for me to leave."

"Where?"

Joe removed his hand. "I don't know."

A banal spirit from Denver or Long Beach had taken possession of Joe's voice. And this new voice made his face look different too. It reminded Eric of the face in the passport snapshot: mouth set as if to contain a hurt, quiet eyes wanting something. Eric had never truly seen Joe's face.

"So you're staying here," he observed to cover his self-contempt, for he felt that Joe would never have come to this if he had simply let Joe be, let him go on being African.

Joe said something, but his voice had gone under water.

"Lost what?"

"The lottery. I'm out."

"What lottery?"

"Ha! Goneril with a white beard!"

A coat came striding out of the gloom, a paper plate extended, a finger wagging. Eric looked into his accuser's face.

"Eamon."

Connelly's complexion was sidewalk-colored, his beard raged out of control. His mouth was smeared with spaghetti sauce. The worst thing of all was that he didn't seem to know it.

"He lost the lottery, can't you see? We're all lottery losers here. They told me I was everything."

"I didn't know you were still here, Eamon." Eric tried to assume a conversational tone. "Jerry told me what happened with Margot."

"You'll see! Look at you, your victory face! I know what goes on." The paper plate shook in Connelly's hand. He was glowing with righteousness. "Your pub parties, your secret lusts. I'm God's spy." He seized the zipper of Eric's parka and shook it. "Through tattered clothes small vices do appear, robes and furred gowns hide all. You tell me to be a man, clean up my act. Your asshole stinks in your Jockey shorts just like mine."

Eric said mildly, "And I've been kicked out just like you." He took Connelly's hand from his parka and held it a moment. In spite of his embarrassment he was strangely moved. "We're brothers, Eamon."

For a moment Connelly lost the flow. Then, as if seized by a new insight, he pulled his hand away and cried, "You don't think I see how you suck each other's cocks and stab each other's backs? I smell it all, ink, blood, semen, you make me sick!"

"Shut up," a voice snarled. "I'm eating dinner." But Connelly would not shut up.

A few months ago they had stood together in the Harp & Plume and argued about Yeats. Eamon Connelly had been pompous, eccentric, raffish. Now he was unreachable, not a brother at all. Reinvention in its purest form looked like this, smeared with spaghetti sauce.

The night he'd heard the news at Jerry's, Eric had had a notion of doing something to help. What happened to that notion? It retreated to a quiet place and disappeared. This was what people did. All the households in Cambridgeport, with their radios tuned to NPR for information about the world, had to shut Eamon out and lock their doors. At all costs the heart had to harden and not see. It was survival. Because once you saw, where would it stop? Decent, fair—how could you live with yourself?

Sick at heart, Eric turned from Connelly's foaming face to Joe. He was on his feet, struggling into his backpack.

"Where are you going to stay?"

Joe seemed to consider whether the question was worth answering. "The airport. I know a guy there."

"Let me find a place for you. I'd say my own house but I can't. But I'll find one. Please let me."

Joe shrugged. They left Rainbow House and Eamon Connelly behind.

At a money machine across Mass. Avenue from the YMCA, Eric withdrew four hundred dollars. There was one more payment left on the construction work, and they had to keep a reserve in case of emergency hospital bills. It was money he didn't have.

Joe received the cash in silence, and in silence they crossed Mass. Avenue together.

In front of the Y, Joe said, "Why are you doing this?"

"Never mind. I have my reasons."

"You haven't been at the house."

"My wife and I are working some things out," Eric said shortly.

"But she's about to have a baby."

"I'm aware of that."

"I mean—" Joe was stunned. He spread his arms. "You have everything."

"You wanted the world to think you're African when you're not. That's pretty strange, too." Joe looked away. "The Community's trying to find you. They want you for Friday night." Joe looked back, panic in his eyes. "What are you going to do?"

"What should I do?"

Don't tell them! Eric wanted to say. Be an African—I won't betray you! But his hope of a magician and trickster had already dropped away, and in this new face he recognized something of himself. He did not know why this young man had become his responsibility. He asked himself what advice Paula would give.

"I think you should let them know who you are."

"They'll kill me."

"I'm going to write down the name of a person I know," Eric said. "I think she could help you with this problem."

He left Joe on the sidewalk staring at the scrap of paper.

Rachel extended the phone. "For you," she told Eric and started out of the kitchen. "Come on, Zach, let's leave Uncle Eric alone."

He already knew. "Jane?"

"I just wanted to see how you're doing."

"Hanging on. And you?"

"I don't know, Eric. I've done a lot of thinking."

He tried to contain his alarm. But she didn't sound angry. "Mm-hmm?"

"Your cold sounds bad."

"It's not so bad."

"You should take care of yourself. How're Jerry and Rachel?"

"They've been great. I try to stay out of their way."

"What's their house like?"

"A cross between Versailles and a spaceship."

She laughed. "Zach driving you crazy?"

"Last night he sat on my lap and I read him a book about dinosaurs five times. I enjoyed it."

"I never thought I'd hear that from you."

"No."

There was a silence. Was she resentful? Hopeful? Decided?

"You've been thinking?" he said.

"Tell me what you've been thinking."

He had convinced himself that she was busy weeding him out of her life, defiantly taking up yoga. That she was better off this way. But the sound of her voice told him Jane was suffering too. It melted his heart and reminded him that she was the one who knew him best and whom he knew.

"I'm lost out here, Jane."

"Are you? Eric, do you know what you've done to me?"

He imagined physical trauma, stillbirth. "How can I undo it?"

"You can't. Are you really lost? It feels that way, but don't you want out? You know, that night, you never said: Let's stay together, I want to be married to you for the rest of my life. You didn't say that. It would have made such a difference if you had."

She would be in her nightgown, huddled under a blanket on the living-room sofa, her face drawn, a strand of hair lying across her cheek.

"I've thought about my role in this." She sounded sad again. "I know I haven't exactly been there for you during some rough times. I admit, I couldn't face it, I wanted you to get over it. If I'd paid more attention, maybe you . . . Eric, I have to go. Guess what? The rats are gone. The new pipe did it."

They had been such a part of his life for so long, he wished he had been there for the end.

"The crew's clearing out Friday, thank God."

"And you're due next Monday. Perfect timing."

"Thanks for getting all that done."

He hesitated. "Do you want me at the hospital?"

There was a long silence on the other end of the line. "I don't know." She hung up.

twenty-one

The night after Joe returned to the YMCA, Mr. Talk came into his room like a secret agent with a plan.

"We need your presence," Mr. Talk told him. "We need to hear your voice." He was picking at his beard; his bald head flesh was thickly grooved. Joe was sitting on the cot but Mr. Talk remained standing. Joe wondered if he ought to get up; it would be easier to refuse on his feet.

"But what can I tell them?"

"Ed is going to say a few things and me too. But they know us. We're identified as leaders."

"This building—I don't come from here, this is not my country."

"Just be yourself." Mr. Talk squatted and laid a hand on Joe's shoulder. "Like that night in small group. This is just a larger scale. You and I need to have the courage to heal on the next level. Both of us, Joe." He stood up. "We have to take what we know to the people. Individual therapy is totally inappropriate for social trauma. Freud is worthless in Africa, and he's worthless in America."

Mr. Talk stopped at the door.

"May I make a suggestion, Joe? Do you have any African clothes here? With a crowd that size you need a visual cue. We're thinking three or four hundred people. That's an extraordinary opportunity."

Joe looked into the eyes with secrets. "Just be myself."

"That's all we want."

When Mr. Talk was gone, Joe lay on his cot and imagined himself standing on a stage in his wax suit. The golden thread was shining ecstatically at his wrists and neck, green and red and yellow shapes swirled about his body. He lifted his hand to his face and took off the mask. Out beyond the lights, a sea of faces gazed up at him. Women were screaming and fainting, men fought to get closer. He saw Missy and Jim Newburg and Kevin and the poet and Mr. Talk and Mr. Action and the people from The Community. He was raising his arms to unbutton his shirt and they surged toward him with eyes rolling back in their heads like sick people possessed. They fell forward, pushing right up to the edge of the stage.

Below the stage, Eric Barnes was trying to hold them back, but they poured past him and up over the stage like a great wave that broke around Joe's feet. Hands rose out of the wave to claw at his embroidered cuffs. They were tearing his clothes from his body, ripping them to shreds. Fingernails sank into his flesh and drew blood. He looked into their faces and saw not love, but tooth-baring rage. He felt himself lifted bodily, and as he twisted in the air he caught sight of Mr. Talk. He was winking. It had been a trick. Joe was not the magician priest, he was the sacrificial goat. They had fattened him up and now they were going to cut him to pieces and burn him and eat him, and not even Eric Barnes could bury him in a tomb. But he had started and now it was too late to stop. He had to end it.

The day of the rally in Building X was also the last day for the crew. Light work, just touch-up and packing tools, and in the late afternoon Joe finished alone. Working at his own pace he vacuumed the new carpet, wiped down the window panes, polished the hardware in his meticulous way. It was a beautiful room they had made, soft and light and quiet. The baby would be safe in here. He was glad to have played a part.

As dusk fell he grew sleepy. He lay down for a moment on the carpet's creamy nap, his African clothes rolled up for a pillow. In the shirt pocket were the wooden figure and a hundred dollars, the money left from what Eric Barnes had given him—the amount he had come here with, three months ago. Half-asleep, he felt that his time in this city had been a dream, another dream like Africa, and getting out would be as easy as waking up, still in his old house, the bed with the corduroy bedspread, and his foster mother about to come into the room. He slept.

Joe woke up with a start. The room was dark. The house was silent. He sat up, the print of the carpet on his cheek, and remembered the window bars. He had taken the hardware off the bolts and put it . . . somewhere. Where?

In the dark he felt his way out of his work clothes and into the embroidered suit and the British Airways windbreaker. Sockless, he put on his African shoes, black slip-ons with downtrodden heels. Then he turned on the light. The room was empty. He looked under the new furniture and along the walls and in the laundry closet, but the hardware wasn't here. He went to the window and pushed the tip of a nutless, washerless bolt. It sank into the wall like a snake disapppearing into its hole. Kevin or his associates could pull off the bars and come in and take everything—take the baby.

Why had he done that? He wasn't a thief. Why?

Joe left the room and went out into the hall. Maybe someone had picked up the hardware without knowing what it was and put it somewhere else. The house was dark and he passed through it like a prowler. In the kitchen the luminous digits on the oven clock said 6:03. He still had two hours. He moved toward the living room. In the corner was a pool of light. Someone was lying on the couch.

Her hand flew to her neck, her mouth opened to scream.

"Oh Jesus! Oh, you scared me."

"I'm sorry."

"I didn't know anyone was here." The wife was wearing a nightgown and bathrobe and slippers. She must have come home when he was sleeping.

"I was just going. I was finishing up the baby room. It's finished now and I'm going."

"I thought you—I didn't know it was you."

I thought you were a thief. A killer. What was she doing here alone? Not reading. The television was off. Her face was pale except for a swollen darkness around the eyes. She brushed her nose with the back of her hand, then ran the palm up under her eye.

She was crying. He had interrupted.

"The baby room is perfect," Joe said, to soothe her.

"Thank you. Thank you for your work."

"The baby will be safe there."

She looked at him and then away, a shadow of fear in her eyes. It wasn't the right thing to say. He was about to ask if she had seen the hardware when she made an effort to sit up, raising her body with both hands. She winced and her mouth opened to draw air.

"I can't believe this."She closed her eyes and bit her lip and shook her head from side to side. The shaking fell into a rhythm of breaths and sobs. "No, stop, stop, stop."

She had fallen into a dream of receiving blows, or words that hit like blows, as if Joe were assaulting her. He stood helpless at the edge of the rug.

"Oh, I don't want it, no, no!"

He took a step toward the couch. "Please—"

"Oh God, what am I going to do?"

She wept and rocked and now and then her face convulsed. The sobs died to moaning that sounded like some strange, tuneless song. When she opened her eyes, she appeared startled to see him.

Joe asked, "What is it?"

She was breathing and staring. He was afraid she would tell him to leave.

"Could you get me the portable phone by the kitchen door?"

Joe hurried from the room. When he came back with the phone, she held his eyes for a moment.

"Do you understand?"

He shook his head.

"I'm going into labor."

When she finished with the phone he refused to go until her friend arrived. He brought her aspirin and a glass of fizzy water, and he arranged the pillows so she could lie down again. When she groaned and seized her belly he panicked, wondering if he would be required to deliver the baby himself, right here on this couch, on a piece of newspaper. He began to hope it would happen. He was grateful to be the one here. She didn't tell him to leave.

"Do they let the father watch the birth where you're from?"

It took Joe a moment to remember where he was from.

"Oh no. No man can come near, not even the father. It is the business of women."

She listened with a vacant stare. "Maybe that's better."

When the pain came back he was bold enough to take her hand, and she let him hold it. She gazed at him with large, moist eyes. The pain made her beautiful.

"I think your baby will be the most beautiful in the world."

She smiled, but there was no color in her lips. "That's sweet of you. I'm sorry, I don't even remember your name."

"Joe."

She nodded. "You're the magician."

Joe could not bear to say that he wasn't.

"Can you make this painless for me?"

"I wish I could. But I cannot." He looked at her womb with regret. "I wish it could be mine."

She jerked her hand away. "What a thing to say!"

"I mean—" His face was throbbing. "Without children, an African is considered nothing. I have no children of my own."

"I'm sorry, I can't have this conversation right now." She checked her watch and struggled to sit up. He had lost her. "Jesus, where's Rachel?"

She left the room and when she came back she was wearing a dress and jacket and he felt like an intruder again.

"He is a good man."

She was trying to put on her shoes. "Who?"

"Your husband."

Her hands froze, she looked up. "Why do you say that?"

"I had no place to stay, no money, and he gave it."

"When did you see my husband?"

"This week. He said he loves you and the baby. This was what he said to me."

Her cheeks colored, her eyes filled. Then her head dropped and she was pulling on her shoes again.

When the friend arrived she regarded Joe with suspicion and

took over. Everything slipped out of his hands and he became un-necessary. There was some debate between the women about what she would need in the hospital. The friend collected a few things from the bathroom in a bag.

"Where's Eric?" the wife said. "Is he at the house?"

"Not when I left."

"I need to talk to him. I want him to be there."

"Jerry gave him his beeper yesterday. Let Jerry handle it, you've got to have this baby."

Joe saw himself as the devoted friend she would always remember for what he had done when she was crying and alone: helped her baby into the world, given her back her husband. His last service was to ease her into the front seat of her friend's Volvo. He stood in the dark parking lot and kept waiting for her to turn and answer his wave, until the car disappeared.

He began walking. It was a dry evening with just a sliver of moon, almost mild for late February but bone-chilling to someone in African clothes with no socks. The streets were empty; he had the city to himself. On entering a strange city at night during his travels, he sometimes felt that the life on the street—the cane-juice vendors, the little boys selling gum, the women giving him sidelong looks—was produced for his own excitement. But tonight the streets were just passages from one house to another. Only what went on inside was real.

He passed buildings with cozy lights glowing in their windows. In each of them a different family was going about its family business. Each house was a world of its own. He longed to be on the other side of one of these lighted windows, among people who knew and loved him. He imagined returning to his foster parents' home after a long time away and being received with love—not as a magician with secret powers that turned out to be a lie, but as himself.

The hardware. Too late now.

Maybe that was his true shape, if he had one—not the friend in the living room, but the thief at the window.

Near Central Square the houses became restaurants and bars. Joe wanted to lose himself in a boisterous room where everyone was allowed and no one noticed. He hadn't eaten all day. He had to get ready.

On the corner over a windowless door, a sign in old-fashioned writing said "Harp & Plume." Loud voices and a bass guitar pounded through the wall. Joe pushed his way in the door and the bodies were packed so dense that he had to turn sideways to wedge through. He stood for some time at the bar holding up a five-dollar bill he'd taken from the wad in his pocket next to the figure with the hollow skull. Finally the bartender came and cocked his shaved pirate's head over rows of rinsed glasses.

"Do you have any food?"

"Kitchen's closed. Bag of chips?"

It wouldn't be enough. "Sure. And a beer."

The bartender waited, then swept his hand across a line of taps. Joe pointed at one and the bartender drew up a glass and pulled the handle.

The chips only made him hungrier. He washed away the salt with beer and looked down the narrow room.

In the back, a band was playing a Bob Marley song. It was a song about the singer's love for a woman, a simple, aching love. Joe closed his eyes and African children were dancing under the mango tree outside his house, two shirtless boys holding hands as they rocked back and forth, a girl doubling over with giggles, and the bread lady's boy quietly watching and tugging on his penis. Joe was standing on his front steps, holding a radio and singing, teaching the children the words.

He didn't want to open his eyes. The sweet mood of the music would end.

A man at the bar was looking at him.

"We love this music in Africa," Joe explained.

The man wore a blond ponytail, and a piece of gold glimmered in his ear. "Isn't it Jamaican?"

"But we love Bob Marley in Africa. You see his face on boys' T-shirts. It takes me back." A clot of words rushed to his tongue. He wanted to talk so the mood wouldn't die because behind it there was emptiness.

"Sounds like you're homesick."

"Oh yes. But I can't go back. I have to live on my memories."

The man turned to a woman standing down the bar. She raised her eyebrows and her mouth shaped a smile as if answering a look of the man's. She was wearing black lipstick on her chalk white face, and the whole rim of one ear was pierced so that black earrings formed a question mark.

The man turned back to Joe. "Let me buy you a drink. No, come on. As our guest in America."

On his empty stomach the first pint had already gone straight to his head. The second beer was passed to him and the man raised his glass.

"Land of the free home of the brave."

"Thank you."

"Your tired your poor your huddled masses."

The woman snorted. Joe gulped deeply. When he looked at the man's face, he was disturbed to see that it had become a cartoon. An invisible hand was squeezing the cheeks together and forcing open the lips like a fish. Joe tried to push the picture out of his mind because it was ugly and made him angry and afraid.

The man said, "My friend Tina wants to know if you know this magician guy who's supposed to be performing tonight." Behind him Tina blew out smoke and laughter. "There's a big event and he's on the card. She just thought because you're African."

"I know him very well."

"You do? Tina, he knows him."

"I know him," Joe said, "but I don't like him."

"You don't?"

"Not at all."

"Really? Tina, he doesn't like him."

Tina leaned forward and draped her arm over the man's shoulder. Her face was a cartoon too, the hair black and short and bristly like a wild pig's back.

"Why not?" Tina asked the man.

"Why not?" the man asked Joe.

"The magic he does is wicked." He would keep talking until their faces looked like faces again. "In Africa he hurt many people. This is a wicked, evil man."

"Hey, Ferber, I like him already," Tina said.

Ferber was surprised. "You knew magician guy in Africa?"

"Oh yes. He was well known as a wicked man and also a thief. He stole so many things. If you go to Africa and say his name, anyone can tell you about his misdeeds. No one there respects him."

"I thought he was some kind of political refugee."

"No. Not at all. This is what he *says*. But he was caught stealing. I will tell you something: he killed a man, a man whose magic was *good*. No African would accept him because his heart is rotten and full of maggots, so he ran away and came here."

Ferber turned to Tina and his ponytail brushed her chin like a fly whisk. "Do you hear this?"

"So magician guy's a creep." Tina looked bored.

"But I mean, it's incredible. The guy had people thinking he was some kind of saint."

"Can you tell me something?" Joe asked. "Can you tell me why such a man known everywhere in Africa as a wicked man is a saint in America?"

"I don't know." Ferber shrugged. "He had people fooled."

Tina leaned into Ferber's ear and whispered something.

"You're gross, Tina. I'm not going to tell him that."

"I'm not gross. I'm neurasthenic. Tell me a story."

"I really think we need to go to this thing. I mean isn't it better than takeout pad thai and our thirty-fifth viewing of 'Blue Velvet'? No really," Ferber said. "Isn't the point that we live like children while real kids are shooting each other and everything's going to hell? I'm extremely concerned about the decline of civil intercourse. What? Oh Tina, you are such a tart, you never declined intercourse in your life."

They had stopped talking to Joe, but it was still a performance for him to overhear. He swallowed the last of his beer and ordered another. He was drunk—he had come in here for that.

One night a young girl was brought to Amouzou with jaundice. Her eyes were yellow and droopy, she slouched as if she had no bones. But when the drums started and the women sang, her weak little body shook, folded, spun under everyone's eyes. She twirled across the dirt and her head rolled, the eyeballs disappeared back in their sockets. No one came to her aid. The clapping and singing increased so that her body ran out of control and she started bumping into people. Suddenly she toppled in the dirt and lay on her side, legs scissored, eyes open but empty as death. Except for the quick rise and fall of her belly, she looked like a corpse. Someone carried the body off. When Joe saw her the next day she was skipping and singing to herself on the way to school.

"Well, Tina, it takes a village to raise a child."

"The village can have it."

"I'm not going to miss out on history. You're free to go pick up some witless hunk who can make you happier than it's in my power."

It was time to go. They were waiting for him in Central Square. But what had made the girl spin across the dirt? Amouzou was inside her, doing it all. The opposite of neutral buoyancy—you floated up, sank down, jerked this way and that with anything that filled you. A pregnant woman; a lighted window; a song; a face. But something stayed, what was it? Just a body lying on the ground like a slaughtered goat?

He had to get back to the moment when he showed Eric Barnes his passport. There was relief then, and it wasn't the same thing as neutral buoyancy. He had tried neutral buoyancy and it didn't work, he couldn't make it last, feelings kept running at him from all sides. But his name was on the passport, and his face. You had to fill in the rest. As he left the bar, he was fighting to hold something of himself that was solid and couldn't be poured out.

People were leaving with him. On Mass. Avenue he saw others heading into Central Square. Trying to keep his balance, he moved through the crowd past the Y, into the middle of the Square, and there were more people out than he'd ever seen. Farther along down one of the streets was an open area of abandoned lots and demolished buildings. The street was packed, with cars parked on both sides, and more cars were jammed on the dirt behind a chain-link fence. Blue signs were posted on the fence. "Tonight changes everything." "You will never be the same again." The building was set back from the street and bathed in floodlights that blazed on its gaping window holes and shadowed insides. Policemen stood behind the fence and around the building, and people were streaming from all directions, drawn by the call of an amplified voice. From half a block away Joe recognized Mr. Talk.

twenty-two

In any crowd Paula suspected that she was the only sane person. The humming press of strangers made her bones feel as small and breakable as a child's; a casual movement of people could crush them like an elephant stepping backward. It wasn't just physical harm that frightened her, it was the crowd's mood. In her session room, one on one, even with Earl, she possessed a secret power, like a lion trainer, that in the last second would save her: She could look in his homicidal eyes and say, "Stop, think." Against reason she believed that everyone could be reached, even psychotics, once she made them feel that she understood, that she was human too. But a crowd had no eyes. It was an ocean whose surges were mindless. Even as a teenager and half-stoned at a rock concert, she kept one part of her brain on the lookout for exit signs, secretly urging the lead singer to tone it down so that the people behind would stop pushing.

She resented having to be the one person who couldn't go crazy. It would be liberating to give in, be lifted and thrown by a wave.

The room she was standing in tonight, near the back of a crowd of several hundred people, was unlike any room she'd ever been in. It was low and vast as a parking garage, and it smelled of fresh cement. It was a brutal room. It had no Cape Cod picture to hate; its dank, hard, bright, dark surfaces offered no human use or reference points. Here and there light gleamed on steel studs that cut the floor space into cages. The window openings, letting in cold air, dazzled with exterior floodlights, but the room itself was underlit by bare bulbs strung alongside pipes and ducts from the ceiling beams and by spotlights clustered around the front. There, among policemen and marshals in shiny blue vests, several rows of people were sitting in folding chairs before a podium and microphone. Paula had spotted a tall man with a black ponytail and she had known that it was Steve Lorenz, her ex-tryst, here on behalf of the city planning office, carrying on his life without her.

The speaker was explaining the position of City Hall. "We'll take every perspective into account. But there has to be a process."

His disembodied voice boomeranged around the room. Everyone ignored it, and an expectant buzz of chatter continued to surge across the floor, mingling with another sound that Paula had become aware of on the second floor, muted by the conrete slab overhead: the howls and laughs of children.

To Paula's right, a man with a ratty tweed coat and a self-inflicted haircut was droning to no one about a secret deal a certain university and a certain developer were scheming to cut with certain officials of local government for property near the river. On her other side a middle-aged couple silently held hands—the man's clenched jawline suggested pain and endurance, the woman had pretty doll-like features and an anxious mouth. Near the wall Paula thought she recognized an inhabitant of the Widener reading room. Clients kept materializing in the half-light and becoming someone else. The crowd had taken on a personality disorder, her least favorite, borderline—voracious, vulnerable, prone to rapid shifts of mood.

Paula had returned from a week in New York, where she had gone to supervise her mother's discharge from the rehab clinic, to find, among other messages, two from Eric. Strangely, the only anger she felt was at her mother, for pulling her away at just the moment her lover was having a crisis, and at herself, for being too mother-absorbed to call in for messages.

Frantic, she tried to find him. From work she called his number and got the answering machine. She called again at night and hung up when his wife answered. She went down to Harvard and searched the reading room at Widener—no flannel shirt, no laptop.

She made two futile journeys to the river. She knew nowhere else to look, scarcely knew him. Their bond had been as thin as string, and he had slipped loose and flown away like a kite. If she had been in town when it all blew up, maybe she could have salvaged something by acting fast. But by now, his messages seemed old. Whatever needed to be decided had been decided.

She entertained no fantasies of digging her nails into his kind, attentive face. She kept waiting to be turned to ashes in a furnace of misery, but instead she went numb; and in this way, to her confused chagrin, she made it through almost unscathed, as if the whole thing had never mattered. This calm felt dangerous. Sooner or later she would pay.

Immediately two things happened. She began spending lots of time on the phone with her mother, cajoling and buoying and finally inviting her to come stay in Boston for a couple of weeks. The second thing was that a rash had broken out on her forehead. It was a vulnerable spot in times of stress but never as bad as this—a bright amoeba of disturbed skin, unconcealable by hair. Every morning before work, she had to spend half an hour with makeup, and in sessions she held her head back from the lamp (most of her clients, preoccupied with the nonstop action behind their own foreheads, wouldn't have noticed if she greeted them without a nose). Tonight she had contrived to position herself in total darkness, the only comfort Building X gave.

Suzanne Martin had corralled her after work, and although Paula didn't want to be part of Fine's cheering squad, refusal would have cost her. On the way over, Suzanne crackled with sisterly irony about Fine's new career as a politician, but near the building her eyes grew large with adoration and potential treachery. Wanting to be seen, she grabbed a chair up front. Paula dropped back into the shadows and looked around for Eric. Too crowded, too dark; if he was here she'd never find him. Anyway, by now his wife probably had him under lock and key.

Paula was disconcerted to find that she didn't want to miss the occasion. Here at last was the audience of Fine's dreams, and she had the butterflies in her own stomach. Hundreds of people were going to hear him. One way or another it would be big, bigger than anything in her own life. Maybe it would give her something else to go on for a while.

The speaker from City Hall finished to a scattering of applause and boos. There followed a void of amplified sound in which the crowd noise swelled and then fragmented like shells bursting across a field.

"What's going on?" someone called out. "Who's the next speaker?"

A disc of light was moving toward the podium like a sunspot. It was a bald head, bathed in the radiance of high-wattage spotlights. Paula saw the blue sweater vest and she imagined Fine padding across the concrete slab in his dark socks, a gleam in his teddy-bear eyes. Her heart was pounding; he seemed utterly calm.

The podium stood a hundred feet from her, and when Fine came up behind it he looked ridiculously small, like a boy of six. The lights bleached out his features, leaving no expression, just the dark curve of beard and the brilliant scalp. The room went on heaving with restlessness. Fine seemed to be waiting for quiet. He leaned toward the mike.

A long exhalation, like a cloud of static mist, rolled over their heads. Fine was breathing hard.

"Why are we all so sad?"

From the small of Paula's back, a shiver raced up her spine. The voice was so familiar, so banal: the voice of staff meetings. Yet it filled the room and silenced Building X as suddenly as if someone had switched off recorded crowd noise.

"Why are we all so goddamn lonely?"

You phony, she thought, but the shiver ran up her back again and out of her body, and she felt it pass like electric current among the people around her. Everyone in the room was listening.

"Why are we so angry and depressed? Look at the person to your left."

Hundreds of heads obeyed. Against her will Paula turned and

was confronted with the crew cut of the middle-aged husband, whose head was turned toward his wife's Shirley Temple curls. In the back of her own head she felt the eyes of the man in ratty tweed. *Come on*, she told Fine, *get it over with*.

"Pretty angry and depressed, aren't we?"

Heads turned back to the podium. He already had them mesmerized. Beneath his composure Paula heard the faint, shrill sound of mania. She was certain that no one else heard it. She could do this to clients, just had to say "You love her, don't you?" and feelings popped open and tears flowed and she cringed inwardly, because it was a cheap, spurious power. But Fine was surveying the room full of angry and depressed people like a glutton contemplating a banquet. His face was coming into focus now. The intense light rendered his flesh pale and soft, but his eyes weren't the teddy-bear eyes at all. They were piercing. She had never seen these eyes and they filled her with a vague fear. She knew she was witnessing the greatest moment of his life.

"People of The Community, do you know why we are all sad and lonely and angry and depressed? You can feel it in this room, can't you? I can. I can because this naked room has no frills and no distractions. This is what we're like without the furniture and the gadgets. Take a good look."

His pace was starting to quicken.

"Do you know why our government is dysfunctional? It's like a parent that doesn't have time for us. 'I love you, you're special,' it says, and it eats up all the love and trust we can give. But when we want it to take us to the park or read a story or just *be* with us, it always has something more important to do, doesn't it? But it won't let us be independent either, it doesn't want us to grow up, it *wants* us to need it. So we spend our whole lives in this dysfunctional parent's house, giving, giving, giving and getting nothing back. *That's* a reason to be sad and lonely and angry and depressed. Who the hell wouldn't be?"

People were nodding, murmuring assent.

He had made Paula think of her mother, her face in the taxi on their way home from rehab, shrunken, lips tight, eyes shifting for something to blame. Yes, she gave gave gave, and most of it was pouring water on sand—but who else would? It wasn't dysfunction, it was love. What did he know about it? Phony!

"Let me tell you something else. Every other institution in our lives has failed us. School makes us feel stupid and throws away our finger paintings, and then Fidelity and AT&T tell us we're expendable and downsize us to our souls, and then our church or temple says it's because we're bad, we've sinned, and then TV fills up our minds with murder and beer commercials, and when we've had too much and start to crack, psychologists put us in a diagnosis straitjacket, *paranoid*, *narcissistic*, and then send us home to families that tell us not to love anyone else, to kill our needs and desires, to feel guilty just for being alive. Every institution we look to for help is dysfunctional! Who *wouldn't* be?"

In front of Paula, a woman was nodding her short head of silver hair. The man with the suffering jawline was rocking gently on his feet, chin nuzzled into his chest like an old man at prayer, while his wife clutched his hand and gazed up at Fine with wide doll's eyes. And in the turbulence of Fine's words, Paula felt her stomach muscles tighten against some pain coming from within.

"What's left?" His voice dropped, but over the PA every consonant hissed and clicked. "What's left is our selves, people of The Community, our battered and resilient selves. It's amazing our selves have endured through all this dysfunction and abuse. So hug your self close, it's a fragile thing and a source of wonderment. Don't neglect it." He was almost whispering. "Be good to your self, people, take care of you, because you're the only one you've got."

The silver-haired woman wrapped her arms around her body—her fingers splayed across her shoulder blades looked like the embrace of another person. The middle-aged couple was locked in a hug. People were talking quietly to themselves. A knot of sadness tightened in Paula's throat. It felt as if they had all come here to mourn together.

Mourn whom? She knew.

Fine paused to sip from a glass of water.

"This is a truth-teller." The man in the ratty tweed coat was talking to himself. "This one knows."

Paula turned toward him. "Anyone could say these things. It isn't hard to poke your fingers inside people."

His mouth fell open: The audience he carried everywhere in his head had suddenly come to life. He turned back to the podium and retreated into his skull. "He's a truth-teller," he repeated, as if this would make Paula disappear.

"If everyone else has failed us," she told him, "then we've failed them, because we're everyone else too. What about that?"

The man held his neck rigid, blinking rapidly.

"It's the *institutions*," a working-class woman's voice answered. "Not us. That's what he's saying."

"But what are the institutions? You and me. Who else would they be?"

"See, you're thinking the way they want you to," the woman said. "You're not free."

"But listen to him! It's just words. What is he offering us?"

Someone shushed them. Fine was speaking again.

"In America, men approach each other on the sidewalk with fear and murder in their hearts. We brace—for what? Laughter. To be ridiculed is to be killed. So we walk around thinking: I can't let him laugh at me, I have to kill him first, I'm doing this to survive. But you're not surviving, because every day a piece of the self dies. And women—a man approaches and you cringe and bolt like deer, because your helplessness enrages you. You're running away from the killer—yourself. But you can't get away from yourself, never, and so you hide inside depression and alcohol, and you're dying from lack of love."

Fine's voice was riding cadences she had never heard. He had them all, every one of them was giving into the wave. Paula saw herself as a small, damaged, murderous creature, curled up, waiting to die, refusing Fine's offered hand.

"Do you know what age this is? This is the age of decline.

Everything is in decline. The roads are in decline, they're full of holes that never get filled. Sixty percent of every major city is off limits to anyone who values their life. Politics is in decline—left, right, meaningless crap, they've both failed us. People are drinking and getting fat and yelling at their spouses in the half hour they see their spouses because they both work late. And you're too tired to have sex more than once every election cycle. Right?" There was quiet laughter. "When was the last time you had sex?" Louder, nervous laughter. "How much foreplay? Did you both come, or were you too tired and anxious?" A few people cackled, but most of the laughter died. "Duration of the average sexual encounter is in decline—I can't prove it but this is my field, I know. Attention span is in decline. So is government efficiency and mean family income and personal security and charitable contributions and voter turnout and creative insights per capita per month and annual gross domestic happiness. That's the sum of all decline and it's in deep decline.

"Am I making you more depressed? Well, it's depressing! So you might as well be depressed and know it. This is the beginning of change. Because, *we can change*. Now I want you all to do something. Close your eyes. Close them please, no cheaters. What I want you to do is think of the thing you want most from life but for some reason can't get. Visualize it. What is it? Maybe a bigger salary, a more understanding partner. A better figure. A lover. Fame. Good health. Focus on it, turn it around. It looks wonderful, doesn't it? You deserve it. You want it so much but you can't get it. What's stopping you?"

Eyes closed, rocked and lulled by the voice, Paula heard Eric say: "But then self-interest takes over." When did he say that? Yes— outside Widener that night. It was raining. She brushed against him to get under his umbrella. Did he follow her out of the reading room, was that how it began? But anyway, he was gone. And better for her because the whole thing was folly and disaster. Why cry for everything you can't get? What if it crawls out of a dark hole to kill you? But here was Fine the hypnotist (tonight Fine had what *he* wanted) offering total fulfillment. If people got whatever they wanted it would be chaos, husbands beating wives, wives castrating husbands, kids left alone by their parents to fight the dog for food and drown in the bathtub, old people shut up in rooms by their children and no one to find the corpse, poor people cut loose and shitting on the sidewalk outside the Problem Place, which would be closed down because no one would give away money, Gladys left to face life without Paula's help. Fine was going to let all this out of the bottle.

And then maybe Eric would come back to her.

"There's a screen before your eyes and on this screen a projector is flashing a series of slides, and each slide is a picture of something that's keeping you from what you want. See them? There's your boss. Your parents, your husband, your wife, your children. Your bank statement. A cop. Your joke of a congressman. This city. Keep them flashing. Your body. Your lover. Flashing. Fate. The horizon. God. Now there's one more slide, the last slide, and I'm going to tell you what it is. Look carefully. You already know what's there. It's your face. It's you. People of The Community, open your eyes and get rid of all the other slides because this is the only one that matters. *You're* what's keeping you from what you want. Just you."

But instead of her own face, Paula saw Eric's under his umbrella in the rain and dark, his lopsided smile, the sudden glance down. Why have I let him go? she thought, her eyes still closed. Why? Because . . . it was easier. You have to survive your own desires. If they keep crying and kicking, leave the room, make a phone call, see a client. But there was that one day of the snowstorm when she left the office and went to the projects to save Gladys—almost high, really, because of him. It ended in a room with the vodka smell and the bloody cotton balls. Then he was waiting in the snow and he reached for her hand and she said yes. But she let him go without a sound, and things grew muffled and dull, and the streets looked like February. But here was Fine saying it didn't have to be this way. She was free to demand love and get it.

"What happened? You betrayed your true self to your enemies. You let the false self into your house and that thief tied up your true self and gagged you and pistol-whipped you and then robbed you blind. Humiliating! But you let it in! And it's murder. We're already dead."

People were sobbing. Overhead, faint children's voices shrieked delight. Paula steeled herself against them, too.

"But you know what? Once you set your true self free you won't believe how strong you feel. You don't need to scream in traffic any more. Multiple orgasms for men and women. And here's the best part, and I want every person in this room to feel it: Now we can start loving each other. Now we can come together without fear or hatred. So get rid of the false self! We've got something wiser and sexier and better."

Liar! These people won't get what they want, she thought, except by luck, by fate. And when the spell broke, they would become her responsibility. They would line up behind Gladys and Earl so Paula could restore them to the lame, compromised lives that Fine had lifted up and dropped and broken into pieces. They would come into the cubicle and eat up all the air until she suffocated. She let Eric go to be available for them. Responsible, helpful, level-headed, chicken!

Paula thrust her fists into her coat pockets. She would turn into Sara Simon. Or grow old in a melodrama like her mother, dreaming up revenges, shamming *gusto de vivere*. No, that wasn't her. She would go quietly, without histrionics. The place on her forehead where all her feelings had erupted would scar, and people would pretend not to notice it. In later years, she would corner startled strangers and say: See? This is what happens.

"Central Square," Fine was saying. "What is Central Square, people of The Community? A place tourists avoid. Eternal urban improvement. The midpoint between two dysfunctional universities. The asshole of this city. Petty crime, fast food, loose garbage. That's the *false* Central Square. The *true* Central Square . . . is us. Me, and you, and the person next to you. It's where we all come together. That's what the name means! Without Central Square, what are we? We work, eat, pay taxes, worry, dream, fail, wear down, endure, die—alone. For what? What are we without each other? But with each other is there anything we can't do?

"They want to take this building and turn it into a prison house of money. We'll all be standing here in a chain gang under armed guard, feeding quarters into a slot machine. We'll be slicing each other up at the blackjack table. Video poker will be lockdown, solitary confinement. The roulette wheel will be the new death chamber. Don't let it happen, people. This building is ours! Don't let the false selves break in and steal it! Look each other in the eyes, take each other's hands, hug each other, and feel the power of The Community!"

Paula felt a pressure of hands on her shoulders. Someone was turning her, pulling her into the soft promise of an embrace. As she looked up for the face under the umbrella her forehead was crushed against ratty tweed.

twenty-three

The crush of bodies jammed Eric in the entrance. People were wedged shoulder to shoulder in a wall of flesh behind, in front, on all sides, and he couldn't move. The voice had stopped, but its echo flowed through the exposed wires and pipes and over the slab floor into their nerves, where it pulsed even after the plump, bearded man came down from the podium and out of the light.

Pinned amid smells of wool, sweat, perfume, and stale smoke, Eric looked at the faces around him. They lied to spare their own feelings, condemned friends for their own failings, turned away from beggars and went home to write a check, always promised more than they could deliver, picked the scab off old resentments, demanded justice only for themselves. He knew them all, and tonight they were his brothers and sisters. Even this idiot who kept stepping on his foot.

The impulse came as swift as desire. He wanted to write, to catch these faces in words. A quickening in the blood. He wondered if it might not be too late. He thought back to the winter days growing shorter and darker, his head achier, bent over the computer screen while love—compromised, temporary, contingent—waited outside the barred window. Not only Paula; a world of strangers. But he had to be forced out into Central Square to know.

Behind him there was a commotion, and he turned to see. Marshals in blue plastic vests were trying to clear the entrance. A surge at his back carried him forward; in front, bodies separated, partial daylight opened. He squeezed sideways between bellies and hips and came out on a narrow shelf of the main floor. Before him, hundreds of people spread outward. He suddenly sensed that Paula was among them and began to scan the backs of bodies and heads, fragments of faces.

Above the floor noise, through the concrete slab overhead, he heard faint cries. He had been hearing these sounds during Fine's speech and thought he was imagining them. But they were real—the voices of children. They came and went like the far-off childhood echoes on a movie soundtrack. To Eric they sounded like souls of the unborn clamoring for life.

Jerry's beeper was clipped to his belt. He had switched it off this afternoon to teach—the thing made a horrible noise and he didn't want it going off in the middle of class. But then he'd forgotten to turn it back on. The beeper charted his movements at all hours, like a sonar device on an endangered sea mammal, or the parolee's electronic bracelet that Jane had said she wouldn't track him with. It had been Jerry's idea, he was pushing Eric to go to the hospital even if Jane wouldn't let him in the delivery room.

And now he was irritated. He didn't want to feel guilty for being here in this crowd, looking for Paula. He kept his hand on the beeper a long time. Finally he switched it on.

"Please let our next speaker have your eyes and ears." The black man in overalls was at the microphone now. "We're privileged to have a guest who comes from a place where the human spirit is still alive. He's got some news coming out of Africa just in time to teach America how to live together and love together before we tear ourselves apart. The human race was born where he's from. We're all Africans here! Make this young man feel at home so he can take all of us back home."

Jags of noise kept spiking up. They sounded hungry, volatile. Unity had deteriorated since Fine ended. The good feeling he conjured had nowhere to go, and the crowd wanted more of it.

Up front, a flash of colors was gliding across the chairs. In the half-light of grays and blacks, the colors were dazzling—yellow, green, red, with brilliant arabesques of gold fringe, as if an exotic and bejeweled bird had been set loose and was fluttering toward the microphone.

"Ladies and gentlemen of The Community."

Maybe it was a trick of amplification, but Joe's voice seemed to have recovered the music of Africa.

"Mr. Talk and Mr. Action have asked me to tell you the story of my life. It is a long story, but Mr. Talk and Mr. Action asked, so I will try to be brief, because these stories save our lives."

A few people laughed uncertainly, as if this might be a comic opening riff. But Eric picked up the note of recklessness and knew something was wrong.

"OK. The story of my life as a maggot."

More laughter, and gasps. A hand gripped Eric's arm: An elderly woman was demanding to know what had just been said.

"I couldn't hear." He moved away to get a better view of Joe.

"From birth, I was destined to be a magician. Now an African magician doesn't perform card tricks at birthday parties. He doesn't saw ladies in two and make pigeons disappear. No, it is more serious. An African magician has a totally different energy."

"He said magician," a man explained.

"I swear he said maggot."

"An African magician can turn men into crocodiles and vipers. He can turn himself into any creature on earth. I did this frequently."

"Do it, do it now," a woman called out. "A crocodile."

"But there is a thing about being a magician I have to tell you, and it is a sad thing. We are not like other people. We live alone because other people don't understand our power. We are not loved. People fear and hate us. They think we are evil. So it is not all sunshine for a magician. When a boy is chosen for a magician, his parents cry. I can tell you my parents cried, because from the day of my birth I wasn't theirs. Magicians don't have parents and they don't have friends. They never marry, they will not know the joy of children. Somewhere in this city tonight, a woman is having a child. But because I am a magician, I cannot be the father."

There was something automatic in the way Joe spoke, as if he'd gone into a trance. A couple near Eric exchanged brisk looks.

"Weird."

"Maybe this is how they talk."

"He doesn't even sound African. I bet he's from Jamaica and he's high on something."

"But let me tell you about Africa. One day, a fever came to my town in Africa that was stronger than any magician. It started in one house and spread to another, and then it spread all over town and even to the little farmhouses in the bush. This fever attacked the soul and turned people like me and you into killers. People who shared seed corn and drank palm wine together on market day took the machete and cut their neighbor and their neighbor's wife and children. They sliced the necks of little girls and chopped old men in two. They ripped open the bread lady and threw her in the latrine. They strung up intestines across the road at checkpoints. The false selves killed the true selves and the true selves killed the false selves, and the fever left behind a pile of corpses and a smell. Ladies and gentlemen, that is your African community."

"Good God," Eric murmured, and he raised his hand to make Joe stop. A hostile stir had begun to spread across the room, an underground rumble that erupted here and there in defiance. A few people who had been laughing at everything were still laughing. Joe didn't seem to register his audience's response. He had gone into a trance that made him eloquent and mad.

"I left, I had to leave, because in Africa fevers are always some magician's fault. I left for America, the real Third World. I came to this city where we are tonight. I won the lottery and you took me into your homes and beds. I got a job and made more money overnight than an African makes in a year, I never saw so much money. Mr. Talk and Mr. Action asked me to speak to you. This is the greatness of America. You could be anyone."

The African voice was gone. Denver or Long Beach had taken possession again. Eric was beset by an image of Joe peeling off his skin like a wetsuit and leaping, all blood vessels and muscles and nerves, into fire that burnt him to ash.

"But the story takes another sad turn. Ladies and gentlemen of The Community, there's a problem. The problem is, my magic doesn't work here. I don't know if it's because of the cold weather, but when I came to America it stopped working. No more crocodiles and vipers. No more neutral buoyancy. I apologize to the people who came for treatments because the sickness is still inside you."

"I want my money back!" someone shouted near the front. More bursts of laughter. More people shouting for their money back, others trying to shout them down.

"I don't have it," Joe said sadly into the uproar. "Kevin stole everything. And I want to tell everyone out there who's looking for magic—don't look at me! I can't help you. Africa can't help you. Africa declines. Untie the true self. Throw the other slides out. Tonight changes everything. I think you should let them know who you are."

Eric heard his own words, outside the YMCA. And he thought of Paula and her Gladys Dill, messing with other people's lives. He had messed with Paula's and with Joe's, and the destruction Joe was piling on himself was even more spectacular than his own. Jeers were spreading from the front of the room toward the back. Amid the scattering of hisses and boos there seemed to be a tidal pull of part of the crowd toward the exit. Peter Fine and the man in overalls were walking toward the microphone, where Joe stood in a blaze of color. When they gestured to him he didn't move, and the two men loitered at a short distance like nervous cops assessing a dangerous suspect.

"One more thing, ladies and gentlemen of The Community, just one more thing. Bear with me. I have an announcement to make. Tonight before your eyes right here in Central Square, I am going to perform my last magic act. This act was suggested to me by my one and only friend in this city, and if he's out there, I'm sorry for everything. With the last ounce of my power I am now going to turn myself into an American."

Eric shut his eyes and saw himself uncorking Joe's little statue and blood gushing out of the head. When he opened his eyes, Joe was spreading his arms like a bird preparing to take flight.

"I would like everyone to watch carefully because this process is happening as I speak. A mysterious and invisible change is taking place inside my head and body. Watch carefully. In ten seconds I will be just like you. No more Africa. Africa declines. Someone else can be Amouzou. Here he is, catch him."

A dark object came flying from the podium into the crowd. A dozen hands fought for it.

"Five seconds. I'm emptying out now. No more neutral buoyancy. Africa is going. Four. Three." Part of the crowd joined the countdown. "Two. One. Zero. It's over. I'm American. I'm just like you. Now everyone go home because Kevin and his. . . ."

The floor noise overwhelmed him. One section was cheering derisively like an audience baiting an abusive comedian. From the far wall came a chant: "Bull-shit, bull-shit." And then the room's collective attention shattered like safety glass into hundreds of pieces.

"He ruined a beautiful thing!"

"Wait a minute, he's trying to tell us something."

"That we're fucking fools. Get your hand off me!"

Joe had retreated from the microphone. The man in overalls crowded him, pointing and speaking vehemently. Jim Newburg had come out of the front row and was attempting to wrap his arms around Joe. Fine stood a few feet away, hands clasped across his bald scalp. Joe turned his face from the men, chin against his chest, shoulders slumped.

The microphone was idle, and in this vacuum the movement toward the exit resumed in noise and disorder. "Jessica!" a woman cried. "My daughter's upstairs!" And as if they had all just remembered, others began calling out the names of children.

Eric tried to fight his way toward the front. He wanted to get Joe out if he could. But too many people were coming at him, one riptide pulling back toward the exit where it broke against the wall of people jammed together there, another surging across the first toward the corner stairs that led up to the second floor. Caught in the eddy of bodies, he could hardly move his legs.

A scuffle broke out in the traffic jam. Eric turned to look.

Thirty feet away, Paula was framed in a window opening.

A floodlight silhouetted her head from behind, and although he couldn't see her expression he knew that she was looking straight at him. He raised a hand but she stood stone still, like that night in the snow.

The current over there was calmer. He had to abandon Joe. It took him a full minute to reach her side.

He said, "I thought you were here." Their eyes met and at once his blood was alert.

"This place is going crazy." Now she was looking everywhere except at him. "What happened to your magician up there?"

"I guess he decided to end it." He almost said, "I told him to," when the thought that it had been disastrous advice stopped him. None of the things he wanted to say seemed sayable. There was a quiver on her lip that he remembered. He was absurdly happy to be next to her.

"Where the hell are the cops?" Paula shook her head as if to clear her ears of water. "I knew this would happen. Fine got them going. I need to get out of here."

"It's too jammed over there. We can get out this way."

She started to let him lead her toward the window opening. He felt a tug on his elbow.

"I want to talk to you, Eric."

Ominous—but he held onto the sound of his name on her voice. "I know. Let's get out first."

The window was set low enough in the wall for him to step easily over the ledge, but the drop was five feet down. Expecting a hard landing, he felt his shoes sink into soft, thawed ground. Paula perched warily on the ledge and he held out his arms for her. She hesitated, seeming to look for another way, then she jumped. He caught her by the waist and for an instant her hands touched his. She felt wonderfully light; a current passed into his body. She disengaged.

Policemen were approaching Building X from the street, where a cop was pulling people by the arm to clear the entrance. Two young marshals in blue plastic vests were screaming at each other.

Eric and Paula moved away from the window and went to stand in the lee of a construction Dumpster. The air had thickened into mist, mingling with a humid breeze that brought the smell of sea brine from the harbor, and with it a sense of expanse. Winter was ending. He had an impulse to take her hand and start running.

"I want to talk to you," Paula repeated as if to exhort herself, holding her head and body at a reluctant angle. "What's going on?"

He tried to engage eye contact.

"Don't look at my forehead."

"What?"

"I don't want you to look at my forehead."

He looked at her forehead and saw nothing. But the demand made her vulnerable; it felt like intimacy. "OK. I won't look at your forehead."

She lifted her chin and waited. Inside, Fine had regained the microphone and was urging people to be calm, but the building kept releasing bodies out into the open air.

"She found out. She told me not to see you, she kicked me out. I tried anyway, I went to your office." He tried to stifle the squeak of self-justification.

"I went to New York for my mother."

"How is she?"

"Angry and depressed, Eric. I'm such an idiot!" She pressed her hands to her eyes. "I was going to pretend I was fine. Nice to see you again, how've you been? Idiot!"

"I'm glad you didn't."

"Really?" She searched his eyes. "I got two short messages from you."

He was tired of evasion and apology but there seemed to be nothing else, so he didn't answer. It was enough to stand with her here, indefinitely.

"How did she find out?"

"She saw one of my letters. I forgot to delete a backup file—I've always been lousy with technology," he said lamely. "She went into my computer."

"Why didn't you delete it?"

"Because I forgot." He had asked himself the same question, with the same suspicion. "People forget some things."

"It doesn't matter. It was inevitable. You're a responsible man."

She said this factually, without sarcasm or bitterness, but it sounded like the very worst thing she could call him. He saw himself limping down the street, fumbling in his pocket for house keys. She was condemning him to a terrible fate: himself.

He wanted to show her that he wasn't what she had said.

"If only I were a bitch," she said. "I should have laid down the law—take it or leave it. Why couldn't I do that? That's what your wife did. She would have won. She won anyway."

"You're not that way, Paula."

"Why are we even talking? There's nothing to talk about."

"You're angry and you have a right to tell me."

"What's the use?" she cried. "It doesn't change anything!"

She turned away. He almost said, "Don't go," but she only walked across the mud as far as the Dumpster, where she hid her face in her hands. From her trembling he knew that she was crying.

He approached with a strange feeling of dread. It wasn't her anger he was afraid of—there hardly was anger. There was despair, which told him that her love was deeper than he had imagined, deeper than his. He could have put the phone back and left her alone. What frightened him most was the knowledge that in this very moment he was losing his chance at her kind of passion.

Paula wept without making a sound, so he imagined her sobs carrying in the damp air to where he stood, transfusing him with warmth, washing away the stubborn casing of self. Even sensing his own smallness he felt amplified by her. He closed his eyes. He wanted to be poured into the body of her love and be dissolved in it.

When Paula turned around, her face was wet but she had herself under control.

"I need to know something." She cleared her throat. "If I'd been here when it happened, would it have made a difference?"

"A difference?"

"Was there a chance—don't you understand?" She wiped her cheek impatiently. "Would you have come to see me?"

"I tried to see you."

"But to tell me what?"

"I don't know."

Why hadn't he tried harder? A responsible man. Once he had gone looking for her and found The Community instead. She was right to distrust it—what a pale imitation of love!

"I want to feel I had some power over you, Eric."

"My God, don't you know that you have?"

She winced and shook her head. "I want to feel I could have changed your mind. Don't you see why that matters?"

"Change my mind from what? I look at you and see my chance at happiness and I can't stand it."

"There's no point in talking. Your life is back to normal. I have to try for the same thing."

The mist had condensed into a prickling rain that gleamed on her hair. Inside, Fine confronted the exodus. "People, if you leave this building it will be death, you'll be committing suicide! It's all death out there! Life is in here!"

"My life isn't back to normal," Eric told her. "I sleep at a friend's house every night. I have no secure income. I don't know whether I have a family or not."

She stared at him. "I thought you were back home."

"Home? Jane doesn't know whether she can stand to live with me."

The news stunned her. "I just assumed that was resolved by now."

"Nothing's resolved. I'm waiting to find out if my marriage is over."

In the shadow of the Dumpster her eyes shone very large. His breathing became quick and shallow. The building, people's voices, the damp night, everything had telescoped down to this face before him. The face under his umbrella. He imagined leaping with her into darkness.

He reached out and brushed the moisture from her hair.

"Paula, let's . . . go."

She turned her face up to his, withheld as if against a blow, yet expectant.

Her look was answered by an insane electronic shriek. She jumped. He started and then froze.

"What the hell was that?" she said.

If he ignored it, maybe it would stop. But a moment later another shriek seemed to be torn out of his stomach.

"What is it?"

He unzipped his parka and turned the beeper off. The phone number shown was the Silvers'.

"I guess it's the baby."

Paula dropped her head and moaned. She looked up, and when she saw him hesitate her expression took on a strange resolve.

"Go."

He couldn't move. In a moment he would explode.

"Go, Eric. Go."

She touched his arm just above the elbow. Then he watched her turn away and walk with brisk steps around the Dumpster, into the flow of people coming out of Building X. In seconds she was out of sight.

He began to run. He ran out of the fenced-in dirt and turned down the street toward his house. He ran to get away from the feel of her hair and the knowledge that he would never see her again. The wind was picking up, blowing warm rain in his face. Soon his trouser legs and shoes were soaked and his throat tingled, weak and sweet.

At a traffic light he crossed without looking and a police car had to brake, honking angrily into its slide. Across the street another squad car was parked outside someone's house—cops were inspecting the front door. A block later there was a third, its blue lights whirling, two policemen sprinting into a house. Eric ran harder, running now to see what the night held for him.

The storm window of his old study was a jagged, gaping square. Pieces of Plexiglas glittered on the sill, and the sash had been jammed open. The iron bars were lying in the parking lot.

He had no keys—the window was the only way. He climbed into his house. There was no sound. As he reached for the light switch in the baby room, he flashed on Jane's body and their baby's lying bloodsoaked on the new carpet. But there was no one.

The brand-new diaper cabinet had been pulled open, blankets and diapers scattered across the floor. The changing table had been violently unhooked, one of its hinges had snapped and it hung limply from the other. Dirty man-sized footprints on the new carpet mapped the intruder's moves: from window to dresser, from dresser out the door.

Eric went into the hall. To work up his courage he screamed, "I'm coming after you!" and the rage in his voice shocked him. He hoped to find the intruder at work and kill him. But the house was empty. Jane was gone.

It was in the kitchen and living room that most of the damage had been done. The television and VCR were missing. Every cabinet and drawer had been flung open, some of the plates and glasses smashed, chairs turned over, the counter scattered with pennies, paper clips, matchbooks, unpaid bills. It looked like the spiteful damage of a frustrated search.

He was an outraged property owner now, taunted by an image of Jane tied, gagged, raped—her eyes accusing. This was his home and he had failed to protect it. He wanted to chase the burglar down with a crowbar, corner him cowering—and then smash, smash, smash into the floor, the way he once imagined exterminating his rats.

A percussion grenade seemed to have blown up the bedroom and closet. Clothes, shoes, sheets lay in heaps. Before moving out he had stowed his computer in the dresser drawer with his underwear— he already knew it was gone, because the drawer was hanging open at a careless angle. Everything he had written in the past few years, the book he never finished, the letter to Paula that Jane found: all of it now in the hands of a stranger.

Eric sat on the tangled mattress. The bedroom suddenly seemed empty, a room burned to a shell, like his demolished study. The sense of violation left him. It was too late for anger or second chances; the intruder had erased everything.

In a daze he went into the kitchen. The sight of the phone reminded him of the reason he'd come home.

Jerry answered in the middle of the first ring. "Eric, it's happening."

"When, when?"

"I've been trying to beep you all evening. Where have you been?"

"I turned it off to teach."

"That thing doesn't work when it's off." Jerry's tone was sharper than Eric had ever heard it. "Where in God's name have you been?"

"That rally. I ran home to call. The place is trashed. Someone got in and just ransacked the place. I think the whole neighborhood got robbed."

Zach was crying in the background. "Just a minute, honey, I'm on the phone with Uncle Eric. Look, worry about that later. Get to the hospital."

Eric was looking around the kitchen. Jane's sweater was draped over a chair. The sink was full of dishes. And the kettle was on the stove. She had made tea. The most familiar sights in the world. At least these had been left.

"Does she want me there?"

"For Christ's sake, Eric!"

"But did she say so?"

"She asked where you were. Do you want a notarized document?" Jerry's voice softened. "Hang up, man. Get to the hospital or you two will never recover."

The rain had let up, but by the time Eric got to his car in Central Square he was soaking. The engine wouldn't turn over and he flooded it. He had become convinced that if he didn't make the hospital in time he would lose his baby and his wife. Not that she would never have him back, but that there would be a complication, a tragedy, mother and child would die. He tried to remember the birth lessons he'd found irrelevant and condescending—there had been a purpose, which was to make sure Jane and the baby survived, and he cursed himself behind the wheel.

Waiting to restart the engine, he saw people streaming down Mass. Avenue from Building X. Central Square was crowded, but the crowd was already dissolving before his eyes. The Community was going home. Some of them would find their houses burglarized; they would go back as homeowners, parents, husbands, wives.

From behind his windshield he looked for the African colors, but Joe wasn't to be seen. Eric told himself that he'd done what he could for Joe.

He gazed out at Central Square for a long moment, trying to memorize the sight of all these people together, sensing that this might be his last view of it, until he was brought back to himself and the night's urgency.

Every distracted driver, red light, and construction detour found him on the road, and he couldn't stay off his horn. At Brigham and Women's an elevator bore him upward with agonizing slowness and released him into the bright, high hallway of the main wing. Men and women in scrubs passed, an old man wheeling his own IV rack. The signs and maps were meaningless—Ambulatory, Emergency, Pike. He was about to approach a young doctor when he noticed the elevator alcove, the metallic letters: "Center for Women & Newborns." The sight of a pregnant girl and her mother waiting for the elevator filled him with irrational hope.

The receiving nurse on the fifth floor was blond, angular, terse; and as she searched her admittance chart for Jane Juneau, her implacability in the face of his breathlessness was a bad omen.

"Room 604. Newborn ICU."

"So then—" Disappointment gave way to alarm. "Why ICU?"

"That's where they go after delivery."

"Everyone's OK?"

Her nod affirmed it. He awaited some further information that would offer a role for him—for everyone to be OK and yet the birth still to happen. The nurse looked at him with quizzical impatience. "Take the elevator one floor up and turn left."

The "up" button gave his fingertip a tiny shock. He raised his head, squared his shoulders, and prepared to see his wife and baby.

It had no name, no sex. Its existence was utterly abstract, an entry on an admittance chart. But it was in the world now, one floor above. The elevator carried him toward it. And though the knowledge was still theoretical, his palms were sweating.

The door to Room 604 stood partly open, an ambiguous invitation. He knocked once and took a step inside.

Rachel was perched on the edge of a bed. Stout, bosomy, competent. To her right, a nurse in street clothes was holding a pink plastic cup. Both women were looking at the same thing, which was the person lying in the bed. Stepping into the room, Eric saw his wife's face turned toward him on a pillow. It had a color he'd never seen—not so much pale as colorless, and drawn and wasted as if she'd undergone a long illness. Her lips were dry and bloodless and slightly parted. Dark puffiness enclosed her eyes, which were shut. Jane's right hand lay curled on the bed and her left rested on her chest, on a white bundle that he knew was their child.

He understood at once that something extraordinary had taken place, shared by these women, and others too, strangers bound together in its common glow. The light in the room looked delicate. He stood outside it and would never get in, however long he lived.

All these perceptions came in an instant. Rachel's eyes shifted to him. She smiled, quietly triumphant. There was no scorn in her look, but a trace of pity.

"Hi, Eric."

"Come on in." The nurse waved cheerfully. "Say hello to your son."

He moved into the room. Jane's eyes opened and looked straight into his without changing expression. She hadn't been sleeping, only resting. She seemed to gaze at him from the far side of a journey that she would never be able to describe. Childbirth had purged her face of all personal emotions—of disappointment, anger, kindness, joy. It conveyed only peace. For the second time tonight he felt himself in the presence of someone larger than himself. He was inadequate to fathom her and felt ashamed, not of anything he'd done but of being so puny in her presence. And he didn't know what to do next.

Then her right hand opened. She was reaching toward him. At once the distance closed. He crouched at the bedside and covered her hand in kisses; it was warm and limp. She smelled of blood and fresh sheets.

"I wish—"

"Don't," she murmured hoarsely. "It was a big mess."

"A big beautiful mess," Rachel said, and he nodded, accepting this, accepting that no matter how completely he devoted the rest of his life to the family that his wife had just admitted him back into, he would still have been too late tonight. And there were other things that he would have to accept—far more things than he could begin to think of now, though he already felt that a new life had taken hold of him.

Jane was struggling with the bundle on her chest. She was trying to give it to her husband. He stood awkwardly, leaning over the bed, and took it against his parka, which was still damp, improvising a hold in the crook of one arm. He was terrified of dropping it, terrified of his own grip. But the infant—eyes closed, the lids thick and marbled, the pink wrinkled serious old man's face swaddled in a blanket and cotton cap—slept undisturbed. A faint, rhythmic stirring said that this bundle was a living thing. Fragile, almost weightless, yet endowed with the same oceanic power as the mother, having made passage on the same journey to becoming a separate person. Holding his son, Eric experienced an emotion so pure and fierce that it shook him. He would give his life to this stranger, would die for him. Volition, choice, his individual self were already canceled. He stood imprisoned in the unbreakable grip of love.

Jane raised her arms, and he moved toward his wife's embrace.

"I'll take him now, Eric."

twenty-four

By mid-March winter was over. It ended abruptly in a week of warm days that raised the first blades of crocus and daffodil. The landscape of ice and black snow melted away, running with city debris along gutters and down through storm drains and emptying near the footbridge into the Charles River, which carried it to the harbor and out to sea.

The end of the rally didn't by itself destroy The Community. Nor did the other incidents of that night: the rash of burglaries in that part of the city, the vandalism of pipes and defacing of walls in Building X, the injuries resulting from the meeting's breakup and from fights that were carried out into Central Square. The public hospital's emergency room was swamped throughout the night; so were the police, who were slow to answer calls for assistance at Building X because so many squad cars had already been dispatched to check on reports of break-ins. The Community, along with City Hall and the Police Department, came under immediate criticism for poor planning and inadequate security. There were even rumors, seeded by the developers and politicians who had always regarded the organization with dislike, and quickly spread through the city's fertile soil of paranoia, that The Community had conspired that night with a criminal element for the enrichment of its leaders. Nonetheless, no one imagined that the long work of building a citizens' group and inspiriting the city's winter face would end in a single night.

But within two weeks, the local paper was reporting The Community's demise. "A noble effort that died of ambiguity," said the editorial obituary. "It was always better at arousing and articulating populist emotions than directing them." The Community had nothing more than longing to hold it together. When its fragile moment came and went unfulfilled, when the spell of African magic was broken and the unity of hundreds of souls undone, those feelings drained out like water without a vessel and sought containment elsewhere.

The rain became fragrant, and the group meetings stopped; the blue signs ceased to appear, although old ones that no one bothered to take down from lampposts and walls continued to haunt the city for months. Perhaps they stayed up as long as they did, damp with spring rain or fading to turquoise in the summer sun, because their questions and enigmas remained unanswered, reminding those who noticed of a time when they had known who their neighbors were, and because nothing else had come along to take The Community's place.

In the middle of March, Paula's mother came to visit. For days Paula had been feeling savagely indifferent to everyone, including her clients, whose problems seemed willfully trivial and stubborn, like pimples under the skin. Most of all she loathed herself, her insomnia, her unexercised body, her period, her monotonously bad mood. But the pleasure of rage continued to elude her. Waiting in the rain for her bus after leaving Eric, she had simply wanted oblivion.

Having already suggested that her mother visit, now Paula resented in advance the intrusion on her own unhappiness. It was unclear who was going to take care of whom.

For the first two days, Paula indulged in regressive collapse. She called in sick and lay under a blanket while her mother cooked pasta and soup in the tiny kitchen. The apartment filled with wholesome smells, her mother talked continuously, her voice was soothing. They hadn't gotten along this well in years.

On the third day, the arrangement fell apart. They woke up mutually irritable, and when Paula came home from work her mother, still in her bathrobe, was noisily rearranging dishes and pots in the kitchen cabinets.

"How can you live when nothing is where it should be?"

At dinner, Paula remarked on her mother's silence.

"What is the point?"

"Of what?"

"Saying anything."

A little later her mother put down her fork. "Terrible *ai funghi*."

"It's fine. What's the matter?"

"We are living, we are breathing. The *ai funghi* is terrible. What is wrong with that?"

A great weariness descended on Paula. This was her mother-in-the-truth, all the wine and melodrama bled out, leaving a small husk without the savor of either blind hope or operatic despair. No more grand tomorrow in which she would start fresh, the past canceled, her old self discarded for a new one. The woman who resounded like a church organ throughout Paula's childhood, bright with laughter or in a towering rage—had she never been more than this?

"Rehab is hard, Mama. But you won't always feel this way. Then things will be better than they were."

"When I went home from that horrible place, do you know what I saw? A ruin. That is my life—failure, failure, failure."

"That's pretty pessimistic talk."

"The truth."

"What about me? Am I one of your failures?"

"I have not been an easy mother. No, of course, why deny? But you were raised with love. Here I can say is my success." A desiccated smile crossed her mother's face. "So this is what I came up here to tell you. Men can take your heart and throw it in the dirt."

"That's not what happened, Mama. It wasn't like that." Paula was afraid that the subject would induce her mother to try luring her into the netherworld of the permanently disenchanted. "Good things happened. I learned about myself. I'm glad for what I learned."

"They can take your heart and throw it in the dirt," her mother said. "Maybe another will make you happy, maybe not. You have work, you are secure. I had only my face and charm. But have children, *carina*. This is what I came to tell you. You must have children. My other ideas all were stupid failures."

Before Paula could reach for her hand, her mother's smile died and she lapsed back into silence.

When Paula picked up the phone and heard Eric's voice, her nerves fluttered in a pointless reflex of hope.

He said that their parting had been chaotic and he hadn't wanted to drop off the map that way. The baby, he told her, was a boy. Fred was getting far more sleep than his parents and consumed all their waking attention. Eric reckoned he'd already changed three dozen diapers—it was like tying your shoes after the first time. There was a sound of crying near the phone. Paula pictured the baby in his father's lap.

He had never written his article on The Community, because his editor had been fired from *Edge*, which already appeared to be backing off its new seriousness. But Fred's father had gainful employment now: A lawyer friend had gotten Eric a job at his law firm, as a technical writer. He was in the corporate world now.

Because of the break-in, Jane wanted to sell the apartment and move out of the city, but Eric had put his foot down.

"This is where I draw the line. It's where we belong. We'll stay in the city."

Paula wondered why he was telling her these things. She decided to pretend she was angry.

"Why are you telling me these things?" Cheap, belated pleasure.

He didn't answer at first. "I don't know who else to tell."

"Wow," Paula said, "new baby, new job. Sounds like the revenge of in on out."

"What?"

But she knew he understood, and as she waited for him to compose an answer she felt sorry. The satisfactions in this kind of thing were vastly overrated. They faded quickly and left a stale aftertaste.

"I'm trying to stop thinking in those terms," he said.

"That's probably better."

"We may not have as much choice as we think." He sounded bemused, amazed, tired. "Oh, I've gone back to my book, when Fred lets me. At least I'll finish it."

She understood why he'd called: not to restart or resolve anything, but just because they had been each other's intimates. For her own sake, she made him promise never to call again.

"Who was it, *carina*?" her mother asked from the other room.

"Just—a client."

"You give them your home number?"

"In case there's a crisis."

Peter Fine was taking an indefinite leave from the Problem Place. At a staff meeting, he announced that his recent public work had left him feeling fragile. He had been overgiving of himself and was going to spend some time finding his center on one of the Lesser Antilles ("These winters wear out our souls"). At the end of the table he looked stunned and diminished; thanking the staff, he wept. Paula saw that his great moment had come and gone so fast and left so little trace that Fine had experienced something close to a death. He had even forgotten to shave above the sculpted curve of his beard, and the grizzle growing on his upper cheeks made him look wild and reckless, like a client. Everyone understood that this was the end of Fine.

Suzanne Martin became the Problem Place's acting director. She delayed naming an associate, not only because the inevitable resentment of everyone not chosen paralyzed her in advance, but also because the Problem Place was about to exhaust all its funding. There were almost certain to be more layoffs, perhaps a temporary closing. Despite the relief occasioned by Fine's departure, apocalyptic gloom filled the basement offices.

"Do they think these people are just going to go away?" Fran exclaimed at the first post-Fine staff meeting. "Don't they know we're going to see more abuse? We should all be retraining for jobs in corrections!"

At the same meeting, Sara Simon announced that she would be leaving at the end of March to prepare her wedding and devote her full attention to conceiving. "We can't all be therapists," she told her colleagues. "If everybody's a therapist who is there to treat? Someone has to raise the next generation of clients."

"Why do you sound defensive?" Fran said. "Women have always had to face this decision. This is your answer, so own it."

"That bitch," Sara told Paula in the stairwell. "I guess I'm a gender traitor."

"You're getting out of the field just in time."

"Fran wants to be Suzanne's VP. She's talking about turning the Problem Place into a women's mental health collective."

In the void left by Fine, a disconcertingly female atmosphere had materialized—oppressively warm, more talktalktalk than ever. "And get rid of Earl? No way." Paula took Sara's hand. "You'll be missed. We're going to be so earnest and party-line without you."

"I'm racked with guilt. This work is *hard*. If I'm not with child by the end of the year I'll look like such a fool. It's not that I don't care about the clients, Paula. I'm not going to register Republican."

"Of course—"

"I just don't relish the thought of spending the rest of my life by myself."

For an instant, Eric was lying on Sara's floral comforter. Paula pushed the image from her mind.

"Well, I'm back in that wonderful state."

"Oh no!" Sara squeezed her hand. "I'm sorry, Paula—I'm so sorry. I can't even imagine how you feel."

Sara looked every bit as disappointed as Paula was.

The next day, the Problem Place was reprieved by a source that everyone, including Paula, had forgotten. A renewable grant of $65,000 was awarded by the Whitset Foundation.

It was an enormous sum, more than enough to cover their lost funding, and Paula bitterly resented Jane Juneau, who had everything, including the power to decide whether the Problem Place lived or died. The grant felt like a payoff for abandoning all claims to Eric.

The best thing would be to hand it out to the clients. Five hundred apiece, lump sums, no strings. It would immediately be blown on clothes or hookers or pharmaceuticals, but so what? Who was to say it wouldn't do her clients more good than talk?

The trouble was, Paula had nothing to fall back on except talk, or surrender; and her will turned out to be surprisingly strong.

She made an appointment with Suzanne Martin.

"I have an idea for part of the grant money."

Suzanne's face composed itself in earnest attention. The grant had sent Paula's stock soaring.

"Our clients need baby-sitters. One of mine has a four-year-old with asthma. They're cooped up all day long in this tiny apartment in the projects. No wonder she's depressed. We could provide day care for our clients with jobs. It would be an incentive for them to work. Isn't that what everyone's telling these people to do? We could expand the front room into that empty closet and your old office. Suzanne"—Paula couldn't stop her voice from trembling—"we have to be a little bit political. Fine was full of crap most of the time, but he was right about one thing. We are part of a community. We can't just be like pit crews changing a tire, or the guys in the corner who slice the boxer's eye so he can go back out there and get the shit beat out of him. Their problems are not all psychodynamic. No one believes anything can be done for them anymore. These people are being cut loose. I'll take the planning on myself."

Paula thought she sounded incoherent. She had taken herself completely by surprise.

"You've done more than your share already."

"No I haven't." She wasn't going to be put off. "All I've done is get us the money," she reminded Suzanne. "Now we need to justify it—to Whitset, the board, ourselves. Another year of muddling through and we'll be out of here. A software company will move in." Suzanne looked terrified. "But if we get out in front on this, people will have a reason to start giving to the Problem Place again. The start of the Suzanne Martin era."

"Describe it one more time," Suzanne said, fingers to her lips, for Paula had just appealed to her only instinct more powerful than fear. By the end of the meeting, Suzanne had agreed to present the plan to the board; and Paula had agreed to go back on staff, as associate director.

Toward the end of the month, she saw her mother off at South Station. The sun was out and the sky looked a deeper shade of blue than it had in months. Spring had already officially begun, but this morning felt like the first real day. People blinked in the sunlight and wore less clothing. In their slack bodies Paula sensed the possibility of foolish vitality, like the brave little crocuses that had rammed their way up through mud the past few days, waiting to be crushed under an April snowstorm or frozen to death.

"Good-bye, Mama," she said on the platform. "Call as soon as you're home." She pressed her mother's cheek against hers.

"Did we have a nice time, *carina?*"

"I loved having you."

"But I was morose."

It was time to obliterate all irritations. "No, you made me feel better."

There was always a kind of desperate cheerfulness in their good-byes. Paula could never turn away until her mother was out of sight—it would be like hanging up on her. She stood peering into the dim window of the Amtrak car: A hand was moving back and forth, and Paula waved in reply, so that one hand seemed to exercise a magnetic force on the other. With a lurch the train began to pull away. But even after the waving hand in the window disappeared, and then the window itself, Paula continued to stand and wave, knowing the hand inside the car was doing the same, long after the train was out of sight.

She took the T to Central Square. A full day of sessions awaited her, starting with an intake. But at the top of the escalator—dedicated, she always noted on a plaque, "to Councillor Hyman Pill, Friend of the Subway Rider and All Mankind"—something made her stop to take in the Square. This morning, in the sunlight, it looked as gay and gaudy as a transvestite. The flimsy patchwork of shop signs jostled along the streetfront in hideous colors and lurid lettering. The slight rise in temperature had brought them to life and she saw them as faces of cartoon grotesques, the coffee shop leering with its tongue out, the used-record store gleefully crazed, the discount clothier slick and sinister. Across Mass. Avenue, the regulars lounged on granite planters trying to warm up in the sun. Pigeons gathered around an old woman with a bag of french fries. A man in a business suit ducked furtively into the magazine shop. Fine's dream was a nice dream, but this was the Central Square she was willing to live with.

On the sidewalk a black man with a shaved head was accosting pedestrians at the top of his voice.

"Hellooo young miss, you look so beautiful today. Young man— young man! Sir, hi ho it's off to work we go. Oh look at you, young lovers, don't leave him, don't you ever leave her. Big guy! Big guyyy! Ma'am, I like that fine spring dress!"

It was the homeless news vendor, selling the homeless newspaper, assaulting passersby right and left with frantic enthusiasm. He reappeared every year at this time, as sure a sign of spring as the frenzied flocks of sparrows. He would keep this pitch up all day, all year, until it got cold again and he disappeared to wherever he disappeared to.

A few people stopped and took out a dollar, but most turned their heads or even left the sidewalk to avoid him. It unnerved them to have their anonymity ripped away—but this morning, Paula felt, there was something more. His insane zest reminded people of the energy rising like sap within themselves, the crude quickening that made their bodies seem shrunken and underused. It was painful and embarrassing to feel this overflow of life.

Better to feel it than not. Better to throw yourself into the mindless stream.

Paula approached, offering her dollar. The news vendor wheeled and his face exploded.

"Oh my God, you look so fine today, Miss Beautiful, you just knock me out!"

The morning's intake lay on her desk and it was a strange one. The last name had been left blank, the first sounded generic. She laughed out loud when she read the symptoms: "Lying, stealing." But the referral stunned her. The name written was Eric Barnes.

Someone was standing in the doorway. Paula couldn't suppress a startle in her chair.

"Are you Joe?"

"That's right."

Although the light in Building X had been bad and Paula never got a clear look over all the heads, she knew that her intake was Fine's magician, Eric's carpenter, who had said all those extraordinary things that night.

"Please sit down."

He came in and shut the door. Looking around the cubicle, he settled his long body in the client's chair without taking off his pea coat—too heavy a coat for today. His fingers interlaced in his lap. He had a thin mustache and his face was handsomely chiseled in the cheekbones. Though he tried hard not to meet her eyes, he kept returning to them.

"Tell me a little about what brought you here, Mr. . . ." She made a show of looking at the file on her desk. "I don't believe you wrote your last name."

He leaned toward her. "Is anyone going to know what I say?"

"It's strictly confidential."

Paranoid, she thought. And yet there was no defiance in his manner. He told her his last name but she forgot to write it down, registering only that, like his voice, it sounded thoroughly and blandly American. No African magician; just another candidate for therapy. What a comedown.

He was waiting for her to say something.

"Let me tell you about how this process works." She didn't

mean to scare him, but his Adam's apple bobbed up and got caught in his jaw. "You can tell me anything you want to. OK? Anything. Whatever comes to mind."

The Adam's apple descended. He sat back, unlaced his fingers, and nodded. He still looked concerned.

"You might get bored," he said.

She leaned forward. A small lead. "Why would you think that?"

"I don't know."

"Do people make you feel as though you're boring?"

"I try to be gone before they have a chance."

She thought this clever and funny, but the tension in his eyes told her to check her laugh. He said everything straight, apparently guileless. She decided to make a leap. "Will that go for this too?"

He looked as though she had caught him in the act of planning his escape. "I don't know. I hope not."

Notepad in her lap, she went through the basic intake procedure. He had never been treated for psychological problems and had no history of substance abuse or violence (these questions seemed to surprise and hurt him). He was currently unemployed, having been released from his job with a construction company, and he was staying at Rainbow House. He answered each question minimally in a low voice that at times became inaudible.

From most black men, in here and out there, she was used to a certain initial suspicion, if not outright hostility, or else an elaborate display of indifference. Not him. He had undone his coat buttons and was fidgeting with one, darting fretful glances Paula's way. He was going to make her do the work. He had turned himself in and now he was waiting for her to pronounce judgment.

This was what Eric had bequeathed her. His parting gift.

She put down her pen and decided to try silence.

"Things have been happening that I don't understand," he suddenly said. "Nothing like this used to happen to me."

She nodded, listening carefully.

"I came back from Africa and kept getting into weird situations. There's this thing in Africa called shape-shifting. It was like I didn't have control. Sometimes I think I might be going crazy."

She waited for him to say more.

"So far—based on what I've said—do you think so?"

He was in deadly earnest. She didn't allow herself a flicker of smile.

"No, I don't think you're crazy." He expelled a breath and sat back. "But I want to hear more about the weird situations. Does it have something to do with"—another false glance at the file—"the symptoms you mentioned on the intake?"

He looked away, toward the wall where the Cape Cod picture was hung.

"Some of that started before. But it got out of hand here."

"What happened?"

He began chewing on a thumbnail. When he answered it was in the direction of the Cape Cod picture.

"I got involved in a hoax. It wasn't my idea. People pushed me into it, they were the ones who wanted it."

During sessions Paula would sometimes flash on herself in a black robe, calmly hearing confession and preparing to forgive and bless. Or tarted up in underwear and garters, willing to be whatever fantasy they wanted, the wilder the better. But until now she had never seen herself uniformed in blue, handcuffs and radio and gun on her hips.

"Why did they want it?"

He shrugged. "I guess they liked me that way. I got sort of famous."

"Sounds like fun."

"Fun? I don't know. Maybe it was fun at first."

"Why do you think they liked you that way?"

"Don't you want to know who they thought I was?"

He was proud of it. Criminals couldn't help being a little proud, making fools of the rest of the world.

"Sure, if you want to tell me. I'm more interested in how it made you feel."

This seemed to disappoint him. But she had made him think of something new.

"Like nothing could bother me. Like . . . I'd never have to get angry again, I'd never have to get upset or sad." Understanding began to break in his eyes. "Stealing, too. I didn't mean to hurt anyone. It made me feel better, that's all. Like nothing could get me."

"Wouldn't we all love that. No wonder people liked you that way." He was biting the end of the nail, cornered again by his interrogator, unwilling to confirm or deny. "What made it stop being fun?"

"It wasn't *me*."

Paula received the familiar shock of encountering a mind in pain. The varieties were endless and strange and often invisible to the eye, but sooner or later they found their way to her. He was a palpable emotional presence now. Her energies began to mobilize. She knew what to do: It was her talent, her best use. She felt a surge of gratitude.

"It must have been lonely," she said. "When no feelings can get you, no people can get you either." Tears sprang to his eyes and he blinked and looked away. So did she, wanting not to overdo it, for he was still elusive. "What do you think you were after, with this hoax?"

"I don't know. Something." The sliver of thumbnail came off and he deposited it in his coat pocket. "I guess something I couldn't have."

"I still don't understand why it couldn't have been you. If people thought you were so wonderful and interesting, maybe it wasn't a hoax. *Someone* had to make them feel that way. Who else was it?"

"I never saw it that way."

"Are you you now, with me?"

Another leap, a risky one, but instinct told her that he was beginning to trust her, partly because she was in authority but more because of what she said and how she made him feel. The tension had begun to leave his filmy eyes. She sensed that he had never spoken this way with anyone in his life and thousands of words under terrific pressure were waiting to be released.

"I guess so."

Paula smiled and nodded. "Good." She glanced at the clock and saw that the hour was almost up. He was alert to her now and noticed.

"Is that it?"

"There's a few things we have to go over before you leave."

"Am I coming back?"

This time she couldn't help smiling. "Well, that's up to you. Do you want to come back?"

His nod was almost imperceptible.

"Does it take a long time?"

"Depends on what you want. It can take a pretty long time. Once a week is sort of a normal starting procedure. We have a sliding fee scale down to five dollars and it sounds like you wouldn't pay much more than that, at least until you have a job. See Cheryl on your way out and she'll schedule you. Your regular therapist will be assigned by the time you come back next week."

She knew that this would stun him and it did.

"It won't be you?"

Paula said in her most professional voice, "The therapist who does the intake doesn't ordinarily become the regular therapist."

"I thought you were the one."

"The staff as a whole makes that decision. I can note that you requested me, but the staff makes the decision."

He sat motionless. His eyes were fixed on her now. "Everybody leaves!"

"What do you mean?"

"Either they die, or get killed, or they just walk off and don't come back. They leave. Everybody."

"People do leave," Paula said. "And it's hard when they do. You think, if I'd just done this or that. We'll talk about it—" She caught herself. "I'll request that we work together, but the staff makes the decision."

He went out like an unrequited lover. Although everything had been done by the book, Paula felt a little guilty, for she already knew that he would be her client, hers, because she wouldn't turn him over to anyone else, because no one else could help him. She could. She knew the cure. If it was a kind of interrogation, she interrogated with love.

Paula put her notes in his folder and stowed it in the file drawer. Her next client was Gladys Dill. In a minute she would come through the door. Paula sat facing the empty chair. This was her post, in this basement. It was her work to sit and hear about the traps people sprang on themselves, the lifesaving checks that got thrown out with the trash, the petty insults that would be spectacularly avenged, the ancient wounds and commonplace failures, the loneliness shared by thousands, the futility of meals in shoe box kitchens, the breakthrough that came back once every six months, the lifelong tic that would be mastered next week, the mornings when it was too much to make coffee, the lovers who deserved to die and the ones too good to live for, the rehearsed quarrels that would never stick to the script, the injustice of the gas company, the drug-free hunger for chemical freedom, the exhausted prescriptions, the broken restraining orders, the world's indifference to misery, the eternal fresh starts. In her cubicle there was enough room for a community of two. At least they had each other.

George Packer was born and raised in the San Francisco Bay Area. He graduated from Yale and has worked as a Peace Corps volunteer in Togo, West Africa, a carpenter in Boston, and a writing instructor at Harvard, Bennington, and Emerson. He is the author of *The Village of Waiting*, a memoir about his Peace Corps years, and *The Half Man*, a novel.

This book was designed by Wendy Holdman.
It is set in Sabon type by Stanton Publication Services, Inc.,
and manufactured by Friesens on acid-free paper.